Secrets of Tarin-Tiran

Secrets of Tarin-Tiran

Trickster's Song ❧ Book 3

Tom O'Bedlam

Podium

Published in 2023 by Podium Publishing, ULC
www.podiumaudio.com

Secrets of Tarin-Tiran

The Gates of Tarin-Tiran

Chapter 1

*T*he wind rippling across the emerald-green grass of the hills around Tarin-Tiran ruffled Robin's hair. He stood on a boulder near the top of a high hill outside the city, looking down at what he could see of the warren of ruined streets below.

Considering the age of the place, it was surprising this much of it was still standing. Magical construction no doubt. Still, even for someone accustomed to the megacities of twenty-first century Earth, this was impressive.

There were soaring towers still thrusting upward toward the sky, and vast avenues which threaded their way through the tangle of smaller streets. Some of these were lush with green grass—nature claiming her due—but still others remained pristine, clean, and clearly paved with broad, flat stones.

Around it all was a massive wall, pierced at regular intervals by gates—these showed the signs of decay. All of them appeared to have been shattered by titanic forces at some point in the distant past, which fit with the bits he'd been able to recover of the city's history. The dream of Tarin-Tiran had been ended at the hands of an invading army, probably under the direction of Urkhan or one of his most faithful and fervent.

Robin felt a flicker of curiosity along his bond with Rerebos.

What do you think? Robin sent the thought winging along their connection. It was so much easier communicating this way! Rerebos was hidden nearby, still one of Robin's many aces in the hole.

It is big. Many places for a good lair. Many places for hidden shinies.

Robin could feel Rerebos's approval.

The bard glanced back over his shoulder to the rest of his party, packing up camp from the night before. It hadn't been difficult to assemble them for the quest, even though this place was incredibly dangerous—well above their average level, in the parlance of his old world.

Drev had readily agreed. The prospect of lost arcane knowledge as well as riches had been enough to secure his presence. Jhess, on the other hand, had come for the riches alone.

Against his better judgement, Robin had decided to recruit Savra to his cause as well. On top of being a talented healer, the woman had divinatory powers and a connection to a goddess sympathetic to Rhyth. Either might come in handy.

He had considered recruiting Fiamah for this expedition. He'd even carefully sounded her out on the idea, but she was busy with something secret for the guildmagister and was reluctant to leave the other Sisters Sharp for any extended period of time.

So, they had brought Savra along, in spite of the screaming willies she gave Robin.

The final member of their party, the replacement tank, had come from an unexpected quarter: Robin's experiences at the Great Library of Noviel. It turned out that Tellurian Vance, slim and elegant appearance aside, was an excellent warrior (and in Robin's mind, still referred to as a tank).

Vance employed a combination of unusual sorcerous gifts, a few curious blessings from one of the bardic deities, and a great deal of study both martial and academic to create his signature style. The scholar had the ability to control paper and parchment and was able to create incredibly strong armor and shockingly sharp weapons from the stuff. Furthermore, in times of great need, he could channel the legendary prowess of individuals featured in popular stories.

Robin had seen him do it thrice already, much to the chagrin of the ogre, the small pack of bandits, and the goblin war party they had encountered on their journey here.

It is good to have minions.

Rerebos's comment almost made Robin snort with laughter, but he managed to control himself. Laughing out of nowhere tended to draw attention, and that wasn't something Robin wanted at this particular moment. Not if it might point people toward Rerebos's presence.

Speaking of shinies, Robin sent the thought to redirect the little dragon's attention toward something useful, *you should go and scout out the nearest gate to see if there are any near there.*

Yes. I shall do that.

Keep an eye out for traps or enemies!

Robin felt rather than saw the little dragon depart. There was a sense of someone being just out of reach in his mind which told him that his familiar had flitted away out of telepathic range.

They'd need to find ways to increase that, eventually.

Robin frowned and pulled up his interface to review his active quests. There were a few related to Tarin-Tiran at this point, but the one bothering him was the secret quest he had been given to find lost knowledge of the illusory arts within the city. The quest goal read:

Successfully make your way past the gates of the city and into Tarin-Tiran.

From what he was seeing, that wouldn't really be a challenge. All of the gates in the vicinity had been blasted wide open, and there did not appear to be dangerous traps or enemies he could see from this vantage, though perhaps Rerebos would scout some out.

"Ready to head out?" Drev called to him.

"Yeah," Robin replied, hopping down from the boulder. "I can't see anything from this far away, but the gates are all blasted open."

"We knew that from the guild reports we read before leaving," Jhess complained.

"It doesn't hurt to verify information." Savra came up alongside the rest of the group, annoyingly as composed and unruffled as ever.

"Agreed," Vance said. The scholar was dressed in a flowing robe which completely belied his status as the party's tank.

The incongruity appealed to Robin on multiple levels.

"So, shall we proceed and see what we can see?" Vance began walking down the hill without waiting for a response.

Robin and the rest of the party followed. Many of them had already braced themselves with longer lasting defensive magics or girded their loins with their customary arms and armor. Drev shimmered slightly as he walked due to the shield of force wrapping around him, while Jhess had her fingertips resting lightly on the hilt of one of her daggers.

Savra and Vance, however, might as well have been strolling through a garden party for all the concern or defensive posture they displayed.

The walls were large. Very large. As Robin approached, they rose up like a cresting tsunami of stone. The sight didn't bother him, though. For some reason, he felt a welcoming vibe from them.

This was not the case with all of his compatriots, however. Jhess pulled her knife and started nervously flipping it end over end in her hand. Ripples of distortion, like heat over a summer's highway, flickered around the tips of Drev's fingers.

Even Savra looked slightly peaked.

"There were some serious siege spells used here," Drev said, pointing to some warping in the stone around the edges of the gate once they finally drew near enough to see.

"And siege engines as well," Vance noted. "Look at the cracks in the foundation and the way the hinges are bent."

Robin looked and filed the information away. This was not the kind of thing that generally made its way into ballads and legends, so his [Bardic Lore] was a bit less helpful than usual, even with [Shard of the Shattered Manymind] to reinforce it.

"I'm more concerned about what might be waiting for us inside." Jhess had stopped flipping her dagger and now held it in a reverse grip, ready to lash out should anything attack them.

Anything? Might as well check in with Rerebos now that they were close. The little dragon couldn't have gone that far . . . unless he'd spotted something shiny running away from him. Then he'd pounce on it like a cat after a mouse.

No shinies. No foes. No nothing.

A mixed bag of news, then, but worse for his familiar than for him.

Robin wished he could consult with Ruprecht, but the dungeon was currently stowed safely away inside his mimic conveyance in Robin's storage space. And there was no way the bard was risking taking that out here and now.

Things have been here recently, though. I can smell them.

Robin stiffened.

Things? What kind of things?

I do not know. The smell tastes a bit like goblin, but muskier.

"Any sign of goblinoids about?" Robin asked casually. "I heard some of the others back at the Adventurers Guild telling stories about ambushes within the city, but I have no idea if they were winding me up or not."

As lies went, it wasn't his worst. It got the job done.

"Nothing yet," Jhess replied, flicking a glance at Savra to see if the seeress agreed.

Savra nodded.

"I think the danger, if any, will come later. When we are already deep inside the walls and have no easy way to get out. Why close a trap early?"

"Thank you for that wonderful sentiment," Drev drawled sourly.

Vance just laughed and strode through the gate.

"Come on, you lot," he said. "We're here for adventure, aren't we?"

Robin followed. Passing through the gate took longer than expected—the walls were *thick*. Fortunately, the gate-passage was also large enough for all of them to walk abreast with plenty of room to spare, though they had to step carefully around all the debris gathered at the edges and across the intervening space of the tunnel.

"What did they move through here? Elephant-drawn, double-wide carriages?" Robin muttered.

Eventually, they made their way through and into the city proper.

Robin blinked in the sunlight as they emerged, and all five of them stood together, taking in the sights.

The buildings were a strange mix of resilient intactness and picturesque ruin, in a style which Robin's mind tried valiantly to chart as somewhere between art nouveau and art deco. There were a great many artistic touches to the architecture, as if the people who lived here saw everything as a canvas.

The streets were a tangle, gentle curves intersected with ramrod-straight lines. Even here, there was a mix of pristine condition and decay, with some boulevards opens and clear and others choked with vines growing up from centuries of accumulated dirt and detritus.

But they were here! They stood upon the streets of Tarin-Tiran, legendary city! They—*wait, tho.*

Robin frowned. He hadn't gotten a quest update. They'd passed through the gates.

Hadn't they?

He opened his interface to check. Nope. The quest line item was still listed as pending.

Huh. So if those weren't the real gates to the city, what were they? Were they even in the right place? Something funny was going on here.

Before he could ponder further, however, he felt a spike of alarm from Rerebos.

Ambush! Big-big goblins coming for you!

Chapter 2

Robin bit his cheek to keep from swearing as the hobgoblin warrior chased after Drev and around a corner.

Right out of Robin's line of sight.

The band had hit the party mere moments after Rerebos's warning, leaving Robin with just enough time to pass it along with a shout of alarm before they were hip deep in melee. It was only a small warband, five to five. It shouldn't have been much trouble, but the hobgoblins clearly had the home turf advantage. They knew the terrain and how to take full advantage of it.

That left Robin's party struggling, for all they had not been caught completely unawares.

Robin shot a glance after Drev but decided not to leave his hiding spot. Drev was a defensive mage of a high caliber—he'd probably be alright. Just in case, however, Robin sent a mental command to Rerebos to spy out the situation and report back.

Then he turned his attention to the battle.

Enough of the nearby buildings had fallen to the strangely inconsistent decay that, although this was technically a crossroads, it was more like a small, litter-choked town square. Robin could see Savra behind Vance, who was squaring off against an absolute monster of a hob and a twisted wretch of a specimen that kept trying to flank him. There was one hobgoblin corpse already on the ground, and Jhess had disappeared chasing another; they didn't want anyone getting away to bring in reinforcements.

Robin kept a close eye on the battle, looking for an opening.

Vance was magnificent in gleaming white armor—paper, of all things, but as hard as steel. He had a sword to match, and both hobs still standing were bleeding from several very fine cuts.

Savra murmured a prayer, and light flared around Vance, who immediately began to move with greater ease and vigor.

"Get the healer, you fool," the larger of the two hobs snarled. [Tongue of the Fallen Tower] allowed Robin to catch the meaning.

He didn't think either Savra or Vance spoke the language, though perhaps he ought not to make that assumption about the librarian-turned-warrior. It was frightening how much that man knew sometimes.

The smaller, roguish hob darted around Vance, skipping around the sword blow the warrior lashed out at him and tucking into a roll to come up close enough to menace Savra.

There!

Robin murmured a quick set of [Whispers from Beyond], and the hob suddenly stopped in his tracks, an expression of horror on his face. Savra was ready and she swung her mace directly at the rogue's face.

It connected with a crunch.

The hobgoblin screamed in agony and fear and backpedaled away from the healer. The larger hob spat out a curse and a threat, but the smaller hob continued to retreat.

"Don't let any of them get away!" Vance shouted.

"I'm on it!" Robin said, casting his voice via a [Lesser Phantasm] so the large hob couldn't pinpoint him; he had accursedly good hearing and better aim. If Robin hadn't had [Healing Note], he might have bled out near the beginning of the battle.

That's what he got for being careless with his camouflage.

Robin willed himself some cover using [Visual Phantasm], a roil of magical-looking shadows dropping down like a sheet between the larger hobgoblin leader and the fleeing rogue. He covered his movements with sounds via [Lesser Phantasm] and trusted Vance to keep the leader busy enough that Robin wouldn't take any major hits.

The bard dashed through the illusory shadows, weaving a bit as he went in a serpentine pattern. It slowed him down, but it also made him a bit safer from the odd dagger thrown his way.

In moments, he was around a corner in hot pursuit of the fleeing hobgoblin. Their speed was fairly evenly matched, and the street the rogue was fleeing down was one of the straight avenues, rather than the curving boulevards. Robin took full advantage of this and began conjuring [Lesser Witch Bolt]s. The flaming playing cards sailed ahead of him and struck the hob in the back, who didn't even stop running to turn and look. Robin had to press harder to try and catch up.

Chest heaving and fingertips sizzling from the magical discharge, it was several more streets before Robin had whittled the hob down to the point where he collapsed, sides heaving, against a nearby wall.

Is Drev alright? How about the others? Robin sent a quick query to Rerebos.

Battle's finished. All big-big goblins dead. The allies are about to come looking for you.

Good. He'd have backup soon.

Robin turned his attention to the hobgoblin wheezing against the wall. This one was still alive, and in no shape to pose a credible threat. Might as well see what information Robin could get from him while he waited for the others.

He invoked **[Lesser Mindreading]**. Time to get some practice in.

Instantly, he became aware of several minds in his immediate vicinity. Most of them were small, probably rodents and insects and diminutive monsters infesting the nearby ruins. One, however, blazed brightly: the rogue over by the wall.

"Who are you?" he asked, playing for time for the spell to grow in power.

The hobgoblin just took two deep, shuddering breaths and hawked a lump of bloody spittle toward Robin.

Dratch.

The name was floating in the rogue's mind, and Robin plucked it from the stream of thoughts as easily as plucking a leaf from a lazy creek.

Robin decided to try several questions.

"Why did you attack us? Are these ruins your base? How many others like you are there?"

Robin put on a good performance of getting irritated as the hobgoblin continued to refuse answering his questions. But even as he did so, the answers drifted to the top of the hob's mind, and Robin was able to easily lift them out.

He had been part of a regular patrol, of which several continually roamed the ruins. The ruins were indeed their base in a general sense, and with a bit more questioning, Robin was able to get the general location of their prime encampment. The hobgoblin then managed to summon enough wherewithal to threaten him with a rock, so Robin ducked the projectile and answered with a **[Lesser Witch Bolt]** to the face.

It was more than the hob could stand. The rogue died then and there, because he had dared to spike Robin's adrenaline.

Robin shoved the thought out of his mind as he grimly crouched down to search the body. Some rations and a few daggers and other blades which had seen better days were all he managed to turn out of the dead thug's pockets.

He discarded the rations. He wouldn't trust them even with [Lesser Phantasm] improving the taste. They hardly looked fit to eat, and he had much better options stowed safely away in his storage space.

The rest of the party caught up to him shortly after that.

"We need to move," Robin said as soon as they arrived. "Get ourselves farther into the city. According to this one"—he gestured to the cooling corpse behind him—"there is a whole group of hobgoblins here. A—what was the word?—hjuncta. It sounded like a cross between a war band and a small town. Hundreds of them."

"Not something we want to run in to if we can help it," Drev observed. The mage had a purpling bruise dawning across his cheek like a sunrise.

Robin muttered a [Healing Note] and set it right. Drev nodded his thanks.

"Hang on to your spells," Jhess snapped. "We're not safe yet. You might need the firepower."

Robin ignored her.

"I know where we can look for shelter, and a way deeper into the city. I got the impression that the hobs stick mainly to this thin outer rim of the place."

Robin stood and began walking, the rest of the party quickly falling into formation around him. He mentally checked in with Rerebos, sending the little dragon a vision of the route he intended to take. There were several locations his research had turned up as potential avenues to the depths of Tarin-Tiran, many marked as leading directly to the dungeon growing in the ruined city.

Robin intended to avoid those. If they could delve deeper into the city without crossing into the dungeon's territory, they had a better chance of finding actual artifacts and remaining unmolested by monsters far above their capacity to handle.

He led the party through the maze of ruined streets and alternatively pristine and crumbling buildings. There were occasional signs of other hobgoblin patrols, but fortunately, they didn't run into any before they arrived at the location Robin had been seeking.

The building itself was one of the remarkably intact ones. Robin got a good feeling just by looking at it. Once, it had been a tavern, and the sign outside was still brightly painted with the image of three crossed staves, all shining silver.

"The Silver Staves," he said. "There should be a passage leading deeper into the city hidden somewhere inside. Come on. If nothing else, it should be a good place to set up camp."

"It does look defensible," Jhess grudgingly agreed. "Those are heavy-duty shutters, and they all seem to still latch."

The party slipped inside so as to be out of sight, then Jhess quickly scouted out the place for traps or monsters.

"All clean," she informed once she reappeared. Then she sneezed, sending dust everywhere. "Well, clear, at least." She glanced at Robin expectantly.

Robin rolled his eyes but began magically clearing the dust by way of **[Legerdemain]**. The things people demanded once they got used to them. He was practically being taken for granted.

"And I'm guessing that is our way down?" Vance pointed to what looked like a large well in the middle of what had to have once been the common room floor.

"Should be," Robin said, going to have a look. "According to legend, it was sealed long before the city fell, but that never seemed right to me. I'm guessing there is some kind of mechanism the owners used, and if we can find it, we can probably get the thing open."

"And if we can't?" Jhess asked.

"Then I've brought along someone who most certainly can, all while also making sure we've a safe place to stay."

Robin pulled the little mimic out of his storage space. It helpfully played dumb and acted like a chest while Robin opened it, revealing Ruprecht's core.

Drev and Vance gasped. Jhess glared at him sourly, and Savra looked as unperturbed as ever.

"Is that a dungeon core?" Vance asked.

"It is," Drev confirmed, stepping closer. "One that looks strangely familiar." He shot Robin a questioning glance.

"Are individual dungeon cores that recognizable?" Robin asked airily. "I don't know that they are. And honestly, you should all be far more respectful of our ally. He's going to be watching our backs and making sure we get further into Tarin-Tiran than any other party that has attempted this city."

"I knew you had to have something up your sleeve, putting this expedition together," Jhess said, admiration and exasperation warring in her tone. "But this is mad, even for you!"

"You're going to need to explain everything in great detail," Drev demanded firmly.

Yeah. There was no way in any number of hells that was happening. Robin just smiled in reply.

There is indeed a mechanism. It's ensorcelled, however, and incredibly complex.

Ruprecht's voice echoed in the heads of everyone present. Robin had to stifle a laugh as Jhess leapt nearly three feet into the air.

"How is he doing that?" she asked.

I have already claimed the structure as my new territory. You are now safely within my demesne.

"I am going to kill you, bard," Jhess muttered.

"What will it take to get that passage open, Ruprecht?" Robin asked, ignoring Jhess's threat. She'd come around.

Eventually.

Unfortunately, it's very complex, and the sorceries are unfamiliar to me. I'll require a great many energies to fuel my assimilation of the mechanism to the point that I can control and, thus, open it.

"What does that mean?" Vance inquired.

"It means we need to lure some hobs in here for our new ally to eat," Robin said brightly. "Now, who fancies a bit of dinner?"

Chapter 3

*T*hey know we're here."

Robin peered out the window of the former residential building he and the rest of the party were hiding in. Down the street, several lengths away, he could see a patrol of hobgoblins making their way carefully toward where he and his friends were hidden.

"They know someone is somewhere in the area," Robin corrected Jhess.

"They wouldn't even know that much if we hadn't tricked that last patrol into following us down Ruprecht's gullet," the rogue snapped.

"That's hardly fair, and entirely untrue," Drev chided. "They have to have found the bodies of the patrol that attacked us as soon as we entered the city. And those corpses hardly bore the marks of an easy death from natural causes."

"Knives are perfectly natural," Jhess muttered, but it was clear she had taken the point.

So far, the party had successfully lured only one patrol to the dungeon growing slowly around Ruprecht. There was not much there in the way of traps—enough for defense and a bit of challenge for the invaders, but that was about it. The party had had to contract with Ruprecht as sort of temporary dungeon monsters. There were a few benefits, and it meant they had an inherent mental connection to Ruprecht when within his boundaries, but even the assurances Jhess had negotiated into the magically binding contract were not enough to set the rogue fully at ease.

"There's something different about this group," Savra said suddenly.

"They have a mage of some kind." Vance pointed to the slimmest of the advancing hobs.

The hobgoblin in question was dressed in simple cloth armor, with odd markings stitched into it. It wasn't quite a language, since Robin couldn't read any meaning from it. It held some significance, yes, but what was beyond his ken.

She also had some kind of wand in her hand. It was long and thin but made of metal; the same metal as the spiked gorget around her neck. The material was brassy and etched with deep runes in some kind of black enamel which had a distinctly sludgy and corroded look about it.

"Have you ever seen anything like that?" Robin directed the question at Vance and Drev after his **[Bardic Lore]** came up empty.

"No," each said in turn.

"Could be some kind of magical focus," Drev offered, squinting as if to try and bridge the distance.

"Or something which compensates for an inability to speak," Vance added. "That gorget design is unusual."

Robin had heard small bits about magical devices designed to aid those who had lost their voice or hand, items which made up for the inability to fully execute the magical formulas and gestures which seemed to control much of the sorcery of this world. This was his first time seeing even a potential example, however.

He hadn't had a lot of time to explore magical markets, after all.

"Either way, it looks like a weak spot," Jhess said. "Less nattering, more battle planning. We need to separate them and lure them after us. How are we going to do it this time?"

"Illusions, again," Robin replied. "How else? It's safest."

"You're becoming predictable," Jhess complained.

"You just want to get the chance to use your knives," Robin retorted. "You're an adrenaline junky—you live for the thrill and the danger," Robin corrected himself before Jhess could ask after the strange word.

He caught Drev and Vance exchanging a glance. Damn. He'd need to be more careful. He likely didn't need to be this paranoid, but too many questions into his past could be inconvenient.

Right. Time to play up the attention-starved bard, then.

Robin stood with a flourish.

"To satisfy our bloodthirsty friend, then, I suggest we try something a little different. I'll bait them with illusions, we'll skirmish, then I'll cover our retreat, again with illusions. We can play hit and run or cat and mouse games with them as we lead them to Ruprecht. That should keep them keen, at least."

"It's an unnecessary risk," Drev began.

"Oh, come on!" Jhess wheedled. "Let me have some fun!"

The party bickered good-naturedly for a few minutes as they made sure all their gear was ready and that they each had a clear idea of the escape routes should anything go wrong, before they slipped out of the building and down a nearby alley, angling across the way to intercept the hobgoblins from their left flank.

Jhess was practically bouncing on the toes of her feet.

Right. Robin needed an illusion that fit with the damage those knives could do; something that looked like a worthwhile foe, not too dangerous but potentially carrying something the hobgoblins would want. Like some juicy haunches or a pouch of gold coins.

So far as they knew, no hobgoblin had survived to report back to the hjuncta what Robin and his party looked like. Ideally, they could keep it that way as long as possible. That didn't mean he couldn't conjure up a convincing adventurer, though.

In fact, he had a model all ready.

Robin willed a **[Visual Phantasm]**, backed with sound from **[Lesser Phantasm]**, to dart from an alley across the street to a patch of shadow he could just see out of the corner of his eye by peering around the edge of the building they were hiding behind.

The sight of the slim rogue caused a shout to go up from the assembled hobgoblins. And if said rogue bore a seedy caricature of Khavren's features . . . well, who would notice in the chaos? Being a rogue *and* an illusion? The knight would tear himself in two if he could see this.

Not that Robin was advocating some kind of **[Resurrection]** spell or anything. No. Let Khavren keep his just rewards in the afterlife. No need to bring him back down here to bother innocent bards—errr, that is, to suffer the slings and arrows of outrageous fortune.

Here they come, he signed to the rest of the party.

Jhess drew her dagger and, choosing her moment, sent it winging toward the lead hob, who screamed in outrage and pain as it hit him in the shoulder.

He should have worn more (or better) armor.

Robin conjured a mocking laugh from the shadows and sent a darting flicker of movement to lead the hobgoblin patrol along the route they wanted them to go.

"I'm going to take Drev and cut past them," Jhess said. "You keep the illusion leading them to us, but from the rear. That way, we can hit them from both sides if we need to."

It was as good a plan as any. They split up, leaving the bard with the seeress and the sorcerous warrior. Vance had conjured one of his paper blades but had yet to summon his armor or invoke any of the great legends to power his prowess. No point wasting magical energies if it wasn't called for, and he could invoke his abilities quickly enough if he needed to.

"You're going to learn something interesting soon," Savra spoke suddenly, looking at Robin.

The bard felt his blood go cold. He *hated* it when she did that on a deep, visceral level. Possibly right down to his shadeling DNA, if DNA was even a thing in this world.

"I'll be sure to keep an eye out," he said lightly, refusing to let her see how much she unnerved him, even though she had to know. She was a bloody seeress, after all. One deeply beloved by her spying goddess.

They moved after the hobgoblin patrol.

Robin kept his illusory rogue dancing in and out of the shadows, kept it laughing and mocking and urging the patrol on. It never seemed to occur to them that they might be running into a trap, though to be fair, the rage quotient in this group seemed higher than average, and Jhess had pegged the leader pretty good with that first knife she had thrown.

But the thing that caught Robin's attention was the mage. It was hard to say for certain, but the bolts of flame she was flinging via that wand seemed to be hitting slightly harder than he would have expected. They certainly seemed to hit harder than his own [Lesser Witch Bolt]s.

It could be her specialism, but something nagged at Robin, made him think it had to do with the wand and gorget combo.

He wanted a closer look.

Was there some way to separate the mage from her companions? Possibly. It wouldn't be easy, though. Mages tended to stick close to the tanks and vice versa. Everyone benefited from that synergy. And they needed them to make it to Ruprecht's territory. The dungeon needed all the life force he could get to fuel his assimilation of the locking mechanism so he could open it and let them deeper into Tarin-Tiran.

Suddenly, the mage whirled and flung a bolt of fire directly at Robin.

Robin cursed and dodged. He'd let himself get distracted and gotten too close. He'd been spotted!

"I'll play rabbit," he said quickly to the others, throwing a [Visual Phantasm] around them to make sure they remained unseen. "Try to lead them back around and intersect Jhess and Drev."

Then he turned and sprinted off down an alley, mentally calling for Rerebos to guide his path from above. It was almost as good as GPS.

It was certainly equally as snarky.

The hobgoblins gave chase—some of them, at least. Maybe they'd split up as well, but Robin could hear at least two sets of feet and two voices shouting after him as he ran, and from the bolts of fire he had to dodge, it was clear the mage was among them.

Left! Now! Fast, fast! Rerebos was all but shouting in Robin's mind.

The bard did as he was bid, reacting almost without thinking. He trusted the little dragon would see him through this.

He pelted down the crooked little alleyway, wincing as sparks splashed against the stone wall near his ear. At least the way was twisty enough to provide some cover, and the mage was not so skilled as to be able to control the path of her missiles. Drev was working on that, and Robin was not looking forward to needing to come up with a counter for that particular trick as he advanced in tiers.

Hurry! They are gaining! Stupid ape, run faster!

Robin put his head down and did just that.

Chapter 4

Now!

Rerebos's voice echoed in Robin's head, and he willed the illusion of a wall across the alleyway behind him right after the mage ran inside. A **[Lesser Phantasm]** cast the sound of running feet headed away down the other branch of the alley.

Rerebos confirmed they had lost the other hob.

It had been a desperate plan, but Robin had had too many close calls during this chase, and the hobs had been gaining. He needed to face them one at a time and make sure he survived. Ruprecht would just have to get another set to snack on. Robin's life took precedence over the dungeon's appetite.

A bolt of fire caught Robin in the thigh. The mage had taken advantage of his distraction in casting the illusion, but had not yet noticed she now faced the bard alone.

Robin sang out a quick **[Healing Note]**. He'd taken more than one bolt of fire as he fled from the two, and now he needed to patch himself up so he was in good enough shape to go toe to toe against this strange mage.

The next bolt of fire missed.

Robin ducked behind cover, throwing an illusory mist around himself, and the hobgoblin mage growled in annoyance. She didn't seem worried, however.

Illusionists? Underestimated? That was hardly uncommon.

Robin began a sort of guerrilla skirmish, moving from point of cover to point of cover, stepping out to fire off a **[Lesser Witch Bolt]** when opportunity presented itself, using **[Visual Phantasm]** to conjure obvious targets, etc.

It was far from a fast engagement, but Robin wanted to test the mage's limits, to see what she was capable of. If there were more like her, all the information could prove invaluable. He didn't think taking this chance was putting him in too much danger, either. She had yet to produce any large or powerful spells; he expected that if she were going to do so, it would have been during the conflict and chase already. That didn't mean there wasn't some trump card she was holding on to, but from what he'd seen so far, he was safe enough testing her limits like this.

The mage answered him spell for spell, always using fire of some kind, be it shaped as a dart, a bolt, an arc, or a lash of even a small explosive ball of flame. (Robin didn't feel the latter was quite worthy of the name **[Fireball]**, for all its similarities. It just wasn't impactful enough. Was **[Lesser Fireball]** or **[Least Fireball]** a thing? He'd have to pay more attention in his studies.) And the fire always, *always* issued forth from the wand she held. She never cast fire with her free hand or spat it from her eyes or mouth. It was always channeled via the wand.

As he fought, Robin noticed something else. The runes on the collar glimmered faintly right before the wand released a spell. More evidence that the two were connected.

I think that wand is a huge weak spot. Robin sent to Rerebos. *Keep an eye out. If you get the chance to snatch it from her, take it. She might very well be powerless without it.*

Yes! I will take the shiny! It shall be mine!

Robin wasn't going to promise that, but he also knew better than to argue with Rerebos during a battle. The little dragon might get too caught up in fighting for what he saw as his rightful spoils of victory. Or worse, he'd begin to sulk and wouldn't bother to try and snatch the thing at all.

Getting the wand from Rerebos later would be a battle in and of itself, but it'd certainly be one with lower stakes than this.

Robin dodged as another bolt of flame nearly took an ear off.

Enough! He had plenty of information. It was time to stop playing around and see about winning this fight.

Robin launched into another offensive, using illusion to mask his movements and his attack cantrips to whittle away at this target, who was surprisingly robust. Far more resilient than any spellcaster had a right to be.

That or Robin needed some more powerful spells, always a possibility. Still, they were coming. He was likely to find several good options somewhere in this very city, in fact.

If he survived long enough to delve deeply enough.

Robin exchanged more cantrips with the mage. He had [**Healing Note**] on his side, at least. The mage didn't appear to have any healing magic at her command; he didn't even see any potions she could use.

The bard ducked behind a pile of rubble to catch his breath. He needed to do more cardio! He was getting winded.

To cover, he conjured an illusion of himself popping up not far away. The mage raised her wand in response, preparing to fire another bolt of flame at him.

Rerebos chose that moment to strike. The little dragon swooped down and snatched the wand from the mage's upraised hand, and in moments, he had darted away with it, concealing himself once again among the shadows of the ruins.

"No!" the mage wailed, clutching wildly at the air.

Robin didn't give her the chance to regain her mental balance. He pressed the advantage, sending a [**Lesser Witch Bolt**] at her. The flaming card sliced her cheek and drew a slim line of blood.

The mage stumbled back. Her eyes spat daggers of hate toward him, and her fingers flexed, but she didn't immediately counter with a spell.

He had been right! Losing the wand definitely had an effect on her combat effectiveness. Robin pressed his advantage.

He cast [**Lesser Witch Bolt**]s interspersed with mocking quips about the loss of her wand, fueling the insults with the sorcerous power of [**Cutting Words**].

The mage quickly began to show signs of exhaustion and wear. This battle was not going well for her, and every time she tried to flee, Robin blocked her exit with illusions, conjuring darkness she could not see through and thus causing her to stumble and fall, or thick clouds of mist that played havoc with the senses.

Robin was going to win. The mage was going to die. She realized that before long, and her face grew increasingly desperate.

Robin didn't let up; he couldn't afford to let the mage escape. Besides, he wanted a closer look at the collar now that he had the wand. What about it so impacted her magic?

Then the mage did something unexpected. She stood stock-still and began chanting, her hands moving through the practiced gestures of spellcasting.

Robin froze. He'd had such an advantage, and the mage had shown no other signs of being able to cast without her wand before this, so her actions caught him off guard.

He should have expected this.

Wild, dancing flames kindled in the mage's eyes, followed shortly by a nimbus of fire that began dancing around her. Robin, currently in plain view, immediately wrapped himself in an illusion and threw himself to one side. Whatever she was conjuring, he had no desire to get hit with it!

The mage howled in hatred and in fury and brought her hands together. An arc of flame, magically intense, roared out from her, heading toward Robin.

No, not quite a flame. It was . . . butterflies made of fire! Their wings aflame in reds and oranges and golds. They were beautiful!

And they were painful!

One after another slammed into Robin, setting his clothing alight and searing into his skin. The bard yelped and slapped at the fiery insects, but there were too many of them to avoid. The mage was pouring out an endless stream of them.

No. Wait. Something else was happening.

Between the flickering of the butterflies and Robin's efforts to evade as many of them as he could, he caught sight of the mage. It was hard to see with so many swirling around her, but she herself was burning—no, she was dissolving into the butterflies!

Screaming. She was screaming. Her magic was out of control!

In moments, there was only the faintest of outlines remaining, until she detonated with a concussive *bang*! Butterflies exploded everywhere, washing over Robin and the nearby buildings, setting everything aflame.

Nothing remained of the mage. Not even the collar.

Not that Robin had time to retrieve it. There were larger problems in his life right now, like escaping the rising conflagration.

He darted away, running along several alleys and streets before he pulled up to catch his breath. He could see a bit of smoke behind him, but it didn't look like the fire was spreading much more beyond the street he had stood on. Probably enough ruined buildings to make effective firebreaks or residual antifire enchantments.

Small motes of flame danced on the breeze. The fiery butterflies. Robin wondered if they'd become a part of the local ecosystem now. They didn't seem to be fading like most spells would.

Strange.

Though possibly not as strange as the notification flickering on the edge of his vision. Robin focused on it and his eyes widened as it provided at least a bit of an explanation for what had just occurred.

Congratulations! New perk acquired! [Touch of Wild Magic]

You have survived an encounter with wild magic, keeping body, mind, and soul mostly intact!
Effect(s): *Having been exposed to Wild Magic, you now have the opportunity to explore this source of power. Wild magic–related classes and peculiarities have been unlocked.*
Be warned, wild magic is even more of a double-edged sword than most power. It can harm you as easily as it can help you.
You also gain a small increase to both your good luck and misfortune stats.

Well. Interesting, but not something Robin really saw himself actively pursuing. But good luck and misfortune stats? Robin didn't recall seeing those.

He opened his interface again just to be sure. No. Nowhere that he could find.

This system must have some invisible stats working within it as well.

Come on, Robin said mentally to his familiar. *We have another hob to hunt down before we head back. Can't have any of them getting away to tell the others what we look like, can we?*

Chapter 5

Robin winced as he massaged his feet. A hot stone, enchanted with a simple heating charm, glowed cheerily in the fireplace at his back. It lacked the crackle and flicker and comfort of a real fire, but the heat was welcome on his aching muscles. He was almost tempted to use a [Healing Note] to remove the last of his discomfort, but he held off. They were still camped in dangerous territory, even if Ruprecht's demesne around them meant the dungeon *should* be acting as a highly effective early-warning system.

She exploded into flaming butterflies? That is not a magical effect I can say I've encountered before.

Ruprecht was taking quite the interest in their encounter. The rest of the party was interested as well, but not to the degree the dungeon was. They'd all heard of wild magic before, in stories and guildhall whispers at least.

"Wild magic can take almost any form at all." Drev was pacing near the western wall. "It's a wondrous and dangerous thing."

"It turned the hamlet of Thrommlet into pudding," Vance said from the chair where he was paring his nails with a deceptively sharp piece of paper.

"That's an old bard's tale." Drev dismissed the thought with a flick of his fingers.

"There's documentation in the library," Vance countered.

"Before this turns into an absolutely *fascinating* argument," Jhess interrupted, "can we get back to the point?"

"Which is?" Robin wasn't quite sure anymore.

"That we're going to have to be much more careful luring patrols here if all of their mages explode like that when stressed," Savra said. Leave it to the diviner to keep an eye on salient bits of information.

"It's wild magic!" Drev protested. "They can't all do that. It would be too predictable."

"True," Vance agreed.

"Just my luck," Robin muttered.

Perhaps the wand can provide some additional insight.

The rest of the party looked at Robin expectantly.

The bard sighed and plucked the wand from his storage space. Might as well let Ruprecht have it his way. It's not like he hadn't already exhausted his creativity and his **[Bardic Lore]** trying to activate the thing. Nothing had worked. Robin didn't think it worked without the collar.

"Here." He tossed it to the ground.

The wand landed with a bit of a ringing sound from the metal used in its construction, and the party watched as it glimmered for a moment before dissolving into the ground as Ruprecht "ate" it. There was a curious lightness that came through the air then, the dungeon's attention absorbed almost completely by the new acquisition. Jhess passed another round of drinks which Robin jazzed up with **[Lesser Phantasm]**, cooling them with **[Legerdemain]**.

Magic was awesome.

"What concerns me more than the possibility of more wild mages," Vance spoke after a long pull at his drink, "is that we have yet to see much of the clerical sort with the patrols."

"Isn't that a good thing?" Jhess asked. "Less healing, easier fights."

"Possibly," Vance said, "but otherwise, the units we've faced so far have been remarkably balanced. Almost like adventuring parties or military patrols. Something here feels off. Like there's a missing element."

"I agree," Savra chimed in. "It is hard to see anything in this city for some reason, but what fragments of visions have come to me point to something important happening."

"What have you seen?" Jhess leaned in.

It was unlikely the rogue to take an interest, but Savra had helped them sort out true treasure from false, so perhaps Jhess associated the seeress's visions with wealth.

"As I said, it was mostly fragments, but some images do recur." Savra frowned. "I have seen a cracked mirror filled with mist and something moving within the vapors. I have seen a rotating spiral of teeth, and an endless expanse of stars. I have seen an iron fist with rust-red nails, clenching spasmodically. What any of it means, I am not sure. My Lady has been enigmatic of late, even for her."

A debate sparked up among the party as to what the images might mean, but before Robin could dive in, he got a hint of his own, likely stemming from that last, import-laden image.

New Quest: [Break the Iron Fist]

Your companion has had visions laden with symbolism that to you warns of Urkhan's presence here in the city of Tarin-Tiran! Investigate to see if your instincts are correct. If they are, do everything you can to destabilize or destroy the grip of the god in this city in exchange for some of the secret knowledge you seek. Break the power of the hjuncta or drive it from the city if you can!
Reward(s): *Increased enmity of the god Urkhan, secret knowledge hoarded by the deity's faithful and kept from those who would reclaim it, and some useful consumable magic items.*

"What do you think, Robin?"

"What?" He blinked away the status screen he'd been staring at.

"What do you think any of it means," Jhess repeated. "Stop staring off into thin air! You're a bard; you should have some lore at your fingertips which might put some of this into context."

"Urkhan," he replied. "The iron fist is Urkhan. I've had enough run-ins with his goons so far that I can tell what his touch on a place feels like. I'd lay a large wager that the hobgoblin hjuncta is under the control of one of his priests or warlords."

"It's possible," Vance conceded. "The imagery does fit. Savra?"

"I suspect our bard is correct. He does, after all, have the experience he claims." A small smile played about the seeress's face. "And I have reason to trust him. The goddess likes him, after all."

"Far be it for me to question the taste of a divine being," Jhess said, "but has she met him?"

"I'd protest, but I don't think it would do any good," Robin drawled, instead heading to claim another drink.

Fascinating.

Ruprecht's return interrupted the conversation. Everyone turned to the central well where Ruprecht's core—and thus, his physical body—was located. It only seemed polite.

Oh. Not the wand. I was making an observation as to your fleshy social dynamics. Not something I get to see up close terribly often.

"And what did you find out about the wand?" Robin interjected, attempting to head off a lecture from Ruprecht or a series of threats from Jhess.

It's next to useless without the collar, to begin with. This is certainly a case of a singular item with two components. Possibly three, but I can't be sure without similarly assimilating a collar.

"That's a pity." Drev grimaced. "I'd been hoping it might have some use in and of itself. We could use every advantage we can find."

Fetch me a collar, and perhaps we'll see what can be done.

"Are you able to get a sense of how an item functions after assimilating it?" Vance was looking on with keen interest.

To a degree. I can see some of the basic runic structures that comprise the enchantment and follow the channels of energy. It was created using a process I don't fully understand, so while I can replicate it exactly and make several copies, I can't alter or refine it in any way.

Ruprecht sounded incredibly frustrated by that fact.

There are some similarities, too, between the runic structures I can see and the ones holding the locking mechanism down here in the well in place.

"What does that mean?" Jhess asked.

"It means we need to lure a mage to Ruprecht properly so our friend can discover more," Savra opined.

That would be most helpful, yes. Attempting to assimilate this mechanism is consuming most of my energies. I'd prefer to expand out a bit more so we have more warning in the event of an attack, but once the process has begun, I must continue it.

Robin suspect that Ruprecht would like enough energy to begin spawning some mimic servants as well, but he kept that supposition to himself.

Jhess would freak.

"We need a better approach, then," he said instead. "So far, we've just been wandering and trying to pull after us whatever patrol we find that looks the right strength. We need to scout properly. We should know where the main camp is, what order their patrols go out in, or which routes they tend to follow. That will allow us to lay safer traps and better lures."

"That sounds like a lot of work for me," Jhess complained.

"I can help as well," Robin countered. "And I'm sure our resident seeress can aid in narrowing down the important areas quickly and efficiently."

Savra acknowledged the point by inclining her head, but then she raised a warning hand.

"I can, though I should reiterate that for some reason, my sight is . . . *fuzzy*, here in this city, and I do not fully know why. Perhaps there are old antiscrying wards blocking my connection to the goddess or warping my skills in ways unexpected. It has not made things impossible, but the difficulty should not be underestimated."

"Trust but verify," Robin said airily. "Following your lead still gives us a direction to search and will cut down on decision-making time. We'll just have to be very careful checking our work. No assumptions."

Robin sent mental instructions to Rerebos. The little dragon was a sharp scout in his own right and had several advantages that the bipedal members of Robin's little adventuring gang lacked.

Wings were only one of them.

It may be that absorbing the collar will greatly reduce the proportion of energies I need to dedicate to assimilating the locking mechanism, if the two are as related as I hope. The sooner that is accomplished, the more I may be able to aid you and shore up our defenses.

Robin suspected he was also keen to expand his influence before the other sentient dungeon within the city caught wind of their presence. The more Ruprecht could assimilate and learn from this ancient bastion of magic and knowledge, the more formidable he would be.

Not that Robin could blame him! He intended much the same thing, after all, though his part of the process didn't require putting down such literal and metaphysical roots.

"Well, what are we waiting around for then?" Robin rose to his feet. "We have our plan! Let's get to it so we can lure ourselves a mage!"

Chapter 6

Robin squinted in the afternoon sunlight. The angle and the direction positioned it perfectly to lance straight into his brain via his optic nerve. It wasn't making his mission any easier.

Either of them.

He and Vance were scouting as a pair while Jhess and Drev did likewise, searching out patterns among the patrols, trying to find the main camp so they could execute their plans. Robin and Rerebos, however, had a secondary mission they were attempting to complete as well: find some key locations Robin had unearthed in his research into Tarin-Tiran before they'd left Noviel.

There were several spots the illusionists in that diary-turned-instruction-manual had mentioned. If Robin could find even one of them, he might be able to pick up some lost or secret knowledge which had survived down the millennia.

Of course, the decay in the city combined with working from old maps and secondhand descriptions didn't make things any easier. He'd managed to find one likely prospect so far, but a cursory inspection hadn't turned anything up, and with Vance along, he couldn't afford to delay and search more carefully.

He'd left Rerebos behind to do so in his stead. The little dragon had a nose for treasure, and if there was something there to find, there was a good chance he would. Also, Robin could always circle back in the future to look more closely if he didn't find any of his other better options.

"Any sign of patrols?" Vance asked.

"Not that I can see in this light. You get anything?"

"Not yet, no." Vance raised a hand to shield his eyes. "I think we need to shift our pathway more to the left. It looks like there might be some signs of activity among the ruins in that direction."

Last time, it had just been natural decay bringing a building down, but this time, they might have better luck. Either these hobgoblins were *very* good at hiding their tracks or he and Vance were headed mostly in the wrong direction.

"I hope Jhess and Drev are having better luck than we are," Robin said, carefully making his way down the pile of rubble he'd ascended. Halfway down, a stone shifted beneath his foot. Robin lost his balance and tumbled, falling at just the right—or just the wrong—angle to hit every protruding edge and corner of broken stone all the way down. He was a bruised and bloodied mess by the time he came to a rest.

Robin coughed and sang out a **[Healing Note]**. That was bad luck. His footing had looked solid.

Bad luck. He was supposed to be encountering more of that as well as more good luck, now that he'd been touched by wild magic. If that had not happened, would he still have fallen? There was no way to tell, and trying to figure it out was a one-way street to madness.

"You alright?" Vance called, hurrying down the pile of rubble to check on him.

"Fine," Robin replied, slowly levering himself into a standing position. "Healing magic is great stuff."

"I'm afraid I haven't any to speak of, really. I can patch up a wound or do a splint, but that's about it." Vance dusted off Robin's back.

"Do you ever think about learning any healing magic?"

Robin was curious as to the answer, but he also wanted to know what Vance thought about his learning process. Robin's system advantage was, so far as he'd ascertained, unique. Not that it gave him that much of an edge, really. There were a lot of much more powerful people he'd already encountered.

"I've considered it," Vance said as they began scouting again. "But it's not terribly compatible with my strengths. Anything I could learn wouldn't be as effective as having a healer or a backup healer along, and would cost more to acquire than the few potions I do tend to use anyway. Most of my resilience comes from my abilities. A lot of the power I channel goes to soaking up damage. When the power ends, a lot of the damage goes with it. It's easier for a legend to bear such wounds than me." Vance smiled.

"How do you decide what to do next, then?" Robin kept his eyes on the task of scouting, but most of his mind was on the conversation. "I mean, you have a fairly unique set of abilities, from what I've seen and heard. That must make it hard. No set training regimen to follow, few to no mentors available to guide your path."

"True, but there's a lot of freedom there as well." Vance paused, holding up a hand. Silence fell before the librarian shrugged and motioned that they could move on again. "But from a practical standpoint, it means I do a lot of research. I look at similar paths, what has been written on them, what has worked, what has not. It goes a long way to establishing some guideposts. Plus, if I get in a real bind, there are specialists in the art of divination or the occasional crumb of divine guidance if one is lucky."

The gods of this world were very hands-on. It was a far cry from Robin's own experiences in his old world, where the gods, if they even existed, were very much a subtle work, mysterious ways kind of bunch.

He wasn't sure which was a better situation, honestly.

"How many of your next steps do you have planned?"

"I'm not sure I'd call it a plan." Vance scratched his cheek. "I've researched some abilities which seem like they'd work well with what I can do, some things I've read others being able to manage that I'd like to master myself someday, but a lot still depends on access. I don't have a sect or a master to guide me and provide training; I don't have endless funds for personal research. Not yet, anyway. So for now, I sometimes have to focus on learning something which I might not have, had I the resources other people have. And it's not like any learning is wasted, for all that we have a limited amount of time and energy."

Not that different from Robin's situation, really, even if Robin had a shortcut that not many others seemed to have. Though he had learned of skill books which could do some of what his interface allowed him to do with experience point expenditures.

Speaking of, Robin flicked open his character sheet.

Yes! He *did* have enough experience to boost his *Survival* a bit. Maybe that would help them track down these patrols.

Robin Parker

Heritage: Shadeling, Paragon
Profession: Bard
Tier: 2 (Effective Level: 7)

Experience: 1275
Spell Points: 15
Bardsong: 7 uses

Properties

Free Ranks Available: 1

Physical
- -Strength: 11
- -Dexterity: 14
- -Fortitude: 11

Mental
- -Intelligence: 17
- -Cunning: 23
- -Resilience: 14

Social
- -Charisma: 15
- -Manipulation: 13
- -Poise: 16

Proficiencies

Free Ranks Available: 1

Physical (9/9)
- -Athletics: 5
- -Brawl: 5
- -Dodge: 8
- -Melee Combat: 5
- -Pilot: 4
- -Ranged Combat: 9
- -Sleight of Hand: 7
- -Stealth: 7
- -Survival: 6

Mental (9/9)
- -Arcane Lore: 8
- -Bureaucracy: 7
- -Concentration: 9
- -Crafting: 6
- -Healing: 6

-Insight: 8
-Learning: 7
-Natural Wisdom: 4
-Perception: 9
Social (9/9)
-Animism: 4
-Deception: 10
-Empathy: 7
-Expression: 9
-Gossip: 8
-Intimidation: 6
-Persuasion: 8
-Socialize: 8
-Streetwise: 7

Peculiarities

Blessing of Rhyth
Tongue of the Fallen Tower
Mark of the Trickster
Chronicle of Infinite Visions
Mask of Myriad Faces
Initiate of the Craft
Illusion Focus
Metamagic Initiate
Improved Familiar Bond

Perks

Wayfaring Stranger
Shard of the Shattered Manymind
Mark of Fairy's Favor
Touch of Wild Magic

Spells

Cantrips* (*no SP cost)
-Lesser Phantasm*
-Cutting Words*
-Legerdemain*
-Lesser Nightmare Curse*
-Lesser Witch Bolt*

    -Minor Repair*
    -Lesser Charm*
Tier 1 (1SP each)
    -Visual Phantasm*
    -Healing Note
    -Whispers from Beyond
    -Minor Enchanted Slumber
    -Invisible Servant
    -Familiar Bond
    -Wizard's Armor
Tier 2 (3SP each)
    -Assume Quality (Special)
    -Lesser Mindreading

Bardsong

Command Attention
Song of Arcane Power

"What are you thinking about?"

Vance's comment brought Robin back to reality.

"What, sorry?" Robin blinked away his interface.

"Just then. You were staring off into space. What were you thinking about?"

"Tracking," Robin answered. It was even the truth, of sorts. "I'm wondering how much I can improve my skills here and how much that might help us with our current project."

"Ah. Good question. Did you manage to come up with an answer?"

"Not a definitive one," Robin replied, "but I think you're right about the direction we need to head."

"Is that because you agree with my assessment or because there's another location you want to investigate on the way?" Vance smiled slyly.

Adrenaline spiked. Vance was too sharp for either of their own good. Robin considered denying it for all of three seconds before deciding that was not his best play here. Might as well keep doing what he had been doing: give a version of the truth.

"I may have used my research time in Noviel to compile a list of likely locations of interest," Robin said loftily. "What of it? I'm simply attempting to maximize my time here! And if I come across a cache of useful supplies or a lost library, well, we all benefit, I assure you."

How could the party not benefit from Robin increasing his personal power? It made it that much more likely they would all survive and prosper.

"And you chose to keep them to yourself because . . . ?" There was a teasing edge to Vance's tone, otherwise, Robin's stomach might have dropped.

"To make sure I'm not wasting anyone's time, of course." Robin sniffed. "Are you going to tell me you haven't done the same? You know that library better than anyone else in the party, and have deeper access. Can you honestly say you don't have a few secrets you hope to uncover here in Tarin-Tiran?"

"No, I can't say that." Vance smiled. "I'm just pleased I'm not the only one! Now I don't need to feel selfish or sneaky."

"Bards are meant to be sneaky." Robin flicked away any shame that might cling to the idea with dismissive fingertips. "It's one of the better ways to survive when we're hardly the offensive or defensive powerhouses of the party."

Before he could say anything more, however, Vance held up a hand and cocked his head to one side.

"I think we've got company."

Chapter 7

Robin and Vance immediately took cover behind the nearest ruined building, Robin wincing as the ragged edges of the crumbled stone bit into him through his clothing. For good measure, he dropped an illusion of rubble on top of them.

He wasn't a moment too soon. A hobgoblin patrol—this one far better equipped than any other they had seen so far—came into view. The leader was a massive warrior, and the mage accompanying them was older, battle scarred, and burned. He carried his wand at the ready.

Wands, actually, Robin noticed. This mage held one in each hand. The one in his left was the same as the others the bard had seen the hobgoblin mages in this city carry, but the one in his right was different. Where the first wand was made of metal, this one was made of wood and finely crafted, with a smoothness to the lines that spoke of a completely different design aesthetic.

Robin really wanted to know what that wand did. Not so much that he was willing to step into view as a target, but still.

Beside him, Vance held perfectly still. The two of them were outnumbered and, to all appearances, outgunned, even if they faced these hobs with even odds.

Robin could feel the uncertainty in the air. Should they stay hidden? Try to run and lure the party after them? It was a very long way back to Ruprecht from here.

Before the silent conversation between Robin and Vance could come to a conclusion, however, the hobgoblins began speaking to one another in their native tongue.

Not a problem for Robin. He held up a hand, a small gesture, and Vance signed recognition. They would wait and see what happened.

"Anything?" the warrior demanded.

"No, boss," one of the others replied. She looked like a scout or a rogue of some kind.

"Some small traces, but nothing that says any kind of invading force is here," added another slim figure, this one whipcord thin with a scar across one milky-white eye.

"Something is taking out our patrols, and I want to know what," the leader snapped.

"They might have deserted." The mage stopped scanning the surrounding area with his gaze to speak. "It has happened before."

"They would not dare!" the second woman in the group spoke. She was brawn, though not so strong looking as the leader, and bore tattoos which Robin couldn't quite completely see all over her visible flesh.

Something about those markings made him uneasy.

"And has Lord-God Urkhan given you any special insight into the matter?" The mage's voice could well have been poisoned silk.

Urkhan! That was why the marking looked so familiar! They were sacred symbols of Urkhan, albeit not in a form he had encountered before.

His **[Bardic Lore]** pinged, confirming Robin's realization and adding some likely suppositions. The woman was probably some kind of battle priest, trained to channel the divine energies of Urkhan into effects that would help dominate and secure the battlefield. She almost certainly would have the same command ability that Gis had exhibited. That could very well be lethal in a fight where he and Vance were outnumbered five to two.

The army that had originally crushed Tarin-Tiran had been under the command of one of Urkhan's favorites. Were these hobgoblins the descendants of a part of that army? One that had never left and instead had set up permanent camp within the ruins of the city they had tried to utterly destroy?

An occupying force was certainly within Urkhan's style book.

"Lord-God Urkhan does not coddle his faithful," the battle priest was saying, practically spitting in disdain at the mage. "The Lord-God Urkhan helps those who help themselves. It is down to us to discover who or what has invaded our territory and crush it or bring it to heel."

"Well, we aren't finding it out here," the scout interjected. "We should either strike out in a different direction or head back. All we're doing here is wasting breath." She all but rolled her eyes at the mage and the priest squabbling.

The rest of the patrol looked to the leader. He glanced around at the buildings, eyes narrowed, before shaking his head.

"There has been nothing fruitful in this direction, today nor yesterday. We head back. Perhaps one of the other patrols has found something."

The hobgoblins grumbled but turned around and started back the way they had come. Robin flicked his fingers through the paces of [Lesser Phantasm] and caused a single illusory word to appear in front of Vance's eyes.

Follow?

Vance hesitated for a moment before nodding in assent. He held up a hand, though, before they moved, indicating extreme caution.

Robin was fine with that. If they managed to stay undetected and find the location of their camp or headquarters or whatever, it would be a prime piece of useful knowledge.

The bard waited until the hobgoblins were safely out of sight before rising to follow them on quiet feet. Vance trailed along behind him, staying back far enough so as not to risk his clumsier tread giving them away, but not so far that he couldn't see Robin or be close at hand if things took a turn for the worse.

Robin sent a mental message, hoping Rerebos was in range.

No response. The little dragon must not be close enough for their bond to work. *Dammit.* He'd have to keep trying; they could really use an extra pair of eyes right about now.

The hobgoblins were moving at a quick pace—not outright running, and they kept their weapons ready, but they darted through the ruins with the air of people who knew the territory, knew it well, and had little to no reason to fear a surprise attack. After all, they had just passed through and knew the area was mostly clear, in spite of their mission to seek out whoever or whatever was disturbing their patrols.

There was no sign that any of them realized one of the reasons was trailing along quietly behind them, moving from crevice to corner, sticking to the shadows, and conjuring illusions to cover his tracks.

Robin was close enough that he could hear the hobs talking to one another, but too far away to catch the meaning. He briefly considered trying to use [Lesser Mindreading] but dismissed the idea almost immediately. The range was less than ideal, and whatever information he picked up would be incidental, not focused like it might be in a conversation or an interrogation.

And he might need those spell energies to fuel combat magics if they caught on that someone was following them.

Though he couldn't hear what was being said, Robin could see how they moved, could see how the group dynamics played out. He watched carefully, drawing on his [Bardic Lore] to help fill in gaps.

The leader—the warrior—ruled with a clearly iron hand, and there was little resentment and nary a whiff of rebellion. The group was very hierarchical, as one would expect from Urkhan worshippers.

There was a lot more fractiousness along the horizontal axis of power, however. It wasn't clear who outranked who, but the mage and the battle priest were both clearly a step above the two scouts or rogues. From their body language alone, Robin couldn't tell if the dislike between the mage and the battle priest was social or personal. If he had to bet, though, he'd bet social. Not many of the legends or tales in his mind spoke in depth about hobgoblin social dynamics, but many of them agreed that as a people, hobgoblins prized order and respected personal power over social power. And if it was endemic to their social structure, it might be something the party could use to even the odds in their encounters with the hobs.

The hobgoblin leader threw up a fist, and the patrol suddenly came to a screeching halt, freezing in their tracks. Eyes were peeled, weapons were poised. Waves of battle readiness rolled off the whole group.

Robin's foot chose that moment to scrape on a stone, of course.

The bard froze, immediately willing a patch of shadow to deepen around where he was crouched behind a corner. It was an imperfect solution, as he had been in the middle of darting to his next hiding place, but it was all he had. He prayed Vance had seen him freeze and was not even now moving closer to the hobgoblins, who were now on high alert.

Each member of the patrol was scanning the surroundings, rotating slowly in place, acting almost in concert so that while each individual scanned a section of the nearby area for threats, no single angle was left unwatched.

It was impressive, but not a good situation for Robin. His muscles trembled with the odd position he had frozen in, trembled with adrenaline, but he held firm. If he didn't move and no one noticed a slightly odd patch of shadow, things would be all right.

Maybe.

More hand gestures from the warrior leading the patrol. The hobs fanned out, taking cover in the nearby ruins, close enough to one another to provide support but far enough apart that they weren't in, as Robin's old dungeon master would have called it, "fireball formation."

A bolt of fire sailed out from somewhere beyond Robin's line of sight, splashing against the wall near the warrior's head. The patrol leader flashed out a quick series of hand gestures, and the group of hobgoblins leapt into action.

There was a whirl of activity as they clashed with . . . another patrol? Robin was so thrown, he very nearly didn't take advantage of the distraction to improve his hiding place.

Nearly.

The two hobgoblin patrols skirmished for a bit, then Robin was thrown another curveball when the fight just stopped and the two forces came together, jovially beginning to talk with one another before joining up to continue on in the direction the first patrol had been originally headed.

This was not a social behavior he had expected. Robin had no idea what in nine different hells that might be, really. It didn't even seem to be something he could take advantage of in the future; it was simply that weird to him.

Maybe it was because he wasn't part of the martial society. Maybe it was because he originated from another, far different world to this. Whatever the reason, one thing was clear: with ten hobgoblins to follow instead of five, this plan had just gotten exponentially more dangerous.

Chapter 8

Robin and Vance were still following the hobgoblins. Sweat, hot and salty, rolled down Robin's face and pooled beneath his nose. The patrol set a truly brutal pace, the two groups of five each pushing to try and outdo the other. It was all Robin could do to keep up.

Thankfully, both groups had agreed to a brief pause to drink from their waterskins and tear at some field rations. Robin's feet were grateful for the chance to rest.

Vance had it easier—the librarian was annoyingly fit. If Robin didn't know better, he'd suspect the man had some way to channel the stamina of legendary figures as well as their battle prowess, but that effect wouldn't last nearly long enough to be a worthwhile expenditure of Vance's magical energies . . .

. . . that he knew of. There was still a lot he didn't know about Vance's particular talents and divinely bestowed blessings.

"What?" Vance asked without looking at him.

Robin started, realizing he had been staring.

"Sorry," he murmured. "Just thinking how much I hate that you seem less winded than I do."

Vance grinned wickedly.

"Don't make me laugh," he said. "Now would not be a good time."

No lie there.

Boss! What are you doing so far from home base?

Rerebos! Robin had to bite his tongue to keep from cheering. It was like a flood of balm to his frazzled soul hearing that little voice in his mind once more. He was going to have to raid his stash of shiny things to give his familiar a present this evening. Hearing the avaricious dragon giving his tiny growl of pleasure at a new acquisition sounded like the exact sort of thing he needed tonight.

Since another hit of that psychedelic mead was at least a world away.

We're trying to follow the hobgoblins in front of us all the way back to their base.

Oooh! Lots of food for friend Ruprecht?

The little dragon sounded pleased at the prospect. Robin knew it was a bad idea to let the dragon get too close to the dungeon—it could create almost unlimited shinies. What being of draconic heritage could resist something like *that*?

Vance was looking at him, head cocked to one side. Robin had the sneaking suspicion that he was raising suspicion. He held up a finger and tapped his temple, then jerked his head toward the hobs. The librarian mouthed the word *Anything?* And Robin shook his head with a rueful look.

He was starting to slip up. He was going to need to start trusting these people a bit more. Too many secrets. It was distracting him, and here, that could get him killed.

Well, he wasn't that far off from leveling again, was he? Certainly not at the rate he was facing danger and discovery in this place. One more level, and then he could get Rerebos more of his native powers. That would make it safe enough to bring him into the party as Robin's *new* familiar. Maybe as something a lot more innocuous looking than a miniature shadow dragon, though.

The hobgoblins began to shift in preparation for moving out again, and Robin used the cover of the noise they were making to risk a few more words with Vance.

"I'll keep following. Stay as quiet as you can. If we get separated, meet back at the fountain three streets back and two over. We have to be getting close. They're too relaxed."

"Just make sure you're not so focused on them you miss any other patrols which might be in the area. The closer we get to their headquarters, the more patrols there will be. Not to mention traps."

"Good point."

Rerebos, he asked the little dragon, *be sure to watch for traps while you're spying on them, as well as for any patrols which might intersect us as we follow.*

Yes. Though I do not like these risks. Risks are decidedly not shiny.

Robin couldn't argue with that.

He exchanged a few more words with the librarian, establishing a signal in case a patrol came up behind them and Vance noticed it before Robin had the chance. He wasn't too worried, not with Rerebos having eyes in the sky, but it was nice to have redundancies when it came to something like, *oh*, basic survival in a hostile territory.

The hobgoblins began to move out. Robin rose and followed, glancing back over his shoulder once to check on Vance. The librarian flicked him a signal saying all was well.

Good. He'd follow in a few moments, staying just far enough behind to make sure he wasn't spotted.

The pace they set didn't make it easy. It was fast and uneven, with lots of pauses to scout ahead or to the sides. If Robin hadn't had Rerebos flying quietly above and ahead, sending updates back along their bond, he might have been caught more than once by the unexpected pauses and detours.

He was so intent on following that he must have missed the first set of signals—whistles from Vance disguised as bird calls. It was only when the sound went deliberately off-key that it caught his attention, and he glanced behind him.

Vance was gesturing frantically. Another patrol! This one coming up from behind. *Fuck.* They did not need this right now.

Then it got worse.

Boss! They heard something! They're turning to look behind them. Get out of sight NOW!

Robin didn't stop to think. He sprinted to the closest alleyway leading away from the broad avenue they had been traveling down. He slipped around the corner and threw himself down behind a pile of rubble, chest heaving, praying he hadn't been spotted.

Are they moving this way?

Not yet. I don't think they saw you. But they definitely think something is behind them. They're going to head that way soon, I think.

Vance! He had to get out of there or he'd be caught between two patrols in front and at least one behind. And with so many eyes, illusions might be tricky; especially with the hobs on as high alert as Rerebos seemed to think they were.

Robin frantically signaled to Vance, urging the librarian to hurry and catch up. They needed to get out of the way, and now!

Vance sprinted for the alleyway where Robin crouched, concealed. The bard's heart beat a frantic tattoo against his ribcage, and he could only wait and watch as the slim man dashed across the open, oh-so-vulnerable area of the street. He couldn't help reaching out a hand.

The librarian grabbed it, and Robin pulled him in and down under cover just as the patrol rounded the corner, blades drawn and sparks spitting from the mages' fingertips.

Robin didn't wait for them to find them. He sent an illusory figure fleeing down an alley at an angle away from them, not in the exact opposite direction—that would make it too easy to follow if the mages sniffed out the illusion—but angled away from the way the alley they were hiding in ran.

For good measure, he used [**Lesser Phantasm**] to conjure the clattering sound of falling rubble and a voice spitting out a loud curse.

He didn't pause to see how well his ruse worked. He pulled Vance after him, and they began running as quickly and as quietly as they could, taking the first turn they could that placed them even further away from the direction Robin had sent his decoy illusion.

Then again. And again. They turned and ran, pausing every so often to check for sounds of pursuit or signs of other nearby patrols. Once they were at the end of their endurance, Vance pulled them into one of the larger intact buildings in the area.

Robin and Vance stood pressed together, frozen in place, listening for any sounds of pursuit. After a few minutes with no signs of it, they relaxed. It looked like they'd gotten away.

"Come on," Robin said when they'd regained their breath. "Let's head up to the roof, see where we are. It's going to be a nightmare navigating back after this."

Fortunately, he had a little dragon who would make things much easier, though he'd be happier when Rerebos was once again in mental hailing distance. The little dragon had slipped out of range during that last mad sprint, probably having to detour around a building so as not to be spotted by one of the mages.

No one wanted to be on the business end of a fireball, not even an airbound dragonling.

They ascended the stairs, not quickly but with more energy than they had a right to. Robin paused at the top, listening and looking before cautiously creeping out to get a better view of the surrounding city. No sooner had he done so than Rerebos's presence exploded back into his mind.

Boss! Boss, look! You're—

But Robin had seen it. How could he not, from this vantage? Across a wide swath of destroyed city, all building reduced to rubble or fortifications, a veritable village—no, a small town of tents and cookfires spread out before him.

They'd found the hobgoblin's main base of operations. There was no question about that.

Robin ground his teeth.

It was so much bigger than he'd feared.

Chapter 9

$\mathcal{R}$obin rubbed his forehead as several voices clashed in disagreement around him. He and Vance were back at the base and, having recounted their discoveries to the others, now had to face the debate about what to do about them.

He took a sip of his drink, cooling it with **[Legerdemain]**. It was not a question that was going to be settled any time soon.

I still do not understand why you cannot give us a more precise estimate of their numbers.

"We don't all sense our surroundings the way you do now," Robin answered drily, with a bit of warning on the end of the sentence. "We have to use our eyes to determine such things. And there were at least three hundred hobgoblins in that encampment."

"He is correct," Savra confirmed. "I cannot tell precisely how many, as my senses are still confused. More confused when directed near the hobgoblins, actually." She paused, thoughtful. "Perhaps, they are somehow responsible for the confusion I sense. Though that seems unlikely."

"Maybe they have something that defies divination *and* there is something about the city itself that frustrates that art," Vance suggested. "It does not have to be simply one or the other. It could be both."

The librarian was sitting next to Robin, likewise savoring a cool drink—Robin made sure to keep it that way. He owed the man that much at least after the day they'd both had.

Well, three hundred would certainly be an excellent start toward expanding our influence in this area.

"You'll get fat," Robin murmured in English.

The building around them shook slightly in displeasure.

"Robin?" Jhess said sweetly.

"Yes?"

"Don't antagonize the dungeon."

"Yes, ma'am." Robin smiled sardonically and fired her a mock salute.

"What I want to know is if there are other encampments like this throughout this section of the city," Drev said, a troubled look on his face. "From your description, it sounds like this is very much a war camp, but they're not enough to hold more than a few neighborhoods of this place. There's plenty of room for others."

"Savra?" Robin looked to the seeress hopefully.

She shook her head.

Robin sighed. He really wanted to take more pleasure in her frustration, but it was as much a problem for him as it was for her, and that just took all the fun out of things.

I suppose we shall just have to do this the hard way. We need more information. It is imperative—our success depends on it. Fortunately, we have an ideal solution at hand.

"What?" Jhess asked, wariness as clear on her face as a freshly painted bull's-eye.

We send in our spy.

Robin didn't like where this was going.

"I presume you mean me?"

Of course. You have the requisite skills. You are equipped both to infiltrate and to understand the native language in question. You can generate illusions to hide yourself in as you eavesdrop. In fact, I'm not sure why you did not simply remain behind to gather information from the start. It would have been much more efficient.

"I'm rather attached to my hide," Robin drawled, "and this plan seems like it has too high a chance of separating me from it."

"Oh, come on," Jhess said. "You live for this kind of stuff. Playing with disguises, acting like a master spy, living by your wits. You can't hide any of that from us. We know you too well."

"You do." Robin glared at her flatly.

Yes. We do.

Robin bit back a retort. As irritated as he was about being gently bullied into this, they did have a point. And Ruprecht knew far more about him than any of the others. Knew about Earth.

And a dungeon was not an enemy you really wanted to cultivate.

Particularly one that was currently providing you with rations, shelter, and defenses.

"It might also give you the chance to get your hands on one of those collars without blowing it up," Drev added.

Jhess laughed. Vance grinned. Robin glared.

"Is that supposed to be funny?" the bard asked the mage.

Drev colored.

"No!" he blurted. "I mean, no. Definitely not. I just meant—"

"I know." Robin sighed. "And you're right. I should probably be the one to do this."

He sent a thread of will through the [Mask of Disguise] resting invisibly on his face. In place of his usual bardic self, a battle-scarred hobgoblin scout sat. Robin pointedly raised his drink and took a noisy slurp.

"Happy?"

"Definitely an improvement in the looks department," Jhess quipped.

Robin shifted to make himself look like a hobgoblin version of the rogue. The smile promptly dropped off her face.

A knife appeared in her hand a moment later.

Robin quickly shifted his appearance again, this time to that of the first hobgoblin mage he'd faced.

No, Ruprecht spoke instantly. *That is not a wise idea. Too many people of power might recognize you. It certainly would not do you any favors in terms of staying unnoticed. Mages tend to draw attention.*

"Not all of us," Drev pointed out.

"You're the son of a crime lord!" Robin exclaimed. "And twice as handsome as you have any right to be. You're hardly one to talk."

Drev colored again and hid behind taking a swig from his own drink.

"Do not attempt to distract us," Savra said. "We were discussing your infiltration attempt."

"We're really doing this?" Robin looked around at the party. "You're going to micromanage *my* infiltration? Tell me *how* that is a good idea? The only one of you who would have anything reasonable to say on the matter is Jhess, and even then, her methods aren't close enough to mine for her to have any really useful advice." Robin noticed Jhess still had her knife in her hand. "No offense."

"I'm not sure if I'll be taking any or not," the rogue sniffed. "We'll see how the rest of this conversation goes."

"We're happy to leave the details to you," Vance said. "We trust you. But I do believe that this is the best course of action at the moment. It's in the best interests of yourself as well as the party to agree."

Oddly enough, Robin thought the librarian meant that. And even odder, the bard was inclined to agree. He did feel like he was slowly slotting into a place where he could trust these people. To a point.

A bard's gotta have some secrets, after all. And what your friends didn't know, they couldn't have tortured out of them.

Robin resumed wearing his own face.

"Fair enough. I think this level of risk does call for an increased level of reward, though."

"What do you want?" Jhess leapt on the suggestion immediately. The rogue always was quite protective of the treasure division.

"Any illusion artifacts, knowledge sources, or magical items that we discover anywhere in or related to Tarin-Tiran are *not* tallied up with the regular treasure and are offered to me. If I want it, it's mine. If I don't, then it can pass into the treasure pool as normal.

That's stupid, Rerebos piped up into his mind from wherever the little dragon was hiding. *Why surrender any shinies at all?*

Because friends are the shiniest of shinies, Robin thought back at him. *And you the shiniest of those.*

Robin felt his familiar preen beneath the compliment.

"That seems like a lot," Jhess complained.

"Just give it to him," Drev said. "This way, he won't try to sneak it from us on the sly or hold back on any of the potential treasure hoard locations he's researched."

"Traitor," Robin told Vance.

"Don't look at me," the librarian denied. "I didn't say a word."

"You're a little bit obvious," Drev said. "And it's not hard to figure out your main areas of interest, given, well, everything we've been through together."

"Wow," Robin said. "Way to weaponize our friendship."

"I still think it's a lot," Jhess spoke up. "After all, how dangerous can it really be?"

She was going to fight him every step of the way on this. *Fine.* Robin was ready for this battle; this was not a line he was going to budge on. Might as well make the risks crystal clear, maybe make it a bit of a performance. If he played his cards right, the others would join together and outvote Jhess.

"What do I do if I'm discovered?" Robin asked. "There are battle priests there as well as mages. How do I prioritize targets? I certainly can't live among them for an extended period of time. I'll be able to fool them for a while, and I'll have mind-reading spells for a bit of my reconnaissance, but my magical energies do have limits. What's the line? When do I call enough, enough?"

I do not know the answers to any of those questions, Robin, but I do know one thing.

"Oh? What's that?" Robin's heart sank. He had a feeling he already knew what Ruprecht was going to say.

You are going to find out for us.

Chapter 10

*T*he smell of game stewing in a broth of wild herbs teased at Robin's nostrils and made his stomach growl. Or was it even his stomach right now? He was currently walking through the middle of the hobgoblin camp in the form of an eminently forgettable hobgoblin scout.

It was an interesting question. How much did he change on the inside when he shifted shapes? Did each of his organs change as well? Was it all the way down to the cellular or DNA level? Was DNA even a thing in this world? He assumed there was some degree of change, especially when he employed **[Assume Quality]**, but there was no way he could think of to truly know for sure. Magic broke, twisted, and bent a lot of the rules as he knew them.

Maybe Savra would know, if her goddess would tell her.

Robin moved purposefully through the camp, though he had no hobgoblin-y reason to be there. You're less likely to be stopped or challenged if you looked like you belonged and if you looked like you're already doing something productive.

The camp or village or whatever it was wasn't huge, but it was far larger than Robin was comfortable with, considering just how many enemies were surrounding him. Rather terrible odds if he got caught.

He'd already identified the salient features of the settlement: the place he was thinking of as the mess hall, though it was more an open firepit with a cooking tent nearby; the larger and largest tents or pavilions which held the officers' quarters and the command structure; and so on.

The hobgoblins of this war camp—and he couldn't really think of it as anything else—were a curious mix of settled and on alert. He hadn't yet been able to confirm the theory that they'd been here since the army that had sacked Tarin-Tiran had, well, sacked the city, but circumstantial evidence certainly pointed that way. They didn't seem to have transitioned fully to a peacetime footing, even though they were fairly relaxed in their war bands.

The dungeon probably had a lot to do with that. Robin had gathered that wandering monsters were very common—he could even see some of the trophies dotting the camp—and their presence was frequent enough that there were a few wounded and several active warriors still trying to win points by bragging about their last encounter.

There was also a sense of wariness to the camp, something which didn't feel usual. As Robin made his way through the place, it was easy enough to pick up on the mutterings and whispers, concerns about the patrols that had vanished without a trace.

That would be because of Robin and his friends.

It was still a faint understirring of unease, nothing that would mobilize the whole camp, and Robin would prefer to keep it that way. Several hunting parties in nicely paced succession—that was what they were after.

Robin kept a sharp eye out, storing away faces and names in his mind. He'd likely need to impersonate some of these individuals in the future if he wanted to successfully sow the rumors that would lead several patrols into the areas his party wanted them in. He'd need to find the scoutmaster as well, and see if he could use **[Lesser Mindreading]** to pull details of how patrols were divided and which routes they were sent along from his brain. The more his party could nip at the edges and keep their location from being discovered, the better.

Robin was also here to sow rumors of a terrible beast, sent up from the dungeon below. They might need a distraction, or possibly even a way to drive the war camp off in the future. Or the idea might not be used at all. In any case, it was something useful to cultivate for now.

The problem was everyone seemed to be doing something. There were no casual gatherings engaged in idle chitchat, and he needed enough people in one place so he could slip in some illusory words, or he'd have to take the face of someone who was really here. This camp wasn't so large that a strange hobgoblin could wander up and join a conversation.

Robin pondered the problem as he carried an armful of supplies from one side of the camp to the other, looking busy. What he needed was . . . *aha!* There.

A patrol was clearly headed out. Robin adjusted his trajectory and pacing to make sure he intercepted them before they made it fully out of the camp. As he walked, he yanked as much as he could about cultures like this one out of his **[Bardic Lore]**. The right attitude would go a long way to selling this.

Right before he made it to the approach, he cast **[Lesser Mindreading]**. He was going to need every advantage he could get today.

"Good hunting," he said as he approached.

"Sharp spears," came the reply.

"Word is there's some sort of beast out there," Robin warned. "Some of the other scouts just back say they've seen signs." He didn't say anything about the missing patrols being connected to the beast sighting. He didn't say anything about the missing patrols at all. It would be considered . . . not a bad omen, precisely, nor exactly in poor taste, but something in that vein. The cultural concept didn't translate perfectly to his own experience.

"What kind of beast?" the patrol leader asked. "Any useful intelligence or is it more scouts jumping at shadows?"

This one was clearly in the mold of Khavren when it came to leadership.

"It's fast, sticks to the shadows, and the one track that was found showed signs of wicked claws. Six of them, possibly seven."

"Dungeon's getting creative again," one of the other scouts heading out with the patrol muttered. "I hate it when it does that."

"It doesn't like people poking around," the patrol mage replied. "So what did you expect? We have our orders; deal with it."

Orders? Poking around the dungeon? *Interesting*.

Robin focused his mind reading on the mage, hoping to catch a bit more information on what, precisely, the hjuncta was up to. The emotions came through first, the reddish-gray of resentment, then a faint yellow-green flash of fear, quickly suppressed. There might have been a thready gold flare of hope, but the dull wash of general cynicism that overlaid the mage's mind made it hard to tell.

"Orders are orders," Robin said, to keep the subject on the top of the nearby hobgoblins' minds. "Whoever is giving them."

The flare of resentment that flashed through the mage's mind then was practically blinding. Robin caught flashes of thoughts that said something like *arrogant outsider* and *but Urkhan commands*.

"Orders are orders," the mage repeated.

Robin dug a fingernail into the fleshy part of his thumb to help him focus. It was a very weird thing to loudly hear one thing in a being's thoughts while the words coming out of their mouth said something else.

There was a fascinating flash of resentment that accompanied the idea of unwanted orders and the image of the collar around the mage's neck, which was interesting. Was the collar more than just a magical item? Or did it have an effect Robin had yet to see? One which would cause the mage to resent it?

Robin filed the idea away for later. There was no way to chase it down now, and none of the regular hobgoblins really gave the mages much thought. At least not that Robin had found so far.

"Good hunting," Robin said again, noticing the irritation and impatience growing in the mind of the patrol leader. "And keep an eye out for the beast."

The flashes of wariness were satisfying as Robin moved away. There hadn't been any suspicion in any of the minds around him, so he didn't think his disguise had been compromised at all.

He crisscrossed the encampment a few more times, always carrying something from one end to the other. When the opportunity presented itself, he'd pause and mention the beast. By the end of the day, there would be at least a few sightings reported to the scoutmaster. Robin had left a bit of evidence that one or more of the patrols were sure to pick up on, and he'd primed a few patrols to specifically be looking. They'd assume it was precisely what it appeared to be, what they'd already heard about.

At least, Robin hoped they would.

He set his latest burden, a bundle of wood, at the end of a pile of stuff destined to fuel the cooking fires. There was a large amount of dried dung as well as the expected wood and dried vegetation. He was looking around for the next obvious errand he could use as an excuse for his presence when a voice interrupted him.

"You there. What are you doing?"

Robin froze, then slowly turned to face the speaker.

Fuck. What now?

Chapter 11

Robin was looking at one of the scout lieutenants. The hobgoblin, tall and rangy with a scar across his nose, was glaring at the disguised bard with obvious impatience.

"Well?" he demanded. "What are you doing? All scouts should be reporting in right now."

Robin could see several funneling toward the large command tent. Rather than risk saying something wrong, he just nodded and headed toward the gathering of scouts. He'd be among a lot of other faces there, and he was likely to pick up some useful intelligence, so he judged it worth the risk.

Certainly, it was easier than trying to make a break for it.

Blending in wasn't really Robin's strong suit, but he was also a shape-shifter, so he made it work. Those shadeling instincts were coming in handy, and the [Lesser Mindreading] wouldn't hurt.

Robin used the cover of movement to cast the spell again, further depleting his store of magical energies. It was unlikely it would last the whole meeting, but a gathering of scouts this large meant there had to be higher-ups present. He might get lucky and sneak a few useful thoughts away from them. Useful to have up in case he faced any unexpected challenges settling in, too.

All told, there were a few dozen scouts assembled when he joined the hobgoblins, enough to mix in and lose himself, so long as he didn't draw too much attention. Murmured conversation ebbed and flowed around him, maybe half of the assembled scouts speaking while the other half stood in stony silence.

Interesting mix.

Silence fell like an executioner's axe the next moment, though, as the scoutmaster stepped into the tent. Robin had ferreted out all of the leadership as a first priority when he'd first infiltrated the camp, so he knew precisely who he was looking at.

The scoutmaster was an old blade, honed thin over many winters of hunting, but holding an edge all the sharper for it. His golden eyes cut through the room, sharp and seeking. Robin forced himself to relax as they played over him.

"Pathetic," he spat. "Not a one of you sharp enough to spot what is killing our patrols. Three! Three patrols have been lost, all without a trace! And none of you have brought me anything more than rumors! Some kind of beast sent up by the dungeon? That's really the best you have?"

Robin swayed, nearly bowled over by the flares of fear and anxiety all around him. The scoutmaster clearly held his position through fear and an iron fist. (Yay, something new and different for the followers of Urkhan.) There were small sparks of curiosity and jealousy as well. Several nearby scouts wanted to know who had managed to find even that much of a hint.

This was not a healthy work environment.

"It's becoming a problem," the scoutmaster continued. "Keep it up, and we'll have the mages pushing to try divinations again."

There was a flash of resentment and anger at that. This time, it was accompanied by mutterings throughout the tent, and phrases like *keep the dogs leashed!*, *bloody menaces!*, and *fucking finger-wagglers!*

Robin rifled through the nearby thoughts, clutching at every fragment of information he could. It seemed like the mages were both generally feared and looked down upon. The collars they wore were seen of as leashes, and the general mood of the assembled was that they—the collars—were a good, reassuring thing.

So, mages were sort of second-class individuals in the hjuncta. *Interesting.* And the collars somehow leashed their powers or allowed the command structure to control them? It was hard to follow from all the fragments, but there was enough to get a general picture.

Now, how could he use this to get some more mages to fall into their traps? He wanted Ruprecht to have a chance to disassemble the thing even more now. It might be twice as useful as they had originally thought.

"It will not be allowed to happen!" The scoutmaster's voice whipped out like a lash and snapped all attention back to him. "You're all going to go out, following the paths of the missing patrols, and you are going to scour this ruin of a city until you find a clue as to what happened. I don't care if it's a beast from the depths of the dungeon, a specter from some ancient war, or a bloody turncoat murdering scum! You will find it and you will do so before the mages gather any more support for the idea of letting them off their leashes enough to try divining again."

Ruprecht was going to need to up the defenses around their main camp. With this many scouts scouring the city in a dedicated search, the likelihood of one of them finding the party's trail and following it back to Ruprecht had just jumped. High.

There were more orders. More complaints. Robin managed to pick up that there was some sort of expedition happening, parties descending deeper into the city, which was what everyone assumed had roused the dungeon. Bit of luck, that. Something to reinforce the idea of the beast that Robin had been sowing.

Unfortunately, his spell gave out before he could probe anyone very deeply on the matter of this expedition. The scoutmaster didn't give many details, as presumably everyone here already knew as much as they needed to. It seemed like it was important to the commander of this war camp, and there was a mix of hope and resentment among the scouts. Hope that there might be riches in it for everyone, and resentment that it was clearly making their lives more difficult.

Robin's eyes searched the interior of the tent whenever he could. Were there useful maps in here somewhere? There had to be, even if most of the scouts knew the nearby area by heart. Commanders liked planning their battles, and this place didn't strike him as one that would employ illusionists to conjure battle maps for strategy meetings.

Their loss.

"I'm sorry, am I boring you?"

Robin froze, suddenly very aware of the attention focused on him from those nearby and, even worse, the attention of the scoutmaster.

"No, sir," he replied immediately, adrenaline driving an ice pick into his neck.

The eyes on him made his skin crawl. This place was big, but not so big that he could indefinitely get away with being a face no one truly recognized. Sure, he looked familiar to most because Robin had carefully sculpted bland, forgettable features, but that didn't mean sustained attention wouldn't unmask him as someone who didn't belong here.

"Then what is so fascinating that you're looking at it rather than listening to me? Hmm?"

Robin's eyes flashed to the canvas of the wall in the direction he'd been looking. He couldn't say anything about the chests he'd been eyeing, or the table with its pile of parchment. The setting sun (could you even call it that, in this world?) painted the walls of the pavilion with shadows from outside.

Shadows. Outsider and outsiders. Robin's mind flashed over what he'd heard so far today, the cracks he'd seen in the hobgoblin society.

"Someone's out there, moving. Sir." Robin jerked his chin in the appropriate direction, even as he willed a shadow to suddenly stand and move rapidly away with [Visual Phantasm]. A shadow bearing the rather distinctive shape of a figure in robes with a collar. He even put a wand in the figure's hand. Might as well make it obvious.

The room erupted in murmurs as several others spotted it before it winked out of sight.

"Spies!" the scoutmaster hissed, eyes narrowing and, thankfully, no longer on Robin. "Well spotted."

Orders were barked out and a set of five scouts slipped out of the command tent to investigate. They'd not find anything, but that didn't really matter. The scoutmaster's attention was firmly elsewhere now.

More instructions were quickly relayed with hand signals; it looked like he had no intention of taking any more risks. Robin bit his lip. He now had no idea what was being said, at all. If only he still had his [Lesser Mindreading] up! But there was no way to recast the spell now, in a tent full of scouts, with the telltale hand gestures and magic words so likely to stand out.

He needed more levels and more metamagical knowledge, and fast!

Luck was on his side, however. Nothing more was said, and the gathering was swiftly dismissed. Robin was able to file out with the others who all quickly peeled off and headed in different directions to accomplish their missions.

Robin found an out-of-the-way nook and swiftly changed faces. He'd just drawn far too much attention to himself, and he didn't want to be around if the scoutmaster decided his moment of insight warranted further responsibility. That was just the sort of good luck/bad luck proposition he was likely to encounter, even more so now that he'd been touched by wild magic.

The *ding!* of accumulating experience was nice, though. That shadeling bonus for solving problems via deception was quite the sweet deal.

Did barbarians get bonus experience for solving problems with their fists, or rogues for solving problems by stealing things? Not something he could really ask. Besides, he had bigger fish to fry. There were going to be several patrols on their way to locations near the party's camp, and likely a few might even follow them back to it. He needed to warn everyone, maybe even lead an extra patrol back to give Ruprecht a bit more to work with in the energy department.

Though speaking of, hadn't he said that absorbing new materials also helped with that? And there were certainly several items here which would be unusual if they were different enough.

Well, extra supplies were always welcome, if not. And it would be doing some small service in terms of weakening the enemy. Maybe he could even sow some discord, get the hobgoblins quarrelling among themselves and blaming one another.

No. No time for something as elaborate as that. He'd just make his way through the camp toward the exit he needed, swipe whatever he could that wasn't nailed down along the way, and hightail it back to camp.

There was a chance that company was coming, and he wanted to make sure that a proper welcome was waiting for whomever—or whatever—arrived.

Chapter 12

*R*obin winced as the screams from the nearby building cut off abruptly. There had been a hobgoblin mage in there, part of the most recent patrol the party had lured to Ruprecht's sphere of influence. Robin wasn't sure precisely what trap or monster had been spawned in there, but it was clearly effective.

Finally! Ruprecht's exultation sounded in Robin's mind. The bard took it as a sign that the dungeon had managed to successfully absorb one of the mage collars he had been after. That should be the last of the patrol, as well. Robin sent a pulse of inquiry toward Rerebos, who had been their eyes in the sky, and received a wave of assurance in response. That was all of them.

Back to base, then. Robin brushed the dust from his clothes, not bothering to use **[Legerdemain]** just yet. He'd pick more up on the way back anyway. Better to wait and clean himself off properly right before entering the hideout.

Robin moved quickly and carefully. There was no telling when another hobgoblin patrol might appear. They had been out in force since he'd last infiltrated the camp, and he wasn't certain, but he thought they were beginning to consolidate their efforts in the area around Ruprecht.

Mixed blessing, that. The increased patrols meant more opportunities for Ruprecht to, well, gather energies and expand, but it also meant more stress on their defenses and a higher chance the party might get caught out by a patrol or patrols that overmatched them.

So Robin doubled-back twice and took care to obliterate his tracks as well as he could, then he dusted himself off, magically, and stepped into the safe haven that was the building at the center of Ruprecht's influence.

He was welcomed by the mini mimic Ruprecht had used to carry himself up to Robin's tavern. The dungeon had invested heavily in enhancing the little guy with any energy he could spare, and now he was not so little anymore.

"Hi, Immi," Robin said, reaching out to scratch the faux wood of the mimic's baseline form.

The thing purred, a deep, catlike sound. Robin had been trying to teach it to assume a monstrous form which could be used to more convincingly leave tracks. The patrols could use some more distraction, and he'd gone to all that trouble to sow those beast rumors at the camp, after all.

Robin conjured a great pantherlike beast with tentacles sprouting from its shoulders using [**Visual Phantasm**].

"Come on, Immi, imitate the kitty," he coaxed.

The mimic quivered in delight and began morphing.

The resultant shapes were horrific beyond description and would haunt the nightmares of any who looked upon them. Mimics were not meant to copy living creatures, after all. It was definitely outside of Immi's wheelhouse.

Well, it was close to getting the feet right, at least.

While the mimic strained, Robin carefully blocked most of his view with a strategically placed interface window. He'd raked in a nice bit of experience recently, and he had some stats to increase. It was too bad he was still too low in level to start investing in boosting his attributes with experience. He'd like a bit more *Dexterity*.

Damn and blast it to all seventeen hells!

Robin wasn't sure which cosmology Ruprecht was referencing, but he was sure it didn't bode well.

"Problem?" the bard asked.

I have assimilated the collars. I understand their functions now, none of which will aid me in understanding, assimilating, and unlocking the mechanisms which seal the lower city away.

"Not ideal," Savra said, "but you have at least gained some understanding. That in and of itself is a blessed thing."

"Yeah." Jhess jumped in. "What do the collars do, anyway?"

It is somewhat complex, but I shall simplify for those in the party who do not possess the requisite arcane knowledge.

Drev looked smug and Vance looked very self-assured, so Robin was certain that Ruprecht had been having some very detailed conversations with those two. He was uncertain, however, if his arcane knowledge was in and of itself up to that challenge, and he was just as happy not relying on his [**Bardic Lore**] in this exact instance. Simple was good. He could start there and make things more complex as needed.

The collars in conjunction with the wands act as a channel for magical ener-gies. I have absorbed three wands and a single collar at this point. Each of the wands has a slightly different enchantment tuned to produce a specific effect. Well, or two. One of the wands was clearly of a much higher quality.

"That cannot be efficient in terms of magical energy consumed." Drev frowned. "The effects would be weaker, and you would be able to cast less spells than you would be able to naturally."

Indeed. Though it is a much more stable way of channeling magical energy.

"Which makes sense, given what Robin was saying about the mage erupting into a conflagration of wild magic . . . butterflies?"

"Yup. Fiery, fiery butterflies," Robin confirmed.

This also matches my own experience. The last mage you brought, the one I was finally able to assimilate a collar from, also attempted to cast a spell when deprived of his wand. His first attempt worked, blinking him out of a trap. His second, attempting to blink through a wall, went wild. The hobgoblin mages seem to have an unnaturally high occurrence of wild magic among them.

"And the collars would allow them to channel it effectively, control it," Vance noted.

"It is part of an ancient curse of Tarin-Tiran," Savra said suddenly, her eyes distant. "Their ancestors were among the army that invaded this place, and the city—perhaps a god?—cursed them for their part in the fall of Tarin-Tiran."

Robin filed that detail away to interrogate with his **[Bardic Lore]** later. That had to be part of the story he was here to uncover. If he could find more details, possibly the place where the curse had been pronounced . . . could he learn to replicate it? Or at least fashion a new spell or two out of the knowledge?

But that is not all the collars do. They also contain a control mechanism. Those who wear them live only at the sufferance of the one who holds the key to them all. I cannot replicate the key without absorbing it, but I can see the general shape of its presence in the enchantments I have absorbed. These mages are all slaves to their commander.

"That fits with what I saw at the camp," Robin offered slowly. "The mages definitely seemed to be mistrusted—makes sense, given the whole wild magic–surge danger—while at the same time were held a bit in con-tempt, which fits with them being a lower class of citizen, even if they are powerful, magically speaking."

"Aren't all mages second class?" Jhess quipped before ducking the bolt of force Drev flicked at her head.

"There has to be a way we can use this," Robin said. "If we can foment a rebellion among the mages—maybe by getting them the key or at least crafting a believable fake they could rally behind—we could seriously gut the power base of the hjuncta!"

Whatever we decide to do, we need to continue luring patrols to us, and quickly, because the collar turned out to be useless for bypassing the gate. I will require far more energies than estimated to get us through, and I don't know that I could do it anywhere else. We've invested too much here in this place. I've quite taken root. The only way forward now is down here.

"We can do that," Robin said. "I can sneak back into the camp and gather some more information while the rest of the party keeps luring the odd patrol to Ruprecht. If I can find the key and approach the mages, maybe we could even cause enough chaos to siphon off a large portion of their forces and catch it in Ruprecht's traps."

I can endeavor to craft a convincing substitute key. There is no guarantee that I will get the physical shape right, but I should be able to imbue it with a convincing fake aura. You may be able to use it as part of a bluff if the commanders of the hjuncta have been too careful to reveal the real key to the mages. They may not even know what it looks like, after all these centuries.

"Unless it is necessary to lock the collars in place," Drev added thoughtfully. "Though even then, they may not be allowed to set eyes on it. We don't know enough about the ceremony involved."

"I can figure it out," Robin spoke with a confidence he didn't entirely feel. **[Lesser Mindreading]** and some targeted questioning could get him close, but it was a dangerous conversation to initiate in any case, let alone when he was infiltrating a hostile force with as much conformity and homogeneity as this one.

"We can make it work," Jhess said firmly. "I'm tired of cooling my heels up here! I want to get down deeper and find some real treasure! There's a mansion in Noviel I've got my eye on."

Then what are we waiting for? Go! Fetch me more hobgoblins to fuel my research! The gates of Tarin-Tiran call!

Robin Parker

Heritage: Shadeling, Paragon
Profession: Bard
Tier: 2 (Effective Level: 7)
Experience: 2755

Spell Points: 15
Bardsong: 7 uses

Properties

Free Ranks Available: 1

Physical
-Strength: 11
-Dexterity: 14
-Fortitude: 11
Mental
-Intelligence: 17
-Cunning: 23
-Resilience: 14
Social
-Charisma: 15
-Manipulation: 13
-Poise: 16

Proficiencies

Free Ranks Available: 1

Physical (9/9)
-Athletics: 5
-Brawl: 5
-Dodge: 8
-Melee Combat: 5
-Pilot: 4
-Ranged Combat: 9
-Sleight of Hand: 7
-Stealth: 7
-Survival: 6
Mental (9/9)
-Arcane Lore: 8
-Bureaucracy: 7
-Concentration: 9
-Crafting: 6
-Healing: 6
-Insight: 8
-Learning: 7

-Natural Wisdom: 4
-Perception: 9
Social (9/9)
-Animism: 4
-Deception: 10
-Empathy: 7
-Expression: 9
-Gossip: 8
-Intimidation: 6
-Persuasion: 8
-Socialize: 8
-Streetwise: 7

Peculiarities

Blessing of Rhyth
Tongue of the Fallen Tower
Mark of the Trickster
Chronicle of Infinite Visions
Mask of Myriad Faces
Initiate of the Craft
Illusion Focus
Metamagic Initiate
Improved Familiar Bond

Perks

Wayfaring Stranger
Shard of the Shattered Manymind
Mark of Fairy's Favor
Touch of Wild Magic

Spells

Cantrips* (*no SP cost)
-Lesser Phantasm*
-Cutting Words*
-Legerdemain*
-Lesser Nightmare Curse*
-Lesser Witch Bolt*
-Minor Repair*
-Lesser Charm*
Tier 1 (1SP each)

-Visual Phantasm*
-Healing Note
-Whispers from Beyond
-Minor Enchanted Slumber
-Invisible Servant
-Familiar Bond
-Wizard's Armor
Tier 2 (3SP each)
-Assume Quality (Special)
-Lesser Mindreading

Bardsong

Command Attention
Song of Arcane Power

Chapter 13

Robin shivered inside his borrowed skin. It was cloudy, and a slight drizzle misted down from the sky, but that had nothing to do with his discomfort. He came from a very rainy island, after all. No, he was shivering because, once again, he had infiltrated the hobgoblins' camp.

It had been harder this time. There was a lot more activity, all of it highly directed. Something had the place all kinds of agitated.

Something was clearly up. For a while, the plan had worked, and several patrols had made their way into Ruprecht's grasp, but they'd suddenly dried up, and Robin had been "volunteered" to find out why.

So far, his investigations hadn't turned up a reason. There were clear signs the camp was being struck, preparing to move, but it was more than that. There were whispers and stray thoughts which made it clear that someone important had arrived at the camp.

Robin grimaced and adjusted the bale of goods he was portering over his left shoulder. It was taking a lot more to look busy enough not to be bothered this trip. Accepting some actual jobs was the price; no dillydallying, just skimming what he could from overheard gossip and mind-read thoughts.

The camp was going to relocate, and soon. Robin tried to get a sense as to where, but no one he was within range of seemed to be sharing that knowledge, if they even knew at all, which, well, they might or they might not.

"... traveling all day. It hardly matters. Get your commanders, summon them to the command tent, and be quick about it. I have ord—information for them. Vital information."

Robin's blood went cold. He knew that voice! He'd hoped never to hear it again, but with his luck, he should hardly be surprised. Especially given the religious predilections of the hobgoblins he'd encountered here in Tarin-Tiran so far.

Gis. Robin caught sight of the priest out of the corner of his eye and tracked his movements as best he could without turning and making his interest obvious. At least the snake was safely hidden behind the evil old man's eye patch.

Gis was headed toward the tactical command tent that Robin had seen the inside of last time he'd been here, when he'd been posing as a scout. There was going to be a meeting there, soon. Robin had to know what was being said!

There was no way he'd be able to get inside, though. He'd have to find a way to lurk nearby, concealed by illusion or, even better, illusion and a bit of real cover. And just to make sure he didn't miss anything, he needed to find a way to sneak Rerebos inside.

That is, if the little dragon couldn't find one himself.

Robin sent a pulse of urgency along his bond with the familiar and felt an immediate response. The little dragon would be here soon. Good. Now, to find a hiding place close enough to the tent which would allow him to hear—possibly even watch by dipping in and out of Rerebos's senses.

First, however, he needed to deliver this bale of goods, and quickly. Robin hurried to his destination, forgetting all about overhearing gossip or the odd snatch of thought. *Thought. Right.* He'd need to find or make a small hole in the tent so he could see in and get a line of effect on those assembled therein. There was no way Gis, at least, wasn't somehow involved in a larger plot of some kind.

Robin ditched his delivery, timing it to coincide with a couple others so it would be easier for him to slip away afterward. All the practice sneaking he'd had so far in this world paid off, and he got away scot-free. Then it was a matter of using the same skills to slink through the camp, changing his appearance to that of a scout looking freshly returned from patrol. Any questions were deflected with the excuse of needing to report in right away.

When he made it to the vicinity of the tent, Robin flicked a quick eye at its surroundings. Last time, there had been very little in the way of hiding places—that would have been tactically unsound. But luck was with him today! In the chaos of disassembling the camp, piles of goods had begun to sprout around the tent like mushrooms.

Robin slipped behind a stack of rough crates and began carefully picking his way around the perimeter of the tent, looking for the best place to conceal himself. About a third of the way around, he found a large stack of supplies covered with a tarpaulin. The way it fell created a sheltered nook, almost like a small tent. Perfect.

Well, almost perfect. Robin conjured a knife from his storage and made a small slit in the tent, working slowly so as not to make more than a minimum of noise. He propped the slit open with a bit of twig and covered the whole section with the illusion that the fabric was undamaged. He'd have to hope the wind didn't pick up. Too much motion might make his little spyhole stand out.

Now, to conceal himself. Robin turned to wedge himself out of sight among the supplies. Slipping inside required a bit of a wriggle, but he managed. Then he layered an illusion over the whole section, deepening the shadows and concealing himself further.

Safe from idle discovery, Robin turned his attention to sussing out what was happening inside. The entrance was currently wide open, letting in a bright wedge of sunlight. It was in front and to the left of Robin's position, good for seeing who was arriving.

Gis was already inside. Robin didn't have a great view of the priest—the tactical table with all of its maps was blocking most of the view in that direction—but the scoutmaster was there as well, pacing back and forth like a stalking lion in a cage.

Robin felt a wary pulse at the back of his mind and the sensation of smug glee. Rerebos was inside already! Robin looked, but he couldn't spot the little dragon anywhere. Good. If *he* couldn't, it meant it was unlikely those inside could either. Well. Less likely, anyway.

The bard carefully and quietly went through the words and gestures to activate the [**Lesser Mindreading**] spell. It took a while to get up and running to the point that he could pick off surface thoughts, anyway.

The first one that came through was a curious mix of impatience and serenity from Gis's direction. Robin focused on the odd sensation. There were two minds there, but slightly overlapping. Gis and his brain serpent, Gehn, if Robin had to guess. So they were somewhat, though not entirely, linked mentally. Weird.

Was that how he and Rerebos would read to [**Lesser Mindreading**]? Something to investigate in the future, perhaps.

Robin focused on the scoutmaster and grimaced. The man was a blank spot. His mind was either too well guarded or Robin had been unlucky, but there was nothing for the bard to pick up there. Though even without magic, Robin could see the tension in the hobgoblin's shoulders and the dagger glances he kept tossing toward Gis. The priest and his retinue ignored all of it.

Retinue . . . or fellow party members? Robin picked up a stray thought which made him think it was the latter. The priest was here with a full adventuring party! What were they after? Not him, surely? He couldn't have caused that much trouble or enraged the priest to that degree, or he'd have had trouble in Noviel, surely.

There were other hobgoblin leaders present as well, but Robin didn't have time for more than a cursory inspection before a new figure swept into the room, the flap of the tent falling closed in his wake.

"General Gar-Soom," Gis greeted silkily, rising to his feet. "Thank you for joining us."

"Dispense with the pleasantries," the commander almost spat before continuing in a more respectful tone, "What news does the servant of Mighty Urkhan bring?"

"So far, none of the passages we have tried have led us to the depths we seek," Gis said, clearly irritated by the fact. "Much has changed since one of my order was last present here."

"Yes," the scoutmaster spoke. "Not all have been so dedicated in their service to Lord Urkhan as our people."

Gis flushed with fury but said nothing. The general smiled broadly and shot an approving glance at the scoutmaster. *Interesting dynamics.*

"Be that as it may," Gis continued, "I have received some counsel which may serve both our aims—and the will of Lord Urkhan."

The hobgoblins stiffened.

Robin fished for Gis's surface thoughts. They wanted to get deeper into the city and avoid the older dungeon that was already here, that much was clear. But what were they looking for? What was Urkhan's will?

He couldn't find it. If the thought was there, it was swiftly being drowned out by the flood of irritation Gis was feeling. The priest really didn't like that these hobgoblins weren't under his command. Or was it that he wasn't properly under theirs?

Who was in control here, anyway? Urkhan usually had clear lines of command, but this looked like a weird sort of parallel power structure. It was certainly different than the last environment he'd seen the priest in.

"I understand you have lost *several* of your patrols." Gis tsked. "Most unfortunate."

"We are narrowing down the area and will uncover the cause soon enough," the scoutmaster said tightly.

"Yes. That's precisely why I am here. That area. Signs point to it possibly containing a way down which would be useful for my purposes—for Lord

Urkhan's purposes." Gis turned and did something on the table that Robin couldn't see.

He risked glancing through Rerebos's senses. The little dragon was hidden high up in the tent and had an almost bird's-eye view. Gis was pointing to a map of the city—pointing to the area near where Ruprecht had rooted himself!

"I suspect there is more, however," Gis continued. "An annoyance, a gadfly buzzing in Lord Urkhan's ear, has made his way to the city. An illusionist." Gis's mouth wrinkled with distaste at the word.

"You think this trickster is responsible for our missing patrols? A sniveling coward like that, defeat our warriors?" the scoutmaster sneered.

"Perhaps," Gis said. "Or perhaps it is as your scouts are saying, a beast sent up from the dungeon below to harry and distract you. It hardly matters from a practical standpoint. The solution is the same in either case." Gis rapped his finger on the map. "You are moving your camp, as your orders from Lord Urkhan command. But you will—that is, *I* [Suggest] you move your people to this area. Occupy it entirely. There is no beast, no trickster, that can handle a force of this size alone, not even with a few allies, if such have been brought or found or made. It is clear this is the place. This is where most of your patrols have vanished, is it not?"

Robin didn't miss the subtle magical force that had been issued out with Gis's "suggestion." The priest had used some kind of spell! Probably on the commander, judging by the way the hobgoblin was nodding.

The scoutmaster opened his mouth to say something but shut it with a shocked click when General Gar-Soom agreed with the priest.

"As you say," the brawny hobgoblin spoke, "we shall relocate there."

The scoutmaster looked like he wanted to protest, but faced with his commanding officer and a powerful priest of his god in agreement, he clearly thought better of the act.

The conversation slipped into logistics at that point, and Robin let his mind wander a bit, heart hammering in his chest. This was huge! There was no way they could handle this many hobgoblins in force!

He had to tell his party immediately! They needed to prepare, to plan, maybe to flee—wait, could they flee? Ruprecht had rooted himself to the spot and wouldn't have the energy to move and breach another door.

Whatever! They would figure it out!

Robin just needed to make it out of the camp alive, first.

Chapter 14

*S*o that's where we are," Robin concluded. "We've got a few hundred hobgoblins soon to be bearing down on this general vicinity, bent on rooting out whatever has been killing their patrols and making this their new base camp."

The bard looked around the room that had basically become Ruprecht's de facto core chamber. They had all gathered to hear his report after he'd returned, solemn and shaking, from his reconnaissance. Now, they all shared his look.

Well, hopefully, he didn't look *quite* that shell-shocked.

"Suggestions?" he asked. Might as well try to focus things on a positive direction.

Silence answered him.

Well, silence and Rerebos.

Kill them all and take their shinies!

That's the plan, he answered cheerfully, *as soon as we can figure out exactly* how *to do that.*

Ah.

Then there was silence.

"Ruprecht can't be uprooted again so soon," Robin said, laying out the facts. Facts were good. You could work from facts. Any time something was known, it removed a bunch of possibility, and it was often very hard to see through an endless haze of possibility.

"And there are three hundred or so hobgoblins coming to this area," Savra added slowly.

Robin glanced to the jewel floating atop a nearby pillar. Ruprecht was strangely silent. Although given that he may be staring down the barrel of his own mortality—at least the destruction of this version of himself—Robin could see how it might be difficult to muster any kind of quippy observation.

Or maybe the dungeon was just pondering a masterful plan to wow them all with.

They will almost certainly shatter me.

Or maybe not.

Robin had never heard the dungeon sound so dejected. So morose. So—human.

"Not if we end 'em first!" Jhess spoke suddenly. "Come on, think! Isn't this basically what we wanted? An all-you-can-eat buffet for Rupee here? So what if it's delivering itself a bit ahead of schedule. We just need to find a way to chop it into small enough pieces to stuff down his gullet." Jhess jerked her thumb toward Ruprecht's gem.

"That is one way of looking at it," Vance said.

Robin shot the librarian a look. Vance looked far too pleased with Jhess's suggestion. Far too pleased.

"I appreciate the sentiment, of course, and applaud the initiative," Drev said coolly. "But I, for one, would appreciate a bit more *how* to go with this *what*, thank you."

"That's for you all to figure out." Jhess shrugged. "I'm the brawn. Most of you claim to be the brains of the outfit. So use 'em."

"We'd need a way to slow them down and separate them," Robin started. "Something they get caught up in before they realize it so there's not enough time to abort whatever attack is coming." He sighed. "And it will have to be more than simple illusion. The priest that tipped them off, Gis, knows me. Knows a lot of the tricks illusion can pull off. And how to counter them."

"The faithful of Urkhan are relentless," Savra said, "though also usually lacking in imagination. It comes with the territory of being so bound to their petty hierarchies."

"Might be something we can use there," Vance spoke up. "You said there wasn't a clear chain of command? Maybe we can get conflicting orders into the mix, gum things up that way?"

"Or use orders to direct the groups where we want them, when we want them." Drev looked thoughtful. "And we know Robin can forge them easily enough."

"The mages," Savra said suddenly.

Everyone turned to her.

"That's all I can see." Her hands clenched at her sides as she stared off into the distance. "This accursed city! I can see that the mages present some sort of opportunity—a dangerous one—but I cannot see beyond that. It is too clouded."

"They're certainly an exploited underclass with a unique power all their own," Robin said slowly. "If we could somehow convince them to rebel . . ."

A key materialized on the ground near Robin's feet. He bent and picked it up. It was ornate and looked to be centuries old, worn shiny and smooth in a few places, as if from the movement of hundreds of pairs of hands over the years.

This is the best approximation of the key that controls the mage collars I can manage at present. It won't do anything, unfortunately, but it will at least read as the right kind of magic, should it be investigated. You would, however, have to be very persuasive, I think.

"No lie." Robin passed the key to Savra. "Can you see anything else when you hold this?"

She accepted the key and frowned, turning it over and over in her hands.

"I see nothing else," she said at last. "But that does not necessarily mean anything, in this place."

"Anything else it might be?" Drev asked. "What else do we know about the mages?"

I have come up with a way to possibly neutralize them. Ruprecht sounded less than thrilled about the innovation, however. *It is reckless beyond belief, and not something we can control the outcome of, but it would almost certainly cause utter chaos among the ranks of the enemy.*

"I like the sound of that!" Jhess smiled evilly. "Do tell!"

There was a sigh like the sound of wind through the eaves before the dungeon spoke again.

I have taken a great deal of time to study the function of the enchantments upon the wands, and have even experimented a bit with trying to alter it, to turn the device into something one or all of us might benefit from. I did not succeed in that.

"But you found something else," Robin guessed.

Yes. I believe I can produce wands that have somewhat the opposite of their intended effect.

"I'm not sure I follow," Savra said with a frown.

"They make the wielders magic *more* likely to go wild?" Vance speculated.

Drev went white as a sheet at the words.

"That much wild magic . . . no! There's no way we should risk that." The mage was clearly agitated.

"I dunno," Robin said. He held up a hand to stop the inevitable objection. "Hear me out. Yes, there's a chance the magic might be as bad for us, if not worse, than it is for the enemy, or that it might even aid them in some unexpected fashion, but there are a *lot* more of them than there are of us. If we don't have any other better options in place, it might be worth trying to force some kind of wild-magic surge among them. It could cause a lot of chaos in their ranks, and with the odds we are facing, that would not be a bad thing."

"It is an impossible thing to predict." Savra was shaking her head. "I am inclined to agree with Drev. We should not risk it."

"It's a moot point if Ruprecht decides he does not wish to produce any of these wildly accursed wands he's described," Vance spoke. "But I agree with Robin that we should have them in reserve as a last resort. The odds are currently too stacked against us. This might even those odds or even tilt them in our favor. The wild magic seems to almost have a specific dislike for the hobgoblins."

It made sense, if it was the result of an ancient curse placed on their ancestors for destroying the city.

Ruprecht said nothing. The party all looked to Jhess.

The rogue blinked.

"What are you all looking at me for?"

"You need to vote," Robin told her. "Ruprecht clearly is waiting to hear from everyone before he weighs in, so you need to vote. Wild magic ace in the hole, or no?"

Jhess looked back and forth between all the faces looking expectantly at her before shrugging.

"I say we do it."

"What?" Drev looked aghast. "It might be suicide!"

"Hundreds of hobgoblins bearing down on us when we can't retreat without leaving one of our own behind is just as suicidal," Jhess replied bluntly. "And none of us are leaving Ruprecht, so what's the difference? At least with the trapped wands, we have a chance of taking the bastards with us. Works for me." The rogue crossed her arms and leaned back against the wall.

There was a sudden clatter as several wands materialized on top of one another in the midst of the party. There was also the ringing *clink* of a small pouch of gold appearing behind Jhess's heel. Robin spotted it, barely, and repressed a smile.

There. I would prefer not having to risk that avenue, however, so can we please get to work designing the most efficient and effective death trap we can in the time remaining to us? I have sufficient stored energies to make substantial refinements to the local area. I think some of you recall how effective I can be with trapdoors and nested tunnels.

No lie there.

"How much area do we have to work with?" Robin asked, conjuring a replica of the nearby area with [**Visual Phantasm**].

I just expanded my sphere of influence. Given that it seems unlikely I will be able to assimilate the locking mechanism before the enemy arrives, it seemed more prudent to have greater control of more area. You are sure the priest does not know of my existence?

"As sure as I can be," Robin replied. "He didn't bring it up during the strategy meeting, and I would have expected that to be something he'd mention as a possible impediment."

"The faithful of Urkhan have limited skills in terms of divination," Savra said dismissively. "Mostly, they rely on demonic forces for aid, and not only are those untrustworthy at best but often the information provided is just bad."

Robin grinned at the professional pride—and professional judgement—in Savra's tone.

"At least there's that." The mage shook his head. "Well, let us get to work, then! The more we can do to ensure that those"—he glanced at the pile of wands like it was a nest of snakes—"see no use, the better."

"When they come, they are likely to come as a unified armed force," Robin informed. "It won't be easy to split them up."

I have some ideas on that front.

Robin broke out drinks and chilled them as the party got down to the serious business of trying to outsmart an invading force outnumbering them by a factor of fifty or more.

How hard could it be?

<h1 style="text-align:center">Chapter 15</h1>

Robin moved among the camp wearing a borrowed form shrouded in the illusory disguise of a nondescript hobgoblin. He'd dumped all of his experience into maximizing his *Sleight of Hand* skill, taken all the tips Jhess could give, plumbed the depths of his [Bardic Lore] for the alternate forms he could use for the largest gains in *Dexterity* and general sneaky skill enhancement using [Assume Quality], and he was still bricking it at this plan. Sure, Ruprecht had made the trapped wands, but *someone* had to get them into the hands—holsters?—of the hobgoblin mages.

That someone, unfortunately, was Robin.

The storage space in his ring was super helpful, at least. Made it much easier to be inconspicuous.

He had the key Ruprecht had dummied up as well, but so far as he could see, there was no easy way to use it. Even though the mages were an abused undercaste and he'd identified the woman most likely to be their leader, he had yet to come up with a plan likely to succeed in fomenting a rebellion among them.

Pity. That would have been a much more elegant solution.

And it would have placed him in somewhat less danger.

Well, maybe.

At least Gis didn't seem to be anywhere nearby.

The hobgoblins were moving in groups. Robin had expected something like the ordered march of an army, all paradelike. Instead, the hjuncta had separated into phalanxlike megapatrols. It made them more mobile and allowed them to sweep the buildings and rubble piles as they went, looking carefully for any signs of foes.

It was a tricky thing to manage. Yes, the groups were large enough and occupied with a task, so it made it technically easier to slip among them with the aim of planting the wands, but they were also much more close-knit, and currently primed to be on the lookout for anything out of the ordinary.

If he hadn't had his **[Mask of Disguise]**, there was no way he would have been able to pull this off. He had to watch the flow of hobgoblins like a hawk, assuming familiar faces just long enough to get near to his target mage, make the switch with the wands, and slip away again. Even then, he wasn't able to switch all of them in any given group—it was too difficult. He hit the easiest marks and moved on.

There was only so much a lone bard could do! Even with his faithful familiar in the skies above providing an extra set of eyes and calling out warnings as needed.

"Here! We've found something!"

Robin faded back as the call went up, shrouding himself in the illusion of shadow and rock so the group could move away from him, rather than having to risk being spotted leaving. It sounded like someone had picked up on the trail Jhess had left to one of the five entrances to the killing zone Ruprecht had prepared. Good. Three of the other groups he'd been with had already found their own leads. The leadership should have sussed out that both the mysterious beast they'd seen signs of *and* a group of hostile sentients were camped somewhere in the ruins nearby by now.

Speaking of, it was time for the most dangerous part of his job: he needed to infiltrate the group Gis was traveling with.

The sun was already setting by the time he slipped into the camp in question. Fortunately, there was enough chaos to offset any routine which might have tripped him up; he just needed to look busy. Plus, there were plenty of shadows to use as cover for switching faces while he was walking through. No reason not to give yourself every advantage when facing your greatest threat, right?

It was harder to make wand swaps here, however. The mages were grouped together and not distracted by investigating nearby ruins or the like. Robin gritted his teeth. He might have to stay here longer and try to swap out the lot after most of the mages had gone to sleep.

Not ideal.

There was a surge of emotion from Rerebos, and Robin slipped into a nearby patch of shadow, conjuring an illusion to cover his presence. He'd sent his familiar in ahead to spy on and track Gis's location and activities. That he was being contacted now suggested something interesting was afoot. Fortunately, he was just inside their telepathic range, the mages being encamped near the command structure where the general could keep an eye on them.

Ol' Snake Eye has gotten some sort of dream message from his patron. Sounds like he knows there is something worth stealing or shattering at the center of the area they've been sniffing around. I think they'll try something tomorrow.

Let me share your senses, Robin requested, slipping into the mind of his familiar.

Looking through Rerebos's eyes was different than using his own. The little shadow dragon saw things in a different spectrum, possibly of light, possibly of magic. Robin could see all manner of shades of black and white and gray, and with his experience, he knew how to identify the blue grays from the red grays and green grays, but it was all a bit strange.

It was very detailed, however, and Rerebos had excellent hearing, and smell and taste as well.

Not that he was happy about knowing what Gis *tasted* like. *Ugh.* Whoever had said all magic came with a price had not been kidding, but this was far from anything Robin had ever expected to pay. It was not something you could unsense.

Gis was in tense conversation with the general. They were clearly committed to invading Ruprecht's demesne, and soon. Scouts had been dispatched to explore each of the five entrances that had been found.

That was fine; they'd expected that. Ruprecht knew how to keep his traps hidden, and moreover, how to plant obvious traps and hidden passages so none of the scouts would be too suspicious.

Let them disarm them. There would be enough real ones left after the decoys had been dealt with to more than handle the job. Well, that was the hope, at least. Some of these scouts were quite accomplished. Higher level than Robin, in the parlance of his old tabletop days.

"We could always take steps of our own to, ah, *aid* the revered priest in this matter." The speaker was one of the mages, probably one of the most senior. As far as Robin could tell, the mages had no single leader, unlike the other casts among the hobgoblin hjuncta. He wasn't sure why, but it was one of the bits of information he'd gathered.

The mage was clearly leaning on the general to try and get permission to employ divination magics. Gis looked less than thrilled, but he'd have that reaction to anything that challenged his authority.

The general didn't look any happier about it than Gis, but from the way he drummed his fingers along his scabbard, Robin suspected he was seriously considering it.

"Very well," he said at last. "Fetch two of your most skilled mages. Skilled, mind you! I want skill, not power. The last thing we need is for something to go wrong with this."

The mage nodded, shot a smug glance at Gis, and hurried out of the tent.

Interesting. So skill did matter to a degree in terms of whether or not the magic went wild? Or did they just hope it did?

While the mage was gone, the general moved to a locked chest with smooth, swift motions, unlocking it with a key he kept on a chain around his neck. From the chest, he drew three white wands, similar to the standard ones Robin carried replicas of, but of a slightly different make. Presumably, they channeled the magical energy into divination, rather than offensive energies like fire or lightning.

"Your mages are likely to have no more luck than I or anyone else," Gis said waspishly. "This accursed place is so saturated with lies and illusion that very little truth can make its way through, even the truth of power."

No wonder Savra seemed so unsettled all the time! Some kind of residual epic enchantment? Covering the whole city? Illusion, so many uses!

The mages returned before Robin had any more time to ponder that. The original mage was there with two others, both younger than Robin had expected, what with the general harping on about skill over power.

Each claimed a wand as the general offered it.

"Find out what you can about what is waiting for us inside that area," the general snapped. "I want actionable intelligence! No nonsense generalities!"

"Yes, General," the mages chorused, raising the wands.

Magic tingled down Rerebos's sinuous neck as the mages' eyes all glowed a white that perfectly matched the wands in their hands. They spoke in unison, and the room suddenly seemed several degrees colder.

"Danger, and opportunity," the mages chanted. "There are . . . five—no, six! Six strangers to this place who have come here. The last . . . the last is strange. He tastes of caverns deep beneath the ground."

"Beast and an invading party, most likely," the scoutmaster muttered.

"What else can you see?" the general asked.

"It is difficult," the mages chorused. "The Veil is thick."

"Then part it! Tear through it! Look beyond!"

The light intensified, pouring from the mages' mouths now as well as from their eyes. Sparks leapt from wand to wand to wand. They were burning a lot of magical energies down there!

"The Veil parts, we see . . . we see the city as it was! Unharmed! Before the coming of Lord Urkhan. We see . . . no, we are *seen*!" There was panic in the voices of the mages.

The light gleaming from them took on a distinctly purple hue, and suddenly, Robin felt something twist deep inside him. He felt a curious, fierce, and exultant joy.

It tasted like the water in the shrine of Rhyth.

And it lasted only a moment.

Gis barked out an order, and he and his two bodyguards leapt forward, dragging their daggers across the mages' throats, killing them all.

The purple light flickered and went out.

"Idiots," the priest spat. "Drawing the attention of a memory like that. Foolish. You should know better than to allow such things here. It's too dangerous. Lord Urkhan is most displeased."

Robin withdrew from Rerebos's mind, shaken and mind roiling with the implications of what he had just witnessed. He was sure, more than ever, that he was in exactly the right place.

Not that he could think about that now. No. There was too much still to do. They had to survive the next few days, and if that was going to happen, he couldn't just hang around and spy on the evil old man.

He still had several wand swaps to make, after all.

Chapter 16

All five groups have now entered my demesne.

The words echoed in Robin's head as he crouched, hidden, in one of the intact structures near the group he was monitoring. Five party members, five groups, so each of them was on their own and nearby in case Ruprecht needed a pair of hands to help herd the hobgoblins.

Robin tried not to think too much about what an incredibly dangerous thing it was to split the party this way. So far, things had gone mostly according to plan with Robin's group, though they were being far more cautious than he had expected. Ruprecht's traps had peeled off several scouts already, though, so perhaps that was the reason. They were being more cautious with the ones they had remaining.

Come on, he silently willed the group, *come farther in.* The party didn't have all day, and the longer this drew out, the likelier it was that something would go wrong. Ruprecht had some truly terrible massive pit traps prepared; if they timed things right, this could end up a massacre, then they'd have the energy they needed to delve deeper into Tarin-Tiran.

Personally, Robin was also hoping this would be the end of Gis as well. Not that he'd been that lucky since arriving in this world.

Robin used **[Visual Phantasm]** to conjure flickers of movement at random in the various alleyways and boulevards. It was difficult to herd a group this size when they were being this cautious, but he needed to keep them moving, at least, and focused on more than simply looking for traps.

Is there any way you can easily steal the speaking stone their leader has? Ruprecht sounded annoyed, his ire echoing off the vaults of Robin's mind.

The dungeon's voice had that particular timbre which the bard had come to associate with one-to-one mind speech.

No, Robin answered back. *There's too many of them. I might be able to distract them and send Rerebos in to try and steal it, but you'd need to promise him something very shiny indeed, I suspect.*

There was a pause as the dungeon clearly communicated with the little dragon.

I suppose it's not vital, the dungeon grumbled. *But keep in mind that it may become so. They're trading too much information about my traps. It's making things far less efficient.*

Robin sent a pulse of acknowledgement. Of course, there was more than one way to solve the problem. The group couldn't report in if they were all dead.

How far to the kill zone? he sent the thought winging to Rerebos, who was keeping watch from above.

Close. Well, close enough if they stop lazing about.

Robin needed to shift them into higher gear. But what could he use as bait or lash that would actually shift these many hobgoblins? Unless . . .

Rerebos, I think we're going to need to steal that communications stone. Ruprecht, can you make me a replica that looks the same but doesn't have any magic powers?

The stone near his feet rippled slightly, and the requested replica rose up, coming to rest near his big toe. Robin leaned down and picked it up, mentally sending it into his dimensional storage space.

Now, what was the easiest way to get close to the leader? Stealth was an option, sure, but a lot of the hobgoblins would be on high alert. Not great odds.

Well, why not be direct? There were messengers and scouts reporting in constantly, so why not be one of them? He could stage a bit of a disturbance just outside of their line of sight with his illusion powers, then take the form of a scout—one of the ones Ruprecht had already dispatched, just to be safe—and simply walk up to his target. Then he'd have to rely on a bit of *Sleight of Hand,* but it seemed the quickest, best chance he'd get at things.

It would also put him in the right position to use **[Lesser Phantasm]** to send some fake orders through the stone and get the group moving exactly in the direction he needed them to.

Of course, if anything went wrong, he'd be trapped in the middle of a hundred hostile hobgoblins, but hey, what was life without a little risk?

Safer. Much safer. And life.

Robin sighed. The things he did for his party . . . and to advance his own goals, of course, but hey, the things he did for his party. And how many parties could claim a dungeon as a member? That had to be some kind of first, right? Where was the title or perk from that?

He cocked an ear, but no *ding* announced a notification. *Oh, well. Worth a try.*

Robin mentally reviewed the area. Ideally, he wanted the group to head down the boulevard three streets over from his current position. Was it better to try and drive them away from here with something terrible like a trap, or down it with something terrible like the promise of the beast they thought they were hunting?

Why not both?

Robin sent Rerebos to flit over the boulevard and fake up some tracks to follow while he quickly conferred with Ruprecht and set an obvious trap to spring in the alley. He shifted to the hobgoblin form he planned on using, complete with several lacerations and a good deal of dried blood, and once he was ready, he set off a large *boom* and the illusion of a puff of dust from the alleyway he was in. He waited several seconds, then stumbled out in his hobgoblin form, coughing for effect as he made his way to the group. Right before he came into sight, he made sure to cast **[Lesser Mindreading]**. There had to be passwords.

There were, and his spell allowed him to pluck them right out of the perimeter guards' minds. He made his way directly to the command structure to report.

Fortunately, the scoutmaster wasn't with this group, nor was the general. One of Gis's lackeys was, however, though the human stood out among the hobgoblins and was clearly being held at arm's length, so to speak.

Robin approached, keeping his mind alert to any hint of suspicion wafting off the hobgoblin commanders or Gis's party member. There was tension there, and resentment, but no suspicion.

So far, so good.

Robin made his report, slurring his words and keeping his eyes slightly unfocused. Hopefully, any discrepancies in behavior would be attributed to the obvious damage he had taken while "escaping" from the traps.

The leader grunted and began debating troop movements with the other two hobgoblins in charge of this particular group. Gis's henchman looked on contemptuously.

"We should slow down, check for more traps," one of the leaders was saying.

"No, we should press on," the other lieutenant urged. "We've finally gotten a glimpse of the beast! If we can destroy it, we'll bring glory to Urkhan."

Robin sincerely doubted it was Urkhan's glory he was concerned with.

The leader, a grizzled hobgoblin well into her middle age, looked unconvinced by either side. She drummed her fingers along the speaking stone at her side.

Robin watched carefully through half-lidded eyes. It was going to be hard to lift if she kept touching it like that.

"It's a pleasure to see such decisive leadership in action," Gis's party member sneered.

Wow. Guy was brave. The only human in the middle of a hundred hobgoblins, and he was insulting their leader? Robin quickly reassessed how much pull Gis must have in this situation. What was the priest looking for in Tarin-Tiran?

Whatever it was, Robin could at least whittle down his support system by eliminating as many hobgoblins as possible. His eyes narrowed. And maybe he could even get Gis's pet to help him do it.

"So you think we should avoid the beast, go slow, track down the traps," Robin said, firmly putting words into the human's mouth.

"I—" The man opened his mouth to reply.

"You think hobgoblins lack bravery? That we can't handle the beast? Is that what you think?" Robin wasn't going to let him say anything. No. This was his confrontation to control.

He stepped in front of the man, really got in his face, making sure the hob leader was right behind him. "You insult our leaders! What makes you think you're so great?" Robin reached out a claw and poked the man stiffly in the shoulder.

The man reacted exactly as Robin had hoped, shoving him back. Robin took the cue and used the momentum to stumble directly into the hobgoblin leader. He twisted as he fell, and as she reached out to catch him, he made the switch between her speaking stone and the fake Ruprecht had conjured up.

"Enough!" the leader barked out as she righted Robin and gestured for the lieutenants to sheathe their weapons. "We are all united in the service of Urkhan! There is action enough for all."

Robin flexed his fingers and used [Lesser Phantasm] to make the stone speak.

If any scouts report a sighting of the beast, pursue! It's been wounded and should be weak. After it with all haste!

Robin hid a smile of satisfaction as that little nudge did it.

The group was ordered down the boulevard, full speed ahead. He tagged along as long as he dared, making sure to reinforce their speed with whatever illusions he could muster, keeping a bit of conversation going through the speaking stone, for example. When they were close to Ruprecht's massive pitfall trap, he let himself fade further into the background until he had the chance to slip into an alleyway and cover his escape with a shroud of illusory shadow.

Then he just had to wait.

It wasn't long. There was a loud *thump* as a large section of boulevard vanished, accompanied by several dozen screams which all cut off quite suddenly. There was a pleased rumble from the building around him, and suddenly, Ruprecht was all but singing through the vaults of Robin's mind.

Ah! Excellent. That will help. The other four groups are proving much harder to herd than this one.

Robin had a quick conversation with the dungeon. Things were not going well. Gis was sniffing out several of the dungeon's traps, and the other megapatrols were all being led by more reliable and knowledgeable hobgoblins.

I'm not sure we'll be able to get them all like you did this group.

"Nothing for it, then." Robin grimaced. "I think we're going to have to try and trigger a wild-magic surge among the mages."

Chapter 17

Robin grimaced as he looked down at the city through Rerebos's eyes. He was currently crouched in an intact home of some kind next to Savra. He'd deliberately joined up with the diviner, expecting that he'd need access to her insights before this was over if they were going to have a chance at coming out on top.

Rerebos was currently focused on the closest—and largest—of the hobgoblin groups. The one that had both the general and Gis at the center of it.

"They have definitely noticed the loss of a fifth of their forces," he muttered to Savra. "They're all being *much* more cautious."

"They're drawing closer to one another, aren't they," Savra asked, her eyes distant.

Yes, Ruprecht confirmed. *And they are communicating back and forth much more regularly and with increased efficiency. I do not know that I will be able to draw any of these groups into one of the larger pitfalls I've prepared. We shall have to risk our desperation gambit.*

"Easy enough for you to say," Robin muttered. "You're not facing untold waves of wild magic, capable of literally anything."

There wasn't much venom in the bard's words, however. How could there be? There was that little voice inside his head that actually welcomed the prospect. More magic? Possibly the greatest, wildest explosion of magic that he had ever seen? Possibly more wondrous than he was capable of imagining?

It was a thrilling—if possibly deadly—prospect.

Robin had to question the effect this world was having on his sanity.

"We'll need to key them to a fever pitch of fear," Savra noted clinically. "Though we probably want to draw them closer to one another before pushing one of them to the breaking point, if possible. There's no telling what the reaction might be, nor the wild magic effect. I doubt a single manifestation will solve the entire problem. We want as many of them simultaneously spooked into action as possible."

"Drev was saying he'd noted a few warding and protective magics among them," Robin said. "If we're lucky, if we set off one or more, the rest might attempt to limit the damage with their own protective spells and set off more or wider effects."

I shall begin making some terrain changes to funnel them into position, but I'll have to leave the actual trickery to you, Robin.

"You've set the tinder, I'll do my best to strike the flint and steel," the bard answered. Then he looked to Savra. "Any tips?"

The seeress's eyes went pale and misty. For a long minute she didn't speak, but her head moved, and her eyes searched among things unseen.

"No," she replied finally. "Not really. This place is too shrouded. I can feel their tension, however. The loss of a fifth of their compatriots has them on edge, as does never having seen the beast. Perhaps you can use that?"

"Possibly." Robin grimaced. What he wouldn't give for some more range right now! "Though I think I'm going to need some help from the rest of the party. I just don't have the reach I need to pull this all off by myself."

"What do you need?"

I will pass the message along to the rest of the party.

"Pressure," Robin said. "Pick off stragglers at the edges or snipe targets of opportunity, but none near enough to the mages to really prompt them into trying to respond with spells. One or two small traps. We want them a little bit bloody, but confident that they're going to eventually wear us down, ferret us out, and win. Ruprecht, if you can alter the terrain so everyone has a nice escape route ready, with plenty of fallback positions to keep up the pressure as the hobgoblins pursue, that would be ideal."

"I will continue to look," Savra offered. "I cannot find much, but the mists which shroud my vision are not insurmountable. Occasionally, glimpses slip through."

"We'll take whatever we can get. Be prepared to fall back and heal, though, in case something goes wrong."

Drev has the most range, followed by Jhess. There was a rumble as a couple buildings suddenly shivered and shed stones from their construction. *I have made them some blinds with escape pathways, as you suggested.*

"Let me get into position," Robin said. "I'll want a retreat corridor right into the center of your demesne. We won't be able to lure them into a large open space, so something near your core with a lot of streets. I'll lure them with illusions of the beast. Oh, and can you arrange some spots with monster blood? Something you can reveal as I retreat so it looks like they've wounded the beast? That should help get their blood up too."

Give me a moment.

Robin could sense Ruprecht working. He exchanged a few more words and plans with Savra, then moved out as soon as he got the word from their dungeon ally. Once he was in position, he passed word to Drev via Ruprecht to set things off. Thanks to Rerebos's eyes in the sky, Robin saw a spray of magical missile, comprised of pure force, lance out and slam into several of the advance guards.

There were shouts and a scramble to shore up the defensive edges of the line which had begun to fray as the hobgoblins advanced. Good enough.

Robin unleashed a terrible screeching roar, like something out of a child's nightmares, pumping his **[Lesser Phantasm]** to its maximum volume. He followed it up with a flicker of movement and a massive form in the shadows, situated at an angle which allowed him to send a **[Lesser Witch Bolt]**, unsculpted, as if it had come from the mouth of the beast.

A few hobgoblins screeched back and advanced, only to be yanked back by shouted orders from their superiors. Together, as one, the hobgoblin patrols advanced. From either side, Jhess peppered the ranks with stones as Vance fired hobgoblin arrows—scavenged from earlier patrols and reproduced by Ruprecht—into the throng. Something about the latter, in particular, seemed to inflame the hobs. There was a lot more surging among the enemies struck with those arrows.

Good. Whatever worked to keep them advancing.

And advance they did, like an inexorable tide. Then they found the blood, and a ragged cheer went up from the hobgoblins, their pace redoubling.

They were solidly hooked now.

The party continued to harry the edges as Robin taunted them with glimpses of the beast. It was brutal, exhausting work, interrupted with mad sprints as he and his party members had to fall back and back before the advancing groups. Slowly, they neared the final position, the streets becoming narrower and the groups growing closer and closer until they were nearly one giant mass, separated only by the space of buildings between the tightly knotted streets.

I think this is as close as we're going to get.

"Tell the others to fall back, then. I'll give them a good scare." Robin squinted at the amassed group, calling mentally up to Rerebos to find him the biggest concentration of mages.

There.

Robin primed them with another few screeching roars, followed by decentralized screams, the sounds of hobgoblin after hobgoblin dying, crying out to their mothers, crying out to their god, in their own language. The death-cries were fake, but the effect they had was very real. The atmosphere became tense, and Robin could see weapons rising, lines firming up.

Time to hit them from the direction they least expected.

Above the group of mages Rerebos had spied out for him, Robin conjured the form of a terrible, three-headed flying chimera. He made it as horrific as he could, to startle and inspire fear. [Lesser Phantasm] gave it a voice, and shouts of alarm went up from the assembled host.

There was a flurry of movement, light glinting off of metal, and the bard prayed it was glancing off of a bunch of unsheathed wands.

"Come on," Robin whispered to himself. "Come on."

Just one of the mages needed to break. Just one. Or all of them. All of them would be good too. *Come on, luck; come on, wild magic perk. Do your work!*

Robin didn't see who first raised their wand and channeled desperate, surging magic through it. He did, however, see the effects; they burned themselves into his mind's eye.

A pillar of crimson flame flowered among the hobgoblins, sparking panic and answering magic in desperate warding gestures which themselves erupted in orange flames and yellow, emerald, cerulean, and violet pillars made of sparking, flickering fire. A conflagration of magic, the pillars of flame coiled about one another and swept across the area, a rainbow of death and destruction, wild and devouring.

Hobgoblins screamed as they burned to ash or were transformed to a twist of roses made of living scarlet flame. Others were turned to stone— jet and carnelian, granite and green marble. Transformation rippled across the assembled, and those who did not die from the titanic forces twisting through their bodies went mad with the strangeness of it all, falling onto one another, biting and clawing like the monsters they had become.

Some vanished; some stumbled away, their touch turning the stones they fell against to gold or lead or something that looked suspiciously like strawberry pudding.

Robin had no idea what had happened to Gis and his party; he had no way of seeing through the varicolored mayhem. Mere chaos had been unleashed upon the world, and while some benefitted, most died.

And where there was death, there was experience, certainly for Ruprecht. The dungeon likely had never gorged on such a tsunami of energies before.

Oh, fuck me, *that is good!*

Chapter 18

 $\mathcal{T}$ he biggest problem with unleashing a tide of wild magic to consume your enemies was that it tended to consume their *valuables* as well. Robin let Jhess hunt down any surviving examples, content in the rogue's determination to wring every last copper out of any situation. She'd deliver what she found for an even split.

Most of it, anyway.

Robin had ensconced himself in the building that had become Ruprecht's core room, the same one hosting the capped well which was also a gate to the deeper depths of Tarin-Tiran.

Ruprecht was silent, the dungeon focused entirely on refining the energies he had absorbed from the hobgoblins and channeling them into the assimilation of the gate mechanism. Robin had no idea how long it would take, but it certainly didn't seem to be the sort of thing that was over and done with quickly, so he had settled in, prepared to be patient.

Besides, it wasn't as if he himself didn't have plenty to think about. His share of experience from the plan had not only given him a level but set him right at the cusp of a second. For a few minutes, he had been tempted to leave things there, to get that next level in a few days when they encountered who knows what new challenges from below, but then, the sensible side of his mind had spoken up. Yes, it would be insanely gratifying to hit two levels in quick succession, but he'd be left in a position where his skills were beginning to fall behind, all that experience burned up in elevating his level alone.

And in Tarin-Tiran? He had a feeling he'd need to keep his skills up as much as possible. Who knew what challenges awaited below?

Robin opened his character interface and began with the easy options. His *Deception* needed to be at maximum. His free property rank went into *Cunning*. The peculiarity that came with level up would be a harder decision, so he shelved it for now.

He increased his proficiencies relating to stealth, observation, and all of his various performances and tricks. The math was incredibly annoying, not because it was complex but because there wasn't enough experience to just maximize everything. He still had to prioritize, and shifting various things around changed what he could and could not afford.

This was going to get even more interesting in four levels or so, when he'd be able to start increasing things like *Strength* and *Fortitude* directly with experience. Hopefully, there would be enough beasts and quests and tricks to try to keep up with the point sink that was coming.

Robin was suddenly very glad he had an experience multiplier that he knew most of the particulars for. His need for experience wasn't going to decrease any time soon, not if he had enemies like Gis and possibly even Urkhan to face.

Improve me next! Improve me! Rerebos's voice echoed in Robin's mind. The little dragon knew he was allocating his gains, and he knew that one of the options for Robin's next peculiarity would enhance Rerebos's own power: [Improved Familiar Bond].

Robin had taken it once already, to increase the range on their connection. Taking it again would give Rerebos an at-will invisibility effect, as well as limited shapeshifting and a breath weapon. It wasn't anything terrible at this point, but it would make the little dragon happy.

And he would be able to reveal Rerebos as his familiar. The trick would be convincing the little dragon to only appear in a more appropriate form. A miniature shadow dragon would draw all manner of attention, most of it in a form that Robin wasn't in the mood to deal with.

Not to mention it would hint a bit more than he wanted at his own nature.

The alternative would give him a little more flexibility with his own spells—Robin had his eye on several metamagic-related peculiarities which would make his spells last longer.

Of course, if he went that route, he'd have to navigate the wrath of Rerebos, and that was nothing to sneeze at.

Was he likely to have that much use for longer spells? Having [Visual Phantasm] and all his cantrips as at-will options certainly negated a lot of the need in terms of illusion trickery. Though it was still annoying to set up.

Only **[Lesser Mindreading]** and **[Wizard's Armor]** would really benefit from increases to duration, and Robin wasn't sure that was quite enough savings to make using up a peculiarity slot worth it. No, the metamagic specializations he was eyeing could wait.

Not that that really eliminated all the other options. There were plenty of peculiarities that would grant him new spells or additional bardsong options which were tempting. Not to mention the various utility power enhancements that would increase his flexibility.

Robin pulled up **[Effortless Illusion]**. It would make him better able to maintain illusions while casting or maintaining other spells. It was quite tempting as well. If he didn't take it now, eventually, he would need to.

He needed more peculiarity slots! Ugh! Too many things he wanted—needed—for the build taking form in his mind.

Improve me!

Rerebos's insistence wasn't making it any easier to think. Robin sighed and went ahead and selected the improvement, sending a pulse of warning along his empathic bond with the familiar. They'd need to be careful until he could introduce Rerebos in a more acceptable form to the party. If Robin was going to have to tell the truth, he'd tell a version of the truth. Harmless tricks were still tricks.

Got to keep in practice, and who knows when it might result in a dab of experience or a useful perk, right?

Besides, Rerebos had proven himself an incredibly useful scout. Added invisibility would only help that, and help keep the little dragon safe. Sure, Robin could resummon him if the shell the spirit of the dragon wore was damaged beyond repair, and it wouldn't have any ill effects at all, but Robin just couldn't stomach the thought of Rerebos getting hurt.

Exultation spilled along their bond. Robin could *feel* the little dragon popping in and out of visibility and shifting forms, which resulted in more than a few pangs of outrage.

A cat? A bat? Such limiting forms! So inferior to my innate scaled glory! This is hardly acceptable.

We'll find you a suitably impressive form that you can use, Robin reassured his familiar mentally. *And your shapeshifting abilities will grow as we ascend the ranks of power.*

More shinies! More spells! More power! Tell that dungeon to get off his lazy core and open those gates!

Robin sent agreement along the bond and left his familiar to experiment with his new abilities. He had a new spell to choose.

Thankfully, he'd already compiled a short list of the obvious options he could access via his interface or from his research at the library of Noviel. He'd hoped to find a few more options here in Tarin-Tiran and just learn them, but that hadn't happened yet.

There were a few illusion spells that seemed standard for this tier, but none of them really sang to him as inspiring options. Most of the meaty illusions would come into play at Tier Three. There were a couple spells that interfered with divinations that he had his eye on, though they were neither of them very powerful. They could mask his nature to a degree, redirecting the spell to follow another creature he designated, but without a lot more magic, he couldn't make either of them last long enough to be really useful on a regular basis. Not yet.

There was also a triggered audible illusion which could come in handy, **[Phantasmal Mouth]**. In spite of the name, it could handle all manner of sounds, not merely speech. And it was essentially permanent, with a programmable trigger. Or rather, it could be made permanent with the expenditure of a lot of magical energy.

It was still somewhat situational, though, and he could get a lot of the same mileage out of **[Lesser Phantasm]**. The trigger and permanency might be useful, but they had no idea what they'd be facing down there.

Robin wanted something more flexible.

So in the end, he went with **[Sorcerous Mark]**. It offered various small buffs, and he could have three of the magical tattoos on his person at any one time to start with. They had a long innate duration, and if he had enough magical energies, he could even apply them to the other party members, if they were willing.

Robin was looking over his character sheet in satisfaction when Ruprecht suddenly spoke.

Finally! There was relief and triumph in equal measure in the dungeon's tone.

The sound of massive tumblers turning rumbled through the floor beneath their feet, and the gate beneath them rose open, revealing a well of shadows.

The depths of Tarin-Tiran waited!

Here endeth the tale of *The Gates of Tarin-Tiran*

Robin Parker

Heritage: Shadeling, Paragon
Profession: Bard
Tier: 2 (Effective Level: 8)
Experience: 175
Spell Points: 21
Bardsong: 8 uses

Properties

Free Ranks Available: 1

Physical
- -Strength: 11
- -Dexterity: 14
- -Fortitude: 11

Mental
- -Intelligence: 17
- -Cunning: 24
- -Resilience: 14

Social
- -Charisma: 15
- -Manipulation: 13
- -Poise: 16

Proficiencies

Free Ranks Available: 1

Physical (9/9)
- -Athletics: 6
- -Brawl: 6
- -Dodge: 9
- -Melee Combat: 5
- -Pilot: 4
- -Ranged Combat: 11
- -Sleight of Hand: 9

-Stealth: 11
-Survival: 8
Mental (9/9)
-Arcane Lore: 9
-Bureaucracy: 7
-Concentration: 11
-Crafting: 9
-Healing: 8
-Insight: 10
-Learning: 9
-Natural Wisdom: 5
-Perception: 11
Social (9/9)
-Animism: 5
-Deception: 11
-Empathy: 9
-Expression: 11
-Gossip: 8
-Intimidation: 8
-Persuasion: 10
-Socialize: 9
-Streetwise: 7

Peculiarities

Blessing of Rhyth
Tongue of the Fallen Tower
Mark of the Trickster
Chronicle of Infinite Visions
Mask of Myriad Faces
Initiate of the Craft
Illusion Focus
Metamagic Initiate
Improved Familiar Bond x2

Perks

Wayfaring Stranger
Shard of the Shattered Manymind
Mark of Fairy's Favor
Touch of Wild Magic

Spells

Cantrips* (*no SP cost)
  -Lesser Phantasm*
  -Cutting Words*
  -Legerdemain*
  -Lesser Nightmare Curse*
  -Lesser Witch Bolt*
  -Minor Repair*
  -Lesser Charm*
Tier 1 (1SP each)
  -Visual Phantasm*
  -Healing Note
  -Whispers from Beyond
  -Minor Enchanted Slumber
  -Invisible Servant
  -Familiar Bond
  -Wizard's Armor
Tier 2 (3SP each)
  -Assume Quality (Special)
  -Lesser Mindreading
  -Sorcerous Mark

Bardsong

Command Attention
Song of Arcane Power

Interlude

An unspecified time ago, above the world . . .

The harmonics of the realmsphere sang through the crystal ship as it knifed through the interstellar darkness. The pilot felt it thrumming through the helm and resonating down to his bones. He bounced his foot impatiently; this was always the worst part, the final bit of waiting before journey's end.

"Proximity?"

4.5 cycles to arrival.

"Status?"

Initial mission remuneration: received. System analysis: complete. Reincarnation protocol: still processing.

The pilot suppressed a groan. It was bad enough he was working for a god of mischief, but he had to go on mission as a blank slate. No memories. Minimal guidance. At least Questar, his ship's A.I. would help guide him.

"ETA on Quest Protocol Integration?"

3 cycles.

Questar's voice, provided by the illusion matrix at the core of the helm, was usually stable, but for a moment, feedback rippled through his words. It almost sounded like a giggle. The pilot frowned. A glitch in the system? This close to the mission?

"Questar. Can you run a full diagnostic without compromising integration of reincarnation protocol?"

Affirmative.

"Do so."

The helm beneath him pulsed with iridescent light, refracting in waves through the visible spectrum. Red-Yellow-Blue. Red-Yellow-Blue. Red-Yello-*Ding!*

Diagnostic complete. All systems operating as expected under dictated protocols.

"Carry on." The pilot frowned. Something—

Planetary visual within range.

Questar projected an illusion of the surface of the world beneath them onto the crystal screen in front of the helm. White and blue and green blossomed in a broad view of the seas and lands. The pilot caught his breath.

"That never gets old." He'd been to missions on worlds across seven spheres, different magics, different kingdoms, different bodies, but the same sense of wonder every time. This one, with its cloud of continents floating through the aethers around the central sun, was unusual, but hardly the weirdest world he'd seen.

"Are we in range of a visual on the initial target location?"

Questar hummed a bit before the view shifted, zooming in closer to a kingdomwide shot. Mountains and forests, roads and fields, a few castles dotted here and there. Fairly standard for a world with this concentration of magic and minimal command of the deeper magitech principles necessary for voyaging between spheres.

At least, that was what his briefing suggested.

"Scan for all known forms of advanced magitech, epic-ranked magics, or supersciences."

It paid to be safe. Sure, he had the information in the briefing packet, but how often were those comprehensive? Clients *always* held things back. Usually it was oversight or incompetence. Sometimes, it was dangerous secrets. In any case, he always triple-checked.

Scanning . . .

The pilot took manual control over the view screen as he waited for the ship's systems to complete their analysis. Where was the city he was supposed to start in? *Ah.* There.

He zoomed in. There was an absolutely massive tower at the center of the place. There had to be magic involved in its construction—the thing was ludicrous, more like a man-made mountain than a proper tower or even a skyscraper. He didn't see any obvious evidence of magitech in the construction, though. Epic magic? Advanced intelligence systems working with just a few higher-level spell chains? Hard to tell.

No active magitech currently detected on target landmass. Some

evidence of degraded or slumbering magitech. Further specificity unavailable based on current data and scanning capabilities. Supersciences not present on target landmass. Epic spells and similar ongoing effects present at above-average levels compared to system data on similar worlds. Estimate several dozen epic-ranked individuals to be present on target landmass. End report.

The pilot pursed his lips. Could be worse. He'd been to cities with mad goddesses overseeing all aspects of the local reality, and some of the rules there were punishing beyond belief if you broke them. Running into an archmage was unlikely enough here. He'd just need to be careful, take care of his new body.

Well, as much as he could, given the circumstances.

In a little more than a cycle, he would be down there, in a new body filled with only a select few preprogrammed memories and the absolute minimum in starting abilities. Anything else would draw too much unwanted attention. Frell. This was going to su—

Reincarnation Protocol established. Limited choices available fitting mission parameters. Suggest option shadeling or option human.

The pilot pulled up each option on the viewscreen. Human, standard biological, flexible, present in large numbers across the target continent. Shadeling, mutable biological, rare, but can possess shapeshifting powers advantageous for infiltration.

"Set choice: shadeling." The pilot had less information than he liked to have, going into a mission like this. Some flexibility would go a long way to making things more survivable.

Plus, it was the option recommended by the briefing material.

Priming Reincarnation Protocol.

The pilot turned back to consider the view on the screen. He'd be down there soon. New body. New memories. New mission. Not long now.

Too bad he couldn't kit his new self out with a lot of magic items. That would be useful, but it'd draw far too much attention. The most he could do was order Questar to seed a few useful items in places they would naturally occur near to his origin point.

That, and to trust luck.

The pilot grinned. Good thing part of his fee for this mission was a massive whack of good fortune and the favor of a god. That was nothing to sneer at!

Quest Protocol integrated. Target Location within range. Connection strong need stable. Reincarnation Protocol primed.

Execute: Y/N?

No reason to put it off; he was as prepared as he could be. He'd just have to trust the guidance he'd programmed into Questar's system interface was sufficient.

The pilot settled himself back down into his seat and made sure the restraints were secure and all the runes around him were glowing with power. Everything seemed in order.

"Yes. Pull the trigger, Questar!"

As his consciousness was pulled from him and channeled down toward the surface, he heard feedback ripple again, gigglelike, through Questar.

Wha—

Descent into Tarin-Tiran

Chapter 1

Robin sent one final **[Lesser Witch Bolt]** sparking off into the darkness, and the battle ended with a small *squeak*! Around him, the floor of the tunnel was scattered with small corpses, the remains of the swarm that had descended on them. Most of them were small, ratlike creatures with clusters of crystal spikes where their eyes should be. Three or four of them had had those but also a small gem glowing on their foreheads, between their eyes.

Jhess was busy trying to pry one out from its attendant corpse as Robin stood there, actually. The thing suddenly gave under the pressure and sailed off into the darkness, hitting the wall with a small *plink*!

"Shit!" The rogue scrambled to her feet.

"What were those things?" Drev asked, prodding one with the end of his staff. The staff didn't do anything yet. Ruprecht had made it for him as part of a test to try and adapt the magical structures the dungeon had found within the wand-and-collar combo of the hobgoblin mages. So far, he hadn't succeeded, but the staff was solidly made, and Drev used it to help keep his footing in the ruined tunnels they had found behind the gate Ruprecht had finally managed to open.

Descending down the well had not been fun, but they'd managed it. There had been enough scraps of the ruined pulley mechanism people had once used that Ruprecht had been able to absorb and recreate one for the party to use. Ruprecht had then closed the gate behind them and reabsorbed the decent equipment to make it harder for anyone who might have survived the wild magic to follow. If they needed to get out without the dungeon's help, Robin wasn't looking forward to figuring that out.

"They appear to be some kind of psirat, but oddly mutated or warped." Vance crouched down for a better look. "That sonic attack, at least, seems the same or similar to ones I've read about. These crystals in the eyes, though, those are new to me."

The other dungeon here had a fondness for crystalline creatures. I expect we will encounter more. There have been hundreds, if not thousands, of years for some of the dungeon flora and fauna to escape his demesne and carve out new niches for themselves in the surrounding territory.

"Not to mention the prevalence of wild-magic surges coming through every so often, which could easily change or mutate them," Robin added after both his **[Bardic Lore]** and his **[Touch of Wild Magic]** perk seemed to *ping* simultaneously.

That could very well alter dungeon creatures and break the relationship between them and their parent.

Was that how dungeons saw the monsters they created? Kind of fucked up if they then sent them to die before the blades and spells of adventurers. Still, Robin wasn't a sentient floating crystal. There were probably alien moralities at play he couldn't begin to comprehend.

At least Ruprecht was on their side.

For now.

"Why can't you just make a bunch of your own monsters? Let them battle it out with these rats," Jhess complained.

"You know Ruprecht is using all of his energies in claiming and expanding his territory, as well as laying traps so it's safer for us to delve here," Robin replied, not mentioning that there'd be a lot less experience going around if they sat back and just let the dungeon do all the work.

And claiming territory like this is ridiculously inefficient, the dungeon complained, not for the first time today. Not even for the first time this hour. *Spherical expansion is so much cheaper in terms of energies expended. I feel so many kinks and bends in my form. Is this what it's like to be over twenty as a meatbag?*

"Language," Robin chided.

Honestly, *meatbag*? After they had both realized Ruprecht had once been human himself? It seemed tasteless. Though it could be Ruprecht's way of misdirecting attention, or even trying to mentally adapt to his new circumstances.

"Which way next?" Savra asked sourly from a fork in the tunnels ahead of them. There were stairs winding off in all directions. This passageway seemed to have been a way for residents to travel between levels. Runic patterns in curling lines that reminded Robin of art nouveau paintings could still be seen, though almost all of them were dark. Only the odd sigil still occasionally sparked with light and life, a testament to the workmanship that had once gone into this place.

Vance, Drev, and Robin all stopped to examine the runic structures whenever they found one, but so far, they'd not been able to puzzle out why these runes were different, or special. Ruprecht might eventually be able to figure it out, once he'd absorbed enough of the place, but there was no telling when that would be, if ever. A lot had been broken or damaged, and there was no guarantee he'd be able to piece together meaning or function from what remained.

"We go left," Robin called to the seeress. "We shouldn't be too far from a passageway or some other kind of entrance to the third level of the city."

"This place gives me the creeps," Jhess muttered as she moved forward to scout things out. "I swear I keep seeing movement in the shadows, but when I get there . . . nothing."

"It's not nothing," Savra said, her voice dark. "There is a presence here. I can feel it, even if I cannot clearly see it through all this . . . fog." She waved her hand distastefully through the empty air before her. "I dislike having my vision clouded so, to feel . . ."

She cut off, but Robin knew she must be talking about how remote and far from her goddess she felt currently. He wasn't sure which instincts were telling him that, but something certainly was. And something in him empathized.

Weird.

"I've heard it as well," Vance noted, though he treated it like he treated everything: as an item of interest. "Curious."

Drev nodded in agreement, purple-white energy briefly sparking at his fingertips, a visual manifestation of the mage's own unease.

"We'll get to the third floor," Robin said, pushing calm and assurance out into his voice. Could any good performer do less? "Ruprecht will claim one of the potential campsites I located in my research, then we'll be safe and set about figuring out . . . whatever it is."

He sounded surer than he felt. Ghosts were not something he'd prepared for; in retrospect, that choice seemed very foolish. Dead city and all.

And he'd had more than enough recent experience with curses, thank you very much. No more of those for awhile, if you please. Nope.

"Clear," Jhess's voice drifted back down the corridor.

They moved forward slowly, but not before Robin noticed that Ruprecht had absorbed all of the psirat—crysrat?—corpses around their feet. He was fairly certain the dungeon had swiped one of the ones with a gem in its forehead before Jhess had noticed it, too. Not that he could blame the dungeon—the place had to be hungry—but his instincts were telling him Ruprecht was up to something

Of course, he was one to talk. Or think. *Whatever*. He had his own agenda he hadn't fully shared with the party. Oh, he'd come clean about having several locations marked out to search for treasure, sure. He'd had to, once Vance had figured out he was looking for something. But he couldn't tell them everything. Not about Rhyth, not about his quest, not about his interface.

If nothing else, keeping secrets and hiding his true motivations made sure his experience gains were tripled. Trickery and lies paid dividends, and Robin wasn't willing to give that up. Not when the world he was in was so dangerous, and faster experience gains meant survival.

Not sure it was super healthy, but it was where he was at right now.

"What in Serenya's name—" Jhess's voice drifted back.

Huh. Robin wouldn't have pegged the rogue as a worshipper of the goddess of sun and healing, but hey, maybe she worshipped multiple deities. It was possible. Not that he even knew who the gods of thievery and profit were.

His **[Bardic Lore]** had several suggestions, but Robin paid the knowledge no attention because at that moment, he also stepped out of the passageway and onto the third level of the city.

"Sweet Rhyth," he whispered under his breath.

This level was in better repair than the surface, though there was still plenty of evidence of decay and ruin. That, however, was not what had caused the party to stand and stare. *That* honor went to what they could see of the ceiling. While in many places the roof of the cavern was shrouded in shadow, several areas flickered with life and light. Huge chunks of stone would suddenly spark to life, and for several moments or even minutes, the illusion of a sky would fill the space, making it feel like they were once more on the surface—or as close to feeling like they were on the surface as could be accomplished when the sky overhead flickered and went fuzzy.

Curious. I cannot be certain until night falls and I can see the stars, but I believe these illusions are mimicking the sky above as it is right now, in real time.

"What?" Robin glanced up and then along the boulevards again. "You know, I read that this city was once known for spatial magics as well." That sparked an idea. "With the right positioning, you could make the entire city, even the levels down here, feel like one continuous piece. Visitors might not even have realized they'd descended belowground when all of this was working."

"Trust your twisted brain to think of something like that," Jhess said, but the words lacked any kind of bite, as the rogue was staring up in awe.

"This is incredibly high-level illusion magic," Drev muttered. "The sheer scale and scope of this . . . I can't even imagine what it would take."

Robin could, but he'd been doing more than his fair share of research into illusion. And while he didn't know the spells or requirements for something of this scale—and permanent, on top of that—he did have his eye on a particularly powerful enchantment that could cover a massive range with an entire illusory environment.

"I honestly thought the descriptions of this place were referring to frescoes or other artworks, not to real magic," Vance added. "This is such a large effect, it's almost unthinkable. Well, not when gods are involved, of course, but it's been thousands and thousands of years since they took a hand directly enough in matters to manifest something like this."

"It could just be a lot of work by a lot of dedicated, entirely mortal illusionists," Robin pointed out, critically eyeing the patchiness of the sky. "Look, it's coming and going in sections. What god or goddess would need to do things in sections? That seems more like mortals with a lot of time and dedication to me."

"We should find shelter," Savra spoke suddenly. "We don't know what else is roaming this section of the city, and we don't have a safe fallback position yet."

"Split up and check the three possible sites Robin has on his map, or go together and check one at a time?" Jhess had a knife in each hand and looked uneasy.

"One at a time," Drev said firmly.

Robin agreed.

The first location they sought out, an inn that Robin had seen in the illusory book back in Noviel (not that he'd shared that particular detail) had long since turned to rubble. No joy there. The second location, a small temple, was standing, but all the entrances and exits had sealed themselves with some kind of magical stone. If it was an illusion or there was a trick to bypassing it, neither Robin nor Jhess could find it.

The third option, however, the personal mansion of a wealthy supporter of the Church of Rhyth, was more promising. It was partially destroyed, yes, but there were still sections standing strong, and even unbroken glass in the windows! Drev was already muttering about trying to figure out the enchantments on *those* with Ruprecht's help.

"Looks solid," Jhess said, popping her head back out after a quick scouting run through the place. "Something in here you should all see, though."

"What is it?" Drev asked, purple-white magic flaring defensively at his fingertips.

"We've got a body."

Chapter 2

Robin followed closely behind Jhess as the party made its way through the ruined mansion. Night had fallen, judging by what they could see from the flickers of illusion that still struggled to shroud the cavern ceiling. An oppressive silence had fallen as they crept inward, knowing that a body lay at the end of their path.

Yet for all that, there was still beauty to be had. The remnants of faded glory still clung to the walls in panels of fine, dark wood and glimmers of gilding. There were even traces of paint still clinging to the whitewash, evidence of beautiful murals or patterning. Robin could almost imagine how it had looked like, so long ago. There, the staircase bordered with orderly rows of dark spindles supporting the banister. Through that doorway, a servants' passage, likely leading to the kitchen. The pattern on the walls restored, all white and blue and . . .

. . . and for a moment, Robin wasn't imagining it as it had been; he could literally *see* it as it had been. And judging from the sharp inhalations of breath around him, he was *not* the only one.

The walls were restored, the windows shining with clear panes and stained glass accents. There was furniture all around, rather than the rubble of detritus and splinters, with expertly appointed little tables sporting various art pieces and other treasures of bric-a-brac.

And as quickly as it appeared, it vanished.

"What," Jhess said slowly, "was that?"

"Illusion?" Robin ventured, though his voice was anything but sure.

"What kind of illusions come and go like that?" Drev demanded. "And why did it look like what this place presumably *used* to look?"

Before Robin could offer a thought, there was a flicker of ghostly light from the top of the stairway to their right.

"Who's that?" Jhess jumped back after sending a knife winging upward.

The light vanished before the knife hit a beam and stuck there, quivering.

"What way is it to the body?" Savra asked, a note of finality in her voice that said she already suspected the answer.

There was a long pause.

"Up there," Jhess finally replied grudgingly.

"Of course," Drev muttered.

Robin quickly consulted his **[Bardic Lore]**. Were ghosts an actual thing in this world? Seemed likely. *Yeah. Ghosts are definitely a thing. Haunted places, ditto.*

The question was, in a city of illusion like this, how likely was it that this was an actual ghost versus the illusion of one? If he was going to try and scare intruders away from his expensive house, he'd certainly consider a permanent enchantment that mimicked a haunting.

But this was also a city that had been brutally invaded and had had many of its citizens slaughtered. If anything was going to cause a raft of ghosts to inhabit a place, that was a pretty good candidate.

Only one way to find out.

"Savra, anything you can do in case that's a real ghost?" he asked.

"Yes," the seeress replied. "That, at least, this place has not taken from me."

"Let's go, then!" Vance urged, beginning to stride up the stairs, eyes sparkling.

The man was far too enamored of adventure.

"So long as it is not an excessively powerful specter, at any rate," Savra added.

Vance, to his credit, only froze a moment before carrying on up the stairs. Savra followed, a small smile on her face, along with Drev, then Robin and Jhess.

The stairs creaked and groaned beneath their feet. Small sparks of light flashed occasionally, a sign of runic structure finally giving way to age. Whatever preservation spells had been worked into the place were on the verge of giving out. Still, the party made it safely to the next level.

Robin glanced down the hallway. It ran in either direction and seemed generally to be in better repair than the ground floor, though it was covered in dust, possibly from when the wall at the other end had collapsed. A gaping hole allowed Robin to see out to the illusory stars twinkling briefly on the ceiling.

"To the left," Jhess called out softly. "Three doors down on the right."

Vance moved forward, quick and quiet on his feet, with the rest of them following closely behind. The door in question was open, and faint traces of Jhess's movements through here on her earlier scouting trip were apparent in the light Drev had conjured so they might make their way more easily.

The light flashed off of something in the room, sharp and bright. Drev sent the light higher, to float near the ceiling, and the alteration in angle made it easier to see what had caused it. It was the corpse. Like the crysrats they had destroyed earlier, the body had crystals growing out of its eyes, but that wasn't all. Small outcroppings sprouted from all across the withered, almost mummified skin, and a veritable forest of spikes had forced their way out of the corpse's mouth and cracked off its jaw.

"That does not look like it was a pleasant way to go," Robin observed.

"There are a few things still on the body," Jhess said, "but I didn't want to touch them. Might still be a curse or a disease or wild magic clinging to him. I thought the experts should weigh in first."

"No magic that I can sense," Drev spoke after several moments.

"Nor I," Vance concurred. "Well, not from the crystals or from the body. There are some items that register, I think. Something around his neck. That ring on his finger. The coin purse on his belt. Wait, maybe it's something in the purse? I can't tell without touching it."

"I do not sense any danger," Savra added, hesitantly. "Though of course I cannot be certain, in this place."

"Well, let's take a closer look, then!" Jhess darted forward, happy enough with the risk levels now to take a chance.

I think we have the chance to stage your entrance to the party, Robin sent the thought winging its way to Rerebos. *There's a small hole in the ceiling of this room. Don your disguise and wait for my cue.*

A wave of assent mixed with a little annoyance and a great deal of excitement came back along their bond.

"There's a mundane satchel here as well," Drev noted. "And some kind of rucksack filled with equipment. Decent stuff, but nothing amazing. Some kind of explorer?"

"He certainly found more than he was prepared for," Savra said before beginning to mutter a prayer for the deceased.

Jhess was focused on carefully removing the equipment from the corpse, doing her best not to so much as brush any of the crystals, just in case. Robin opted to search the room for hidden compartments, or at least a hiding place where extravaluable discoveries or supplies might be stashed.

Who didn't like hiding a few trinkets away?

"There's a book in here. Some kind of journal," Drev called from where he was examining the contents of the satchel. "I've never seen one like this. And the writing implements are strange."

Robin glanced over and froze. Drev was holding a clickable ballpoint pen. And the red journal in his other hand was clearly mass-produced. Another world traveler? Robin wondered what Ruprecht would say when he found out. The dungeon was amassing energies, preparing to expand in the needed direction when they found a suitable base. He'd not be pleased to have missed out on this moment.

"I cannot read the script," Drev said. "I don't even recognize it."

Now he had both Savra and Vance looking over his shoulder in interest. Drev waved a hand toward the bard.

"What do you make of this? Anything you can piece together? Ring any bells in any stories or ballads you might know?"

Robin accepted the journal, gingerly opening the cover. The cover was textured like leather, but he could feel the fake plasticine nature of it. It was strange, and for a moment, he felt almost homesick, but it was a distant, hollow feeling, more like the idea or echo of an emotion than the real thing.

It was in English. Most of it, anyway. There were sections that were clearly encoded on top of being in a foreign language. Paranoid much?

Not that he could talk.

"I'll need several minutes," he said. "There is a lot here, and I don't think it's all in the same language." Code was almost a language all its own, right? Close enough.

Robin quickly scanned through it. Yeah, this was definitely another case of a displaced individual. The book opened with a short paragraph addressed to a potential reader. It listed several key facts, several names and dates. Robin felt the hair on the back of his neck rise.

This person—call him Red—was from a world very like Robin's. Or like Ruprecht's. Some of the big events overlapped, like the world wars, but there was also something about a plague? And a cure? Red was certainly frustrated about having been cooped up for a long time, and had apparently been whisked here just as he'd been able to safely go outside again?

Robin could practically feel the frustration emanating off the page in waves.

Different president, however, than Robin expected, even though the dates were very similar to his experience.

He suddenly found he couldn't look at the corpse. What if it had once looked just like him? Just like Ruprecht? Before the crystal and the mummification?

Not a pleasant thought.

Looked like Red had appeared here months ago, possibly even a couple of years. This was hardly a reliable account of experiences, more like a mad jotting of notes and important information. Red clearly knew he was working with limited resources.

There was no mention of a system, an interface, or any kind of prompts like that. Lots of gut instincts that turned out to be right, though. Maybe there was some sort of guidance in place, but it worked subtly because Red was clearly too paranoid to ever trust something as obvious as Robin's own interface?

There was more, however. Some of it immediately useful. Several sections of the city were mapped out, taking up several precious pages. Different locations were clearly marked, and there were several notes alongside. Unfortunately, most of these were in some kind of code. Robin's **[Tongue of the Fallen Tower]** was of no help. There were some mentions of apparitions and ghosts that he could read, but nothing helpful like how to avoid, detect, or defeat them.

Annoyed, he flipped back to the beginning of the book, looking for any clues as to some kind of code or cipher key. This was someone from a world very like his. This was no coincidence. Some power or powers were clearly playing a game, and Robin would like very much to know the stakes. His life depended on it.

There wasn't any mention of Rhyth or Urkhan that he could see, unless it was encoded in one of the mysterious sections he couldn't simply read. He really needed some kind of key.

"Is there any other text on his body," he asked while rereading the opening page. He should have been paying more attention to the rest of the party, who had been watching him avidly.

"Wait, can you read that?" Drev asked, looking at him intently.

"I can recognize some words," he hedged. "Something about ghosts?"

Rerebos, that's your cue!

Robin did not want to go too deeply into answering that question, and his instincts worked at the speed of thought to avoid it.

There was a flutter of wings, and a small shape dropped through the hole in the ceiling. Jhess's knives were instantly in her hands, but thankfully, the rogue refrained from throwing them immediately. A purple-white shield flared into existence around the party, and the light revealed more details.

A sleek black-and-white cat was standing on the floor. He had four white socks, a white chest, and a white tip to his tail. There was a blue-black sheen to his fur and the feathers of his wings when he flared them.

Rerebos was standing there looking like nothing so much as a cross between a tuxedo cat and a magpie. He quirked his head at the party, then sat down and began grooming himself, studiously ignoring everyone else.

Nicely done, Robin sent.

"What is that?" Jhess demanded.

Rerebos looked up, quirked his head to one side, and simply responded, "Mew?"

Chapter 3

I think," Robin said slowly, making a show of looking from the book to the winged cat and back, "that it might be our deceased friend's familiar."

It was a blatant lie, but no one else could decipher so much as the odd word from the journal he was holding, so it worked as well as any other explanation. Better, really, if Robin was going to "bond" with Rerebos in this disguise and make him his own familiar.

Robin pulled a morsel of food from his dimensional storage and crouched down, holding it out to Rerebos.

"Here, kitty, kitty, kitty," he sang softly.

Rerebos cocked his head at him but didn't approach right away. *That's right. Play it a bit coy. Gotta keep the performance convincing.*

"Are we sure it's safe?" Jhess asked, not sheathing her knives. "We're in a city which apparently held more than its fair share of illusionists and shapeshifters, and we've already dealt with more than the usual number of insane dungeon monsters."

"I do not sense any ill intent," Savra said slowly.

Rerebos hissed at them.

"Well, no more than I would expect," the seeress amended.

Nice touch, Robin sent to Rerebos, *but don't push it too much. We need to reel them into accepting you quickly so we can crack on with finding out what else there is here.*

A disgruntled wave of assent came back in reply. Rerebos defluffed himself a bit and took a cautious step forward, nostrils flaring at the morsel of food in Robin's outstretched hand. He took it gingerly and began a rasping purr.

It sounded like a set of rocks with the hiccups tumbling down a mountainside. A very tiny mountainside. Clearly, the little dragon needed a bit more practice in that department.

"Too bad this little one can't tell us what our friend was up to." Vance carefully crouched down next to Robin.

"Do the supplies tell us anything?" Robin slowly extracted another bit of meat to tempt Rerebos with. A small one. The little dragon was going to make himself sick at the rate he wolfed them down.

"Not much." Drev sighed. "The mundane supplies we've found are fairly general, but Savra's insight into what the magical items do might tell us more. At least in terms of what kind of adventurer he was."

"The journal is likely still our best bet," Vance said.

Rerebos chose that moment to leap up onto Robin's shoulder and settle in, claws pricking sharply through the fabric of the bard's shirt. He was going to need to invest in some leather epaulets if Rerebos was going to be spending any amount of time in this form. His shoulder would kill him otherwise.

Rerebos made a small *kek–kek–kek–kek* noise.

"Good boy," Robin said softly. "You want to stay with us, eh? Good Rere."

"Ree-Ree?" Jhess asked, raising an eyebrow but sheathing her daggers.

"It's kind of what that noise sounded like," Robin replied defensively. "Don't you think?"

"I think we need to get back to figuring this whole mess out," the rogue answered. "Put your nose back in that book and pull out something useful, eh?"

"Aye-aye!" Robin snapped off a mock salute and cracked open the book once more.

And like Jhess's words had been a benediction, the book fell open once more on a section of the hand-drawn map, and his eyes alit upon a passage he'd not yet read. Perhaps it was random chance or the hand of Rhyth from wherever forgotten gods dwelled or the influence of his wild magic perk, but the first section of the note was in English before it abruptly shifted to whatever cipher the writer had been using about halfway through.

Found another control point. This one is in much better repair. I think I can repair it and restore some limited functionality to the—

Interesting. He'd been trying to repair something in the city? Why? To figure out how it worked? To answer some kind of quest—

As if the thought had summoned it, a quest notification appeared before Robin's eyes.

New Quest: [A Touch of Restoration]

You've discovered that another worldwalker had a quest to repair some of the damage done to the city. What did he know that you do not? You need to figure out why and decide if you wish to take up his quest as your own. The journal may have some clues for you. It may not. Crack the code. Discover the secrets. Find the control points. Unriddle their secrets. The rewards may be more than you can imagine . . .

Reward: *Lost knowledge, greater access to the depths of Tarin-Tiran, and since you're a greedy little thing motivated by material gain, maybe even a magic item or three.*

Robin blinked away the notification after reading it twice. *Well. That was something.*

He opened his mouth to speak but was preempted by Savra.

"He was clearly some form of caster," the seeress informed. "The necklace contains a pearl which can temporarily boost the efficacy of one's spells for a few minutes each day. I suspect he'd not be wearing it were it not useful to him in some way."

Good news and bad news there! That was exactly the sort of thing Robin was after, but it would also be useful for Vance and Drev and Savra. That was a lot of competition.

"I suspect some of these sachets have a similar effect if the drug inside is consumed." Savra clearly didn't approve of this, but she didn't move to destroy the things either.

Robin suspected that would be a bit of a risk/reward situation. No way to really tell what the balance was without knowing what side effects there might be from the drug, or how addictive it could be.

"The ring offers some form of protective enchantment," Savra continued. "The pouch has a storage enchantment on it and, I suspect, some kind of antitheft measure. Then there is this."

Savra held out her hand. In it was an ancient-looking coin, thick and gold and had clearly been cast with the image of someone important on the side, but the years had worn away the fine detail, so the figure just looked misty and indistinct. The seeress turned the coin over. On the other side was a sigil which looked like it might once have resembled a pair of scales. Savra closed her hand over it once more.

"This appears to have some form of simplistic divinatory magic imbued into it. Though the enchantment itself is potent, I think the questions one might ask are somehow limited."

"I'll let you sparkle-finger types fight over the items, and I'll just take the gold from his pouch, shall I?" Jhess said, claiming her portion of the salvage.

Savra clearly wanted the coin, to judge by the way she gripped it so tightly. Robin could get on board with that. Drev would probably want the protective ring, and he'd be the one most likely to be able to use it most effectively, freeing up magical energies for more attacks, possibly.

Robin wanted that pearl necklace. Badly. But would Vance be willing to take the storage bag? It wasn't that terribly rare a thing, dimensional enchantments of this nature. You could buy similar pieces in Noviel, though this one looked like it was of finer workmanship. And it clearly had a history.

Maybe Robin could use that. Vance *was* a sucker for a good story.

Then the negotiations began. It began easily enough, falling out as Robin had predicted with Drev and Savra, but Vance was clearly eyeing the necklace. Before Robin could launch into his plan to make the pouch look more attractive, however, Vance threw a spanner in the works, turning to Robin with a fiendish look in his eye.

"Look. You want the necklace. I want the necklace. We both know that. I'm willing to make you a little extra deal, however, and take the bag instead, *if* you make it worth my while."

"I'm listening," Robin said cautiously.

"That journal is fascinating, and I suspect it holds a great many secrets. I think you're going to unriddle them. I want a copy—an *honest* copy—in your hand once you've cracked it. With nothing left out. Annotations of any information you understand enough to clarify. What do you say?"

Robin's mind flashed through the options, the lies and the tricks and the dodges he might employ.

"You'd have to swear on your god, of course," Vance casually added before Robin could open his mouth to agree.

That complicated matters, particularly in a world like this. That would not be an easy thing to do.

On the other hand, if he could pull off any trickery in a situation like this, it would surely result in a bumper crop of experience points. And he did trust Vance. More or less.

"I could do that," he said, stalling for time, a thoughtful look on his face.

Maybe he could commit without actually getting to the bit about swearing. He'd need to try and distract Vance with something tempting, though. A good faith offering of sorts, maybe.

"These maps," he said, opening the journal, "they look like they represent sections of this city. There are notations in several locations. I think our friend Red here was trying to find something or fix something. I can read some of the words on the page, but these sections remain a mystery. I think they have been encoded somehow."

"But it does show us that there are spots of interest, here," Jhess pointed out. "Could be treasure."

"And do any of these locations match up with the ones you researched yourself before we came to this place?" Vance asked him.

"I don't know." Robin blinked. He should have thought of that. "I'll have to check."

"That would be the smartest place to start, certainly," Drev offered. The mage was only partially paying attention to the discussion, engaged as he was with examining his own prize, the ring of protection.

"Let me see." Robin turned his attention to the map.

Yes. There were at least three locations he could definitely say he'd want to look at from his own research, and another two which might fit. It was hard to say, between the general level of decay the city had experienced and the hand-drawn quality of the map.

He went ahead and pointed out the three he was certain of to the rest of the party.

"This place seems solid enough, ghosts notwithstanding," Savra opined. "It should serve well as a base. Excellently so, if Ruprecht can make some repairs to the structure."

"It's certainly convenient to the three locations Robin has just pointed out," Vance added. "I think." He turned the journal back and forth in his hands and squinted at the map.

Rerebos began grooming himself from his position on Robin's shoulder. With a quick mental suggestion from Robin, he began to purr loudly.

"I think our little friend here approves," Robin declared. Might as well nudge events along a bit. They had a lot of work to do, and he wanted to get his hands on that necklace! Of course, the party might need just one more little nudge.

Robin sank down into a nearby chair with a sigh. Thankfully, it held up under his weight. A small puff of dust escaped, but otherwise, it remained solid.

"Nice workmanship," he noted. "Solid and comfortable. Could use a bit of a cleanup if we're staying, though. Are we staying?"

He looked around at the rest of the party.

"We'll make this our base, let Ruprecht settle in, and then head to the first of the locations Robin has identified," Jhess said decisively before anyone else could offer an opinion. "That's our best chance at finding something useful. And Savra's right. This is a good location, so long as she feels she can keep the ghosts at bay."

Robin bit back a smile. It looked like his distraction ploy had worked. Now to just . . .

"Right after Robin makes his vow," Vance spoke.

Curses! Foiled again!

Chapter 4

I really don't understand why he likes you so much," Jhess complained as they trudged down the ruined street, clambering over the rubble and shattered stone.

"He's my familiar," Robin answered, reaching up to scratch Rerebos between his fuzzy cat ears. "And he likes me! Isn't that right, cutie?"

I will end you for your impertin—oh. Oh! Right there!

Rerebos began purring loudly. Robin didn't even bother to hide his grin. Of course, as soon as he did so, he stumbled, nearly sending both himself and Rerebos for a nasty tumble.

Fortunately, his reflexes managed to kick in. Phew! Robin couldn't wait until he could start sinking experience into his physical properties. A higher *Dexterity* seemed like a very nice thing to have right about now.

"Eyes on where we're going, please," Savra called from behind him. "It feels like we're close."

"We are," Robin confirmed, after taking a moment to glance around. Even with the decay and ruin, he recognized the place from the visions of the illusory book in the library of Noviel. "In fact, we're here. Look."

The location they'd decided to try first was a small public square, although there were seven sides to it, so maybe square wasn't the right phrase. Anyway, there was an ornate fountain in the center of it. In Robin's memory, it flowed with ever-shifting iridescent waters, and the walls of the surrounding buildings were inlaid with intricate mosaics.

The memory was far from reality.

Sure, there was still a fountain at the center. It wasn't even all that damaged, though no water currently flowed through it, and some of the mosaics were still intact. The ground was littered with brightly colored shards of stone, however, like someone had upended a hundred jigsaw puzzle boxes.

There was a flicker of movement, a wisp of a humanoid shape appearing and disappearing in the corners of his vision.

"Savra," Jhess called out, "some local spirits want you to come out and play. Tell them we're busy."

The seeress clutched the holy symbol at her neck and began to chant. The apparitions flickered and vanished as she finished, and Jhess motioned the party to continue forward.

Robin headed toward the mosaic. He suspected that whatever magic had once operated there would be bound up in the picture, since he recalled it moving in his vision from the book. Sure enough, there were runic lines of force etched onto the stone. He could even see where the lines of the mosaic had once followed them. Keyed into them somehow?

Robin examined what he could still see of the image, cleaning it carefully with [Legerdemain]. The colors blossomed under his attention. There should be a blue chip there, so . . .

He crouched down and began to sift through the rubble, picking out all the glints of blue he could find. After a few minutes, he had a nice pile of them and began the painstaking process of trying to fit one into place. After a few false starts, he found a match, and the line of force sparked, faintly, as he pressed it into place. There was still magic here! The enchantment hadn't been fully destroyed by time.

A shout of alarm caused him to drop the fragment of stone, however. A flickering image had reappeared. Savra called out another chant, but it vanished before she got even a few syllables in. A suspicion began to creep into Robin's mind. He fished around for the fragment of stone he'd dropped. *There.*

Robin carefully reapplied it to the wall. The magic sparked to life once more, and a flickering image reappeared. Savra began to chant, but Robin pulled the fragment of stone away, breaking the magical circuit or whatever it was again.

"Wait," he called out. "I think I've got something here. I don't think we're seeing actual ghosts. Look. Wait for it."

He placed the fragment back on the wall. The figure flickered to life once more.

"I think there's some kind of recorded illusion here," Robin explained. "Jhess, help me gather the mosaic fragments. Vance, Savra, see if you can make anything of the lines of force you see. Drev, watch our backs."

The party set to work, carefully examining their surroundings and gathering up the pieces of broken mosaic. Even Rerebos helped, though Robin suspected some of the shinier bits might have vanished into the familiar's hoard, and getting them back—should he need them—would prove expensive.

With a suitable collection acquired, the party set to work, Robin arranging the pieces as best he could from his limited memory of the mosaic in his visions, Savra adding insight where she could with her divinations—aided by the coin she had recently acquired—and Drev and Vance offering opinions based on the lines of runic inscription they could see revealed by the missing mosaic pieces, and theories on how those lines likely extended under the existing sections.

It was the most annoying jigsaw puzzle Robin had ever done. Sure, they could make reliable guesses as to the color, but the tiny fragments weren't nearly as distinct as puzzle pieces, and there were a lot of them, with no guarantee they had all the ones they needed. Still, they managed to patch together a small section, linking three of the lines of runic power with the small pieces of stone, held in place by Drev's growing mastery of magical force.

Robin clicked a final piece into place, this one with a bit of gold still shining on it. As soon as he did, the ruins around them flickered to life, pictures and forms taking shape out of thin air. It was a three-dimensional illusion, more real and convincing than anything else Robin had seen thus far.

Or it would have been, had it remained constant. It flickered in and out, stuttering a bit like a streaming video across a bad connection. But even with that, there were details to be seen. The ghostly form from before resolved itself with a shocking clarity into the form of a tall, slim individual garbed in ridiculous robes. As Robin watched, he found he could tell that the attire was mostly illusory. Part of a show.

"ie—Nilsiir—glo—kha—"

There was sound as well! Stuttering in time with the flickering of the image. The figure—Nilsiir, Robin presumed by the way they turned at the sound—whirled to face someone. Something? Someone and a lot of backup forces. From his position, Robin couldn't make out the leader, but the flickers of hobgoblins in the background suggested this was an image from the fall of Tarin-Tiran, somehow captured in a looping illusion.

Yup. Definitely hobgoblins. Robin could see several of them clearly now as they advanced on the defiant Nilsiir.

"He looks like some kind of priest," Vance said quietly.

"He is," Savra confirmed. "Look at the Holy Symbol."

"Which one?" Drev asked. "He has them all over."

Now that they had been drawn to his attention, Robin looked. And blinked. It was a strange symbol, and it almost shifted beneath his eye, like one of those optical illusion drawings from his old world.

Even before his [Bardic Lore] pinged, he knew. This was one of Rhyth's symbols! This was a priest of Rhyth! Possibly even a high priest, judging by appearances. Though, with illusionists, that was always a dicey proposition at the best of times.

"Leivniz—"

Was that a name? The person at the head of the hobgoblin forces? Robin struggled to pick out more details, but the illusion was so incomplete it was a losing proposition.

"ex—ed—from—not—"

He couldn't make out all the words, but the expression of distaste and disappointment on Nilsiir's face was crystal clear, even with the flickering nature of the illusion. The hobgoblins moved, advancing on the priest. Nilsiir, for their part, didn't give any ground. Conversely, they smiled—a mocking, taunting smile—and raised their fingers before their lips in an incredibly rude gesture.

Nilsiir's fingers parted, their lips split, and a torrent of riotous rainbow beams of light blasted forth from their mouth in a broad cone, enveloping the advancing hobgoblins.

Chaos and death ensued. Hobgoblins caught fire or began to melt as if acid had been poured all over them; others froze solid or turned to stone, while still others simply vanished or collapsed, frothing at the mouth and choking.

A bolt of black-and-white lightning sheared through Nilsiir's form, but it passed through the priest entirely, leaving them—to all appearances—unharmed.

Some kind of projection? Robin's mind whirred. And what was it about that spray of prismatic light which seemed slightly off to his eye? There was some kind of advanced illusion magic at play there. Of that, Robin was certain.

And if he hadn't been, the notification that appeared before him would have made him so.

Congratulations! Prerequisites for [Shadowcrafter] met!

You have learned of the illusionist's secret weapon, called [**The Mirror's Revenge**]*, from the Queen of Air and Darkness. Now, you have seen it in action. You now have access to the* [**Shadowcrafter**] *class.*

Note: *Gaining levels in the* [**Shadowcrafter**] *class will eventually give* [**The Mirror's Revenge**] *as a bonus peculiarity, but taking levels in this class is not required to learn said ability.*
You are free to learn it as any illusionist-focused caster possessing the [**Illusion Focus**] *peculiarity.*

Interesting. Robin blinked away the notification. So he was definitely on the right track, coming here. Then the illusion flickered one last time and vanished with a small *patter* of falling mosaic chips as Drev's spell ran out.

"Did you see that?" Drev was breathless with excitement. "That was incredibly high-tier magic! At least Tier Seven or Eight! Do you think we can trigger it again? I'm sure we can learn a few things just from watching that image, seeing those gestures and those effects . . ."

Judging by the unexpected perk he had received, Robin suspected the mage was correct.

"Here we go." He picked up the mosaic shards and replaced them just as he had done before, with Drev's force magic holding them in place.

The scene reformed, just as it had before.

"What else can we see if we use different pieces?" Vance mused.

"We're not experimenting with that until we have all of this down," Drev shot back. "Are you insane? We might get something completely useless."

"We'll be careful," Robin said, raising his hands to placate the quarreling magic users. "But you know this isn't the only thing we have to do now, right?"

"What else?" Jhess groaned.

Robin grinned.

"We need to find more of these locations and see what else we can discover!"

Chapter 5

"*F*rell," Robin muttered as he looked through Rerebos's senses at the next location the party intended to explore in their hunt for more illusory knowledge. The location in question had once been a market gallery of shops, but now, it was a nesting ground for some of the monsters which had escaped from the living dungeon threaded throughout the city.

The shopping arcade had been colonized by a small band of humanoids that looked rather like goblins, save for their strange blue hue and the crystalline shimmer to their hair and nails. The most curious thing, however, was their complete lack of communication. Robin had been spying on them for a while now, and there hadn't been so much as a peep from any of them, nor any sort of gesturing or pantomime communication.

That didn't mean they weren't interacting or coordinating, however. Robin could see that they were communicating somehow—maybe pheromones or light patterns or telepathy—because they divided food among themselves, and the duller ones seemed to cower before the more brightly glimmering ones.

They will move quickly when threatened, Rerebos observed.

It was a strange thing, mentally communicating with Rerebos while also sharing the little dragon's thoughts. Not quite a double-echo sort of feeling but close. Like Robin could hear a whisper of the thought in both his projected mind and his brain at the same time.

But do you think we can scare them off?

I do not know. Rerebos flitted to another shadow for a better vantage point. *They seem the sort to be weak and scatter before a threat, but also the kind that will guard their territory most jealously. Though I hope they do not flee.*

Robin could *feel* his familiar's eye glitter with avarice.

Many, many shinies . . . Rerebos whispered to himself, looking at the goblinoids' bodies.

Robin was more interested in the mural. This one had the least amount of damage he'd seen so far. There were still several pieces missing, both scattered throughout and in a pattern that looked curiously similar to the rune lines he'd seen beneath the other murals the party had investigated.

He *really* wanted a look at that mural. But to get to it, they needed to clean out the nest of little blue goblins first. He'd like to assume they wouldn't be too tough, but assumptions like that were a good way to get a guy killed.

"Where's a nice fireball when you need one?" he muttered to himself, returning his senses to his own body.

"What was that?" Jhess asked.

"Lots of little blue goblin-looking types," he answered. "A whole nest. Crystal protrusions, again."

"Like the rats?" Drev looked thoughtful. "Could indicate they also employ some kind of mind magics."

"Ugh," Jhess groaned. "Those are the worst."

"At least it looks like they still have plenty of vital organs for you to stab them in," Robin said. "They're not walking automatons made entirely of crystal and brass."

"Don't tempt the gods!" Jhess glared at him.

Robin raised his hands in a placating gesture.

"Do we have any kind of area-effect magic that is useful on a large number of beings at once? I can hold them spellbound for a while, but I doubt it'll last through the time we'd need to experiment with the mural." Robin looked to Drev. Vance was more of a self-enhancement kind of magician.

"How many are there?" Drev scratched his chin.

Robin twitched his finger, and a **[Visual Phantasm]** modelling the area and its occupants materialized.

"No. Too many. I'd need another tier at least before I could hit all of those with one spell."

"We could snipe them?" Jhess suggested. "Or wait until most of them are asleep and just . . ." She drew a finger across her throat.

"I suspect not enough will be in slumber at any one time to make that strategy effective," Savra said, flipping her newly acquired magical coin. "Sniping them from concealment or scaring them away are the two most favorable options, though both seem to be a mixture of both weal and woe."

Robin would prefer simply scaring the little buggers off, but the way Savra said it made him think that if they did, they'd likely run into the blighters again, possibly at a less favorable time.

"We could snipe with illusory cover," he suggested. "Do both. Take out a chunk of them by casting spells through a monster apparition I conjure. If we time it right, we could eliminate a chunk of them, scare off another chunk, then see where that gets us? Maybe a hydra? That has plenty of heads."

The party roughed out a plan, and Jhess went off to scout good positions. The shopping arcade, although damaged, still had plenty of support on its upper level, even if the stairs had long since been choked with rubble. Between Jhess, Rerebos, and the rope ladders each of them had packed, it was simplicity itself to scramble up while the blue gobbos were looking elsewhere.

Savra took a position on the left-hand side with Vance. Jhess and Drev to the right. Robin and Rerebos took a while longer to get into position, as the archway above the entryway to the arcade was treacherous and the last thing Robin wanted was to fall and break something right before their ambush.

Finally, he was in position.

It began with [Lesser Phantasm]; a few noises that slowly grew in volume, a scrape of something large against a building, the tumble of a pile of stones, the hiss of scales over cobbles.

Jhess was making faces at him, but Robin ignored the rogue. This was theater! If you wanted to convince your audience, you needed to get at least some of the details right.

He followed up with a flickering shadow, another few tactical sounds, then a great huff-huff-huffing before the used [Visual Phantasm] to cause a large reptilian head to snake its way into the shopping arcade.

The blues definitely noticed that! Robin could see a ripple of alarm go through them as they began to scatter. Best not give them a chance to organize any kind of defense.

Robin channeled a [Lesser Witch Bolt] through the illusion as the hydra opened its mouth. The flaming projectile lanced outward and slammed into one of the blues.

Direct hit!

The target didn't go down, but Robin could see he'd done more than a little damage. Before he could fire off another, however, a bolt of force came out of nowhere to finish it off.

Right! The others needed illusory cover as well. Robin tweaked the [**Visual Phantasm**] to add two more heads, writhing and snapping in front of his party members. He followed it up with a growling roar. The blues, for their part, fell back but didn't run out of the arcade. They seemed to think that the hydra might be too big to fit inside.

Robin bit back an oath. Not what the party needed right now.

His eyes scanned the crowd. There had to be a leader, someone bolstering the weaker-willed members of the group. None of them immediately stood out, but maybe if he gave them a little nudge . . .

Robin picked a few cowering targets from among those blues that were clearly the most afraid. As the hydra roared and snapped and fired off occasional bolts of force or fire, Robin peppered each of his chosen cowards with [**Lesser Nightmare Curse**] to really ramp up the fear.

"Come on, come on, break, you bastards," Robin muttered.

He began to throw in a [**Lesser Witch Bolt**] every three cantrips. He was on his fourth cycle before one of the blues finally broke, screaming while running away as another blue was roasted in witchfire. One of the others, slightly smaller but with a few more crystalline protrusions, threw out its hands, and the air rippled as a blast of pure psychic energy tore through the arcade. It gnashed at Robin's mind, but he managed to shrug off the effects.

Rerebos was not so lucky. His familiar, still in his flying feline form, suddenly slumped off Robin's shoulder, the bard barely managing to catch him in time.

Robin willed the heads to all snap and point at that one. That had to be the leader. He followed up the action with another bolt of witchfire, but the expected bolts of force from the other two heads didn't follow.

Fuck! Who had gotten caught in that mind blast?

Didn't matter. That leader needed to be crushed, and crushed as soon as possible. They were clearly holding the whole group together.

Robin fired off a [**Lesser Witch Bolt**] and followed it with a [**Whispers from Beyond**]. If he got lucky, making the leader flee would cause all the rest to follow.

He didn't get lucky.

Clearly, the little blue bastards all had highly developed wills. He was just fortunate that none of them had bothered to interact directly with his illusions yet. If they did, they likely stood a higher-than-average chance of noticing that they were, well, an illusion.

Robin spammed a few more cantrips, scoring a couple hits with his witchfire. While the leader still stood, the rest of the blues were clearly getting seriously agitated.

Fine. Couldn't take out the leader without some stronger spells, he'd double down and try to get some of them to flee with his maddening whispers.

It was nice having a bigger pool of magical energies to work with.

Not all of the blues were as resilient as their leader. First one, then another succumbed, fleeing while screaming away from the hydra. A half dozen others that Robin hadn't targeted followed.

That rattled the leader. The little figure started waving their arms wildly and jumping up and down. Then there was a flicker of movement, and the leader collapsed!

The rest of the group broke at that. Whatever force had been holding them together was gone, and the blues scrabbled to escape, trampling a few of their numbers to death in their panic.

Robin kept the illusion going, mentally directing one of the heads to start snuffling around the nearest corpse, then he carefully made his way to the main level, Rerebos's unconscious form held carefully in the crook of his arm.

Shrouding himself in shadow, he made his way to the corpse of the leader. When he got a bit closer, it was clear what had felled the creature: one of Jhess's daggers.

"Nice shot," he said, hearing the faint scrape of leather on stone behind him.

"Thanks," Jhess grunted. "Thought we were sunk when Drev collapsed and the force bolts stopped flying."

"Vance succumbed as well," Savra informed, joining them. "Though I expect they shall rouse themselves soon enough."

Robin nodded, carefully examining their surrounding for stray enemies. There were none.

"Right," he said. "Let's get everyone up and running again, then see what this mural has to tell us."

Chapter 6

$\mathcal{T}$he mural in front of Robin depicted a golden vision of Tarin-Tiran—at least, they thought it was Tarin-Tiran—as a center of trade and wealth. It made sense, considering it boasted some kind of shopping arcade, though any actual evidence of such had long since been looted by invading forces, wandering monsters, and opportunistic adventurers.

It was surprisingly intact, compared to the other examples the party had seen so far in the city, protected by location and, presumably, the kinds of monsters that had burrowed here over the eons. Drev and Vance were running their fingers carefully along the tiles, attempting to sense out the runic structures behind it. All around them, the storefronts lit up in flickers so fast it was impossible to see precisely what the old illusions had been of, but they seemed to be signs, possibly even a form of advertisements?

"There has to be something . . ." Drev was saying when suddenly, a fully immersive illusion bloomed all around them. "Ah! Got it!"

Once again, the party could see a vision of the city under siege. The image still had missing sections, but the flow of it was much clearer, and those absent pieces were overall minor.

"There's the priest again. Nilsiir." Savra pointed.

The image of Nilsiir stood in the entrance to the arcade, one hand reaching out for support from a nearby pillar. The priest seemed to have been running or otherwise exerting themselves.

"I think this is later in the narrative," Robin said, moving around to examine the priest's trembling figure. "They look exhausted. And the hobs outside"—he glanced at the small bit of the illusion he could see extending past the entrance of the arcade—"look to be in worse condition than we've seen in other illusions."

"Leivniz," the illusory high priest spoke. "You will not take this city. Not whole. Not as you want it, subjected to your edicts and demands. There is too much of—"

The illusion flickered.

"Sorry!" Drev called. "It's sucking up a lot more energy than the others. Let me . . ."

The image flickered back into being. This time, the party could see who Leivniz was. There was a figure standing opposite Nilsiir.

She wore the robes of a mage, though in an archaic style that rang distant bells for Robin's [Bardic Lore]. Her colors were black and white, and the seams were precise, straight lines. Even after what had clearly been a pitched and protracted conflict, the whites remained white and the blacks fully black. No dust dared smudge either color off its exacting adherence to shade.

"You cannot win, Nilsiir," the mage was saying. "This chaotic, lawless place will finally fall in line. Finally see the light of order and reason so that we may pursue a greater accrual of knowledge—"

"You don't want knowledge," Nilsiir interrupted. "You want control. Control! In this place. What fucking nonsense."

"Melusk agrees with me—"

"Melusk?! *Melusk?!* You can't be—ah." Something flickered in Nilsiir's eyes. "That's what that meant." The high priest straightened to their full height. "I'm sorry, my dear, but I cannot allow you to proceed with your plan. Though it cost me and this city dearly, I'm afraid I'm going to have to fuck shit up, as it were. Good luck catching me before I do!"

With that last mocking word, Nilsiir vanished, even as a maelstrom of force erupted in the spot the priest had been standing.

"Find him!" Leivniz snapped to the nearby forces as she drew a crystal ball out of a pocket it had no right fitting into. "He cannot be allowed to—"

The vision cut off, then restarted.

"I think that's all we can get here," Drev called. "But I'll check some other parts of the runic structure to be sure."

"This makes no sense," Vance observed, coming to stand in the spot where Nilsiir had been just a moment ago. "The illusion runes we're working with predate the conflict we're seeing. How can it be recorded for us to find?"

"Specialist illusionists can reshape existing illusions, permanent or not, pretty much at will if they had a hand in constructing them," Robin explained, thinking about some of the things he had discovered via exploring his character options and raiding Noviel's library for information on the art of illusion. "Tarin-Tiran seems to have fostered a very advanced school of illusion of some kind. They might have had masters capable of altering even illusions they didn't create. Like those." He pointed to the mural.

"Well, if that is the how, what is the why?" Savra asked, walking gingerly over to where the Leivniz had appeared. "Why immortalize these pieces of the city's fall?"

"Posterity?" Drev offered. "So someone would know what happened?"

"I'm not sure if we'll know why unless we can figure out who, and then understand that being," Robin said thoughtfully. "If it was Nilsiir, well, they were clearly going to do *something*, but we don't know what."

"Yet," Vance added. "We don't know what *yet*. Each of the illusions we've uncovered following Red's journal have led to a different piece of the story. If we keep following them, we'll likely get even more."

"Does it even matter, though?" Jhess complained. "It's not like the map is leading us to uncovered troves of treasure. It's mostly been minor skirmishes with annoying monsters."

"It's not led to much treasure yet," Robin admitted, "but again, it's *yet*." His mind worked furiously in the background. They needed—*he* needed— to follow this story through to the end. If Jhess got antsy, it might endanger that goal. "Think about the swag Red had on him. He had to get some of that from here. It just fits too well with the place. And there is no way Nilsiir would have let an invading army walk away with the treasury of the city. They had to have had a place to hide it. It's the center of a culture of illusionists! There's almost certainly a well-hidden vault somewhere with untold riches in it."

It wasn't even a lie. Robin firmly believed that. And it seemed he had allies in his goal, to boot.

"I agree," Drev said quickly.

"Yes," Savra chimed in. "There is definitely great treasure to be found by those clever enough and daring enough. However"—she frowned, staring at the enchanted coin she had been flipping—"there is great danger as well."

Shinies?! Rerebos spoke excitedly in Robin's mind.

Yes, shinies. If we are clever and patient, Robin answered.

The familiar was not the only one so swayed by the idea. Jhess was always eager for more treasure, even if Robin did not know the reason. He suspected there was something more to it than mere avariciousness.

"What kind of treasure are we talking?" The rogue looked to their diviner, clearly intrigued but not quite willing to cede the point just yet.

"Well, we can see that they've used gold in a lot of their decor"—Robin pointed to the mosaic—"and clearly, some of it has survived. I've also read that Tarin-Tiran was famed for its artists and artwork. There have to be a few examples which have survived."

"Adventurers often lack the eye to discern what is valuable due to its aesthetics as opposed to simply because it is crafted of valuable metals or minerals," Vance agreed.

Another ally. Nice to have. Robin would take any support he could get.

"And if we're investigating artistic works, like the mosaics, it's likely other works of art might turn up," Drev added thoughtfully, but it was clear the force mage was less keen than any of the rest of the party, as evidenced by his following words. "Though I'm inclined to seek out more esoteric repositories of knowledge, myself."

"I suppose you can sell books for a decent enough price," Jhess grunted.

They were straying away from the point, which was persuading Jhess to support the continued investigation of the murals. Robin was certain the party was keen enough to continue based off a simple majority vote, but it would be easier if Jhess was enthusiastic in participating.

"Tarin-Tiran was also known for having a supply of metals and minerals for craftsmen to use in creating wonders both magical and mundane. Probably comes from digging your city down so far into the earth. There are probably some of those around."

"That's all well and good," the rogue said, eyes sparkling with a mixture of greed and mischief, "but who's to say what is left and what's been carted off long ago?"

"That I cannot see," Savra replied, flipping the coin a few more times. "But I can say there is great treasure to be found if we continue along our current path of investigating these murals. Though the danger grows along with the potential reward."

"That's true of any good dungeon crawl." Jhess shrugged. "All right. I suppose we keep doing what we're doing."

"Don't mention the dungeon." Drev shuddered melodramatically. "Ruprecht is all well and good, but the living dungeon here in the city is incredibly old, and I don't want to think how powerful and dangerous."

"But how rewarding might all that power and danger be?" Robin teased. "If Ruprecht is anything to go on, the more risk, the more reward!"

"Red certainly made investigating the murals work for him," Savra said. "But I do wish we knew more about where he got his information."

"Maybe he was a diviner as well? He did have that coin on him, after all," Robin pointed out.

"Perhaps." Savra looked at the relic in her hand. "I suspect we will never know."

"That's a terrible attitude for a diviner to take on!" Robin chided her.

"I'm going to search these shops before we leave," Jhess spoke up. "There might be a safety box hidden away that was missed."

"I foresee no danger in staying to search," Savra replied after consulting her coin.

"I'll trace the runes through the mosaic again, if we're pausing for a bit," Drev said.

"I'll help Jhess search," Vance offered. "I'm a bit low on magical energies at the moment. I need time to replenish."

Rerebos gave a little feline chirrup and flitted off to follow Jhess. Robin hid a smile. The rogue would be lucky if Rerebos didn't try to swipe any and all shiny things she uncovered, worthwhile or not.

Robin stayed where he was, however. The mystery of the city was tugging at his mind, and he wanted some time to think through what they had seen. What was happening? And who had changed the murals to record the invasion?

Was it even the truth they were seeing?

Maybe he should check his character sheet and see if there was any-where he could apply some experience to help him—and thus the party—unravel this mystery a bit further. He should have enough experience to raise *Insight* and *Arcane Lore*, at least . . . maybe a few other skills . . .

Robin Parker

Heritage: Shadeling, Paragon
Profession: Bard
Tier: 2 (Effective Level: 8)
Experience: 4750
Spell Points: 21
Bardsong: 8 uses

Properties

Free Ranks Available: 1

Physical
- -Strength: 11
- -Dexterity: 14
- -Fortitude: 11

Mental
- -Intelligence: 17
- -Cunning: 24
- -Resilience: 14

Social
- -Charisma: 15
- -Manipulation: 13
- -Poise: 16

Proficiencies

Free Ranks Available: 1

Physical (9/9)
- -Athletics: 7
- -Brawl: 6
- -Dodge: 9
- -Melee Combat: 6
- -Pilot: 4
- -Ranged Combat: 11
- -Sleight of Hand: 9
- -Stealth: 11
- -Survival: 8

Mental (9/9)
- -Arcane Lore: 10
- -Bureaucracy: 7
- -Concentration: 11
- -Crafting: 9
- -Healing: 8
- -Insight: 11
- -Learning: 9
- -Natural Wisdom: 5
- -Perception: 11

Social (9/9)
- -Animism: 5
- -Deception: 11
- -Empathy: 10
- -Expression: 11
- -Gossip: 9
- -Intimidation: 8
- -Persuasion: 10
- -Socialize: 9
- -Streetwise: 8

Peculiarities

Blessing of Rhyth
Tongue of the Fallen Tower
Mark of the Trickster
Chronicle of Infinite Visions
Mask of Myriad Faces
Initiate of the Craft
Illusion Focus
Metamagic Initiate
Improved Familiar Bond x2

Perks

Wayfaring Stranger
Shard of the Shattered Manymind
Mark of Fairy's Favor
Touch of Wild Magic

Spells

Cantrips* (*no SP cost)
- -Lesser Phantasm*
- -Cutting Words*
- -Legerdemain*
- -Lesser Nightmare Curse*
- -Lesser Witch Bolt*
- -Minor Repair*
- -Lesser Charm*

Tier 1 (1SP each)
- -Visual Phantasm*
- -Healing Note

-Whispers from Beyond
-Minor Enchanted Slumber
-Invisible Servant
-Familiar Bond
-Wizard's Armor
Tier 2 (3SP each)
-Assume Quality (Special)
-Lesser Mindreading
-Sorcerous Mark

Bardsong

Command Attention
Song of Arcane Power

Chapter 7

I've just about got it," Drev said, a look of concentration on his face as he stood with one hand pressed against the remains of the latest mosaic the party was investigating.

This one was in the ruins of a small temple. Robin had already ransacked the place for hidden caches of knowledge, but aside from a few small scraps of scripture carved into the walls, he'd come up empty. Jhess had done slightly better, finding a nest of things that looked like winged packrats. Their nest had had a respectable collection of shiny things.

Currently, the rogue was going through the pile, pocketing anything which looked truly valuable and flipping the worthless bits of glass and polished metal to Rerebos in his magpie-cat form.

"There!" Purple-white motes of light danced along Drev's fingertips as he managed to temporarily activate the runic structure behind the mosaic.

This image was the clearest yet. Nilsiir stood by the altar, restored to its full glory in the illusion. Robin's eyes tracked the inscriptions around the base. In reality, they were cracked and worn away in many places; here, they were intact. He filed it away in his memory, more scraps of the faith of Rhyth to add to his collection.

The high priest stood panting by the altar, crouching behind it for physical shelter as much as he must be leaning on it for metaphysical and metaphorical support.

"Ah, here comes—what was the name?" Drev was watching an approaching figure, flanked by two sets of hobgoblin mercenaries.

"Melusk," Vance replied, studying the figure. "Some kind of important political figure within the city hierarchy, I think."

"I still say he could just be a powerful merchant," Drev opined.

"There is no reason he cannot be both," Savra pointed out. "Now quiet. They are speaking."

"It's over Nilsiir," the illusory shade of Melusk was saying. "You have been run out of all your hiding places, and the city is under my leadership now, with the full support of the merchant council, Leivniz's faction, and the priesthood of Urkhan."

"And I suppose you want me to surrender now and act the part of defeated leader to legitimize your destruction of this city?" The illusory shade of Nilsiir stood shaking their head sorrowfully. "You may have been the doom that came to Tarin-Tiran, Melusk, but you'll have no satisfaction from it. The city's treasures shall not be yours, nor shall the people bow down before you and your foul and petty tyrant of a god. I've hidden the treasures where you shall never find them, in trust for the city's future renewal, and the people are even now fleeing your army. Your victory here will ring hollow, and though your god has seen his will done, you will see nothing beyond these four walls."

"Your pretty tricks can't touch me," Melusk sneered. "I'm protected against all your magics, warded against the greatest tricks your mewling sorcery can muster."

"Ah, Melusk, you great, pompous pustule on the ass end of idiocy, you've lived in this city all your life and you've not managed to pick up on any of the precepts of our greatest cultural art?" Nilsiir stepped out from behind the altar, tossing a small bag of coins in their hand. It landed with a heavy *clink* each time they did so. "Never assume that the trick is happening where the magician directs your eye"—the illusion of the high priest vanished, only to reappear as an army of duplicates, one for each of the hobgoblins surrounding the politician—"and never, ever forget that the true power of illusion is understanding the art of misdirection."

Melusk cried out as the army of Nilsiirs all pulled daggers and began burying them in the politician's body. The original illusion reappeared by the altar and shook its head.

"Why would I waste spells on you when all it took was a pouch of gold and the promise that whosoever dealt you the fatal blow could have your old rank? Your little army may all be faithful to Urkhan, but does not your god teach that only the strongest hold power, and that if you fall, it is only due to your own weakness?"

"I will kill you," Melusk rasped, summoning a serious flare of hate to hold on to consciousness while the blades slammed into him repeatedly. That, or the protections on the politician were truly impressive—though clearly no match for two squads of determined hobgoblins with spell-breaking daggers.

Nilsiir ran a hand along the altar and sighed.

"I'm afraid you're already far too late. Even if you do manage to return from the dead somehow, I'm afraid you'll find I'm already dead," Nilsiir informed cheerfully. "I'm not going to let you wankers have any joy from this little catastrophic invasion, and my life was the price. I may be walking, but I'm just as dead as you're about to be. *Ta-ta!*"

The image of Nilsiir vanished, but the illusory scene played on until Melusk's torn and bloody body finally ceased moving. Then the hobgoblins—no longer wearing the image of Nilsiir—fell upon one another in a mad scramble to seize whatever power was left up for grabs by Melusk's death.

"Well, at least we know the good stuff is probably still hidden somewhere," Jhess said cheerily.

"That's your takeaway from all of this?" Drev looked at her.

"What? Self-sacrifice spells are a big deal! Everyone knows that! There's no way a curse of that magnitude would be countered so easily. I mean, look at this place! The wild magic, the living dungeon?" Jhess shook her head. "There is treasure here, somewhere deep."

"And you think we'll be the ones to find it? Why?" Vance looked intrigued.

"Because not only do we have a diviner on our side but we're not an invading horde, we do not worship any of the gods that any old ghosts knocking around this place might resent, and we have an actual bard and illusionist on our side." Jhess grinned. "Oh, and of course, we have our own living dungeon as an ally. How could we not eventually find the hidden treasure?"

"That reminds me," Vance said. "Once we're done here, we really need to round up some more monsters to lure back to Ruprecht's killing grounds." He looked at Jhess, eyes dancing. "Our ally will need fuel if he's going to help us delve as deep as we'll likely need to."

"I can send Rere out to scout for some," Robin offered, nudging his familiar mentally.

Rerebos yawned at him, but after the mental promise of more shinies, bestirred himself to flit out of one of the ruined windows to scout around for monster activity.

Robin moved to the altar and began to examine it carefully. There had been something about the script that was tugging at his subconscious. He ran his fingers over the stone. Smooth, like cold silk.

"What are you looking for?" Jhess asked.

"I'm not sure. I thought I saw something in that illusion." Robin crouched down and tried to follow the script based on the fragments still visible.

"Nilsiir did say they were leaving stuff behind. Presumably, they'd want the right sort of person to find it." Jhess hopped up near the altar to join Robin in searching.

"And you're just that sort of person, I take it?" Robin smiled to take the bite out of his words.

"Definitely! The exact right sort of person to take care of all that poor, orphaned treasure!"

Savra flipped her coin.

"You're right to keep looking," she said. "I can't see if you'll find any-thing, but . . ."

"Bingo!" Robin's hand found the word he was looking for. He channeled a bit of magic into the spot, using **[Lesser Phantasm]** to make the word glow.

Nilsiir's face appeared in the altar, the curving lines of script serving as his mouth, and two sockets where precious gems had long since been pried out as his eyes. Robin recognized this spell! It was one he'd been considering!

"Tarin-Tiran must live again! So seek the silver star! You're on your way, from the path don't stray, but stop to pray where the brute holds sway!"

The language was that of old Tarin-Tiran—Robin had found enough examples of it so far to recognize it. None of the others could read or under-stand it, and he'd let them know he could follow fragments.

"Something about a silver star, a danger—maybe a strong one, like, physically strong—and something about keeping to a path?"

"Well, we've been following the path laid down by Red, even if that's not the one that was meant," Vance pointed out.

Savra flipped her coin.

"Good and bad, in great measure, if we keep to it," the seeress said, "but I think it is the best course of action for now."

Rerebos chose that moment to flit back into the building and let loose a triumphant meow. He'd found suitable prey for his friend Ruprecht, giver of shinies!

That was their cue.

"Come on, y'all," Robin urged, heading out. "We've got some monsters to wrangle!"

Chapter 8

*U*nder Ruprecht's power and influence, the ruined manor had been fully restored. In fact, it was restored far beyond any degree necessary for the party's purposes. Ruprecht, however, was having none of anyone's objections.

The energies are mine to use as I see fit.

"Not when we're the ones risking our lives to bring you dinner!" Jhess protested.

Robin noted that while the rogue was irritated, it didn't stop her from lounging in the lap of luxury Ruprecht's efforts had provided.

If I don't have something to do, I'll go absolutely insane, and right now, all I have to do is restore this manor house! I'm saving absolutely everything else for expansion when you finally *decide on which direction you wish to head next.*

"We're getting close," Robin said, raising a hand to gently pat the nearest wall. "Just a few more spots on Red's map to investigate, and if we're lucky, we'll know exactly where we need to go to claim the treasure."

Robin flicked his fingers, and a **[Visual Phantasm]** of the local area in miniature appeared. It was hazy and misty in many places—the areas he had not yet explored—and small red dots marked the locations he had translated over from Red's map. Those the party had been to already were ringed in green. There were also a few blue dots, locations he'd marked based on his own research and hopes. He'd persuaded the party to investigate two of them—those were ringed with white—but aside from a few more fragments of not-yet-useful knowledge, neither location had had much to offer.

Then, thinking carefully, Robin flushed the area that Ruprecht maintained as his territory in a light gold. There was an immediate brightening in the atmosphere of the manor house.

I approve of your color choice.

Me too! Rerebos added. *Shiny!*

"This is where we are, right now," Robin said, marking the manor with a silver star. He started there and went around the map, explaining the various markings and his rationale for including them.

"What about the entrances we've found to"—Jhess shot a glance at the walls around them—"the other D-U-N-G-E-O-N?"

I can spell, you know, Ruprecht observed drily in their heads. And *I am quite capable of maintaining my composure in the face of mentions of other living dungeons,* thank you. *I'm hardly a child.*

Robin wisely chose to leave that hanging without response, and instead, added small black archways in the two locations they suspected were entrances to the great dungeon consuming Tarin-Tiran.

Really? Ruprecht's voice was suddenly poised and distant.

There was a small rumble beneath them, and the party froze. A sound like the jingling of coins cut through the air before silence fell again. The party exchanged glances.

"What was that?" Jhess demanded.

I have felt the presence of the other dungeon ever since we arrived on this level, but it was a distant thing. Now that you've drawn my attention to those locations, that sense has sharpened. But it also feels . . . incorrect. The map seems wrong—well, incorrect—to my senses. So I have made the executive decision to use some of my stored energies to produce a pair of scouts.

"You can do that?" Vance asked with interest. "I've heard of dungeons disgorging monsters, of course; an endless wave of maddened, bloodthirsty—" He coughed. "That is, I did not realize you could marshal scouts as well."

It is somewhat more expensive and riskier than most dungeons are willing to entertain. There is a high chance that the scouts might break free or be killed, and I will receive no intelligence from them until they return. And many dungeons— not me—are notoriously parsimonious.

Robin bit back a laugh. Ruprecht? Not parsimonious? Yeah, and Scylla and Charybdis *weren't* all-devouring monsters.

"Why scouts?" Jhess asked. "I could probably answer most of your questions."

Are you attuned to dungeon energies? Ruprecht's mental voice all but rang with a heightened tone of shock dripping sarcasm all over the nice, clean floors. *I had no idea you were so accomplished! And here I thought I was the only dungeon occupying this space.*

Jhess burst out laughing, and the atmosphere around the party went slightly hazy with Ruprecht's amusement. Robin really didn't understand *that* relationship at all.

However, in all seriousness, I do believe the other dungeon, as you term it, may be far closer to this location than is indicated by those tunnel entrances.

"How much closer?" Savra asked. "I presume from your tone that it might be a problem?"

I am not so proud as to believe I would easily prevail in any form of direct dungeon-to-dungeon combat. It is likely that if I draw too near, the other dungeon may bridge the distance between us and seek to subsume me to fuel its own growth.

"That happens?" Robin blurted out before his **[Bardic Lore]** informed him that yes, it did happen. Rather regularly, in fact.

Indeed.

The party looked somberly at Robin's map. They might have quite fewer options for progression through the dungeon than they'd thought if they had to tiptoe carefully around the other dungeon.

"How long until the scouts return with useful information?" Drev inquired. "Best-case scenario?"

It should not be long. I imbued them with qualities for speed and stamina, and most of my creatures are inherently good at stealth options.

Robin knew what that was like, as a fellow shapeshifter.

The party fell into discussion while Savra began producing food and drink. This was a council of war of a sort, and they needed to keep their strength up. And their spirits. Robin made sure to add nice touches of flavor to all the dishes and drinks as he could, keeping up a steady flow of cantrips. His hands were really incredibly limber at this point. Oh, the ivories (and other things) he could tickle right now!

He refused to let the song about the piano man start earworming him, however.

Eventually, Ruprecht announced that his scouts had returned. The dungeon's voice was troubled, and Robin felt his blood thicken in his veins. Things were about to get heavy.

Meet! Rerebos chirruped, demanding the scout be brought before the party to deliver its intelligence, even if only Ruprecht would be able to understand it. Robin was just glad the little cat-bird hadn't started talking to everyone and had restricted himself to mental communication with himself and Ruprecht.

Ruprecht complied with the request, and soon, two very sleek-looking mimics—full treasure-chest size—galumphed up the stairs. Jhess jumped a little at their arrival.

"Those little feckers are *quiet*," she said. "Nicely done!"

Thank you. Now, please shut your mouth so I can concentrate on retrieving the intelligence we require.

Robin suddenly felt an echo of the connection he and Ruprecht had shared, back during his first foray into the dungeon. There was an image appearing in his mind—the map! *Ah*. Ruprecht wanted him to just . . .

The bard twitched his fingers (mostly for effect), and the map shifted. A translucent black suffused the area Ruprecht was outlining for him, the likely extend of the other dungeon's reach.

It was . . . extensive.

Not everywhere, true, and not universal. But there were fingers of it stretching out in many directions, some the size of bloody fjords if the sense he was getting from Ruprecht was correct. Any one of those protrusions would be large enough to swallow Ruprecht's current area two or three times over.

"That," Jhess said, "is a big dungeon."

"Dangerous, too," Vance added. "Though I did a great deal of research on it before we left Noviel. The outer reaches shouldn't be beyond our skills. Going too deep, however, would be all but inviting death and disaster. No party from Noviel has ever made it to the greatest depths and returned to tell the tale."

"On a scale of one to ten, with one being your average apprentice at the guild and ten being the guildmagister, what are the highest rated teams that have tried?" Man, Robin would really kill to have a universal system to translate power into levels for this question.

"The guildmagister is probably punching at about the sixth or seventh circle of power, I'd say," Drev opined. "I don't think any parties higher level than him have attempted the dungeon."

Oh, right. Tiers were still a thing.

"The most effective spells at piercing illusions are all—at a minimum—fifth circle," Savra said. "Though here, I'm not so certain they would be perfectly efficacious. Even as it is, certain seventh-tier illusions can fool most of them. In many cases, it comes down to individual power comparisons. Skill and environmental factors count for a great deal, even with the aid of magic."

The party debated relative virtues of spells among themselves for a while, with Jhess rolling her eyes the whole while before Robin brought them back around to the point.

"But the highest tier group of individuals to make it back alive from the dungeon," he asked. "Who were they, and do we know how deep they made it?"

"We do not know how deep," Vance replied. "Especially given the illusory nature of everything we've found so far, even if they had measured properly, they might have been mistaken, fooled by the dungeon. It's all but impossible that it wouldn't have all manner of illusory traps and misdirections at its command."

"The highest tier party I know of included Khavren's mother," Drev said with a faint sign to ward off evil. "This was perhaps two decades ago. I think they averaged the seventh tier? Though Khavren's mother was only fifth or sixth herself at the time. And as it was, not the entire party made it back."

Maybe Khavren'd had a bit more justification in mistrusting shape-shifters and illusionists than Robin had realized. The man had still been a bigoted dick, but maybe there was more to the root of his psychoses than terminal Lawful Stupid.

However, as you said, the outer reaches should be safe enough. The dungeon will not place the greatest threats upon its borders unless it is feeling threatened, and I cannot imagine what might threaten a sentience of that level. They will want to lure as many monsters and adventurers and patrols in as possible, so there will be little resistance and tempting rewards at the edges. It should be possible to engage in a few careful, bold forays and emerge relatively unscathed and at great profit.

"And if we want answers to everything Red recorded in his journal, we will have to do so," Savra pointed out. "Look."

Robin looked. Based on the intelligence retrieved by Ruprecht's mimics, at least two of the remaining red dots were distinctly inside the other dungeon's territory.

"Did he brave the dungeon and mark those locations, or has it expanded since Red died?" Drev wondered.

"Does it matter?" Jhess demanded. "What are we going to do now?"

"There's only one thing we can do," Robin said lightly. "We're going in and coming back out with the answers we need."

He paused, then added a little sweet to the bitter news.

"And as much treasure as we can scam out of the old bastard!"

Chapter 9

$\mathcal{T}$he dungeon entrance could have been any other tunnel or doorway in the vastness of the ruined city. Robin studied it alongside the rest of his party. It was a simple archway of crumbling stone, but given the control dungeons tended to have over their demesne, it was likely that a cruise missile wouldn't dislodge so much as a pebble on a direct hit.

"I don't like how innocent it looks," Jhess complained. "Those are the ones you have to watch out for. Give me a dungeon with skulls on pikes or ominous vapors issuing forth any day."

"Weal and woe, both in great measure, if we enter here," Savra said, studying her coin. "I'm guessing from the way the futures shift, there are many branching tunnels inside; many opportunities for things to go wrong."

"And many opportunities for them to go right!" Vance added brightly.

"Are we sending the cat-bird in to scout?" Jhess asked, prompting Rerebos to arch his back and hiss in alarm.

"I don't think Riri approves of your suggestion," Drev replied wryly. He squinted into the entrance. "I don't see any obvious lurking monsters. Jhess, can you do a quick trap assessment?"

It should be safe enough for them in the outer fringes of the dungeon's territory. Dungeons had instincts which drove them to lure people in, and death on one's doorstep tended to discourage that.

Robin stepped closer, the gloom on the inside of the archway no barrier to his vision, though the tunnel sharply cut perpendicular quite soon after the entrance, so what he could see was limited. The walls and floor were worked stone, all of which matched what had been used in the building around them, yellow and squared. The architectural style, however, was off. There was no reason for a corridor to suddenly branch off so aggressively.

"No traps," Jhess reported after a careful examination. "I'll head in and—"

"Hang on," Robin interrupted, suspicious of the setup. Something was off here. "How about we look for hidden doors? There and there." Robin pointed to the wall where the passageway would continue straight on in a normal building, and at the wall opposite the direction the open passage ran.

"You think this is another Ruprecht-style place?" Jhess grimaced. "Just what we need."

"We're in the capital city of a highly illusion-focused culture," he replied. "I think the odds are somewhat better than average that we'll run into a lot of this kind of shenanigans."

Jhess grumbled but began a careful examination of the walls, Robin doing the same. However, while Jhess was searching for mechanical triggers, he was looking for more illusory means of concealing entrances and exits.

There was a *click*, and the wall swung open in front of Jhess, directly opposite the obvious corridor.

"Found one," Jhess announced triumphantly.

There was no way it was only one. Not here. Not in this world so fascinated with multiples of three, in a city of illusions. Robin's mind flashed back to the concealment of that little shrine to Rhyth he had awakened in—it seemed like a lifetime ago. He moved his hand along the wall where *he* would conceal a door if he was building this place. It felt solid. Still, illusion could fool all of the senses, so he also *pushed.*

His hand went through the wall.

"One here, too," he called over his shoulder.

"Fascinating!" Vance was staring at Robin's arm, which appeared to have sunk up to the elbow into solid stone. He reached out to touch the wall. "It feels completely solid!"

"That is a Tier Seven effect, at least," Savra informed somberly.

"Well, we knew this place would be something else before we left Noviel," Jhess said. "But that doesn't answer the real question here. Which way do we go?"

The party fell into a quick, quiet debate, stepping back out of the dungeon to do so. There was no way it wasn't aware of their presence, but there was no reason to telegraph their every move. Delving in living dungeons was much more dangerous than exploring other kinds. Even if there were limits to the actions they could take against an adventuring party within their demesne, smart ones could and did stack the board, shifting monsters around or—like Ruprecht—building traps that circumvented some of their limitations.

Thank you, **[Bardic Lore]**!

Because this was, predominately, an information-gathering sortie, they agreed to scout carefully down each passage, with Robin mapping it as they went before deciding which one to follow deeper. The central corridor seemed the most probable one to bear fruit, both because it was most likely to lead to the spot marked in Red's journal and because of the nature of the concealment on that doorway.

So they left it for last. The other two were quickly assessed to a distance of a few hundred meters. A couple potential deadfalls and one magical trap altered to look like a malfunctioning artifact from the ruined city were all they found down the first one. The one behind the hidden door Jhess had discovered was a bit more interesting; it was styled as some kind of long-lost thieves' hideaway. It made no sense that it would be here, but Robin had to assign points for thematic effort. Jhess had managed to uncover a couple small coin pouches, so she was happy.

While the party continued searching, Robin sent Rerebos a couple quiet instructions via telepathy, and his familiar popped out of sight and flitted down the third passageway to scout ahead.

The little dragon in disguise reported that the corridor was uninteresting but that it ended in what appeared to be some kind of hidden temple, possibly the same location marked in the journal.

Robin bit back his excitement. Whatever the place had been, the dungeon had claimed it as its own. There was no telling what changes had been made.

Didn't mean he wasn't raring to get there and find out, though.

Movement! There is something here! Alarm flared through his mind as Rerebos spotted a flicker in the shadows.

Stay out of sight! We'll be there soon, Robin sent back.

"Next one?" he asked aloud, using a hand signal the party had established for silent and discreet communication to indicate there was likely some kind of enemy or ambush ahead.

"Next one," Jhess confirmed, pulling her dagger. To keep it casual, she began flipping it idly in her hand.

The corridor was almost as empty as Rerebos had indicated. *Almost.* Jhess found two trip wires and a pressure plate; Rerebos, as he flew, tended to miss out on those details. They were simple enough for the rogue to bypass, however.

"This is too easy," Jhess complained under her breath.

Robin agreed. Whatever was in the temple Rerebos had found was likely much, much worse than they imagined, to keep the balance. That was the only thing that made sense. Not that he fully understood the dungeon mindset; the only reason he understood as much as he did was from his time with Ruprecht, and even then, the dungeon had once been human—had once possibly been a version of himself! How that translated to the thinking of other living dungeons was something he could only make educated guesses on, **[Bardic Lore]** notwithstanding.

Soon enough, they made it to the entry of the hidden temple. Robin paused as the party scanned the room for threats.

Any more movement?

No. I have watched the shadows and seen nothing. Rerebos didn't sound reassured, however.

Robin pulled a small bit of rock from storage and flicked it into the center of the room. It *plinked* across the floor, the noise suddenly loud in the oppressive silence, but nothing stirred.

"Magelight," Jhess suggested.

Drev complied, casting a small sphere of purple-white light high above to hover near the ceiling of the room. It was higher than it had any right to be, actually; more a cathedral dome in miniature than a modest hidden temple.

The light glittered off of dusty gold and flared in several inset gems. Probably glass, Robin thought critically. Not that that would stop Jhess from checking every single one.

Still, there was no movement.

Vance, the most durable of them, conjured sheets of parchment around himself like an armor. They flexed and took on the hue of night, with small motes of light swirling within them like stars. A massive shield appeared in his right hand, similar in appearance to his armor.

Something about the ensemble seemed familiar. There was a story—*ah!* His **[Bardic Lore]** pinged. "The Ascent and Fall of Noxon, Paladin of Ipherea." Noxon had been renowned for his defensive raiment, and though whatever it was that Vance conjured out of legend with his magic was usually but a pale imitation, even the imitation of something great could be formidable in its own right.

Hopefully enough to protect them from whatever was out there.

Vance didn't immediately conjure the sword of silver starlight which should accompany the shield of night, but Robin was sure he could call it forth in an instant if need be. Keeping something like that manifest no doubt was quite the drain on one's magical energies.

Thus warded, Vance stepped into the room. This time, Robin's eyes caught a flicker of movement in the shadows. A flaming card—the manifestation of a [**Lesser Witch Bolt**]—appeared ready in his hand.

"All is not as it appears," Savra warned.

Well, that was telling the sailor the sea was wet.

"More light," Jhess called.

Drev responded with a barrage of orbs of glowing force. That was a new one! Robin wondered what made the spell different.

Whatever the purpose, the effect was to banish many of the shadows while simultaneously casting new ones. Robin's eyes were lucky enough to catch the full-on movement this time, with none of the natural darkness in place. A figure coiled and thrashed in annoyance before darting toward first one, then another of the shadows cast by Drev's magic. As the orbs moved, however, so did the dark spaces, and the thing was forced to follow if it wished to remain mostly hidden.

Which it would do, if only to increase the effectiveness of its attacks. It had two legs, two arms, and the general shape of a hobgoblin, but it was, all things considered, just a shade of that actual being.

Literally.

It was another motherfucking shadow!

Chapter 10

*T*he party took up defensive positions, spreading out along the inner wall of the temple so as not to be in—as Robin still thought of it—fireball position. No one wanted to get hit with an area attack.

"Watch for others," Savra warned. "Undead of this kind often dwell in groups." Then she raised high her holy symbol and began calling upon her goddess to rebuke the undead thing before them. Her features fell into sharp relief, and Savra took on a strange angularity, as if all ambiguity had been leeched from her body.

Robin conjured the illusion of light blazing brightly through the room. Motes of starfire glittered and danced in the air like an aurora, threading through and around Drev's globes of forcelight. Vance conjured a sword of light, and Jhess looked sourly out at the incipient battlefield. Her daggers were unlikely to find much purchase on an incorporeal enemy, and Savra didn't seem to be available to offer any kind of blessing which might help with that.

"Watch your shadows," Robin shouted. "Some of these things can step right through them and stab you right in the back!"

"Someday," Jhess muttered.

There was a flicker of movement as the shade revealed itself, lashing out at Drev from the pool of liquid darkness cast by the altar. The mage was ready, however, and three bolts of force leapt from his fingers and lanced toward the shadow, aiming unerringly for its sinuous form. The missiles slammed into the shadowy form, but not having a physical existence, it was difficult to tell how much damage they may have done to the shadow.

It *did* change, however, shifting its outline from a hobgoblin soldier to that of Drev, a two-dimensional doppelgänger of darkness.

Robin didn't want to think about what that might portend.

Nothing good, probably.

Vance uttered a battle cry and attacked while the thing stood there staring at Drev. The blade of light arced toward the shadow, but it split apart, allowing the sword to pass harmlessly through thin air before rejoining itself. Fortunately, Robin had been ready, and he managed to score a sizzling hit with a **[Lesser Witch Bolt]**, but this thing was not behaving like the last shade he'd fought. Something was different.

The shadow skittered along the edge of the room, coming near to Savra and then dancing away. The cleric tossed a bolt of white fire at it, but it managed to coil out of the way.

"We're going to need to attack it in waves," Vance called. "One of us will miss, but if the other can anticipate and land a hit, we can whittle it down."

Hopefully the thing didn't speak the language, but Robin wasn't terribly hopeful.

Ugh. Why was telepathic communication so far away?

Because it wasn't his specialty, and he wasn't looking for work-arounds in his interface. He had enough on his plate with the illusions and the bardsong and everything else.

He really needed some combat bardsong options.

Vance and Savra fell into a rhythm as Robin moved closer to work with Drev. Jhess took the odd shot with one of her daggers when the opportunity presented itself, but the rogue was forced to act mostly as a distraction in this fight.

Hits from white fire and sword of light landed, the odd witch bolt or missile of force, bit of shadow sprayed into the air and dissolved, but the thing didn't seem to be getting any weaker. It stayed dancing at the edges of the room, keeping well away from the light emanating from Savra's holy symbol, and the party just didn't seem to be making much headway.

"Fuck, that thing is fast," Vance complained after his sword of light slashed through the air a moment too late.

It was fast, and it seemed to draw power from the shadows in the room, though something about its movements was niggling at the back of Robin's brain. So he watched. He counted the shadows. And then his eyes widened.

The thing was going for the shadows cast by Robin's illusions! It was mostly ignoring the ones cast by the other light sources in the room. At least, he thought so. It was kind of hard to keep track.

"Going to get a bit darker," he warned. "I need to test something."

Robin cut his illusion of dancing lights, and the overall illumination in the room fell; not drastically—most of the light had been coming from Drev's efforts, after all—but there was a noticeable difference.

The shadow thing turned and hissed at Robin, assuming his silhouette, as revealed by the billowing of the coat. And honestly, could anyone else here cut such a dashing figure? Even through a mirror in two dimensions?

It was clear it changed shape to that of someone who had hurt it in some way, like the first time it had done so with Drev. So why had it changed now? When all Robin had done was remove his illusory light and the accompanying shadow? The only thing which made sense was that it was worse off without the illusion Robin had provided. It had to be gaining power from it somehow.

Weird, but they were in Tarin-Tiran, capital city of a whole civilization built on illusi—*of course!* This thing somehow fed off the magical energies that produced illusions! There probably used to be some kind of divine illusory fresco in here which it had fed off of, but with the city advancing in ruination, its food sources must have been slowly drying up.

"Try hitting it now! See if it gets weaker!" Robin called.

The party fell to it again, with blade of light and flaming spell; with force missiles and raining hell.

And the thing still wasn't going down. Oh, the magical attacks were having an effect, to be sure, but it was always less than it should be, by a large percentage. Maybe because the thing had fed off illusions for so long it was only quasi-real itself.

Frustrated, Robin called upon **[Visual Phantasm]** and fired a bolt of pure light like a laser right through the thing.

That *hit*. And it hit *hard*. The illusion of pure light burned through the shadow like a hot knife through butter. The thing keened in pain and vanished into a nearby shadow, taking a hit from both Savra and Drev in its haste to flee. Vance was too far away with his sword of light, unfortunately.

So magic hit, and illusory magic hit harder when it was shaped in a way that directly opposed the shadow. Was it actually part illusion at this point?

Robin put aside the idea of an illusory life-form to focus on the matter at hand. His hit had driven the shadow mad with fervor, and it had surged up behind Savra to slash at the cleric with its nails, completely ignoring the effects of the holy symbol. Which made perfect sense if it wasn't actually an undead shade of a lost soul but the sentient illusion of one!

Robin called out a **[Healing Note]**, hoping to offset the damage as Savra slumped to the ground, eyes staring blankly into the middle distance.

Vance and Drev struck with their magic as Jhess howled and slashed at it with her daggers while the shadow sank out of sight.

"Grab Savra, fall back to the corridor," Robin called.

Jhess sheathed her daggers and hefted the cleric before moving back. Vance and Drev covered her, taking shots at the shade as it tried to manifest from the shadows at their feet. Robin conjured the illusion of a flash-bang to temporarily drive all shadows from the corridor, then sealed it off with a unidirectional plane of light so the shadow couldn't see them—or more importantly, any of the shadows in the corridor with them.

"What is that thing?" Jhess hissed in frustration as she tried to shake Savra out of her catatonia. Whatever the shadow had done—some kind of mind-influencing attack—was keeping the cleric trapped somehow. They had to hope Savra's will won out in the end; that was usually the way out of illusory attacks. That, or the effect might end if they killed the creature.

Fortunately, Robin had an idea for that.

"I'm going to try something," he said. "Watch my back. If it manages to shadowstep in here or out of the room, this won't work."

Vance raised his sword of light, and sparks of purple-white light danced at Drev's fingers. They had his back. Robin nodded slightly and turned his attention to the room in front of them; he could see through his own illusion easily enough. The room was now mostly shadow, with a lot of them now stretching away from the plane of light he'd conjured to block the door.

Robin murmured to Drev, and the mage's dancing lights still orbiting the room vanished.

It made it easier to count the shadows.

"Let's see how you like this," Robin muttered, a smile crooking the corner of his mouth. He'd had a little idea that was part party and part blender.

What they needed here was a little Disco Inferno!

Robin bent his mind and his will to the room in front of him, conjuring a disco ball. But not just any disco ball! This one was a whirling blaze of laser death, with beams of cutting light lancing out from every single facet of the thing.

The light moved so quickly shadows barely had time to form before they were disrupted, and the burning light danced a dance of death across every surface of the room and all the intervening space, whirling and slicing, cutting through mostly air but also the strange illusory darkness that made up the substance of the thing lurking in the temple.

The scene was begging for a musical underpinning, but Robin didn't have any more attention to lend to the effect. Missed opportunity. He should have prepped the **[Lesser Phantasm]** beat in advance. It would only have lasted several seconds, but as it turned out, those few seconds of total concentration were all that he needed.

The shadow creature dissolved under the onslaught of illusory beams. The bits of it that were cut off from the main body of the creature dissolved into nothingness, and soon, there was nothing left but a small scrap of shadow trembling in midair, as if too terrified to move.

Robin morphed the [**Visual Phantasm**] into another flash-bang and blew that last little remnant to oblivion.

Then he let the illusion drop.

"Right," he said, glancing over at a blinking Savra, who seemed to be coming out of her stupor. "Let's see what that thing was guarding, shall we?"

Chapter 11

Robin examined the altar, Rerebos perched on his shoulder, as the rest of his party examined the remainder of the temple for traps, hidden doors, lurking monsters, or other surprises. So far, they hadn't discovered anything, but Robin would willingly go without spouting a single lie for a month if there wasn't another secret door in here somewhere. This had been a temple of Rhyth—or at least, the dungeon had given it that appearance—and no temple of Rhyth, real *or* fake, would be without multiple means of entrance and egress.

"Look," Jhess called, the sharp-eyed rogue pointing to something near the wall.

Robin reluctantly left his examination of the altar and moved to where she was pointing.

"I think there has to be a secret door here," the rogue said, sketching out a rough shape with her hands. "*And* I think our friend Red was here as well, since this place became part of the dungeon. See? Right there."

Robin followed Jhess's pointing finger. There was a small line of what looked to be red clinging to the wall, wedged into the slightest of cracks. It could be a scrap of material torn from Red's clothing. It wasn't a large piece, but it was possible. Not proof, but a bit of circumstantial evidence didn't hurt when it fit with the other pieces they already had.

"Any idea how to get it open?" Vance asked.

"I was hoping the bard would have some ideas." Jhess was looking to Robin.

Robin ran his fingers over the wall.

"Not yet," he replied. "Maybe after I examine the altar fully."

He moved back to the altar. There was something here, beneath the alterations. This was not the way it should look; he was certain. An instinct, perhaps echoed by **[Bardic Lore]** or **[Shard of the Shattered Manymind]** told him that while it was mostly the same, there had been changes made. Here, a sacred word had been carefully rubbed away. There, a bit of mosaic had been permanently fused together, turning the runework behind it to useless slag. He suspected the dungeon.

However, it wasn't all gone. Something had preserved part of it, which meant there might be a way to bridge the gap in the magic, to access whatever was still hidden here. Had Red found it? Was that why it was marked like this? Or was the dungeon toying with them, knowing somehow why they were here and what they might be after?

Robin reached out and fidgeted with the intact portion of the mosaic, running his senses along the magic he felt still flickering in the fragments of the runic structure, and an idea popped into his head. Well, why not? It was still illusion at its core. Maybe there was a trick to be turned, here.

He closed his eyes, calling to mind with near-perfect recall the other runic structures he'd seen hidden behind the mosaics. Then, he carefully filled in the gaps left by the fused stone and conjured the *illusion* of what he thought the runes should look like, completing the circuit, so to speak.

It almost worked. Fragmentary images flashed in and out of being. Shards of light coalesced and dissolved in a maddening, non-Euclidean display. Discordant voices sputtered and howled from a void of darkness and light.

Robin cut the illusion, and blessed silence fell again.

"What in Galurar's name was that?" Jhess demanded.

"I tried fixing the runes," Robin replied with a wince. "I don't think I got it exactly right."

"You don't say?" Jhess massaged the bridge of her nose.

"But you did elicit some kind of response," Drev observed. "What did you do?"

Robin explained.

"Fascinating," Vance chimed in once Robin had finished. "Shall we try again? Maybe Drev and I can cross-check your work?"

"If you think it will help." Robin waved his hand and conjured the illusory structure he had used once more—safely away from the other runic lines so there was no repeat of the sonic hell they had all just experienced.

"That should have worked," Drev noted thoughtfully.

"So why didn't it?" Vance asked.

"Because you are all missing something," Savra spoke up, flipping her coin. "Though the answer should be somewhere in this room."

"The dungeon has clearly changed something," Robin said. "It kept most of it for, what, aesthetics? Because it had to? Or it didn't want to spend extra energies converting things fully? Whatever the reason, the thing that's going wrong is probably linked to that."

"So we look for differences," Jhess offered offhand. "Grains of wood running the wrong way abruptly, or two kinds of stone next to one another where they shouldn't be, things like that."

"Yes, it's likely the changes are physical in nature," Drev said excitedly, "based on what we now know about dungeon conversion thanks to Ruprecht."

"Spread out," Jhess ordered. "We'll divide the room into sections, and we'll each go over it one at a time. That way, we're all looking and we all have a chance to spot something, but we don't have to waste time."

The party did as Jhess directed and there was silence for a while, broken only intermittently by occasional false alarms as one party member or the other thought they had found something, only for it to be discounted when the others came to examine the area more carefully.

"We really need a geomancer," Jhess complained. "No offense, Drev."

"None taken," the mage replied. "I don't really get on well with stone."

Grathilde would have hated this, too, Robin reflected. Though her air currents might have been able to find minuscule cracks between stones. Actually, what if the differences they should be looking for were the less visible ones?

"Drev," Robin started, "how sharp are your magical senses?"

"Above average," the mage answered.

Drev had a tendency to terminal modesty, possibly because his father was so boastful, so if he said he was above average, he must be very good.

"Can you tell the difference between dungeon magic and preexisting illusions?"

Drev blinked.

"Yes, that should be possible. Dungeon magic largely resonates of transmutation or conjuration, while illusion vibrates on a completely different wavelength. I'll start scanning the room that way."

"Start with the altar," Robin suggested. "I nearly had it, so hopefully the alteration is minor, and we can figure out how to compensate for whatever the dungeon did."

Drev's eyes began to shine with a white-purple glow, and he moved to carefully examine the central stone. His hands hovered over the surface, and Robin could see him tracing parts of the runic patterns in the empty air where they wouldn't connect and conjure anything.

"Here," he said after several minutes. The mage pointed to a patch of stone which looked indistinguishable from the rest of the altar, as far as Robin could see, before etching a quick rune in midair. It glowed whiter on one side, and more purple on the other.

"Sorry I can't get it more precise than this. I lack your fine control of imagery," Drev apologized to Robin. "But here. This is the issue. The rune was changed, but because it changed along the support line here, it only looks different along the branch points."

Robin examined the rune. Yeah. He could see that. Like erasing the curve of the letter *P* and adding two branches to turn it into a *K*. He wasn't sure what that did, magically speaking, but he could see how it would change things.

He consulted his **[Bardic Lore]** and **[Shard of the Shattered Many-mind]**, and then conjured four possible runes.

"Which of these four do we think is most likely the original?" he asked.

Drev and Vance began arguing, with Savra occasionally interjecting after consulting her coin. Robin was tempted just to cycle through all the options and hope to get lucky on the first try, but considering the terrible sounds and noises that had prompted last time, maybe that wasn't the best idea. He had been touched by wild magic and there was no telling what horror he might accidentally summon if chance decided to turn against him, rather than for him.

"This one," Drev said at last, conjuring a rune like a forking branch. "I'm not sure how much interference we might get from an overlay, but this is probably our best shot."

Robin stepped back up to the altar, studying the new runic structure before conjuring it above the spot to check it first. When he was satisfied it was as close as he could make it, he carefully lowered it into place.

Sparks immediately flew, iridescent and hissing, before the surface of the altar shimmered and changed, becoming some kind of map.

"Yes!" Jhess's fist pumped the air.

Robin's eyes scanned over the map. Part of it he recognized as matching the mapping he'd done for their foray into the dungeon so far. So, had the dungeon altered the altar to provide a hidden map? Or did this predate the dungeon and was some strange functionality of the altar? He wasn't sure how that squared with the faith of Rhyth. Unless Nilsiir . . .

A flickering image appeared, stuttering in and out a bit, though not nearly so much as on previous occasions. It was Nilsiir, and this time, the high priest looked beaten and bruised, the jovial air of defiance he had maintained so long just a fading ember.

"That fucker Urkhan has won," the high priest said dully. "I'm leaving this message with the last of my power—the last of Rhyth's power in this place—in the hopes that one day, someone will find it and work to restore Tarin-Tiran. I have—a guide—" The image and sound began breaking up, stuttering. Robin resisted the urge to deliver some percussive maintenance to the altar. Habits from another world . . .

The image suddenly clarified, becoming clear and strong, and Robin felt electricity dancing along his fingertips as the illusion seemed to stare him straight in the eyes.

"The city is damaged from the invasions, and likely from however many years have passed. Find the nexus points! Restore the connections! Return the city to life, and you will unlock the legacy of Tarin-Tiran, the treasures I have hidden away from those autocratic fuckers that have stolen so much—"

The illusion flickered out for a long moment before returning.

"Do—not—trust—"

Then the image was gone, leaving only the map softly glowing on the surface of the altar.

"Don't trust who?" Jhess demanded.

"Or what?" Robin mused, looking at the walls around them.

No one had an answer to either question.

Chapter 12

*T*he secret door gave a *click* and swung open as Jhess pumped her fist in jubilation.

"Further in?" the rogue asked, a hopeful look on her face.

"Great fortune and great danger await," Savra said, eyeing the coin in her palm.

"Further in," Vance opined, with Drev agreeing a moment later.

"Might as well," Robin agreed, following the will of the party. "But slowly. We've had a warning, and it would be foolish to completely ignore it, even if it might be a trick."

"We'll be fine." Jhess waved away the concern. "Between you and Savra, we've got it covered."

The seeress and the bard exchanged a skeptical glance but followed close behind as the rogue began scouting ahead, Robin sending his familiar a mental directive to back Jhess up.

Glancing behind him, he saw that Vance was wedging the secret door open. Good thought. Getting trapped in the dungeon was not the way any of them wanted this little expedition to go.

The corridor behind the secret door was much the same as the one which had led to the temple space. Or it was at first, until Robin noticed several small veins of iridescent crystal beginning to grow in the walls around them. At first, it was simply as if they had been growing in the cracks between blocks of stone, but soon, small outcroppings of the stuff appeared, almost willy-nilly.

Jhess carefully chipped a bit free with one of her daggers after Drev cautiously scanned it with his senses and proclaimed it unlikely to explode.

"It looks like the stuff growing out of those rats' eyes," Robin said. "Maybe try not to cut yourself on it. It might take root."

Rerebos stopped scratching at the exposed shiny immediately upon hearing that. Robin bit his cheek to keep from laughing. Laughing at a dragon was not something one did, ever, and expected to escape unscathed.

The tunnel system still mirrored the layout of the city outside. It wasn't quite a grid, but there was some suggestion of hallways and corridors, of streets and alleyways. They couldn't see any of the city proper, as Robin might expect, which made him all the more certain that the shenanigans the dungeon was pulling were both extreme and dangerous.

He double-checked the markers they were leaving. Everything still seemed in place, both chalk marks and small scratches in the surrounding stone. And magic, when they could manage it.

"I think we should have another [Mystic Mark] here, Drev," Robin called. "I can just barely make out the last one from here."

Drev chanted a quick incantation and pointed his finger at the wall next to Robin. His magic glowed its usual purple white, but this time, the color was echoed by a small outcropping of crystal near Drev's hand. The mark appeared, but Robin was too busy staring at the crystal. Had he imagined that? The thing had gone back to its regular glimmering self as soon as Drev had finished the incantation and the mark had appeared.

"Did you see that?"

"See what?" Jhess asked. "Anything good?"

"The crystal glowed the same color as Drev's magic," Robin explained, resisting the urge to reach out and prod it with a finger.

"It doesn't look any different than any of the others," Jhess complained after looking at it for a minute. "Are you sure?"

"No, I'm not. That's why I asked if you'd seen it!" Robin snapped.

"Cast an illusion at it," the rogue suggested. "See if that does anything."

It wasn't a bad suggestion. Robin thought for a moment, then conjured a small statue of a dancing mouse to hover in front of the small outcrop of crystal. Rerebos made an acquisitive cry and launched his cat form at it, only to swoop right through as if it were not there. Because it wasn't.

There was no reaction from the bit of crystal, however.

"Must have been a trick of the light," Robin said, unconvinced.

"Come on," Vance called. "The next location on the map's just ahead! It should be around that bend in the hall."

The party moved ahead, eager to finally have something to do aside from track their progress and be paranoid about losing their way. They moved perhaps a bit faster than they should have, and it was only a warning from Rerebos echoing in Robin's head which raised the alarm.

"Wait!" the bard called.

His outburst saved Jhess from falling through an illusion and into an open pit. Rerebos had spotted it by flying through the thing, but for land-bound sentients, it would have been a far more effective trap.

Jhess pulled out a ten-foot pole and began running it through the floor until she found the boundaries of the pit. Then she cross-checked the walls in a similar fashion, thoroughly testing them all to ensure there weren't more hidden traps or hidden passages. When she found none, she banished the pole back to her storage and pulled out a ladder which, with a little direction from Rerebos via Robin, she managed to lay across the pit so the party could bypass the trap easily enough.

"Thanks," Robin said as Jhess stowed the ladder back in her personal storage space once everyone was across.

"Standard equipment, standard solution," the rogue replied. "All part of the service." She flashed an irrepressible smile. "And thank *you* for spotting it." Jhess reached out to scratch Rerebos behind his ears where he sat on Robin's shoulder.

"Uhhh, I think you should come see this," Vance's voice drifted back to them. "We're definitely in the dungeon proper now."

Robin and Jhess turned to follow the sound of their teammate's voice. Vance, Drev, and Savra were in the next room, staring around themselves warily.

Stepping inside, Robin could see why. Gone was the pretense of artifice and city ruin. This chamber looked like it was a part of a naturally grown cavern, although they would have had to be translocated who knows what distance in order for that to be accurate. No, the dungeon had clearly created this, modeling it after natural caverns; perhaps ones it had subsumed long ago and were far below where they actually stood.

The rock walls were rippled, as if from the passage of water over eons, and the whole place was lit with a pale glow from several large crystal veins in the walls. It wasn't a small space, either. It was a vast cavern, easily large enough to fit a small ocean liner or a large village within it. Pillars of stone like trees held up the ceiling, and there were vast areas shrouded in shadow: the perfect place for ambush predators of all sorts.

"Does this still match the map?" Drev called, doubt creeping into his voice.

Robin conjured a replica of the image from the altar.

"Seems to be," he said, squinting at it. "It was hard to see what it might be from the map, but the distances and turnings seem to track. Not sure if this was supposed to be a coliseum or some kind of stadium before? But the map definitely had this as some kind of large structure. And there should be some kind of nexus of runes beneath it or near the center, I think."

He could really use some help from the quest notification box right about now, but the thing was stubbornly silent. Robin opened his interface anyway, just to be sure. He even flipped to his character sheet, in case there was something hidden there, some new perk or peculiarity that might point the way.

Robin Parker

Heritage: Shadeling, Paragon
Profession: Bard
Tier: 2 (Effective Level:)
Experience: 4750
Spell Points: 21
Bardsong: 8 uses

Properties

Free Ranks Available: 1

Physical
-Strength: 11
-Dexterity: 14
-Fortitude: 11

Mental
-Intelligence: 17
-Cunning: 24
-Resilience: 14

Social
-Charisma: 15
-Manipulation: 13
-Poise: 16

Proficiencies

Free Ranks Available: 1

Physical (9/9)
- Athletics: 7
- Brawl: 6
- Dodge: 9
- Melee Combat: 6
- Pilot: 4
- Ranged Combat: 11
- Sleight of Hand: 9
- Stealth: 11
- Survival: 8

Mental (9/9)
- Arcane Lore: 10
- Bureaucracy: 7
- Concentration: 11
- Crafting: 9
- Healing: 8
- Insight: 11
- Learning: 9
- Natural Wisdom: 5
- Perception: 11

Social (9/9)
- Animism: 5
- Deception: 11
- Empathy: 10
- Expression: 11
- Gossip: 9
- Intimidation: 8
- Persuasion: 10
- Socialize: 9
- Streetwise: 8

Peculiarities

Blessing of Rhyth
Tongue of the Fallen Tower
Mark of the Trickster
Chronicle of Infinite Visions

Mask of Myriad Faces
Initiate of the Craft
Illusion Focus
Metamagic Initiate
Improved Familiar Bond x2

Perks

Wayfaring Stranger
Shard of the Shattered Manymind
Mark of Fairy's Favor
Touch of Wild Magic

Spells

Cantrips* (*no SP cost)
   -Lesser Phantasm*
   -Cutting Words*
   -Legerdemain*
   -Lesser Nightmare Curse*
   -Lesser Witch Bolt*
   -Minor Repair*
   -Lesser Charm*
Tier 1 (1SP each)
   -Visual Phantasm*
   -Healing Note
   -Whispers from Beyond
   -Invisible Servant
   -Familiar Bond
   -Wizard's Armor
   -Minor Enchanted Slumber
Tier 2 (3SP each)
   -Assume Quality (Special)
   -Lesser Mindreading
   -Sorcerous Mark
Bardsong
Command Attention
Song of Arcane Power

Nothing.

"It's too dark in here," Jhess said quietly. "Anything could be up there lurking. Do we try and flush things out with a quick flash? Or lure them into trying to attack an illusion?"

"What are the odds there's something up there?" Drev inquired.

"What are the odds there *isn't*?" Vance countered gaily. "This is a dungeon! We had to solve a puzzle, find a secret door, and follow a map to get here. Do you honestly think this place is empty?"

"No," Drev answered reluctantly, punctuating his admission with a sigh. "But I was hoping."

"Best options for defensible positions?" Robin asked. "I don't trust something not to change if we do rustle up some trouble. I want some fall-back options in case we end up trapped in here."

Jhess made a sign for warding off evil.

"There and there," Savra said, pointing. "That one has cover from whatever may be lurking above, as well as plenty of room to move and keep those three pillars between us and whatever might spring out from the sides. That little hollow near the wall will be good if we need something at our backs while we fight. We could break in either direction from there, and retreat if needed."

"Sounds good to me." Jhess's daggers appeared in her hands. "Twitch those fingers, boys; rustle us up some trouble."

"Hopefully not too much," Drev said drily.

"Let me see if I can tempt anything out with an illusion, first." Robin called up [Visual Phantasm] and added some sound with [Lesser Phantasm] in case there was an echolocation element in play. It wouldn't be the first time.

A copy of Rerebos's winged cat form flitted up and began darting among the stalactites, yowling in distress. A susurration of chittering answered, and flickers of movement began to shift in the shadows, but whatever it was was too fast or too shy to expose itself easily.

Then the illusion vanished.

"What the fuck?" Robin stared at his hand. The feeling of magic in his fingertips had cut off abruptly, and his extremities began to tingle.

The quality of the light around them shifted slightly.

"What happened?" Vance glanced from where the illusion had vanished and back to Robin.

"My magic just . . . stopped? I'm not sure." Robin flexed his fingers. "At least we know there's definitely something up there?"

"There's definitely something going on down here, too." Jhess's eyes narrowed. "Drev! I think we're going to need some light. I can hear something moving above us!"

Drev's fingers flexed, and several spheres of purplish-white light began to spiral up from his outstretched hand, driving back the shadows.

Or they started to. As the magic rose, the crystals embedded in the floor and nearby stalagmites flared the same color as Drev's magic, and the spheres first began to wobble and then to spin before they began exploding, one into a shower of pink daffodils, another into a small puddle of acid, and a third into cerulean bubbles which giggled as they floated away before popping with a wail of disappointment.

"Fuck me," Robin swore. "Wild magic!"

And that's when the monsters above chose to reveal themselves.

Chapter 13

*T*he party had already fought rats with crystal symbiotes growing from their bodies, but now they faced a far more dangerous—but curiously rhyming—foe: bats with crystal growths. Though it wasn't the eyes that were the focus now, as had been the case with the rats, but instead the fangs and the vocal cords as well, judging by the unholy crystalline wailing that sprang to life as the flock of crystal bats took wing.

"We need to retreat, now," Drev declared. "We can't fight those things with wild magic as a threat backing them up! Too many things could go wrong. We need better ground to make a stand. Crystal-free ground, by the looks of it."

"This whole place is riddled with the stuff!" Jhess said, daggers in hand. "We'd have to run all the way back to the temple, at least."

"And we're where the map told us to be," Robin said. "We're on top of part of the secret. Vance uses magic to fuel his transformation, but the spells that do work seem to remain stable. We can fall back to the entrance where there are fewer crystals, we all load up on our defensive spells there and hope none go awry, then we can advance again, see how many of our cantrips go to plan. Even if they go wild, it should be unlikely that the amount of magic in itself is dangerous." Robin paused, remembering how the spells of the hobgoblin army had fused into a gigantic chain reaction of wild magic. "As long as we don't use too many spells and blanket the area in too much magic, we should be all right. There aren't that many bats."

Saying there weren't that many bats was akin to saying that there weren't many pieces of hay in a small haystack. Sure, compared to the whole field, it wasn't much at all, but it was still a lot of individual stalks of hay.

Still, rhetorically, it worked. Make the problem seem manageable, define the steps needed. It was easier to see the way to defeat a foe if you broke it down into smaller enemies.

And that's what Robin and his party were facing: a swarm of small enemies. All together they were a threat, sure, and triply so in an area of wild magic where Robin, Drev, and Savra were a bit more limited in what they could contribute, but a horde of bat was still just bats.

Even if they did have strange crystalline powers.

"So we fall back, do what we can, try a sortie or two, and if it all goes pear-shaped, we retreat. If it works, we deal with the bats then investigate this place. Sorted." Jhess twirled her daggers. "Let's get to it!"

So the party did, falling back to the entryway as Robin shrouded them with the illusion of darkness. The spell worked, but Robin winced, noticing that several of the crystals seemed to soak up the quality of darkness as he did so.

He pointed the effect out to Drev. Vance, as a scholar, would have been better, but the librarian was busily incanting his spells, calling upon the legends of warriors past to lend the mage their power and abilities.

"What do you think that might mean?"

"Maybe there's a threshold," Drev mused. "The hobgoblin's wild magic reinforced itself, so maybe there is some sort of level at which things change? A certain number of spells before there's an outbreak of wild magic? If we could predict it—"

"Wild magic is never predictable," Robin cut in. "If it was, it wouldn't be proper wild magic. If there is a level, it changes or is constantly in flux. We might be able to ride a trend, but it will be like riding a shark or a tiger or a tsunami of lava—we're never going to know when it is going to turn on us, and a mistake like that could be even more devastating because it's so hard to predict."

"Ready," Vance called out.

Drev sighed and went through the motions for his force-armor spell. It flickered to life around him without an issue, though Robin noticed several nearby crystals spark to life with the color of Drev's magic.

"I think we're definitely headed toward that eruption," Robin pointed out. "Let's proceed with caution."

"The crystals further away do not seem to have reacted. Maybe proximity is also a factor," Savra noted, hands clenched around her coin.

"I suppose we'll find out," Robin said as Jhess lost patience and charged into battle.

The rogue dashed for the cover of a nearby pillar of stone and began lashing out with her daggers, flinging them at the swarm of bats. Each dagger found its mark, but there was no way she alone could take out the whole group of them. She'd run out of daggers first.

Robin risked running to a different pillar, spacing himself out from the other magic users in the party. If their theories were right, it was safer not to overload any one area with magic.

Cantrips flew into the air—bolts of pure force, balls of divine fire, flaming playing cards—felling bats left and right. Vance was a bloody eye at the center of a tornado of razor-edged fangs and flapping wings, his sword glowing a deeply disturbing white that thirsted for blood like a bone in the desert.

At first, nothing happened, and it seemed like their strategy was working. But as the spells flew, the crystals glowed more and more brightly until, at last, there was a *fzzt!* and the stored magic discharged in a coruscating webwork like spun lightning, transforming everything it touched to glass-clear crystal.

Fortunately, Robin, Drev, and Savra were out of the area of effect. Jhess was nimble enough to escape entirely unscathed, in spite of being quite near the point of origin. Vance, however, was not quite so lucky.

The warrior mage attempted to dodge, succeeding for the most part as he danced between a bolt just as it forked around him—maybe he was burning his magic to conjure the legendary luck of the Great Gray Hero, Maus—but the coruscating energies caught his sword just a handspan above the cross guard and transformed both it and two-thirds of Vance's flowing hair into crystal as clear as glass. Vance swore but called out that he was fine before he took a dagger and cut the crystal free form his hair before the fine points could shatter and dig deeply into his flesh. The sword dissipated back into paper.

Well, the bits that had not transformed did. The crystal remained, tearing itself free to shatter in an explosion of razor-sharp shards on the ground. And they were not the only ones. Several bats had been caught in the discharge as well, transforming to high-speed crystal bombs that exploded on impact. No member of the party—save Jhess—managed to evade the flying shards; everyone was bleeding from thin, superficial cuts.

As he winced and levered himself back up, something caught Robin's eye. There were lights pulsing in the crystals, moving from one to another in a spiraling pattern like a galaxy glimmering within the stone of the cavern . . .

. . . and the core of that galaxy was a spot in the middle of the ground, a bit off center. The lights briefly outlined something that could be a trapdoor or another passageway before disappearing from sight.

"Look!" he called to his party members. "Something's there!"

"Make a note and we'll deal with it later," Jhess shouted back. "There are still a lot of bats we need to deal with first!"

"Just watch out for the spells and the crystals! That crystal lightning was no joke!" Vance, for once, had a serious expression on his face. Apparently, the loss of his hair wasn't something he could so easily laugh off.

The party—more cautiously now—went about exterminating the rest of the bats. Robin managed to confuse them a bit with strategic auditory illusions, but they seemed far less susceptible to that trick than he'd expected. Maybe they were using the nearby crystals to navigate? Not just sound?

In any case, eventually they managed to mop up the rest and pause for a breather. Once they had recovered, the party moved cautiously to investigate the area where Robin had noticed the lights disappearing.

"It was somewhere around here," he muttered before conjuring the small illusion of a dancing globe of light.

Nothing happened, so he conjured three more. That made the crystals gulp down the magic, and he was able to follow the traces to the exact spot.

"Bit reckless," Drev said, but the mage was far more curious than he was afraid.

"There's some kind of hidden passageway here." Jhess was running her hands across the stone. "I think I can . . . there!"

There was a *click*, followed by a circular section of the floor sliding out of the way, a set of stairs coiled around the passage revealed in its absence. Crystals, larger than those in this cavern, studded the walls and provided light.

"There's a room at the bottom," Robin said, squinting a bit in the light. The ability to see in the dark was still coming in incredibly handy!

"Well, we've come this far. Might as well see what we're working with." Jhess pointed down the hole. "In you go, Ree-Ree."

Rerebos, who had resumed his perch on Robin's shoulder, puffed up and hissed at her.

"Can you block the mechanism?" Drev crouched down next to Jhess. "I don't fancy this thing sliding into place and trapping us down there."

"Eh, maybe. Give me some more light." Jhess reached for the edge.

Drev, perhaps automatically, complied, conjuring a bright globe of magelight.

That was a mistake.

The nearby crystals immediately sucked up the light, and with it, Drev's magic. This time, there was no delay before those selfsame energies were warped, twisted, and released back into the air around them. There was a shuddering rush, and a cylindrical wall of stone slid into place—or was conjured by the discharge of magical energies from the nearby crystals—cutting the party off from the cavern around them.

Cutting them off from the path back!

There was no way out except possibly by delving more deeply into the dungeon.

The dangerous, far-too-high-tiered dungeon.

Fuck.

<h1 style="text-align:center">Chapter 14</h1>

Robin hissed in frustration and let his hand fall from the stone blocking the party's way back to the cavern and the tunnel that led to the temple. The thing wasn't shifting, and he hadn't been able to find any mechanism to cause it to open once more. Jhess, with her superior skills at finding traps and hidden doors, might still turn up something, or Drev, with his superior magical senses, but Robin was tapped out.

Instead, he descended the newly revealed stairs. Even if trapped, they had found a hidden room which collected vast amounts of magic. That had to be good for something. And it had been marked on the map, so it was important somehow. Might as well investigate that since they were here and clearly not heading back any time soon.

The place looked like a public bathhouse. The stairs had spiraled them down to a sort of entrance location, but the cavern they were in now was large and vaulted, with low stone walls—just high enough for a bit of privacy here and there—winding throughout the space.

A large circular pool dominated the center of the space, with several smaller ones around the perimeter and within the mazy coil of low walls Robin had noticed. Most of them were long empty, the mosaic work around them cracked and warped, with fist-size outcroppings of crystal marring things even further. The central pool was full, however—although, based on the way the contents glimmered and moved of their own volition, Robin suspected it wasn't with water. Liquid magic? Some kind of enchanted acid? A resting ooze just waiting to rise up and engulf them all?

Most of the potential options that had sprung immediately to mind were . . . not good ones.

No water ran through the room, even though Robin could see the channels that should have been filled with it. There weren't any flickers of illusions, either, which was decidedly eerie after spending so long in the ruins of Tarin-Tiran, where fragments of illusions were almost ever present, even after ages of decay and ruination.

Careful! Robin called telepathically to his familiar.

Rerebos had spotted the shiny waters of the central pool and was fluttering above them curiously. If the little dragon in disguise had had a way to scoop them up, Robin was sure an attempt would already have been made, regardless of the potential consequences. At least the pool made no move to form a pseudopod and lash out at the winged cat flying above it. Robin didn't completely rule out the ooze threat, but he did reduce the odds in the tally he was running in his head.

I see tunnels, Rerebos announced. *Three of them, at the edges of the cavern. One looks natural, one has an ornate archway, and the other is some kind of worked stone.*

Robin could feel his familiar's opinion of each. The last one, the worked stone, came with a bit of withering disdain. The work must not be that great; otherwise, it would have triggered Rerebos's greed like the ornate archway clearly had.

"I can't find anything," Jhess said disgustedly. "You finger-wagglers having any luck?"

"No," Drev answered.

Vance shook his head.

"My vision is still unreliable," Savra replied sourly, "but I suspect we're not likely to be able to return that way."

"Well, there are other exits nearby," Robin reminded the party. "We established that before we chose the entrance we did. The others were further away or looked less reliable, but they do exist. We can try and work our way around to one of them if we have to. Might even be easier than boring through several feet of solid stone."

"What is that?" Vance interrupted the burgeoning discussion to point at the softly glimmering central pool.

"I have no idea," Robin said. "But I suspect it's dangerous."

Jhess froze in the act of reaching out to touch the stuff.

"It's intensely magical, whatever it is." Drev was squinting at the pool. "And it doesn't appear to have any kind of magical signature I recognize."

"Maybe it's just pure magic? Filtered by the crystals somehow? The wild magic explosions could be a side effect of pulling away whatever gives a certain bit of magic a signature or resonance." Robin hummed a bit as he thought.

"Resonance. That's a nice term for it," Drev said. "I like it!"

"Thanks." Robin didn't mention he'd stolen it from a tabletop RPG from his old world. Not like there was anyone here to contest him or push a copyright violation or anything.

"Trust a bard to use a word like resonance." Jhess shook her head, but her smile said she was just teasing.

"Why don't you stick a dagger in that stuff," Robin shot back. "Let's see if it does anything." He paused. "But maybe tie a bit of string to it before tossing it in. Probably safer not to be in direct contact with it. Just in case."

Jhess looked alarmed, but a look from Savra calmed her nerves. Though with both Drev and Vance clamoring for the experiment to go forward, Robin wasn't sure how.

Those two agreeing on something dangerous and related to magic was usually a good reason to be nervous.

"This might even prove to be the way to reverse the block trapping us here," Drev mused. "It smacks of a certain sort of puzzle favored by living dungeons."

Robin didn't think it was *that* likely, but it was worth a shot. Might as well exhaust the options here before deciding which of the three tunnels to take.

He quickly compared them to the mental copy of the map they had found in the temple and the one in Red's journal. Either the natural tunnel or the stone one seemed likely to lead to the next location that overlapped on both maps. The ornate tunnel was probably their best bet for the fastest, shortest route out of this place. Although with dungeons, it was all but impossible to tell. Ruddy places did ridiculous things with spatial dynamics.

Jhess, having properly tied her knife to a piece of string, tossed the weapon into the pool, skimming it in so as to minimize splash damage. The pool exploded with coruscating light, and the dagger dissolved into steel-gray sparks which whirled through the air like fireflies before winking out of existence.

Jhess was left holding a much-shortened piece of string.

"Right. Don't touch the pool of condensed magic," Robin said. "Message received."

"We haven't tested enough things to definitively say that," Vance protested.

Drev concurred. "Throw some meat in," the mage demanded.

"Me?" Robin blinked. "Why me?"

"It's your turn, and aside from Jhess, you're the one with the largest supply of contraband supplies."

"I beg your pardon!" Robin acted affronted, but he materialized a small bit of steak nonetheless. "Contraband? This is . . . emergency rations for my familiar!"

"Sure." Jhess smirked. "Rations you packed in Noviel knowing you'd just happen to find a familiar? Pull the other one."

Robin forced a laugh. He had come a bit too close to letting something slip there. Rerebos the adorable flying kitten was a familiar everyone could get behind. Rerebos the miniature shadow dragon? That was a dicier prospect.

He tossed the gobbet of meat into the pool. Once again, it hissed and fizzed, it's true nature sublimating into something wilder, more unusual. In this case, a small gobbet of pink slime hauled itself up out of the pool of its own volition and scurried away into a crack even as Jhess tried to smash it beneath her heel.

"That is definitely going to come back and haunt us, someday," the rogue declared sourly. "Unless we get out of this dungeon sharpish."

"But we have a way out." Drev snapped his fingers. "We just need to figure out how to use it."

"I don't follow," Savra said, frowning.

Robin did, but only because he'd been part of far too many dungeoneering parties in his world and had played with far too many people whose idea of a fun game was trying the weirdest things they could imagine to get out of a situation, forcing the DM to contort into more and more twisted a pretzel as they tried to keep the game on some semblance of rails.

The really fun ones gave up, went with it, then figured out how to make it *look* like it was all part of a grand plan to begin with.

"He wants us to splash the stone blocking our way with a bunch of that." Robin gestured to the pool. "But there's an obvious problem there."

"Anything that touches the pool changes." Savra nodded. "How do we transport the liquid the required distance without mishap."

"That's the million-gold-piece question," Robin said, flashing an insincere smile.

"Any suggestions?" Jhess asked. "Because I've got nothing. And you're not getting any more of my daggers!"

"We shouldn't spend too long coming up with things either," Robin warned. "That's a good way to get stuck down here. Right now, we have no idea where to head next if we're ambushed and have to flee. If we can't get that stone open, we're going to need another route out of here."

"Jhess can scout us one, and Savra can help with her divinatory powers." Drev flicked his fingers dismissively. "We've got a potential solution right here that's also a prime candidate for research. Do you have any idea what we might learn by studying this?"

The excited mage wasn't completely wrong. And the idea of some more secrets or perks was definitely tempting.

Robin sighed.

"I'll send Rere to help scout the tunnels. He's already spotted three, though Jhess might find a hidden one. I'll see if I can think of any ballads or legends which might offer a solution to a problem like this."

"I'll work with Jhess and divine our best course of action," Savra said. "No, I will not aid you in unlocking the secrets of this pool." She held up a hand before Drev could protest. "You have quite enough inquiring minds as it is."

"Fair enough," the mage conceded, deflating a bit.

The party split to perform their respective tasks, Robin keeping part of his attention with Rerebos. He still hated to split a party, too many years of gaming convincing him it would always end in disaster. And it was probably right to be paranoid. A dungeon was not a dungeon master, but it was a damn close approximation. And they'd already tripped one trap.

Be careful, Robin sent to his familiar, following the words with a surge of affection and caution.

Robin got back a surge of emotion that was a mixture almost more appropriate to a resentful teenager: embarrassment, irritation, and a trace of love.

He took it.

"Right," he said, turning to the mage and the librarian. "Let's get creative. Now . . ."

Chapter 15

It was, in no uncertain terms, an unmitigated disaster. For thoroughness, they had tested glass, wooden, and paper containers; all of them had dissolved with unexpected and unpredictable magical effects. They'd even tried to move a small sample of the stuff with Drev's force magic, the mage conjuring a shallow disc of force to carry the liquid across the intervening space.

The results of that particular experiment had nearly killed them all. The liquid had absorbed the force magic and, well, exploded, scattering splashes of raw, unadulterated power across the cavern, which had reacted with the stone to set off a chain of random magical effects. Robin was still trying to wring the watery flan from his hair. The stuff was somehow resistant to his cleansing magics! Honestly. It wasn't worth it.

So he said as much.

"We're running out of time. We need to move on to the next option." Robin flicked away a gobbet of congealed caramel.

"I suppose you're right." Drev sighed. "We're not making any progress toward dissolving that barrier, are we? Still, we have learned quite a lot about the nature of magical resonance." The mage brightened.

"So our next objective is, what? Escape, or investigation of the final node on Red's map?" Vance framed the question, but it was clear the librarian preferred the more exploratory option.

Maniac.

But Robin agreed. They were this close now. The thought of coming back here after escaping once? The very idea strained his belief in all the luck deities in this and his own universe.

"Investigate," Jhess said.

"Agreed," Savra chimed in.

"Looks like it's unanimous."

"You didn't let me vote," Drev protested. "And Vance hasn't said which he actually prefers!"

"Please," the bard responded. "As if it isn't obvious? The two of you are so thirsty for knowledge I'm surprised you didn't try to move the water by drinking it down and pissing it out on the stone later."

Drev paused, mouth open, with a calculating look on his face.

"No!" Jhess chided. "Don't even think about it."

The things people were willing to do for knowledge. Or power. Robin suppressed a grin.

There was no question as to how valuable discovering what had happened in Tarin-Tiran was. Someone would pay for the knowledge. But aside from that, it was a puzzle, a mystery, and *that* interested the whole party, not just Robin, who had a mysterious quest linked to discovering more about this place.

That left them to decide the approach.

"Natural or worked tunnel?" Robin asked. "Either one could do it, with the caveat that we have no idea how this dungeon has twisted up the passageways."

"They both head off in the right direction," Jhess said. "Found a few traps along each length. I went ahead and disabled them in case we needed to make a fast exit for any reason."

A wave of irritation and pride came from Robin's familiar.

Yes, Rerebos, I know you helped as well. The whole party does.

The cat began purring from his perch on Robin's shoulder.

"And what will be the deciding factor?"

That began a debate. The party was split as to which way was the better bet. Savra consulted her coin, but aside from confirming that they should definitely *not* proceed down the ornate passageway, it did little to confirm which of the other two was preferable. Both ways offered good and bad omens in messy, near-equal measure.

Robin was so absorbed in the discussion that it took him too long to notice the surreal mist that had begun rising from the pool of distilled magic.

"Oh, that cannot be good," he said, pointing to it. "Considering what it does when it touches things, I suspect we need to make a hasty exit, *now*."

"Which way?" Jhess asked, already moving. It was clear the rogue had no interest in any more research and testing.

"Natural stone," Drev said.

"I still think the worked-stone passage is more likely," Vance argued.

"Boys, boys!" Robin chided. "You're both very smart and very insightful. However, we no longer have time to debate. It's one or the other."

"Natural stone," Savra spoke up, looking at the coin in her hand.

"Another divination?" Drev asked with interest.

"No," the seeress replied. "I just assigned one side of the coin to each way and flipped it. Complete randomness."

"That's one way to do it," Robin said. "You heard the lady! Let's get moving! Natural stone."

The party made a beeline for the passage, the fog nipping at their heels the whole way. Strange sounds and lights came from inside the mist, but nothing Robin could quite make out. Nothing he was willing to linger behind and see. Though a small voice at the back of his mind asked why the fog wasn't causing more wild-magic surges if it was spread so thin. How was any of this place still standing? Maybe it was just the nature of the enchanted pools and the stone in this area. The dungeon could have enchanted it somehow? He didn't know enough about wild magic, but the rising fog was awfully convenient, somehow.

And wasn't that what he did when he used illusions? Make them amorphous, dangerous, something no sane person would want to test? They were in a city of illusion, which had spawned a living dungeon somehow. There were all manner of possibilities.

But the voice wasn't so loud that it made Robin pause to investigate. No, he kept pace with the rest of the group and headed for the designated passageway. As soon as they went through, Drev used a disc of force to block the entrance. It wasn't a proper wall, but he could angle it enough that, if everything went well, it would keep the mist from rolling in after them. Hopefully, they would be far enough down the tunnel when the fog hit that whatever wild magic resulted, it wouldn't kill them all. It was a calculated risk, but Jhess had already discovered several traps. They couldn't afford to run from the fog head-on into a hidden deadfall or pit trap.

"This place is vicious," Jhess said.

Robin sent Rerebos to help scout ahead. They'd need all the help they could get!

"Any sign of the fog hitting the shield?" he asked Drev.

"I haven't felt the spell warp or vanish," the mage replied, "and we haven't been hit with a wave of lemmings made of cheese or anything, but it's hard to say."

I would like to eat a cheese lemming!

Rerebos was *very* interested in that idea.

Toasty . . . he all but hissed in Robin's mind.

"I can see some tendrils," Vance shouted. "It's still flowing after us, but there's a lot less of it. And it seems to be moving more slowly."

"It's still coming, though," Drev complained. "And why didn't it react with my force disc?"

Robin would like to know the answer to that as well. He almost asked Jhess to toss another dagger in, but realized what the rogue would probably have to say, so he pulled a pebble out of his dimension storage and carefully chucked it at the next tendril of fog he could see behind them.

Nothing.

He tried again.

This time, the pebble erupted into a small burst of gray maggots. They immediately fell to the stone and began burrowing in. Robin shivered. Imagine what they might do to flesh!

"It looks like when it's diffused like this, it doesn't react as much or as severely."

"No studying!" Jhess bellowed from where she was disarming a trap just ahead of the rest of the party. "We want to lose the stuff, not give it a chance to catch up."

"Is the tunnel still heading the way we need it to?" Savra asked, ever practical.

Robin consulted the map and the notes he'd been keeping in his head.

"So far, yes," he replied. "But shout if you notice any sharp turns coming up."

"Drev should play rear guard, as his force disc might be our best warning of a fog increase," Vance said. "I'll cover Jhess as she scouts. Savra, Robin, take the center positions and back us up and keep us in contact."

"On it," Robin agreed.

Savra nodded.

The party made its way down and down the tunnel, covering ground quickly when they could, pausing every so often to allow Jhess to deal with a trap.

"Nothing too complex yet," the rogue said with satisfaction. "We can't have gone too much deeper in, at this rate. Things would be getting much worse if we had."

Robin confirmed that against the mental map in his head.

"We should be over halfway there by now," he informed. Robin didn't like how few branches the tunnel had had so far, but as it was still generally running in the direction they needed it to go, he supposed he shouldn't complain.

But it made him feel like something was—

"Guys," Jhess called out. "I think we have company!"

The rogue pointed ahead of them. Robin followed her finger. There was a pale figure standing there, in the shadows, and even though the darkness was no match for Robin's sight, the figure remained hazy and indistinct.

More ghosts? Not unusual in a ruined city that had seen a lot of violent death. More illusions? Not unheard of in Tarin-Tiran.

Robin tried to look through Rerebos's eyes. His familiar was substantially closer to the apparition than he was; closer even than Jhess. Then he swore, causing the party around him to all recenter their attention on their bard.

There was mist swirling about the apparition's feet, and a whole bank of fog billowing behind it!

They were trapped between two fogbanks!

Chapter 16

*R*obin conjured a flaming ace of spades, the blue light from the witchfire surrounding it casting the scene in an eerie luminescence. The ghostly figure didn't react, but the fog around its feet swirled and advanced slowly.

The bard sent the **[Lesser Witch Bolt]** flashing toward the mist, rather than the figure. The card exploded with a *snap* and *crackle* of eldritch flame, but the fog around it did not respond. No wild-magic surge. Just a bit of swirl to it from the disturbance of the impact.

The figure raised one arm and crooked its hand in a beckoning gesture.

"Oh, hells no," Jhess muttered.

"We've got wild-magic fog advancing on our heels," Drev called out. "I think there's more of it!"

Classic rock and a hard place. Robin looked around desperately for a hidden third option. A trap with an escape tunnel hidden within it, maybe, or a secret door in the walls, floor, or ceiling? But this wasn't one of the classic dungeon crawls; this was no tabletop fantasy. This fantasy was very real, and the dungeon around them was very alive. Unlike a friendly—or even malevolent—dungeon master, the living dungeon of Tarin-Tiran had no motivation to tailor itself to Robin's party.

"Savra," Robin spoke. "Any insight?"

"Behind us is only woe; ahead is a mix of utterly terrible signs and portents and great rewards," the seeress replied, flipping her coin several times. "I cannot see any more than that."

"Great," Robin muttered.

"Forward, then," Vance said cheerfully. "Perhaps new discoveries await! Or great treasure."

That last was clearly for Jhess's benefit, though Robin felt Rerebos perk up at the idea through their bond.

The party advanced, slowly. The apparition fell back before them, never seeming to move but always a set distance ahead of them.

"That's fucking creepy," Jhess murmured, daggers clenched tightly before her.

She wasn't wrong.

"Fog behind us is advancing faster!" Drev exclaimed. "My force disc has run out."

Fuck.

The mist ahead of them still hugged the edges of the corridor, but they were able to pass through it. Robin hated it, but it was a chance of danger here versus the surety of it behind, so the party hurried forward.

Too quickly.

There was a sharp *click* beneath Jhess's foot, and the floor beneath both Jhess and Vance vanished. Savra, Robin and Drev were far enough back that they were spared.

Robin flung himself forward and grabbed Vance. The librarian was tall and thin, but he was still heavier than Robin could easily manage as he slammed to his stomach and began to slide toward the edge. Jhess had managed to catch herself on the edge, hanging by her fingertips.

"Let me through!" Drev rushed to the edge and looked down, conjuring a disc of force beneath Jhess to keep her from falling further, but the spell was too limited to levitate her up.

Savra had not been idle. She'd pulled out a length of rope, already knotted for climbing, and tossed one end to Jhess, looping the other around herself and Drev before dropping her center of gravity to compensate for the downward pull.

"Quick as you can," Robin said through gritted teeth. He had a grip on Vance, but he was caught at the very edge of the pit, and there was no way he could haul the librarian up. Vance looked up at him, his easy expression for once nowhere to be seen.

Robin couldn't blame him. The bottom of the pit was filled with a sea of glittering green mist, and a sea of stone spikes rose up from those depths. If that fog wasn't acidic as fuck, Robin would eat his hat. Not that he had a hat. But if he had one, he'd eat it. If that fog wasn't acidic.

"I think I'm losing my grip," he muttered.

Vance looked up at him, eyes wide. Robin gave him a reassuring smile in return.

"My mental grip, not my grip on you. I got you. I got you."

Rerebos flitted overhead, sending waves of alarm through their familiar bond. That wasn't helping, but Robin didn't snap at the little dragon. There's no way that would help.

Jhess managed to climb out of the pit, and Drev relocated the disc beneath Vance. Robin almost sighed with relief, but the intake of breath caused his grip to loosen, just a hair, and he clamped down on Vance, on the edge of the pit, and on the breath in his lungs.

The rest of the party, now with Jhess's help, lowered the rope once again, and working together, they managed to haul the librarian up.

The party, as one, fell back from the pit, taking deep, gulping breaths of air.

"That was close," Drev said.

"Too close," Vance offered.

Robin couldn't blame the librarian for his reaction, but he couldn't help but wish for Vance's reassuring nonchalance in the face of danger to return. It was apparently more effective than he had realized.

"Fog's coming," Drev informed between heaving breaths. "We need to move."

Robin groaned and pulled a couple long planks out of his dimensional storage, dropping them across the pit trap. The party crossed quickly, but when Robin went to retrieve the planks, the mist had already reached them on the other side, and the boards exploded into a slithering rain of snakes, cascading down into the pit.

Looked like he had been right about the acid!

The apparition was still beckoning them onward, and the mist behind them was spilling down into the pit, slowly filling it and covering the nightmarish sight of hundreds of snakes slowly dissolving as their skin and flesh sloughed off their skeletons.

Robin had just enough time to wonder if the acidic fog would eat away the bones as well or leave them behind, polished clean and sparkling as a trophy for the dungeon, before they were moving again, following the apparition.

"Where the fuck are the branching tunnels? Where are the options?" Jhess muttered with irritation. "This makes no sense. Dungeons don't act like this."

Something about that sparked the small voice in the back of Robin's mind, which had been muttering about the pursuing fog. It agreed. Something more was going on here.

Before he could say anything, however, they stepped forward after the apparition, and an entire chamber materialized around them. One moment, all that was ahead was more corridor; the next, they were several meters into a large room.

Illusion. How many branching passages had they missed for not carefully checking every inch of wall? No wonder the fog had driven them! If they'd had the time, the party would have probably found other options.

Yet here they were. Where they had intended to be. Robin checked his mental map against the journal just to be sure. Yes. This was the place.

Did the dungeon want them here?

It was not a comforting thought.

The cavern they found themselves in was a vast one, once again. And again, it seemed to have something to do with water. If it were in Robin's old world, he'd have guessed it was some kind of water-processing center. There were pools and tanks and pipes running all over, many still showing the signs of intricate runework and enchantment, though time and the actions of the dungeon had long since broken whatever residual magic had run through the lines.

There was also an elaborate mosaic here, or the signs of where one used to be. The perimeter of the space was scattered with mounds of broken pieces of colorful stone, with a few sections remaining intact. These were all water themed, reinforcing Robin's instincts.

"Any sign of the fog behind us?" Jhess asked.

Drev retraced his steps and glanced through the illusion.

"Not yet," he said.

"I'll have Rere keep watch," Robin offered, sending a set of mental instructions to his familiar.

The party relaxed a fraction, no longer having to deal with quite so many issues at once. Now, all they had to deal with was the apparition and the mystery of the room. Hopefully, the fog would stay penned by the pit trap.

"Savra, could you keep an eye on our misty friend while Vance, Drev, and I check the runic structures in here?" Robin asked. "Jhess will watch your back."

"You know it," the rogue said, spinning her daggers in her hands.

The magic in this room was by far the most complex they had so far encountered. Part of that seemed to be because there were multiple areas of magical knowledge involved in the workings. There was more than illusion magic at play here.

"Conjuration, transmutation, illusion," Drev murmured, his eyes gleaming purple white with mage sight. "This is some intricate work!"

"And of a style I've not seen before," Vance added. "This is ancient."

"I'll try and mark out what I can of the illusion threads," Robin said, conjuring a [Visual Phantasm] of the relevant markings. There would likely be small alterations to try and pick out, things the dungeon had done or changed that shifted the way things worked, like in the temple.

The three most magically inclined members of the party worked in silence while Savra investigated the apparition and Jhess stood general watch. It was the work of hours. Fortunately, there was no sign of the wild-magic fog that had pursued them.

Eventually, Rerebos got bored and started complaining in the back of Robin's mind. He suggested his familiar go scout to see what had happened with the mist, and the little dragon agreed after a little persuasion and the promise of a shiny to add to his hoard.

"Anything?" Robin called at last.

"The apparition is just moving around the room in the same pattern, again and again, like a cart on a track," Savra replied. "I can sense no ill will, but cannot divine anything about it either."

"I think the conjuration has to do with moving water to and from the city," Drev said.

"And the transmutation purified it, both as it flowed in and before it flowed out," Vance added. "How, I'm not quite sure, but I can identify the purification bits of this runic structure, at least."

"I think I've got most of the illusion plucked out and replicated." Robin gestured to bring his [Visual Phantasm] into being before the others to illustrate his point. "Here, here, and here, things look like they've shifted, somehow. Probably the dungeon's work. Not sure what the right changes to the runes are, but here are my best guesses." Robin gestured again, and a second set of runes appeared, glowing white to the originals' blue so the differences were clear.

Drev and Vance studied the structure.

"You're the illusion expert," Vance finally said. "From what I can see, it looks solid."

Robin mentally checked in on Rerebos. The little dragon reported he was on his way back, and that there had been no sign of the pit trap or the fog when he'd returned to the site on his scouting mission. They should be secure from the stuff for a while, at least.

I tire of standing watch. Rerebos's voice was firm. *Set another watchman if you worry about fog from that direction. I will seek shinies in this new chamber!*

"I think it should be safe enough to try some repair, and see what happens," Robin said, shooting a glance to Savra for confirmation.

"I cannot see the outcome of this course of action," the seeress replied with frustration. "Nor whether it might bring good or ill." She sighed. "But from studying the apparition, I do not think it will pose a danger in this case. We should stay vigilant, all the same."

"No lie," Jhess muttered.

"Right," Robin confirmed. "Keep an eye out. I'm going to see what we might get."

He double-checked his work before replacing a few key mosaic fragments, gathered during his examination of the runic structures around the room.

At first, he didn't think anything had changed, but then Savra gasped.

Robin turned to look, following the seeress's gaze until he saw what had prompted her reaction: the apparition had taken on greater clarity.

Robin blinked.

Was that Nilsiir?

Chapter 17

*I*t *was* another illusion of Nilsiir, High Priest of Rhyth in the days when Tarin-Tiran had flourished. This time, something was different, however, and it was not hard for Robin to put his finger on precisely what that was.

Nilsiir was staring right at them, eyes flicking from one member of the party to another. The high priest opened his mouth and began to gesture wildly, but no sound issued forth.

A look of consternation drifted across the illusion's face.

Illusion? Ghost? Some combination of the two? A trick of the dungeon?

"What is happening?" Robin whispered to the rest of the party.

"I was hoping you had some ideas about that," Vance whispered back.

Jhess had her daggers out, while Savra was flipping her coin and frowning at it as it came down on edge time and time again. Sparks of purple-white light danced across Drev's fingers as he readied himself for a magical defense in case things got serious, fast.

The illusion of Nilsiir began pacing around the room, squinting at various details, walking through inconvenient obstacles, and generally muttering in discontent.

Robin wished he was better at lipreading. Would [**Tongue of the Fallen Tower**] work with lipreading? Probably not.

"What is it doing?" Jhess asked, keeping the point of one of her daggers continually trained on the illusory priest.

"It looks like they're . . . looking at things?" Robin answered. "Maybe looking for something?"

Nilsiir looked at them and glared.

"Wait," Jhess said. "Can it hear us?"

The illusion nodded and rolled its eyes. The rogue threw a dagger through it.

Nilsiir just sighed and tossed back a look that said, *Really?*

"Can you understand what I'm saying?" Robin asked.

Nilsiir nodded again before the illusion moved its hands through a few gestures. Nothing happened, and they grimaced.

Robin froze at those gestures, though. He recognized them. How could he not? He used them every time he went to cast **[Lesser Phantasm]**.

He stepped forward cautiously and mirrored the movements, conjuring a small image of the figure he had first seen in the shrine he'd awoken in when he'd first arrived in this world: a shadowy figure that from many angles just seemed an outcropping of stone.

Nilsiir smiled broadly upon seeing it and looked at Robin with renewed interest.

"What was that?" Vance asked.

"Something I saw in a—book about a shrine to Rhyth, once," Robin answered. "I figured, if we're seeing a sentient illusion in a city dedicated to the god, what else would be better to show we're friendly?"

"Are we?" Jhess asked bluntly.

"Hey, the more allies we have down here, the better," Robin shot back. "There's a living dungeon all around us that wants us dead, for one, not to mention the other monsters roaming these ruins. If Nilsiir here has access to their old memories, it could be invaluable. Why not try to make friends?"

"It's your funeral," the rogue said. "Just make sure it isn't ours as well."

Robin smiled grimly at that.

Meanwhile, Nilsiir had discovered Robin's floating illusion replicating the runic structures within the room and was examining it with great interest. The reaction when they discovered the bit highlighting the change Robin had just made caused an extreme reaction. The high priest began gesticulating wildly, trying to draw Robin over.

He went. He was trying to make friends, after all, and who knew what he might learn?

Drev and Vance followed, curious, while Savra and Jhess were more cautious. Rerebos was staying out of sight, just to be on the safe side, but Robin could feel the fascination rolling off the little dragon in waves.

Nilsiir was gesturing at the rune Robin had altered to try and reactivate the original functionality of the place. They were drawing a shape in midair with their hands; it looked mostly similar to the rune Robin had shaped, from what he could see, but maybe there was a slight difference. It was hard to tell from guessing at the lines left by an illusion.

But that gave Robin an idea. Using [Lesser Phantasm], he carefully traced the movements of Nilsiir's hands. The illusion, catching on to what Robin was doing, slowed their movements so the bard could more easily follow. When the image was complete, Robin willed it over next to the rune he had altered for comparison.

They were slightly different!

Robin raised his hand to make an alteration to the runic structure, but Drev's voice pulled him up short.

"Wait. Are you sure you want to do that? We don't actually know what that will do." The mage's voice held a note of caution.

"No," Robin answered. "But as it's my magic fueling the change, there's a very good chance I could cut the energies before anything truly catastrophic went wrong. The runes aren't that different. The effects should be very similar to what's already happening. We've seen that in other places we've tried this experiment, after all."

"True," Drev said. "I merely thought it wise that we consider everything carefully before attempting anything. This is . . . unprecedented."

"That we know of," Robin added.

"Savra?" Jhess asked.

The seeress flipped her coin. It came down on its edge once more.

"I cannot see. Whatever effect has been confusing my divination has been almost insurmountable since we arrived in this room. Something is interfering." She shot a suspicious glance at Nilsiir.

The illusion ignored her entirely, focused on the runic structures floating in front of it before the high priest took the decision entirely out of the party's hands. They reached out and grasped the glowing rune formed by Robin's [Lesser Phantasm], sliding it into place in the illusory structure and displacing the one Robin had originally conjured in the relevant place.

"Ah, there we go," Nilsiir said. "Much better." He turned to the party. "Thank you. Light and shadow, but it's been a long time since I've been able to speak freely!"

"Erm, happy to help?" Robin managed to find his voice before the rest of the party.

This was not like the visions they had seen before. There, the illusions had been static things, memories of a past, endlessly repeating themselves on a loop. This was a real-time interactive illusion, the likes of which none of them had ever seen. This was verging on fully awakened, holographic artificial intelligence, to borrow some ideas from Robin's original world.

"There is not much time," Nilsiir said. "I have no idea how long your little patchwork job here will last with the titanic energies involved in this room. Particularly now that Silinir has made so many strange changes." Nilsiir shook their head. "I have no idea what has warped him so, but it is . . . unsettling, to say the least. Oh, what year is it?"

A stammering Drev told him.

Nilsiir raised one elegant eyebrow.

"Really? So long? I'd have thought . . . never mind! You are here now! You can—"

Nilsiir suddenly flickered in and out of focus, flashing between their current form and the ghostlike apparition from before.

"What's wrong?" Vance asked, looking from the illusion of the high priest to the illusion of the runic structure Robin had conjured.

Robin didn't have an answer. There was a tingling in his extremities which felt ominous, so he quickly banished the illusion and reconjured it, hoping that would both stop the sensation and restore some semblance of normalcy to Nilsiir.

It did.

"Well, that was unpleasant." The illusion shuddered.

What did a sentient illusion feel? At first, Robin's mind rejected the idea, but then something clicked, and he saw easily how such a thing could be. On one level, illusion was all about fooling the senses, so why could it not fool senses which were themselves illusions?

Hey, he had turned the pages of an illusory book with illusory hands. This shiz was weird.

"And while I appreciate it, your efforts will not last. You need to make some restorative changes to the runic structures in this room for me to last long enough to tell you anything useful at all." Nilsiir somehow managed to look pale without having any blood. Or body, for that matter.

"And why should we trust you?" Jhess demanded

"You shouldn't," Nilsiir replied, a look of surprise on their face. "Sweet shadow and shade, you don't just go around trusting anyone you meet, do you? That would be the height of idiocy!"

Jhess blinked.

"Ironically, that makes me want to trust him," she complained.

"Still foolish. I'm an illusory apparition in a living dungeon." Nilsiir shook their head. "Bind me with an oath, if you can, or find an agreement that can bind both parties with things each want. Honestly, what do they teach adventurers these days?"

"Why don't you start," Robin challenged. "What do you want?"

"I'd like to remain in control of my faculties, to begin with," Nilsiir responded crisply. "I've spent quite enough time as a drifting ghost in this city as it is. The place is in ruins! There is much that can be done to restore this place, to find the missing voices that should be sounding, even now, through the stones."

The illusion looked troubled.

Robin knew the high priest meant Rhyth. And if this was truly the ghost of Nilsiir, somehow . . . think of the secret knowledge that Robin might be able to access! This was a priceless opportunity, worth any risk.

"And what do we have to do to make sure you get it?" Robin asked.

"Nuh-uh, not yet." Nilsiir shook a finger at the bard. "That knowledge can be turned against me too easily. I'm no novice at this. Tell me what you want, and then we'll see if we can proceed."

"Knowledge," Robin replied immediately, a word echoed by almost the entirety of the party. Jhess's response was more along the lines of asking for the knowledge of where the best treasure was.

"Interesting." Nilsiir's eyes flicked across them, lingering a moment longer on Robin, holding the bard's gaze. "Not your usual adventuring party."

"That's true enough," Robin said. "Is that enough for us to continue, or are you after more specifics?"

"It will suffice for now. I think I have enough of your measure." Nilsiir winked at Robin.

Oh, this was a dangerous game. This person was dangerous, even dead. But there was something about them—a spark of divinity, perhaps? They were compelling, charismatic, and Robin felt something within him respond favorably to the priest's antics. He recognized them.

There was a trickster there, with a flicker of fear hiding behind the mask of joviality. He'd worn that mask before when he'd felt that fear.

"If you would make the following alterations to the runic structures, please, we can get started." Nilsiir gestured, forcing Robin to outline the illusion's quick gestures in light once more, in far more intricate detail.

It was a slow process. Several times, Nilsiir insisted on going over the details exactingly, until the image was perfect. Vance joined in the project enthusiastically, Drev with a bit more wariness, but the lure of new and advanced knowledge of magic proved too strong a lure for them to resist. Even Savra drew close, eyes and ears sharp for useful magical lore.

And none of them were disappointed. Nilsiir proved very happy to share what they were doing. Robin watched several notifications flick past before his eyes as various of his skills received experience discounts just from listening to Nilsiir and carefully executing the illusion's instructions.

After a few hours, enough of the work had been completed that a tipping point was reached. Nilsiir suddenly cried out in exultation, and the room rippled around them. Robin felt it: illusion magic of a tier he had not yet encountered. It rippled throughout the room, and everything *changed*. The runic structures rewrote themselves on the walls, and then Nilsiir did something. Robin didn't know how he knew, but he did. Was it [**The Mirror's Revenge**]?

It had to be! How else could illusion be made temporarily real. And this illusion was so titanic, so far-reaching, that for it to be made real, even for several seconds, was staggering.

Nilsiir cracked their neck with an audible sound, then they reached out and ran their fingers across the stone, prying a small rock from the new mosaic and tossing it from hand to hand.

"Much better." The high priest smiled. "Now, let's get down to business! Silinir—what you call the living dungeon—is not going to be happy about losing a chunk of his territory like this. We'll need to move soon."

Chapter 18

"How much do you know?" Nilsiir asked briskly, striding about the room as it reshaped itself to their will.

If Robin's perusal of potential high-level illusion spells was correct, Nilsiir was likely employing **[Supreme Mirage]** or something similar. **[Supreme Mirage]** was an illusion so encompassing, it could even fool the sense of touch, and had an inherent quasi-reality to it, such that even someone who saw through the illusion or was otherwise immune to its effects could successfully climb, say, an illusory ladder conjured by it.

It was at least a Tier Seven effect.

Robin wanted that knowledge, that power. And while he would be unable to wield it for some time at his current rate of progression, he had no doubt that someday, *someday* it would be within his grasp.

Especially if he could convince Nilsiir to teach him.

"We've seen pieces of the invasion, many of the illusions you encoded recording the final days of Tarin-Tiran," Robin began. "The hobgoblin army of Urkhan—"

"We ran into their descendants on the surface," Vance broke in to add. "Were you responsible for the curse of wild magic that afflicted their spellcasters?"

"Did that last? Excellent!" Nilsiir beamed.

It wasn't lost on Robin that the illusion hadn't directly answered Vance's question. Something to file away for later.

"We've seen the mage, Leivniz, at the head of the army. She used to be an influential figure in the city, right? Oh, and a few glimpses of

Melusk. He was some kind of politician or councillor, maybe a mer-chant, right?"

"Yes." Nilsiir's lips drew into a sharp and distasteful line. "Traitors, the both of them, though Melusk was by far the worse of the two. He was a true Disciple of Urkhan, for all he worked in secret. The Iron-Handed god may pretend that he always conquers through force alone, but he has no compunctions about slow corruption from within as a means of achieving his goals. He's always been sneakier than people realize."

"You talk about him as if you'd met him," Savra marveled.

"That's because I have. I was one of Rhyth's Disciples. Not the first, obviously. I'm not *that* old."

Robin's **[Bardic Lore]** pinged helpfully. Disciples were the faithful of the gods, of any class or profession, that closely embodied the deity's personality, ideals, or portfolio. Or sometimes they just vibed with their divine patron, like a hyped-up, sugar-daddy type relationship. Though those instances were less common, and if the ballads were to be believed, almost always tragic, in the end. Disciples had vastly enhanced powers, always something relating to the deity in question's main portfolio or areas of influence, and were often used as go-betweens to carry messages to other deities or to intervene in affairs on the deity's behalf.

"So, you've gathered a fair few pieces," Nilsiir continued. "Allow me to try and fill in a few of the gaps." An illusion bloomed before them all with a wave of Nilsiir's hand. It was Tarin-Tiran, the city in miniature, presumably as it had been in its glory days. "Tarin-Tiran was a marvel, and not even I know the full history of the place. It began as a Church of Rhyth, however; that much is known. A church turned into a flying citadel. Eventually, the citadel settled here at Rhyth's decree, at the edge of this land, and grew outward and downward and through, becoming the city as I knew it. The city that would fall to the treachery of Urkhan."

Nilsiir's face grew thunderous.

"We were tricked, and that was the city's undoing."

And Rhyth's, Nilsiir's voice whispered in Robin's mind.

The bard held himself very still, betraying no reaction. Was he getting a more involved version of the story? And how was Nilsiir doing this? Some kind of figment, in all likelihood; that class of illusions were seen only by the spell's target.

"Melusk," Savra said. "He was the traitor that betrayed you from the inside."

"Yes. We do not know how Urkhan turned him, but it was most likely his vanity and ambition. Then Melusk went to work on Leivniz, preying upon her love for order and precision. Tarin-Tiran was a joyous, free place, but not one overly given to hierarchy and strict order."

It was messy. No surprise there. But Robin had seen the architecture, the magical achievements. The place had also been a wellspring of pure creativity, art, and beauty.

"But we were the Church of Rhyth! The preeminent specialists in illusion and misdirection. We should have seen what was happening before it was too late." Nilsiir's shoulders slumped. "But we did not. And so Tarin-Tiran fell."

And so did Urkhan usurp the greater portion of Rhyth's power and cast our god into the Outer Dark, to become Lost, harrying and slaughtering the clergy across all the lands until our power was broken, scattered, and also all but lost.

Robin's mind fizzed with the revelations Nilsiir was bestowing upon him. The story of Tarin-Tiran spun before their eyes, an illusion accompanied by Nilsiir's commentary. Threaded through it all, however, was the conversation the high priest was casting directly into Robin's mind, where there was no chance of it being overheard.

Will you take up a quest from me, Robin, to restore some of what Tarin-Tiran was, that I may secure it for Rhyth's return? For our god is a canny one. His will moves unseen throughout the world, even now. I can sense it in you, in the journal of the one you call Red, and even in the sentient dungeon calling itself Ruprecht.

Oh yes. That was an easy one. Rhyth had already been kind, helping him survive—begin to thrive, even—and the chance at more power was alluring in its own right.

Good. We will discuss in more detail soon, but for now, here is an advance upon my goodwill.

Knowledge flooded Robin's mind; mystic words and sigils, gestures and the ways in which they all combined to reproduce the effect Nilsiir was using even now.

Congratulations! You have learned the spell [Lesser Figment]!

But the knowledge didn't stop there. The secrets as to how the sentient illusion was casting and manipulating multiple illusions at once also exploded into Robin's mind. It was, of course, a trick, ways in which to quickly shift the mind to keep both illusions moving by alternating your attention. Like spinning two plates at once, you had to get something in motion first.

Congratulations! You have gained the [Effortless Illusions] peculiarity!

And then, as if that were not enough, the experience galvanized something in his mind, and he heard the characteristic *ding!* of a level notification.

He'd have several more choices to make as soon as he could spare the attention.

Fascinating, came Nilsiir's voice. *What a curious illusion enchantment you are under. Useful though, from what I can see. Combined with some form of guardian spirit? How delightful! Though it is not of Rhyth's devising; I would know if it were.*

Wait. What illusion? The notifications he saw? Robin had long suspected they were a form of illusion only he could see, a figment, but an enchantment that caused them?

His mind whirled. Too much information, too quickly.

Nilsiir seemed to sense it.

I shall now reward your companions as well, as they seek knowledge themselves. Rest. Think upon what you have learned. We will speak more in this manner soon.

Robin felt the high priest's presence withdraw. His mind screamed at him from a dozen angles and unanswered questions, but he shoved them all aside.

The important thing was that he'd leveled and he had choices to make to secure his power. He wanted to get to it while Nilsiir was distracted. The high priest had been helpful, true, but they were also the high priest of a trickster, and therefore, there was only so much trust Robin was willing to extend on so short an acquaintance.

He pulled up his character sheet. The knowledge granted by Nilsiir was there, all right. His level and available pool of spell points had also increased. Everything seemed to be in order.

Robin quickly selected **[Metamagic Specialty: Duration]** for his peculiarity. If he had access to Nilsiir's tutelage, it would be useful in the near future, if not immediately, and it was required for some of the more advanced tricks he should soon have access to, as soon as he advanced to Tier Three.

Which was suddenly quite a bit closer.

Robin briefly swore at how he hadn't been able to fully optimize his experience expenditures to boost his skills, but there wasn't much he could do about it, so he set the irritation aside.

There wasn't even enough experience over the level cap to increase his *Deception* up to his new maximum!

Whatever.

Spells. He wanted to review the specifics of [**Lesser Figment**], but who knew how long he had until Nilsiir's attention returned to him? No. Better to make a choice from one of the spells he was already considering. [**Phantasmal Mouth**] would do. Good for messages and distractions, and the additional permanency option was a nice extra. Done and done.

Robin scanned over his options once more. There wasn't much else he could do right now. He closed out of his interface and focused back on what the party was doing.

Vance and Drev were comparing notes on the magical knowledge they had received. Jhess was . . . playing with a bit of shadowstuff in her hands? Just what had the illusion revealed to the rogue?! Savra looked disgruntled, but there was a glow about her suggesting she had somehow regained a measure of her divinatory powers. Robin hadn't seen light with that particular quality since before they'd arrived in Tarin-Tiran. Perhaps Nilsiir had shown her a way around whatever quality of this place blocked divinations.

"Now," the illusion spoke, "if you are agreed and willing to delve a bit deeper into the dungeon, you may help me solve the problem of Silinir's madness."

"The living dungeon?" Savra glanced at the illusion.

"Yes, though before he became this living dungeon, he was my friend and a guardian spirit of the land which came to be the guardian spirit of the city. He has subverted several mechanisms intended to keep the city safe from invaders, and changed countless other runic structures that control the magic of this place."

"Is that why there is so much wild magic everywhere?" Drev asked, curiosity glimmering in his eyes.

"Partly," Nilsiir said evasively. "There is, as you mentioned, a curse involved as well. But Silinir's efforts are not helping matters, and if left unchecked, he might one day consume the entire continent. He was, after all, first a spirit of the land. His power is . . . deep."

"What do you want us to do?" Jhess asked.

Robin squinted. She was suddenly very accommodating. Something was up there.

"Restore some of the runes to their original function. Now that I have stabilized this area, I can ensure Silinir does not reclaim them easily. Then I can keep the dungeon in check and resume my stewardship of the ruins."

And see to their eventual restoration, when Rhyth returns.

Robin felt a smile well up inside himself at the thought.

"I can promise you more knowledge and even some of the lost treasures of the city as payment," the high priest continued. "There is much that is still here, untouched. I can guide you and your living dungeon ally along hidden ways that Silinir does not yet control, though there will be great danger; I will not lie to you about that."

"That's something, at least," Savra said drily.

Nilsiir just grinned impishly at her.

The party fell into a debate; it wasn't a long one, however. They could all see the advantages here, even if Savra and Jhess showed a few signs of resistance.

"Well?" Nilsiir prompted. "You have delved into the subterranean reaches of Tarin-Tiran. Are you ready to go deeper still and learn some of its oldest secrets? To uncover some of its lost treasures?"

Fuck *yes!*

Here endeth the tale of *Descent into Tarin-Tiran*

Robin Parker

Heritage: Shadeling, Paragon
Profession: Bard
Tier: 2 (Effective Level: 9)
Experience: 50
Spell Points: 27
Bardsong: 9 uses

Properties

Free Ranks Available: 1

Physical
    -Strength: 11
    -Dexterity: 14
    -Fortitude: 11
Mental
    -Intelligence: 17
    -Cunning: 25
    -Resilience: 14
Social
    -Charisma: 15
    -Manipulation: 13
    -Poise: 16

Proficiencies

Free Ranks Available: 1

Physical (9/9)
- -Athletics: 7
- -Brawl: 6
- -Dodge: 9
- -Melee Combat: 6
- -Pilot: 4
- -Ranged Combat: 11
- -Sleight of Hand: 9
- -Stealth: 11
- -Survival: 8

Mental (9/9)
- -Arcane Lore: 10
- -Bureaucracy: 7
- -Concentration: 11
- -Crafting: 9
- -Healing: 8
- -Insight: 11
- -Learning: 9
- -Natural Wisdom: 5
- -Perception: 11

Social (9/9)
- -Animism: 5
- -Deception: 11
- -Empathy: 10
- -Expression: 11
- -Gossip: 9
- -Intimidation: 8
- -Persuasion: 10
- -Socialize: 9
- -Streetwise: 8

Peculiarities

Blessing of Rhyth
Tongue of the Fallen Tower
Mark of the Trickster

Chronicle of Infinite Visions
Mask of Myriad Faces
Initiate of the Craft
Illusion Focus
Metamagic Initiate
Improved Familiar Bond x2
Effortless Illusions
Metamagic Specialty: Duration

Perks

Wayfaring Stranger
Shard of the Shattered Manymind
Mark of Fairy's Favor
Touch of Wild Magic

Spells

Cantrips* (*no SP cost)
   -Lesser Phantasm*
   -Cutting Words*
   -Legerdemain*
   -Lesser Nightmare Curse*
   -Lesser Witch Bolt*
   -Minor Repair*
   -Lesser Charm*
Tier 1 (1SP each)
   -Visual Phantasm*
   -Healing Note
   -Whispers from Beyond
   -Minor Enchanted Slumber
   -Invisible Servant
   -Familiar Bond
   -Wizard's Armor
Tier 2 (3SP each)
   -Assume Quality (Special)
   -Lesser Mindreading
   -Sorcerous Mark
   -Phantasmal Mouth
   -Lesser Figment

Bardsong

Command Attention
Song of Arcane Power

Interlude

Meanwhile, elsewhere in Tarin-Tiran . . .

Gis scowled. The hobgoblins before him, the remnants of a scouting party, cowered before the priest's wrath. Two bodyguards, part of Gis's party, stood to either side of the Disciple of Urkhan.

All of them were safely ensconced in a hidden chamber, one of many that Urkhan's former Disciple, Melusk, had secreted throughout the city, cut off and warded from the main magical constructs which powered and guarded the place. There was a thick layer of dust over everything, marked only by the fit of rage Gis had fallen into when this chamber, like all those before it, had failed to contain any useful information on the artifact the priest was seeking.

And now, the scouts reported that most of their group had fallen prey to the living dungeon and been wiped out.

Useless insects!

Gis rubbed his temples. The task his god had given him was no simple one: descend into the depths of this accursed city and retrieve a powerful artifact which had been in the care of Melusk when the city had fallen. If Gis was unsuccessful, there was a chance that forces from within Tarin-Tiran could birth the city anew, and Urkhan was insistent that that never happen.

His priest did not know why, but it was not for him to question the motives of his god. That Urkhan desired it was reason enough.

Still, from the little he had experienced of this place's residual magic, Gis agreed with Him. This chaos was never to be allowed to spread. It too easily could challenge the rightful rule of Urkhan's faithful across the continents.

He'd seen as much when Basgar had lost that accursed keep near the Borderlands.

That blasted bard!

He was here, too. Gis knew this. Urkhan had revealed it. The last thing the priest needed was that meddling fool anywhere nearby. If anyone was likely to wake the city's slumbering powers, it was him. Gis even suspected he'd been behind the disappearance of five full companies of hobgoblins. The evidence was all wild magic, but something in his gut told him the bard was to blame.

Gehn agreed; Gis could feel it where the serpent brooded within his skull. And Gehn enjoyed an even closer connection to Urkhan than he himself did.

"Your orders, sir?" one of Gis's bodyguards spoke.

"Spare them," Gis said irritably. "They still have their uses."

As much as he would have liked to behead the two imbeciles before him, they had at least been smart enough to escape the dungeon, to return to him with information. And there were not enough hobs left under his command that he could afford to indulge a fit of pique and kill these two.

As the hobgoblins scrambled away, stammering their thanks, Gis stalked over to a chair salvaged from the detritus of the room and flung himself into it. He sat there, brooding on his plans.

They had to delve deeper—that was a given, at this point. He had hoped Melusk hadn't kept the artifact in the deepest depths of the city, but apparently, that had been a foolish hope. Gis growled. If the man weren't already dead, he'd track him down and kill him himself for the annoyance.

Smug bastard.

Not that Gis had ever met the man, but it came through in his journals, his writings; those things the Church of Urkhan had kept safe for a day like today, when an expedition to this accursed city became necessary.

"Our route, sir?" one of his bodyguards asked.

"Down, obviously," Gis snapped before sighing and elaborating. "There are three pathways we could take, but we'll have to risk the more obvious one. We'll likely need Melusk's escape route ourselves later, and if we use it to pierce the living dungeon's territory, that will be it. The dungeon will know about it and subsume it faster than we can make use of it. No. That is our escape card, and we cannot risk playing it now, howsoever more convenient it may be. We'll take the deep roads, the winding path that has been carved out of the living dungeon's territory by rebels, wild magic, and what few of our agents remain, feral or loyal as they may be."

"And the other group? The infidels and interlopers?"

Yes. The bard and his allies.

"We keep an eye out for them. If we can remove them for the glory of Urkhan, we shall, but that is not our main purpose here, and nothing must endanger that. Any deviation risks the greater mission, and this city cannot be allowed to begin resurrecting itself. Urkhan forbids it."

Gis was the newest of Urkhan's Disciples. This was a chance to prove himself. To show his power, his strength, and his ability to dominate lesser beings.

It was not going well, so far. Yes, he had assumed command of the hobgoblins. Yes, he had defied the living dungeon and survived all the monsters that had flung themselves at him. Yes, he had spat in the eye of the wild-magic surges threatening to consume everything he hoped for.

But he did not yet have the artifact His Lord required. He did not have the bard's head on a silver platter before him.

He did not have his unalloyed victory.

But he would.

Gis would descend into the depths of this accursed place, find the artifact left by his predecessor, and use its power to destroy any hope of this place ever rising again! He would conquer the living dungeon, destroying it or turning it to his will!

What a weapon that would be for the glory of Urkhan! What an achievement! That alone might secure his glory and fuel his ascent through the ranks of Urkhan's Disciples.

If he was strong enough, ruthless enough, he might even unseat the First of His Order and take her place as Right Hand of Urkhan!

So the priest sat and dreamed of glory, even as Robin and his party delved more deeply themselves guided by Nilsiir, not suspecting the evil that moved to meet them from above while Silinir awaited their challenge from below . . .

Secrets of Tarin-Tiran

Chapter 1

Robin grimaced and used **[Legerdemain]** to clean the blood splatter off of himself and the rest of his party members. The corpse of a large minotaur-like creature lay cooling rapidly nearby, with Jhess busily trying to figure out the best way to harvest its crystalline horns.

The party had made their way three or four more levels down toward the deeps of Tarin-Tiran. Ruprecht, guided by some insights from Nilsiir, had carved out a spiraling, sporadic domain as they went, carefully avoiding those areas claimed by the other living dungeon, Silinir.

"That would have been a good one to feed Ruprecht," Robin observed as Jhess triumphantly brandished the first of the two horns.

Their dungeon ally needed a steady influx of energies claimed from living beings to fuel his efforts and expansion, and the crystalline-horned minotaur had been a tough fight. It had to have had a lot of life energy to offer up.

"We've sent him plenty of monsters," Jhess replied. "Can't let him have all the fun. Some of us need to work on developing our skills as well." She shot the bard a significant look. "We can't always rely on having a dungeon along to help us do the heavy lifting."

She wasn't wrong. Ruprecht wasn't the most mobile of allies, after all, and he was as much a trickster as Robin. Relying overmuch on the dungeon would be foolish, no matter what kinship Robin might feel with him because of their odd, shared connection.

"How far are we from the target location? We have to be close," Drev said.

Robin reviewed the map Nilsiir had given them. It'd have been easier if the illusion had been able to travel with them, but that wasn't possible. Nilsiir was currently limited in the places they could manifest, though if Robin and the party succeeded, they'd be able to increase that number and occasionally have contact with the living illusion.

The quest notification he had received after they had agreed to help Nilsiir listed three main repair objectives. They weren't too terribly far apart, all things considered, but their progress was slowed by the need to try and avoid large chunks of territory claimed by Silinir.

"It should be a few hundred feet ahead, in a medium-size chamber which according to Nilsiir was once a theater of some kind." Robin was eager to see the place. It was important because it was a nexus of illusion magics keyed into the runic structures that underpinned Tarin-Tiran's existence, but it was also a place where illusions were used at a high level of sophistication to produce miraculous entertainments. There was no way he couldn't learn a lot in a place like that, maybe even snag a couple of performance-related perks.

Robin found he rather missed being in front of an audience. He'd have to rectify that after this adventure wrapped up.

"Well, what are we waiting for?" Jhess asked, stowing the second of the crystal horns in her dimensional storage.

"You," Robin replied bluntly. "We were waiting for you to loot the corpse."

"You should have helped, then," the rogue shot back, unashamed and unabashed. "Let's go! There's more treasure to be found!"

"And great danger," Savra added suddenly, her eyes distant. "We should move carefully. Something is stirring in the darkness. Something that seethes with hatred."

"Oh, yay," Robin said drily. "Something new and different for us! Deadly monsters lurking in the darkness. Love that Tarin-Tiran isn't afraid to go full-on cliche. Love that energy for us."

The party looked at him oddly. The bard just shook his head.

"Humor from my land," he explained. "Never mind. Let's go. *Carefully.*"

I am advancing down the tunnel ahead of you. I have garnered sufficient energies from my other efforts to make up some ground here.

Was that a bit of a waspish tone in Ruprecht's mental voice? Surely not. The dungeon couldn't be that annoyed they weren't hand-feeding him every single meal, right?

Right?

Robin made a mental note to have some more conversations with

Ruprecht, and also secure something valuable to feed the dungeon in addition to the monsters they sent his way. It never hurt to be generous with alien entities who could exert control over your nearby reality to a shocking degree.

The party made its way forward, cautiously checking the shadows for unexpected surprises. Ruprecht assured them things were safe, but with the magical nature of Tarin-Tiran, it didn't hurt to be too careful. The party had already run into a summoning trap which had dumped a small pack of glittering-scaled kobolds upon them. That had been within Ruprecht's boundaries, too. It seemed like, while he could assimilate a lot, magic took a great deal longer than mundane materials, and the advanced magics of Tarin-Tiran—possibly warped by Silinir—were stubborn, persistent, and sneaky.

Exactly as one would expect.

So the party moved cautiously, Robin possibly less so than the others, keen to reach the theater and the riches of knowledge it might conceal. His quest notification had implied—though not promised—that there might be such opportunities for going along with Nilsiir's plan.

The high priest's words also still niggled at Robin's brain. What precisely was this system which allowed him to manipulate his powers and offered guidance—possibly manipulation—in the form of quests? Illusion, divination, there was a lot of very high-level magic bound up in whatever enchantment was upon Robin, and while it might be manipulating him, it also offered him a great deal of power and a lot of say in how he accrued, shaped, and used such power.

"Careful," Jhess warned.

Robin had nearly put his foot down on a pile of loose gravel, which might have sent him sprawling and almost certainly would have resulted in a bit of noise which might have alerted whatever was dark, dangerous, and waiting for them up ahead.

He nodded his thanks to the rogue and adjusted his gait, resolving to pay more attention to his current problems and less to hypotheticals brought up by the words of an illusory high priest of a trickster deity.

Put like that . . . yeah, Robin definitely needed more information before coming to any sort of conclusion.

There was less wear and tear on their surroundings, deeper in the city. The fighting had hit less hard here in this area, and the buildings were less exposed to the elements. There was much to admire in the smooth shifting between architectural styles as they made their way along.

Some of the enchanted lights still worked, though whether that was down to craftsmanship or the influence of Silinir, Robin couldn't say. He kept his eye sharply tuned for any evidence of runic structure or eldritch knowledge. Even if he couldn't decipher it right now, his power of recall might make it possible to do so in the future, when he was more advanced in his facility with magic of all kinds.

Speaking of magical knowledge, Robin cast a small illusion of the runic structures Nilsiir had instructed him to memorize before embarking on the quest. Theoretically, they would help repair the damage time and the living dungeon had done to these key locations, allowing Nilsiir to manifest and regain some control of the surrounding area. If Robin and his party could restore all three, Nilsiir had promised them not only that they'd be able to open one or more of the hidden treasure vaults of Tarin-Tiran for Robin and his friends, but also that the illusion might be able to curtail some of Silinir's excesses, making the city safer to explore.

"What do you think of this whole proposition?" Robin murmured to Savra as they walked. "How far would you trust Nilsiir?"

The seeress looked at him, and Robin was pleased to see a hint of surprise cross her face.

"I would not trust the high priest as far as I could throw him," she answered wryly. "And yet, helping him is—from what little my vision can see—the correct course of action for us. It will be dangerous, true, but I see great opportunity there as well, perhaps even wealth whose value outweighs any dangers we might face." She weighed Robin with her eyes. "Curious that you would ask me my opinion on this now."

"I agree it's worth the risk." Robin shrugged. "Doesn't mean I don't want to make sure there isn't an angle I've missed, and you're the other person here most likely to spot such a thing."

"I think it would be overall a good thing for Tarin-Tiran to rise again," Savra said after a moment's consideration. "My Lady would approve, I think."

"It must be hard, being cut off from her voice in this place, of all places."

"It is. However, it is also very . . . instructive." Savra grimaced. "I think perhaps that may be part of the value I am to take away from here. A bit more self-reliance, a bit more caution in thinking through the visions I can see, though they are fragmented and unsure."

"I do wonder what that's like, sometimes," Robin admitted. "Feeling such a close connection to your deity. I imagine it's nice, but I suppose part of that depends on the deity in question."

"There is almost always a euphoria to it," Savra replied. "Even in the case of the foulest of gods, goddesses, or deities. The touch of the divine is primal; it is a connection to an aspect of all creation, and that is always a powerful thing."

"The sublime and the grotesque," Robin murmured, half-remembering something from an art history course he'd audited for a couple weeks but never actually took.

"Exactly so." Savra nodded. "It is more intense if you have a connection to the aspects your deity represents or embodies, of course, like a sailor who truly loves the sea connecting to a goddess that represents it, but the feeling will be there even if he instead came mind to mind with a god of the lonely desert. It is like looking upon a beautiful untouched forest from a great height or being carried into the air for the first time when flying. There's something primal and wondrous, even if the experience may also be terrifying. It is hard not to respond to that, as a person of almost any kind or heritage."

Before they could continue, their conversation was interrupted by Ruprecht.

We've got company up ahead!

Chapter 2

Robin sent Rerebos to scout. The little dragon slipped into the shadows, going invisible for good measure. Ruprecht had been held back from advancing into the target room proper by the presence of another team of adventurers, and Robin had a sneaking suspicion who Rerebos might see if he got close enough. His stomach jumped off a cliff into a bottomless chasm when it was confirmed.

Gis. The evil old man was here, with bodyguards and backup no less! They were ransacking the place, tearing it apart in search of something.

Don't get too close! Robin sent to Rerebos as Gis's eyes suddenly pierced the shadows where the little dragon was hiding. *He has some kind of familiar in his head. I'm not sure how much it sees, but it can sense lies.*

I will rip the pretender from the foul priest's skull and claim its skull as my rightful spoils of victory!

Robin sensed a wave of hatred emanating from his familiar. Not that he didn't agree, but he was a bit surprised at the depth and quality of Rerebos's ire. He could sense that part of it was a dislike for what the priest and his snake stood for, but the larger share was for how Gis had harried Robin in the past.

Which was a bit touching, as most of those bad memories were from *before* Robin had summoned his familiar.

"What do you see?" Jhess whispered.

Robin recounted what he saw through Rerebos's eyes. Then, after a moment, he added what context he could.

"Gis is a priest of Urkhan. When last I saw him, I'd recently pissed him off quite a bit by ruining him and his god's plans to take over a local keep. He has a snake that lives in his left eye socket—"

"Seriously?" Jhess looked green. "That's disgusting."

"It fits his personality," Robin observed drily. "It also has some ability to magically sense lies—"

"I'm sure that was fun for you," Vance interrupted with a smile.

"Can we be serious, please?" Drev pleaded. "We've got enemies on all sides, including a dungeon that wants to eat us!"

I assure you I have better taste than that.

Robin hid his grin.

"He's a devout follower of Urkhan, and that he survived Basgar's failure at the Keep says how much his god values him."

"He's very dangerous," Savra said slowly. "I cannot see much around him, but his connection to the one he serves is incredibly strong. He may even have risen to disciplehood, if he did not have it when last you met."

"I don't think he did, but I can't say for sure." Robin shook his head. "I don't know enough about it to be certain, but he does have more of an aura around him, now." Robin glanced again through Rerebos's eyes. "Yeah. There is an extra gravitas to him, a feeling of iron. He's definitely more powerful. Besides, he was taking all the orders before; now, he's giving them. Something's changed."

"What about those accompanying him?" Vance asked. "Can you tell us anything about what their capabilities might be?"

"Two big guys in full armor, real dark-knight stuff. Black metal, spikes, the whole *fear me, I'm a bloody tyrant, rar* vibe. One has a massive hammer—a maul, maybe?—and the other has a nasty-looking mace. No blades that I can see."

"The faithful knights of Urkhan tend to use blunt instruments rather than blades," Savra noted, "as those weapons more purely express the power of force. Blades have connotations of requiring skill or finesse, and Urkhan prefers expressions of simple power over everything else. I think we need to assume they may be Dark Paladins or have some form of magic to enhance their combat capabilities."

"Agreed," Vance said. "I've met the type before. Seems likely. What else?"

"Two hobgoblins in leathers," Robin continued, "moving nervously around the perimeter. I'm guessing they're scouts of some kind. They look scared of the others they're with; we might be able to scare them off, take them out of the picture with minimal effort."

"Or just stab 'em when they're not looking," Jhess said, casually flipping a dagger.

"There's a brutal-looking woman with scarred cheeks in some very businesslike robes," Robin continued. "Some kind of mage, I'd guess."

"Scarred adepts," Drev jumped in. "They would fit with the ideals of the Church of Urkhan: channel bodily force to produce magical effects. They tend to play mostly with elemental tricks—fireballs, lightning bolts, your basic energy manipulations. It can be effective, but you don't need any real skill. Very basic magical workings."

"Any others?" Jhess asked. "Or is that it?"

Robin hesitated.

"I don't see anyone else," he spoke slowly, "but I'm not sure. There might be someone else in reserve? They've got a lot of brute force, but there's no way they can bash their way through this dungeon on main strength alone. There are too many traps and tricks. Is there any way he could be that powerful? Because if he is, we might need to abandon this part of the quest for now. Go fix another of the target areas, then return to this one after they've left."

Robin winced. Gis and his crew were doing a lot of damage to their surroundings, tearing apart seats and benches, ripping decorative paneling off the walls, defacing runic structures when they revealed themselves—there might not be enough left to salvage when they were through with the place!

Not only was that a huge loss to history and, more to the point, Robin's personal accumulation of knowledge, but it might cause them to fail their quest! Nilsiir had given them the know-how to effect minor repairs, but something that was seriously damaged or destroyed? That would be beyond them.

Robin passed along what Gis and his minions were up to, as well as his concerns. As much as he would love to sneak in there, bloody the priest's nose, and then lure them all back as a snack for Ruprecht, it was up to the party to make an assessment of what should be their course of action.

Because it *could* end in a slaughter.

"You don't think we could take them face-to-face?" Vance asked, running a thumb along the edge of a paper blade.

"We might be able to," Robin conceded. "But we're outnumbered and have no way of knowing how much divine punch the old geezer is packing. That's hard to counter."

"Can we find out? Test them somehow?" Drev suggested.

Robin looked to Savra. The seeress looked dubious.

"I can try," she said, "but my powers are hindered down here."

"There are one or two things I could try as well," Robin admitted grudgingly, "but I'd need to get closer, undetected. I can't do as much from a distance as Savra can."

The seeress looked at him for a moment as if sifting his words before she nodded like she had found something.

Robin bit back a hiss. Why the fuck did she have to do that? It was bad enough that just being in her presence gave him the heebie-jeebies.

"Right, while she's doing her thing, what are our other options?" Jhess asked.

"Baiting them into chasing us through a series of death traps designed by Ruprecht," Robin said immediately. "He's one of our best cards, if we can set up a play where he can bring his strength to bear."

"Dangerous," Drev observed. "We might not be able to get away, or they could prove too powerful, as you said, and have no trouble circumventing Ruprecht's traps." Drev reached out to press a hand to the wall. "No offense. Your work is exemplary, but we do need to consider all scenarios."

No offense taken. However, I, too, would dearly love to bloody the nose of that walking pile of excrement.

Robin perked up his ears at that. That was some serious dislike there. That sounded . . . personal. Had Ruprecht had a run-in with Gis as well?

"Sounds like we still want a slightly better assessment of their capabilities," Vance said.

"We could lead another monster to them, send it in and see how they deal with it," Jhess suggested.

"If we can find one," Robin added. "Don't get me wrong, I love the idea, but we may not have time. They're destroying the place now. If we want to preserve it, we might not have time to hunt down some cannon fodder."

"Every divination I have turned to the question of whether our facing off with the group in the room right now ends with a mix of weal and woe," Savra started, eyes distant, "has shown there is great danger. I think overall the danger is greater than the reward, but not so great that bracing them would spell certain doom."

"So we're probably slightly outmatched, but there's a chance we could still trick our way into a victory," Robin concluded. "Got it."

"It is uncertain," Savra said unhelpfully.

"Let me see if I can sneak closer and get some more solid information." Robin sighed. "But we should have a plan for if they spot me and this all goes tits up."

The party outlined a strategy quickly, and Ruprecht, though limited in energies, set to creating some limited traps and hidden passages they could use to escape if things went truly wrong.

Robin made sure he had the plan solid in his mind, checked with Rerebos that Gis and his lackeys hadn't changed their behavior in the meantime, and then moved slowly down the corridor, wrapping himself in shrouding illusions and assuming a form more suited to stealthy movement.

He quickly and quietly cast his mind-reading spell; it might not reveal exactly how powerful they all were, but with some luck, he'd find out what they were looking for and what, if anything, they might be afraid of could be lurking down here in the dark with them. That would be useful knowledge for the upcoming confrontation.

And it would hopefully tell him exactly how to screw over the evil old man and his wankstain of a god. With extreme prejudice. Because not only did Robin owe Gis a bad turn or three for their past encounters, it sounded like he owed Urkhan more than a few bad turns for what the god had done to Rhyth and Tarin-Tiran.

"Here we go," Robin muttered as the spell settled into place.

Chapter 3

Robin crept carefully into the room, his flesh changed for that of an elf suffused with grace and dexterity, and his shadow spun around him by illusion into a slowly shifting field of darkness that blended with the interplay of light and shade all around. Nary a sound slipped from the soft soles of his bare feet, and the stone beneath his toes was cool and eerily smooth.

Flesh on stone. Robin smiled. Brought back memories.

And at least this time he wasn't *fully* naked.

Gis had been there as well. The thought snuffed Robin's burgeoning good mood like a cold wind snapped out a candle. And the evil old man was, if anything, even more dangerous now.

Focus.

The priest was in the center of the room, sourly surveying every move his compatriots made. The two largest brutes, melee specialists by the looks of them, were taking a break-it-now, search-the-rubble-later approach. Robin carefully dipped into their minds, as they were likely to put up less resistance than Gis or the caster-types, and were less likely to notice him teasing at the edges of their minds.

They didn't notice. Robin concentrated. They were definitely looking for something specific. A passageway? Leading to some kind of secret chamber. And in that chamber . . .

"Anything?" Gis snapped.

"No, sir," the smaller of the two brutes answered. "Not yet."

Robin bit back a curse. They were looking for something, but Gis had interrupted the chain of thought before he could get a good sense of what it was.

"Keep looking," Gis ordered, punctuating his irritation with a sigh. "Eyes sharp! The passage must be here somewhere."

The fighters simply nodded and resumed their destructive search. While their faces were placid, Robin could feel the irritation and resentment simmering in their thoughts, tempered with more than enough fear to ensure they obeyed Gis's orders, for all that they resented the power the priest wielded over them.

They were also entirely focused on finding the hidden passage, with no thoughts straying to the ultimate goal of their search. Robin bit his cheek. He had to put the irritation somewhere, and it wasn't like he was wearing his own body anyway.

It still fucking hurt.

He was going to have to risk reading the mage—whose eyes glimmered with magical energies as she searched with more esoteric senses—or Gis himself.

Robin decided to start with the mage. Still safer than the priest, though he'd have to move very carefully. He had no idea just how much her enchanted eye might see.

He brought the shroud of shadows closer around his body, minimizing the surface area of magic which might possibly betray his presence to the woman in robes. He knew from talking to Drev that magical energies were intense, and it was hard to sense them very far out with enchanted vision. Savra affirmed it was the same for diviners, though the seeress had been a bit smug about just how much further their sight could pierce compared to those of dilettantes or initiates of other magical traditions. Still, Robin knew he could get close enough to try dipping into her mind without being spotted by her mage sight. If he was careful.

If he was lucky.

There was a whisper of sound as a pebble beneath his feet shifted. The hobgoblin scouts' ears twitched. Robin froze.

If he didn't stupidly give himself away by not paying attention to where he was going.

Or was it something else? Misfortune, perhaps?

Robin felt a twinge in his [Touch of Wild Magic] perk. Was it simply bad luck? The scales balancing out all the times he'd squeaked past disaster? Or could Silinir somehow sense him thanks to that [Touch of Wild Magic] on his soul? Had it drawn the dungeon's full attention?

Whatever the ultimate case, Robin could wrestle with it later. For now, he had to deal with some increasingly alert hobgoblin scouts.

Robin twisted his fingers through the gestures of [Lesser Phantasm] and cast the faint sound of stone scraping on stone down the tunnel to his left. Not the one opposite him, and not the one leading back to the rest of Robin's party. Either of those would just be asking for trouble if the scouts were truly suspicious.

The hobgoblins shared a glance. Something passed between them, a flicking of the eyes, and one moved to investigate the tunnel. The other stayed in the room and began to methodically search, moving carefully around the perimeter and sweeping for unseen creatures. Looking for an invisible monster? Robin dipped into the hobgoblin's mind and confirmed that was indeed what the scout suspected.

Worse, the hob's focus on finding a hidden enemy meant there was no hint as to what Gis and his party were actually looking for here in the depths of Tarin-Tiran.

Robin moved slowly in a spiral, carefully treading his way among the destruction and suspicion to come to rest in a nook behind the hobgoblin, in an area the scout had already searched. It wasn't a perfect hiding place, but it would take the pressure off.

There was no hope for it. He would have to risk reading Gis's mind, even if he had to try and lean on his [Touch of Wild Magic] in the hopes of gaining a small advantage in piercing the evil old man's mental resistance.

And he managed it! Robin slipped into Gis's mind like a fop into a sewer: slowly, resentfully, and cringing at the filth all around him.

The surface layer of Gis's thoughts was all emotion: impatience, irritation, lust for power, and the desire to hold something in his hands.

That had to be it! Robin tried to follow the thread, the desire for something. It had to lead to what they were really looking for!

And it did. For one brief moment, Robin *saw* what it was that Gis sought. It was a crown of black iron, roughly wrought and pitted, with what looked to be crude runes stamped into the circumference and filled with blood-red enamel.

A flash of a face. Melusk? What did the politician have to do with this crown?

A sense of reverence. Urkhan? There was a sense of respect—reverence, even—for the crown. Religious regalia? A divine artifact of some kind?

Robin longed to know more, but any further knowledge was held more deeply within Gis's mind, beyond the reach of his spell. The only way to get at it would be to ask questions, to pull it to the surface.

The bard briefly contemplated using **[Lesser Phantasm]** to try and replicate one of Gis's other party members' voices asking a leading question. It would get him a snippet more information as Gis's mind reacted before suspicion shut everything down. But it would be only a snippet, and then Gis would be warned. He would know someone was here; someone who suspected what he was after. That would make him infinitely more dangerous in a second.

Even as it was, suspicion was rising in Gis's mind. The old priest shook his head in irritation and squinted into the shadows.

"There's something here," he snapped. There was a ripple of force in Gis's mind, and Robin fell back into the wall with a gasp, his mind reeling from the backlash of the priest's iron will. "Find it!"

Robin winced and began moving slowly and carefully away from where he'd been hiding. There was no way the scout hadn't heard that gasp, and he would be zeroing in on the area.

Being able to fly would have come in really handy right now. Robin cursed himself for not assuming the form of a winged elf. That would have served his stealth purposes just as well, though his flight would have been clumsy and cost him a great deal in terms of magical energies. And even then, the sound of his wings might have given him away anyway.

That gave him an idea.

Robin quickly twisted his hands through the gestures of **[Lesser Phantasm]**, and the sound of wings moving across the cavern and away from himself softly whispered through the cavern. The bastards immediately refocused, allowing the bard to fall back toward the tunnel that would lead him back to his party.

As he did so, he got a better look at the damage Gis's party had caused already. Rock was cracked and broken, mosaic pieces scattered wildly all over the room. It would take a great deal of time or some very efficient uses of magic to sort that out and restore it. Some of the runic structures exposed by the search had also been deliberately defaced with chisel marks and cracks from blunt weaponry.

What a mess.

Robin's lips tightened into a thin line. There was no way they could allow this to continue! The bastards would do so much damage they'd never be able to repair the place! They'd fail Nilsiir's quest almost before they'd even begun!

He needed to get Gis and company away from here, quickly repair the place, and fall back. Nilsiir could then control the area and keep the evil old man from finding the passageway he sought.

The longer Gis was kept away from that crown, the better. Robin longed to know what it was—what it did—but that was a mystery for later. Now was a time for action. For dealing with the immediate problem.

He sent a thread of will through [**Visual Phantasm**], losing the protection of his illusory shadows but trusting in the shield of actual darkness to keep him safe. He needed to signal the rest of his party. They were going to have to take steps.

Plan C. Come in hot. Be ready to fall back fast.

Chapter 4

Robin needed a distraction. No, he *was* the distraction. He just needed an idea that wouldn't get him skewered or put him in the line of whatever ability Gis regularly used to usurp the will of other beings.

The rest of his party would attack soon; Robin needed Gis and his mooks to be looking the other way when that happened. If they could do some serious damage, take one or two of Gis's team members out right away, it would go a long way to making this encounter a survivable one. They might even win it.

Although, as Gis seemed to have gone through some kind of power-up, that might be a fool's hope.

Well, there were entrances to and from Silinir's territory all through-out Tarin-Tiran. You could never be too far from one once you descended beneath the surface level of the city. Might as well use that.

Robin concentrated. Something phantasmal but still fitting with the crystalline, wild-magic flavor of the area would be ideal. Phantasmal horde of crystal rats, perhaps?

His fingers flashed through the gestures of [**Lesser Phantasm**], and a chittering arose, sounding as if it were drifting down the tunnel on the opposite side.

"Ugh," the woman in mage's robes complained. "Sounds like more of those rats. Haven't we squashed enough of them yet?"

Robin used [**Visual Phantasm**] to add flickers of light flashing in the shadows down that tunnel; enough to imply the presence of the glowing crystals embedded in the rats' skulls, at least.

The hobgoblins began sniffing suspiciously, throwing glances at Gis as if expecting the priest to say something.

He did.

"You." He pointed at the leftmost scout. "Go and deal with this. It's just a few rats."

The hobgoblin looked like he would like to argue, but he clearly knew better than to do so. He headed toward the tunnel while the rest of Gis's party returned to their search.

That wouldn't do. The whole group needed to be distracted. Time to amp up the threat.

Robin added the sound of a minotaur's roaring, a deep, crystalline reverberation beneath it. The sound was fresh enough in his mind, after all, and *that* would make Gis and his minions pay attention. Especially if Robin backed up the sound with a bit of terror of his own making.

The bard uttered [**Whispers from Beyond**], weaving it into the gaps in the illusory sound he had conjured and targeting the mage. It was a slightly tougher target, but safer than Gis. Besides, something told Robin that the two meatheads in Gis's service might have some kind of fear resistance. Just an instinct, but he might as well follow it.

The mage staggered, face blanching white as whey, and the sooty red light that had been building around her frame to enhance her strength flickered and died.

The melee specialists had drawn their weapons and were already advancing toward the tunnel, grins of anticipation on their faces. Gis stood behind them and to one side, impatience radiating off his thin frame. The scouts were crouched athwart either side of the tunnel entrance, clearly taking up positions to flank or hamstring targets as the opportunity presented itself.

Everyone was focused on the tunnel, and that was the moment when Vance charged in, making a beeline straight for the staggered mage. The librarian had clearly been paying attention, and the glory of a warrior of legend flared around him like a corona. Purple-white missiles of pure force flared around him, also lancing forward to strike the mage.

The sword of paper flew, aimed straight for the woman's neck, only to be brought to a halt at the last second.

"Freeze!" Gis shouted, stopping Vance in his tracks. The immobility only lasted a few seconds, but that was long enough to arrest the librarian's momentum and for the mage to stagger away.

Robin trusted Vance to handle himself and immediately launched an attack on the priest while he was distracted. This time, he did gamble on [**Whispers from Beyond**]. Anything else he had would do a bit of damage or distract, but if he could get that spell to land, it would take Gis out of the battle for several crucial seconds.

It didn't work. Gis's will was too strong.

"Bort! Cliv!" Gis's voice was the lash of a whip. "Pay attention! There is a threat at our heels!"

The meatheads turned from the tunnel and, after sharing a glance, one took up a defensive position between the tunnel and Robin's party while the other moved—impossibly quickly—to engage Vance.

It was not a good matchup. Vance was all about skill, but his opponent was a mountain of a man who used brute force for both offense and defense. Given time, Vance could wear his opponent down, use the gap in skill to maximize on small mistakes, but Vance wasn't going to have that time. The mage was recovering, and Gis had shaken off Robin's spell with no obvious effects. The party was outnumbered physically, and definitely couldn't match the magic most probably at Gis's command right now.

Even as Robin watched, the priest incanted a spell, and roiling chains of mist began to spiral out from him. Shades—half-seen figures bound in some kind of spectral service to the priest—wailed at the ends of the chains, clutching and grasping at any who came near Gis, and the effect spread out a few dozen feet from him.

Robin quickly and quietly fell back, trying to avoid getting caught in the effect. He didn't know what it did, but it would likely reveal his presence, and that wasn't something he was prepared to risk.

Vance was also falling back before his opponent's advance, and the recuperated mage was powering back up, the red nimbus around her deflecting most of Drev's bolts of force. Daggers flew through the air as Jhess took shots of opportunity guided by Savra's insight, but soon, Robin's friends would go from holding their own to being driven back by Gis's force.

Robin called on **[Whispers from Beyond]** **once more,** but he chose a new target: the hobgoblin scout cowering near the tunnel. They needed a distraction to cover their retreat.

This time, the spell took, and the hobgoblin screamed in horror as the impossible sounds sank into his ear and began twisting his brain around itself. The scout took off running, slamming wildly into the wall before ricocheting off and sprinting away down the closest tunnel.

"What—idiots!" Gis shouted.

The party fell back, following their plan.

Well, most of them did. Robin wasn't in position, driven too far to one side by Gis's spectral defenses.

"After them!" Gis snapped. "No! You too. Leave the idiot," the priest snapped at the hobgoblin as he made to chase after his companion.

Reluctantly, the hob turned to follow Gis's orders.

Robin filed that away in case it was a potential weak point. For now, he focused on staying still and silent and not getting caught. If he was going to be stuck on the other side of Gis from his party, he wasn't going to take any chances, though he would take any opportunity to stab the old bastard in the back that presented itself.

He followed behind, trailing Gis's group as they chased after Robin's party. The bard used **[Visual Phantasm]** whenever he could, trying to keep Gis and his minions from getting a solid line of sight on Robin's companions.

"They've got that illusionist with them," Gis growled at one point, loud enough for Robin to catch. "Has to be him. Lord Urkhan . . ."

The priest moved out of range, and Robin cursed but followed. Ahead of them all, his party took potshots and dodged what turned out to be traps. Gis and his party were terrifyingly efficient at circumventing most of the challenges Ruprecht had cooked up along the way. They didn't see all of them, but there was enough defensive magic at hand to blunt the worst of the damage, and Gis's dark gifts from Urkhan were enough to force the body to heal, even though the pain of the priest's care was clearly excruciating.

Robin didn't imagine a bone being commanded to heal would do so in any way that was pleasant, and the screams of pain from Bort or Cliv or whoever it was seemed to agree. They still moved with terrifying speed and efficiency, and Robin catalogued each and every power he witnessed, every trick they pulled. No one had yet spotted him, and he was gathering valuable information even when his mind-reading spell had long since expired.

It continued this way for several minutes while Robin grew increasingly worried. Gis had grown in power, notably and visibly. His companions were nowhere near as powerful, but each of them was worrying in their own way. And though there was clearly fractiousness between several of them, Gis's iron-handed rule always quashed dissent before it could impact their overall effectiveness.

Much.

But there was little sign that Robin's party was going to escape pursuit. Gis was too much of a dynamo, his healing energies and irresistible commands continuing to drive his compatriots on even when they might have otherwise stopped.

Then something stopped them.

Well, not so much stopped as catapulted them in an entirely new and unexpected direction: straight down. The entire floor of the tunnel suddenly vanished, falling into the darkness and taking Gis and company with it.

Robin barely managed to stop himself from rushing over the edge, he had been following so quickly on their heels, worry for his party gnawing at his gut.

Rocks crashed and rumbled, tumbling down into the dark. Briefly, Gis's magic lit up the shadows with a crimson flare, but that vanished quickly.

Then there was silence.

"Hey, bard!" Jhess broke it a moment later, calling from across the pit. "You all right over there?"

"Fine, yeah," Robin called back. "What happened?"

I dropped them down a shaft that intersects with Silinir's territory. I couldn't expand too close to it, lest I risk alerting the other dungeon, so I have no idea how lethal or not it might be, but it should at least distract them for a good while.

"And they can't climb or fly back up?" Jhess asked, fingering the edge of her dagger.

No. I collapsed a deadfall and sealed the tunnel on top of them.

"Old one-eye isn't going to like that." Robin smiled. "Well done, Ruprecht!"

Still, they had no confirmation that the priest was dead. That was a sobering thought. And it meant they had very little time to waste. If Robin knew anything about Gis, it was that the old priest was as persistent as he was mean.

"We need to move," he indicated. "We can't count on our enemies being down for the count, and with what I learned from their minds, we can't afford to let them get ahead of us."

"Why?" Savra looked at him sharply. "What did you see?"

"Nothing good," Robin said, striding off into the darkness. "It's like this . . ."

Chapter 5

*I*t's no use," Robin sighed. "They've done too much damage."

The illusory construct he had been trying to stretch across the chamber collapsed. Robin massaged his temples. He'd strained to focus and make it work, but even without running out of magical energies thanks to [**Visual Phantasm**] being free to cast, it was too much.

He only had so much mental energy and imagination to burn at any one time.

The party was back in the chamber their quest had directed them to. Unfortunately, the damage was more extensive than Robin had initially estimated. No matter what he did, he was unable to conjure enough illusions to cover the damaged sections.

Fucking Gis.

"Not much of use here, either," Jhess complained from where she had been rummaging through the packs Gis and his party had left behind when they'd pursued them to an inevitable and hilarious pit-trap drop.

Well, hilarious from Robin's perspective, anyway.

"I mean, sure, there's a bit of food, some rope, and other dungeoneering supplies, but it looks like all their best gear was on them."

"Any journals or maps?" Vance asked.

"Not that I've found," Jhess replied, kicking the rucksack nearest to her.

"Let Ruprecht eat it," Robin suggested. "He can recreate anything useful, and maybe if there's a secret inside that we missed, his assimilation can find it."

"So what do we do next?" Drev asked, practical as ever.

Robin watched Rerebos flitting throughout the chamber in search of shinies.

"I think we try to find one of the other locations Nilsiir gave us and repair it," he said.

With a sense of sick dread, Robin pulled up the quest log and looked over it. His heart sank when the relevant lines flickered into being before his eyes. It was not ideal. The part pertaining to this location had been crossed out. A clear failure. There was no way he was going to be able to fix this place, even with help from Ruprecht, assuming the dungeon managed to assimilate all the territory. There had just been too much damage.

But maybe not all was lost.

He brightened a little when he noticed the quest itself didn't seem to have failed, which meant that there were other locations they could find and repair to complete it! They just needed to get to the next one before something else happened to it, then Robin and his team could talk to Nilsiir and get some alternate options.

He suggested as much to the party, sans the bits about his personal quest.

"We have what, two other options?" Jhess asked. "Flip a coin," she suggested with a shrug.

As one, the party looked at Savra. The seeress had already tossed the coin into the air where it spun, glittering, before coming down in her hand. Twice more she flipped it. Three times flipped. Three questions answered.

"Either one," she said. "There is great danger and great opportunity in each direction. I can't see much of a difference."

Great danger and great opportunity in every direction. Sounded like Tarin-Tiran to Robin!

He conjured an illusory map for them all to consult.

"The closer one is almost directly below us," he began before Ruprecht interrupted him.

It is possible that your pursuers from earlier survived their fall, and if so, there is a chance that places them substantially closer to that location than we are.

"And the other is further away but on this level," Robin followed up smoothly, though his stomach flip-flopped a bit at the thought that Gis could be both alive and beating them to their next target as well. There couldn't be *that* many places left which suited Nilsiir's needs, not without trying to wrest more territory from Silinir, and Robin certainly didn't relish that idea.

"Go for the one on this level," Jhess spoke. "Less competition."

"It'll slow us down a great deal, though," Drev objected. "Look how we'll have to travel to avoid Silinir's demesne." The mage pointed to the route Robin had marked out as the safer option.

"Still," Jhess said.

The party began arguing the merits and flaws of each option. Robin wasn't really happy with either one, but found himself coming down in favor of the slightly slower option. It was safer, and they definitely needed a win where they could speak with Nilsiir.

In the end, they agreed to go for the slower but safer route. No one really fancied another go-round so soon with Gis and whichever of his party members had survived. And there was no way Gis at least hadn't survived. Nine hells, Robin wouldn't be surprised if Gis turned out to be the only survivor but somehow managed to use the bodies of his compatriots as bait or bribes to dominate a whole replacement party of monstrous beings.

Seemed like the sort of thing Gis would manage to do. Especially since Urkhan seemed to value him so much more highly now.

The party moved slowly toward their destination, with Jhess and Rerebos scouting ahead and luring various weak monsters back to fuel Ruprecht's expansion. More challenging foes were dealt with by the party together. There were old traps and deadfalls, and in one instance, a cloud of living crystalline spores flowing on the subterranean breeze.

That one got away.

Probably a good thing; Robin had limited healing, and he wasn't certain Savra's powers extended to dealing with fungal infections or other parasites.

Eventually, however, they found their way to the section of city marked on Robin's illusory map. It was a place of red brick and slate, of iron lampposts with shattered glass still clinging to them like jagged and decaying teeth. Most of the buildings here had more extreme levels of obvious deterioration. Brick, unlike stone, didn't weather the eons so well.

Robin wondered what that said about how intact or not the runic structures maintaining the city were in this place. This much decay argued there would be a lot of degradation in the magic to compensate for.

"This way." Robin pointed left. "There should be a sort of town square or something down there, over by that pile of bricks."

"You're going to have to be more specific." Jhess moved nimbly over the fallen walls all around them. "Seems like it's more brick pile than street, honestly."

Robin just pointed, attention on his own footing.

Jhess shrugged and moved ahead of the party, Rerebos circling her head. The rogue had little problem with moving through the uneven terrain.

Robin considered shifting to a form better suited to it, but then decided to conserve his magical energies. There was no way wherever they were headed to wasn't the lair of *something*. It wouldn't be a quest if it were a simple move-and-repair job. No. Something nasty would be living there. He was sure of it.

Better to conserve his strength for now.

"Oh, you have *got* to see this," Jhess called from ahead.

Robin quashed the urge to hurry. He'd get there soon enough. It could wait.

But then he got there, and he mentally kicked himself for not being able to see it sooner.

The building the party was staring at sat in the center of a spacious square. Four roads—one on each side—led up to it, with what looked to be row houses in varying states of decay lining the sides and corners between, though none of them were as bad as others the party had passed so far.

But that alone wasn't the remarkable thing. No, that honor went to the soaring gothic stonework of the building in the center. It looked like a very large church or a very small cathedral, in aesthetic if not in layout.

The stone was blackened in places, to be sure, but there were also glorious stained glass windows in a riot of reds, purples, and golds. Without light from within, Robin couldn't make out what the images might be, but he could at least catch glimmers of color by Drev's magelight.

And it was intact. Pristine. Robin couldn't see any decay at all, in fact. Either there was a very good illusion in place, or the magic here was still going strong after all these centuries.

Very strong.

"It looks like a church," Jhess said, stating the obvious for everyone.

"Doesn't feel like one," Savra murmured thoughtfully. "Doesn't feel like one at all."

"Are we close enough to be sure, though?" Robin asked, even when at his core he agreed with the seeress. Something about the place didn't feel sacred nor holy, although it might have at one point; it did have that air about it. He'd been to enough bars and stayed in enough hostels in converted church grounds. He added, "Or it might have been deconsecrated and given over to another use."

"I suppose that is possible," Savra conceded. "It's not common, but it does happen. Places change. Gods leave."

"So what do we think it is now?" Vance asked, eyes avid with curiosity.

Robin grinned. So what if there was a monster waiting for them inside? This was Tarin-Tiran! This was an adventure! And once they sorted that bit out, they could have another audience with Nilsiir and get him one step closer to the completion of his quest!

"Why don't we find out?"

Chapter 6

Robin slowly eased himself through the door. Drev had checked for wards, and Jhess and Rerebos had scouted ahead and hadn't found anything, but Savra's divinations and Robin's instincts said there was still great danger within.

Still, nothing ventured, nothing gained.

There was something here. There had to be. If they couldn't see it, that just made it more dangerous, not less. Robin quickly opened his character sheet and checked his experience levels. Didn't he have some room to expand?

Oh, yeah. Plenty of points to play with.

He quickly maxed out both *Perception* and *Insight* to give himself the best chance of spotting anything hidden, then, to be safe, maxed out *Stealth* as well.

What else? He couldn't quite afford to max out *Dodge*, but it might be useful. He could take *Dodge* up two ranks, *Healing* up three, or *Arcane Lore* up a single rank, and still have his emergency experience buffer.

Robin went with *Dodge*. An ounce of prevention was worth a pound of cure, after all, and both Vance and Drev were here with their stores of arcane knowledge; plus, he had **[Bardic Lore]**. *Dodge* was probably the smartest move right now.

And hopefully, they'd be getting a lot more experience soon.

He ran an eye over his character sheet once more in case there was anything else, but all the lowest hanging fruit had long since been plucked. He was in it for the long experience haul now, unless he somehow replaced a skill or something.

Robin Parker

Heritage: Shadeling, Paragon
Profession: Bard
Tier: 2 (Effective Level: 9)
Experience: 50
Spell Points: 27
Bardsong: 9 uses

Properties

Free Ranks Available: 1

Physical
-Strength: 11
-Dexterity: 14
-Fortitude: 11

Mental
-Intelligence: 17
-Cunning: 25
-Resilience: 14

Social
-Charisma: 15
-Manipulation: 13
-Poise: 16

Proficiencies

Free Ranks Available: 1

Physical (9/9)
-Athletics: 7
-Brawl: 7
-Dodge: 11
-Melee Combat: 6
-Pilot: 5
-Ranged Combat: 11
-Sleight of Hand: 10
-Stealth: 12
-Survival: 8

Mental (9/9)
  -Arcane Lore: 10
  -Bureaucracy: 7
  -Concentration: 11
  -Crafting: 9
  -Healing: 8
  -Insight: 12
  -Learning: 9
  -Natural Wisdom: 6
  -Perception: 12
Social (9/9)
  -Animism: 6
  -Deception: 12
  -Empathy: 10
  -Expression: 11
  -Gossip: 9
  -Intimidation: 8
  -Persuasion: 10
  -Socialize: 9
  -Streetwise: 9

Peculiarities

Blessing of Rhyth
Tongue of the Fallen Tower
Mark of the Trickster
Chronicle of Infinite Visions
Mask of Myriad Faces
Initiate of the Craft
Illusion Focus
Metamagic Initiate
Improved Familiar Bond x2
Effortless Illusions
Metamagic Specialty: Duration

Perks

Wayfaring Stranger
Shard of the Shattered Manymind
Mark of Fairy's Favor
Touch of Wild Magic

Spells

Cantrips* (*no SP cost)
  -Lesser Phantasm*
  -Cutting Words*
  -Legerdemain*
  -Lesser Nightmare Curse*
  -Lesser Witch Bolt*
  -Minor Repair*
  -Lesser Charm*
Tier 1 (1SP each)
  -Visual Phantasm*
  -Healing Note
  -Whispers from Beyond
  -Minor Enchanted Slumber
  -Invisible Servant
  -Familiar Bond
  -Wizard's Armor
Tier 2 (3SP each)
  -Assume Quality (Special)
  -Lesser Mindreading
  -Sorcerous Mark
  -Phantasmal Mouth
  -Lesser Figment

Bardsong

Command Attention
Song of Arcane Power

Robin closed the sheet.

"Fascinating," Vance said, drawing the attention of the rest of the party.

"What is?" Savra asked, running her eyes over the same bit of wall that Vance was looking at but clearly not seeing what had so excited the librarian.

"You can see two distinct architectural styles, here." Vance pointed, and Robin saw both brick and stone, but the brick was filling the curve of what once had probably been an arch.

"So the church used to be more of an open space," the bard said, crouching down to run his fingers lightly over the seam.

"Yes, and they changed it into a small series of private rooms all around the perimeter." Vance pointed at a series of doors.

The center of the space was still soaring and voluminous. There was a space where an altar or pulpit would have been directly opposite them, and through the shadows filling the space, Robin could see a crumbling ruin of some kind. *Looks like the altar didn't make it.*

Though why would it have still been an altar if the church had been deconsecrated and given over to another purpose? Because clearly, there had been some structural changes.

"Drev, can you enchant this with some light?" Robin pulled out a small hunk of crumbled brick.

"Sure." The mage passed his hand over it, and the brick suddenly glowed with reddish-purple-white light.

"Rerebos," Robin called softly, holding the now glowing chunk of brick up. "Fly this outside the window and around it for a bit. Maybe we will get a better sense of what's going on here if we can see what the images on the glass are."

The party fell into defensive formation, ready to retreat out the door if the light awakened anything untoward.

Silence reigned and nothing happened until Rerebos managed to circle the church and carry the light behind the stained glass windows. Then, the beams lancing through the glass unveiled the images immortalized forever in the glass.

That all of the glass itself was intact was a minor miracle in and of itself, but the craftsmanship of the scenes was on another level. Robin stared at the beautiful forms and colors, attempting to pick out the story.

There was a beautiful woman at the center of it, with hair as red as fire. A series of lovers, a string of broken hearts; it looked like the relationship equivalent of the trials of a deity. And several of the images were, ah, much more explicit than Robin would have expected from a church in his world.

Though, honestly, the main image used in one of the major religions from Robin's world was literally an explicit scene of torture, so maybe this wasn't that different. Just sex instead of violence.

The light shining through the final panel, the one showing the woman smiling and weeping all at once over the body of a dying figure—though with her heart unbroken—fell upon a large candle and sparked it to life. A blood-red flame began to dance, and the shadows in the space receded, far more than they had any right to from the light of that single flame.

"Well, that's creepy," Jhess spoke.

The party remained alert, but still nothing moved from the shadows to attack them.

"Closer?" Vance asked.

"Closer," Drev and Savra agreed.

"I'll watch our backs," Jhess said. "Robin, watch the shadows."

"Always." Robin squinted. "Were those mirrors always here?"

There were several mirrors he could see now, each one mounted on one of the doors leading to the newer additions to the space, the smaller rooms.

"I don't think so," Vance replied with a small frown.

Robin was about to ask if it would be too dangerous to look into them or not when the music began. It was soft, pleasant, and sent sparks skittering along the pit of his stomach.

A flush worked its way up to his cheeks.

"Well, that's a first." The rogue tugged at the collar of her tunic. "I've never heard anything like that before."

"Nor I," Robin agreed, cocking his head to listen.

A few bars in, and his **[Bardic Lore]** dinged. There was something about this sound . . . *ah!* It was similar to his own bardic music options, but this one seemed to be threaded with notes that elicited a very particular response in the listener.

Robin looked once more at the imagery in the stained glass window, at the small private rooms, and felt a tightening in his trousers.

"I think this used to be a very nice brothel," he said.

"And at least some of the magics are still active," Drev observed, shifting slightly in his robes.

"Indeed," Savra confirmed, her eyes bright. "I wonder . . ." The seeress turned and went to gaze into one of the nearby mirrors. Upon seeing what was reflected, she gasped.

The party immediately tensed. Sparks danced around Drev's fingers, and a blade and shield of parchment appeared in Vance's hands, but nothing happened. Savra just moved to another mirror to look into.

Robin, curious, followed, glancing into the mirror closest to him.

Cherry, the dryad from Wyndham Wood, stared back at him, though she was less terrifying in this incarnation.

Robin backed away and looked into another mirror. This time he saw Eli winking at him. The next mirror had his first boyfriend. The one after that his first girlfriend. The one after that held Vance's face.

He flushed. So, the mirrors showed, what? Desires? What happened if you went inside the room? Well, what else, in a high-end brothel in a city known for its illusions.

"Who are you seeing," Robin called casually to Savra.

"The first few mirrors showed me people I used to . . . know," the seeress called back. "But now I'm seeing people I've never met, yet somehow, they still seem familiar?"

The rest of the party moved forward to cautiously look into the mirrors. Drev, Vance, and Jhess confirmed the same. They began by seeing past romantic partners which quickly gave way to strange faces that nonetheless seemed familiar.

"I don't like it," Jhess complained. "Feels like someone is spying on my memories."

"I don't think it's anything so invasive," Drev said, one finger hovering over the mirror, not quite daring to touch it. "But the mirrors do seem to key in to our desires, somehow. That much seems clear, based on the first few faces each of us saw."

"Which means that the faces we see after must be . . . what? Future loves?" Robin shook his head. "Savra? That would be your department."

"I sense no temporal magics like that in these mirrors," she replied. "But in this place, my senses are not always perfectly reliable."

"So if these are not images of both past and future, what are they?" Vance tapped his chin thoughtfully. "If this is a brothel, then perhaps—"

"They are faces and voices that will suit your liking without being drawn from the ranks of those you already know," a new voice, musical and liquid, joined the conversation. "Though I am afraid I may not have the power to grant you such desires, in this day and age. I am no longer what I once was."

Robin turned, his fingers halfway to conjuring a bank of illusory mist to hide in, when he caught sight of the figure standing at the other end of the room, just in front of the candle burning with a crimson flame.

It was the woman from the stained glass windows!

Chapter 7

"Hello," Robin said, at a loss for what else to do when faced with yet another illusion that didn't seem to have the sense to stay simply that. "I'm Marq, a rising star of the bardic order, and these are my friends."

He went around and introduced everyone with a false name.

Better safe than sorry.

"I am Fiara Sunbrow," the woman replied with an easy smile. "Welcome to the Blushing Rose."

Her figure was enough to make a stone blush, let alone a rose or a man! Robin had to fight not to stare. Her skin was smooth and unblemished, and had a pale ocher hue to it that complemented the fiery shades of red and orange of her hair. Her figure swelled and curved in a way that made him ache to wrap his arms around her and fit himself to her like she was the missing piece that completed the puzzle that was his life.

She was, in a word, stunning.

"Thank you," he managed to say.

Something about this illusion—this woman—was spellbinding. Robin found it hard to think through the roseate glow that hazed his thoughts as he looked at her. The blood coursing hotly to his extremities didn't help much either.

At the back of his mind, a thread of story struggled to get his attention. If this were his old world, he'd say his brain was struggling because the blood it needed to function was somewhere else at the moment, but who knew what his biology was like, here.

[Bardic Lore] flared, finally making its way through the haze shrouding his mind and better judgement. He knew this story! And several more recent variants! Fiara Sunbrow had been a dream, or an illusion, or a memory—different stories changed it, but they all agreed she had not been a living woman when the story began. But there was also a man, Fionn Nightheart, who wanted, more than anything else, to find True Love.

Robin's eyes flicked to the stained glass mural above the altar. Was that Fionn depicted there? The story was old enough; it seemed to match. There, on the left, was the man all alone. Slightly to the right, he was asleep, possibly dreaming. Was that an indistinct whorl of color above his head? Then there, Fiara's face appearing from the chaos!

He glanced back and forth. Yes. That was her face!

The rest of the story had Fionn seek so long, to believe so strongly in his vision of love, that it'd first appeared in his mind, then in reality itself. The stories all disagreed on how it had happened, but if this was a story from Tarin-Tiran, a place where they'd already discovered other sentient illusions, then Robin could see how the magic had first taken form.

But it hadn't been enough for Fionn to have the image of his love; he needed it in reality. His belief had been such, his faith had been such, that the illusion had taken physical form, had become a woman in truth. And their love had shaken the world with its purity.

Until Fionn had died. Some stories called it tragedy, an illness no magic could cure, while others laid the blame at a conspiracy of jealous lovers who wanted Fiara for themselves, but the story had ended tragically.

Robin's eyes flicked to the final image of the stained glass. Yes. There was Fionn, lying dead, his head in Fiara's lap. And Fiara, after . . .

The bard blinked. The story rang in his head. He looked around at their surroundings, at the former church. Or was it former? Ancient culture in his own world had had sacred prostitution, and what was Fiara if not the embodiment of the idea of love. Of desire.

Such force and blessed power had True Love that, if he was right . . .

"You're a demigoddess," Robin blurted.

Fiara laughed sadly.

"Perhaps I was, once, but there is very little of me left. Some spare scraps of power which keep this place holy; a single memory of love so perfect it took a dream, made it real, and raised it up to a throne of divinity." She colored. "Well. Demidivinity."

"My lady," Savra said, reverence suddenly suffusing her voice.

Robin glanced at the cleric out of the corner of his eye. Interesting. He tended to think of the seeress as just that, a seeress, but she was a woman of faith first, a seeress second, and a healer after that.

His mind began to hum with the refrain of "Sexual Healing."

"My regards to your mistress," Fiara said softly to Savra. "I always loved her eyes, you know. So beautiful."

Savra began to tremble. Robin flashed a glance at the rest of the party and indicated they should fall back. Let Savra have a moment with the being who had known her goddess face-to-face.

"Let's let her have a moment," he murmured. "Jhess, check the place out for traps or monsters that may be hiding in this place. Can't be too careful. Vance, Drev, let's see if we can uncover what the runic structures powering this place looks like. We still have a mission, and I want to know if we can complete it without disturbing anything."

Unlikely, but they wouldn't know until they looked. Robin gazed around the church. Unlike the other locations they'd visited, everything was intact. The runes would be hidden, hard to find.

"I'll take the altar," he said. The most complex runes should be there, and there was something Robin wanted to do anyway.

The party split apart, and Robin made his way up to the altar, careful not to look in any of the mirrors as he passed the doors of the small rooms to either side. This was a holy place, one that had stood since Rhyth had been an active power and given his patronage to this city. It was likely Fiara knew—had known—him as well as Savra's patron.

The altar held a comb, a candle, and a mirror. Robin's breath caught in his throat as he approached. Was there a chance . . . ?

If there was, he'd want a bit of privacy.

Robin called upon [**Visual Phantasm**] and shrouded himself and the altar with a whirling vortex of shadows. He then used his [**Mask of Disguise**] to cover himself in the illusion of himself and invoked [**Lesser Phantasm**], together with his memories and both [**Bardic Lore**] and [**Shard of the Shattered Manymind**], to create—or recreate—a brief prayer to Rhyth.

He expected—well, he didn't know what he expected. A sense of peace? A vision? A whisper in the dark?

Robin got none of those. He stared at the illusion of himself reflected in the mirror. Same eyes. Same hair. Same rakish smile . . .

Wait. Robin had seen the smile before he felt it creep across his own lips, as if he himself were the mirror instead. A spark of something flared briefly in his heart, and visions of mischief suddenly rampaged across his mind.

A moment of pure inspiration.

And then it was gone. He couldn't even be sure he'd actually connected with Rhyth, or the memory of Rhyth. This was a place of illusion and desire—the other mirrors had already shown him that. There was no way he could truly trust what he saw or sensed in this place.

And yet . . . Rhyth was a god of illusion. This had been his sacred city. If there was anywhere he could catch a whisper of the god's memory, it was here.

Robin decided it didn't matter if it had been real or not. The effect on him was real, and that was enough. He didn't know why he felt such a connection to Rhyth, but he could feel it growing, and the thrill of his new powers of illusion and shapeshifting . . . fuck, they were exactly what he'd always wanted from magic. Fun and beauty and wonder. Maybe the limitations on them were annoying; maybe the hard numbers the system showed him took some of the magic away from the magic, but it was still wonder and creation and magic!

And he could only imagine what it would be like if Rhyth was found once more.

Maybe he could ask Nilsiir what it was like. Fiara might also know, a bit. Probably not as much as the high priest, but still.

Robin ached to talk to Fiara himself, and not just because basking in her presence, staring at her form, made him feel alive, made him feel sexy and vital and primal.

What could she tell him about Rhyth, as she was telling Savra about her goddess?

Robin forced the thought aside. He wasn't just before this altar to reach out to the Lost God. He was here because this had to be the nexus of the enchantments on this place, and he needed to get a look at them.

He kept the illusion shrouding him around the altar, and before he did anything which might offend her, the bard paused and decided to make an offering. Robin leaned in and whispered an abbreviated version of the story of his first crush, the first time he had dreamed of love, into the mirror on the altar. It might have been his imagination, but he thought it shined a little more brightly, after.

Right. To business.

Robin called magical energies to his fingertips and extended his magical senses out around him. It wasn't easy, trying to sense magical flows like this, but thankfully, they were mostly illusion, and so matched well with his magic. It made it easier to feel how the energy flows in the place moved.

And he had been right! There was a big knot of energies here! Robin used **[Lesser Phantasm]** to try and recreate an image of what the runes here might look like, but it was hard going. The runes were complex, and not being able to see them made his task next to impossible.

What he did see didn't reassure him. It felt like there were several places where Fiara was keyed into the runes here. He wouldn't have recognized them if he hadn't so closely examined the changes Nilsiir had made to the last place the high priest had taken over.

Could Robin figure out a way to alter this structure without hurting or even destroying what was left of Fiara? Would Nilsiir even want her to still be around? Robin thought the priest would prefer if she persevered, as another piece of the Tarin-Tiran that was, but there was no way to ask. And could they afford to skip over this place as well? Try to find the next one and hope it was repairable? That there would be enough places beyond that to complete their quest? They'd already lost one to Gis's destruction.

Did Robin have to choose between the demigoddess and the high priest?

Chapter 8

Robin mentally reviewed the amount of magical energy he still had at his disposal. Was it worth casting **[Lesser Mindreading]** in an attempt to get more information out of Fiara? Or would attempting to read the mind of a demigoddess, even one as lessened as Fiara, be the height of stupidity?

No risk, no reward, but there were risks and then there were *risks*.

It was better to ask first, Robin decided. The reading of minds was already a complicated ethical issue; no need to get caught up in those weeds right now. For all he knew, Fiara would happily share the information he wanted.

Besides, she was a demigoddess. No need to pick that fight before he had to.

Robin let the illusion around him fade as he walked slowly back to the rest of his party, mind awhirl. Savra seemed to have finished whatever conversation she had been having with Fiara, and the seeress was positively glowing.

"Fiara," he called when he drew near enough. "How much do you recall of the city before it fell?"

"Ah," the demigoddess said. "Trust the bard to ask a question like that."

She smiled, and Robin's bones turned to water. He almost used his shapeshifting abilities to assume a form better suited to standing, then he remembered he couldn't turn himself into a tree. Or a rock.

Not that it would be that much of a shift, considering.

Robin subtly adjusted his trousers.

"We've encountered several visions of the fall of Tarin-Tiran," he continued, "and given the nature of the place, we were wondering how close the apparitions might be to the historical truth. If it's not too painful to recall those times, that is," Robin added hastily.

"No, not too painful, though I'd already encountered the greatest pain of my existence, so my perspective may be rather different than that of another; Nilsiir's, for example. I expect you've seen visions of them?"

Robin nodded, choosing not to speak in case it revealed that they'd more than seen the High Priest of Rhyth, and Fiara began to spin out tales of Tarin-Tiran from before the fall. Simple things, like what day-to-day life had been like, as well as songs and tales popular in the era. Robin felt his **[Bardic Lore]** drinking deep from this well of new knowledge. He paid particular attention to those bits of Rhyth's worship that came up in passing: festivals, holy days, behavior of the priesthood, and so on. It was with great reluctance that he spoke up to shift the conversation when a familiar name came up: Melusk.

"Melusk was involved in the illusions we saw as well," Robin said. "Melusk and Leivniz. What can you tell us about them?"

He really wanted to know more about Melusk, but still wasn't quite ready to show his whole hand yet.

"Melusk, yes, I am very familiar with." Fiara had a slight smile. "He was one of my regular patrons, actually." Her face hardened. "Given his hand in the fall of Tarin-Tiran, I'm ashamed to say I did not see it coming. I took his desire for control to be a simple sexual preference, not an aspect of something more."

"His devotion to Urkhan," Savra said unexpectedly.

"Yes." Fiara's hair began to rise and dance like flame. "The God of Tyranny, who has no room for love for anyone but himself and his own power in his heart."

"We've heard he had an artifact which helped him bring about the Fall," Robin nudged. "And that he managed to keep several rooms and chambers concealed within the city, hidden even from the master illusionists of Tarin-Tiran and Rhyth's priesthood."

"True," Fiara confirmed. "Though he did not speak of them."

Robin bit back a curse. He had hoped to find some extra information. You'd think the insight of a demigoddess—

"But perhaps there is something I could do," Fiara added thoughtfully.

Had he spoken—thought—too soon? Robin glanced at Fiara, hoping the demigoddess would elaborate.

"He was here," she said. "He indulged in his desires here. And such a thing is too primal not to leave a mark of its occurrence. There might be enough of his presence left to call an illusion of the man he was at the fall of Tarin-Tiran back to us to answer some questions. If I can muster enough power."

Fiara looked at Robin.

"And if you decide to be a bit more honest with me about what your intentions are in this place."

Robin froze.

"Nilsiir sent us," he replied a moment later. If Fiara could see he was hedging with the truth, the smart play was to give her what she wanted. "They need us to alter the runic structures here so they can manifest and take control of the local area. They didn't say anything about you being here, though."

"Nilsiir?" Fiara frowned prettily. "Enough of them is left to still exert influence?"

Robin and the rest of the party waited with bated breath to see if this news was welcome or not. An angry demigoddess was not at all what anyone wanted to be dealing with.

Fiara began pacing the perimeter of the church. Brothel. *Whatever.*

Robin felt his heart begin to thud in his chest, hammering faster and faster. They were trapped in a room with a demigoddess who likely hadn't interacted with anyone in centuries. There was no telling what she might do.

Fiara suddenly froze, disappeared, then reappeared directly in front of Robin.

He managed not to yelp. Barely.

"You seem like the sort who enjoys making a deal, bard," Fiara spoke. "And I can smell the faintest of sparks of Rhyth's power in you. So, in the memory of one who was kind to me, and in the hopes that one I thought lost might return and restore this city and my own fortunes, I will offer you a deal. Find a way to restore any measure of my power to me, howsoever small, and I shall aid you in your quest."

Robin blinked. That was . . . reasonable? At least in terms of what she was asking for; he had no idea as to how difficult actually executing the task might be. Divine power didn't seem to be a thing that was simply left lying around, after all.

"I'm willing to make the deal," he answered, grabbing for some time to think, "but I would like some time to think over the best way I and my friends might fulfill your request."

"Take what time you need," Fiara said. "The amenities here will be open to you while you debate." Then she vanished, although Robin had the eerie feeling that every image of her throughout the temple was watching him.

"Well," he started, turning to Savra. "Any secrets of the gods and how they gain and amass power you'd like to share?"

The seeress pursed her lips and gave him a look.

"I'm not trying to cheat anyone here!" Robin protested, oddly feeling accused. "I want a win-win-win situation."

"And if one doesn't exist?" Drev asked pointedly.

"We don't know what does or does not exist yet," Robin shot back. "That's why I'm asking for options."

"She already has a temple, and some relics," Jhess observed. "Not sure if we could provide her with any more, even if we have picked up a bit of treasure."

"She does lack a congregation," Vance spoke slowly. "Although I don't know how we might address that issue."

"I cannot divine anything related to the divine, nor would I attempt to even if I could," Savra said. "All I can offer is that you would do well to treat fairly and honestly with Her Holiness."

"Right. Give me some time to think," the bard murmured to the rest of his party and began pacing through the temple.

Several thoughts warred for attention in his brain. A few seemed like solid prospects, but everything kept coming down to time and nearby resources. The congregation thing seemed best. Gods drawing power from mortal worshippers seemed like a no-brainer. The problem was, Tarin-Tiran was chock-full of monsters and scarce on potential converts.

He couldn't really convert; that would be an easy solution if he could. Fiara hadn't set a limit on how much power she needed in order to help them, so even the little he might offer should be enough. But while he really enjoyed sex and the bonds of love, he couldn't really see himself converting to Fiara's worship. And while he could offer her prayers and devotion, something told him it wouldn't be quite enough to register.

Faith as power was a strange and nebulous thing.

Part of him, small and fearful, whispered that perhaps he could offer to Fiara that tiniest mote of Rhyth's power that he apparently carried within him, but no. There was no way he would do that. No way he would give that up.

If she would even accept it.

Robin shoved the thought away—it was a nonstarter, anyway—and he felt something in him relax as he dismissed the possibility.

Fine. Onto the next thing.

They also didn't have time to find a new temple location or hunt down relics from Fiara's past which might hold fragments of her power, like that shrine of Rhyth he had woken up in. Robin's eyes strayed to his surroundings, seeking inspiration. Rooms, the trappings of a temple turned holy brothel, the altar, stained glass windows . . .

He paused. There, above all, was Fiara's story; the story which had made her a goddess, elevated her to divinity. *That* was a powerful thing. But was it a thing that helped her gain power? Could he increase her power by spreading that story?

But that ran back into the problem of converts. The only potential candidates they had seen so far were the hobgoblins, and most of them were firmly in Urkhan's grip. Even if he could pry a few free, it would take time, and that was in incredibly short supply with Gis and his party possibly nearing Melusk's hidden chambers and the artifact the traitor had left behind.

Something prodded at him from his subconscious. Something Fiara had said? Or hadn't said.

Yes! She hadn't specified a time limit on when he should return the power to her. Could he argue to her aid on credit, maybe by swearing a binding oath that he would share her story far and wide?

Robin examined the idea. It would get Fiara some more followers, inevitably. Especially if he helped things along with some manipulation and illusion to make sure a few matches appeared, as if made in heaven. He could even use his *Crafting* skill and his new **[Phantasmal Mouth]** spell to create icons that relayed the story of Fiara. Well, snippets of it. Maybe whatever equivalent of short prayers she had.

And if she didn't like the idea? If she demanded something now?

Robin's eyes strayed to the altar. Well, there was always the oldest of prayers: sacrifice. Fiara probably wouldn't want blood or death, but he had experience points he could offer, as much as it would pain him, or even a perk, if such a thing could be offered up to the demigoddess.

All he could do was ask, really.

Chapter 9

I accept your proposal," Fiara said, "provided you swear upon your faith."

Savra gasped and looked at Robin.

The bard winced internally. Clearly, this was some sort of big thing. His **[Bardic Lore]** pinged, agreeing that this was dangerous and important but providing only fictional and exaggerated versions of what it might mean, rather than concrete mechanics.

What he wouldn't give to be able to read the *Dungeon Master's Guide* for this universe!

"But I will also require something to increase my power now," the demigoddess continued. "I will not aid you in bringing Nilsiir here in a state where I cannot be certain of matching or exceeding their power."

Right. Sacrifice was back on the table. Robin was about to open his character sheet and look once more for what he might give up when Jhess spoke.

"I will devote myself to you, Lady, to be your true and willing servant. I offer you all my memories of lost love, all my hope of restoring one who loved me so that I may love her in return." The rogue stepped forward, unsteady on her feet, all customary grace drowned in a clear case of nerves.

Fiara looked at Jhess and smiled softly.

"There, now. Was that so hard, my child?" The demigoddess reached out to take the rogue by the chin and draw her eyes up to meet her gaze. "Thank you. I accept your service and your sacrifice. And I shall do all I can to answer your prayers for love."

Robin—watching the exchange uncomfortably, as it seemed such a very private and intimate thing—caught a glimpse of a woman's face other than

Jhess's reflected in Fiara's eyes. He didn't recognize her, but from the way Jhess's eyes were glimmering, the rogue did.

The rogue kept a lot of secrets, and he'd known she had an ulterior motive for amassing such a hoard of wealth, but he'd had no idea it had to do with personal tragedy and lost love!

Robin turned his head to the side, averting his gaze to give Jhess and Fiara a bit more privacy. Vance caught his eye. The librarian had likewise averted his gaze, seemed to also be surprised by Jhess's revelation. The two of them looked at one another for a long moment, wondering which secrets the other was carrying.

"It is done, then," Fiara spoke.

Robin turned to look at the demigoddess and felt his heart nearly stop in his chest. Before, her visage had been affecting, but now it was an order of magnitude more extreme. His body reacted instantly, even as his heart began to ache with loss and longing.

"Do we have a deal, bard? Will you swear upon your faith to spread my story as we discussed?"

Robin paused, looking from the demigoddess to Savra. The seeress just stared at him with wide eyes.

Fuck it. He needed this. And he had no intention of breaking his word anyway.

"I so swear."

Robin's veins suddenly sang with crimson fire. He felt the words write themselves upon his bones, and it was agony and ecstasy, the touch of a divine hand on him, body and soul. Every sense he had was amplified, turned to overdrive as sensations of all kinds tore at his mind in their intensity.

In his mind, Fiara's voice whispered like a lover's caress.

And think not to betray this oath with any of your patron's tricks. I know Rhyth of old, and I will know if you use any of his customary means of slipping the consequences of an oath.

Robin gasped and was almost blinded by the blazing blue light which appeared with the notification before his eyes.

Advanced Knowledge Unlocked! [The Trickster's Oath]

A demigoddess has rudely laid hands upon you, body and soul, binding you with a terrible oath. However, in the process, she has revealed to you the existence of a way to avoid the consequences of breaking an oath. Your attempts to discover this knowledge for yourself in the future will benefit from a greatly increased chance of success.

"Yes, my lady," Robin managed to say aloud, blinking away the notification.

"Then you may proceed with your attempts to complete Nilsiir's request when ready." Fiara gestured, and the runic structures powering the temple revealed themselves.

Robin pulled out a waterskin from their emergency supplies, used [Lesser Phantasm] to give it the sting and burn of eighteen-year-old scotch, and slammed back several swallows.

"Right," he said. "To work, then. Drev, Vance, why don't you help me while Savra and Jhess entertain our gracious host."

Jhess would be in no shape to help them spot inconsistencies, even if she had had the magical know-how for it. And while Savra would be useful for her divinatory skills, Robin felt Jhess needed the seeress by her side more than they needed her double-checking the magical work he, the librarian, and the mage did.

And so they began. It was mentally taxing, and by the time they had a workable model of the changes they wanted to make, they were nearly exhausted.

"This isn't going to work," Vance sighed regretfully.

Well, an *almost* working model.

"It'll work," Robin said. "Nilsiir won't have the control they had in the last space, but they should be able to manifest."

"That won't be enough for them," Drev pointed out. "No way."

"They can take that up with Fiara, then," Robin snapped. "Or you can. I'm not going to."

He waited to see if either Vance or Drev would take him up on that offer. When neither said anything, Robin crossed his arms and continued.

"No. It's not perfect, but it should work. And there's a *chance* Nilsiir will be able to work with Fiara to finish, once they're here. They have a lot more knowledge than any of us, after all."

"If they and Fiara don't try to kill one another on sight," Drev muttered.

"Yeah, that's not helping." Robin shook his head. "Look, they're both remnants of the old city. Both want this place restored. There's a bigger chance of them working together than coming to metaphysical blows. I think, at most, we'll get some catty sniping."

"Fine," Drev replied. "Just do it. But I'm going to have a shield ready to cover our retreat if this goes pear-shaped."

"I wouldn't have it any other way."

Robin didn't bother waiting for Vance to add his opinion, he just called up both [Visual Phantasm] and [Lesser Phantasm] and made the necessary illusory changes to the runic structure. Neither alone were enough to cover the space needed.

It took some quick timing, but Robin was sure he—

The magic connected, surging along the illusory conduits and arcing across the gaps to ground themselves in Robin's eyes. His world went blue and black, and he lost the words for colors as darkness claimed his mind. His last thought before it did was that he'd definitely miscalculated somewhere, but damned if he was going to tell Drev he had been right.

When he came to, the first thing Robin heard was Nilsiir's voice, strident and full of ire.

" . . . botch job! Now I'm trapped here in one of these ridiculous sex mirrors! What do you intend to do about this? I'm going to fry that idiot bard once he wakes up!"

Robin wisely decided to keep his eyes closed for a moment longer. He could hear Nilsiir, so presuming he wasn't dead or hallucinating, his fix had worked. Somewhat. Trapped in one of Fiara's mirrors, though? That didn't make any sense.

He went over the sequence of runes again in his mind. It was easy; they were practically burned there by the feedback.

Yeah, there was no way he could have known that a mishap like this would result. Maybe wild magic? But no. **[Touch of Wild Magic]** didn't so much as quiver at the thought.

"All right, then," Robin spoke, opening his eyes. "Fry me. Unless you're ready to come clean with the bluff and stop tricking everyone for no good reason."

Fiara's laugh, ringing and high and bright as gold, rang out.

"I told you he'd figure you out," the demigoddess said. "Pay up!"

A bet. Sure, why not? Robin sighed and clambered to his feet.

"What's my humiliation worth, then?" he asked.

"Above your pay grade, I'm afraid," Nilsiir replied. "Suffice it to say that Fiara and I have worked out an arrangement that should make everyone happy. Well, except for you and your friends. I'm afraid it means a bit more work for you; perhaps some additional hazards to face."

"Great," Robin muttered sourly.

The rest of his party didn't seem too upset, however. Robin wondered why, but didn't want to ask in front of the high priest and the demigoddess. That's when Robin noticed the additional figure standing quietly in the center of the room.

It was Melusk!

Or the illusion of him, Robin decided at once. There was no way the actual man could be here; if he were, he wouldn't be acting so docile. Fiara or Nilsiir, or possibly both, had to have conjured up this specter.

"Well, that's new."

"In light of the information gathered here," Nilsiir said, "I am amending your task list. There are some additional locations I need you to repair on the way to uncovering this reprobate's hidden stronghold." The illusion of Nilsiir appeared next to Melusk and flashed a rude gesture before its eyes.

"Between the two of us, we have found three likely locations for Melusk's hidden sanctuary," Fiara spoke. "And with the aid of Savra, we have been able to ascertain that the Disciple of Urkhan survived and is headed toward Melusk's hiding place as well."

"You'll need to deal with that, too," Nilsiir noted airily, as if he were telling Robin to mow the lawn or pick up milk from the store. "So that's the bad news; priest of Urkhan bent on destroying what's left of the city using something nasty Melusk left behind. Well, not literally destroying. Trying to wipe out what's left of the soul of the city."

"You mean yourself and possibly Fiara," Robin said.

"Yes," Nilsiir confirmed. "Bad news, as I said. But there is some good news! Although it comes with a tad more bad news, too."

"What's the good news?" Robin asked warily.

"You can easily beat the fucking priest of that wankstain of a god to where he's headed," Nilsiir replied cheerfully. "Plenty of time to get there first, find whatever Melusk left behind, and destroy it. Maybe even to plant a trap for him. There's a shortcut you can take through the ruins of the city to ensure you get there first."

That sounded too good to be true to Robin, so he asked the obvious question.

"And what's the bad news?"

"You're going to have to brave the depths of Silinir in order to make use of said shortcut."

Chapter 10

Robin crept carefully forward, every breath meticulously controlled, every step as light upon the stone as he could make it. He and the rest of his party were moving slowly and quietly through the depths of Silinir.

Whether or not the dungeon sensed their presence, they did not know. Ruprecht, unable to accompany them, had agreed to attempt to distract Silinir by expending some of his store of accumulated energies conjuring new monsters—the dungeon had been evasive on the details of what kind—to test the other dungeon's boundaries in a way that Ruprecht assured them would have Silinir thinking an interloper dungeon was planning to attack and make a play for territory.

If Ruprecht could keep Silinir's direct attention off of them, they stood a chance of slipping through hostile territory without facing a deadly encounter. They were deep within Tarin-Tiran now, and the monsters Silinir had on these levels were likely to be formidable, to say the least.

Rerebos, invisible, was scouting ahead on silent wings. Jhess was checking every inch of the corridor for traps, with Savra assisting. The coin almost never stopped spinning in the air, the seeress consulted it so heavily.

Robin massaged his left shoulder with his right hand. Nothing had happened yet, but the strain of constant focus was beginning to wear on all of them. The bard consulted his mental map. And they had so much further yet to travel.

It was a narrow extent of Silinir's domain which Nilsiir had directed them to. Several tunnels, a few large chambers, and they could be through to the pocket Fiara and Nilsiir had ascertained contained one of Melusk's safe houses.

That the location was free of Silinir's influence was apparently a big clue.

They had made it down long stretches of corridor, passed through one large chamber, avoided or otherwise circumvented a few traps, and avoided one combat by hiding in Robin's illusions. The lone tuvyux had passed by, nearly suffocating them with its stench, but at least that meant it couldn't smell them over itself.

Jhess's hand shot out in a signal; there was another large cavern ahead. Robin stopped moving long enough to look ahead through Rerebos's eyes. The little dragon had paused before entering but was close enough to see much more than Jhess could, especially since he could see through the dark as if it were nothing. Still, Rerebos couldn't see everything; the entrance to the cavern was a large crack with an overhang above it. There was no way to tell what might be lurking above, and most of the vision to either side was obstructed by the stone.

What he could see of the floor ahead, however, was worrying. It was relatively smooth, but it was laced throughout with holes in different diameters. The largest Robin estimated at the size of his fist, so there wasn't really a worry for falling through, unless the stone was weak enough to collapse from their weight, but the tuvyux had come from this direction—Robin could see some glimmering slime from its passage—so if that hadn't collapsed the place, they should be safe.

Unless there was some kind of dungeon-invader trigger to it.

Robin left Rerebos's senses and advanced with the rest of the party, moving carefully as Jhess checked for traps. She glanced at him and made a gesture once the party was gathered about the entrance. The bard nodded and flexed his hands, conjuring some test illusions: a small mouse scurrying around the edges of a few of the closer holes; a few quiet noises—first just some skittering, then the sound of footsteps on the stone. Finally, Robin pulled a small rock out of his storage and tossed it into the room. It clattered across the floor before hitting the rim of one of the holes and falling down into it.

The party stilled, cold and motionless as a grave, waiting to see what response, if any, the pebble provoked. The sound of cold scales over stone whispered faintly through the cavern. There was something in those holes, certainly. What it was, however, refused to reveal itself.

Send a magelight over the hole. Robin used **[Lesser Phantasm]** to paint the small words in the air in front of Drev. Maybe that would provoke more of a response than his illusions.

The mage nodded slightly, and soon, a bobbing sphere of light was dancing through the cavern. The shadows it cast, though Robin and Rerebos could see through them, made it difficult to tell if there was something moving in a particular hole or if it was just the interplay of light and shade.

Can you scout inside, just up and over the overhang? Slow and careful, Robin mentally sent to Rerebos. *I can promise you many shinies.*

Many, MANY shinies, came the reply, tinted with equal parts resolution, anxiety, and the hunger for lost power.

Robin imagined that yes, if one were accustomed to the might of a dragon, being trapped in a smaller version of your own body on an alternate plane would make one long for what had been, if not lost, temporarily set aside in the pursuit of other gains.

To Rerebos's credit, he sent Robin a pulse of defiant courage before he snuck into the cavern proper. The bard shared his senses as he did so, getting a wider view.

There was nothing on the ledge above the entrance, thankfully, although there was a bit of hair and signs that *something* occasionally laired there. Or rested there.

The holes were confined to the floor; there was no sign of them on the ceiling—nor of anything else, really. Robin looked at the lack of stalactites with some apprehension. Something about the whole cavern was just a bit too sculpted. Could mean it was a special project of Silinir's.

Is that another ledge above the exit? We should check that out.

Rerebos grumbled at Robin's implied order, but after carefully checking around, the little dragon flew across to inspect the aforementioned ledge.

It was almost a mirror of the other, down to the small hairs scattered about, and both ledges were far more natural looking than the cavern itself. They had rough stone instead of smooth, and natural outcrops which might have once been stalagmites . . . actually, that gave Robin an idea!

Come back to the rest of the party, Robin told Rerebos, who sent his assent and carefully began to flit back while Robin relinquished the little dragon's senses and turned to his party, conjuring an illusion to illustrate his plan.

They had plenty of rope and string in storage. They could secure one end to an outcropping on the ledge above, have Rerebos run a guide string across the cavern, then use that to pull the rope into position. Between Vance's ability to boost his strength and some judicious spells from Drev, they should be able to secure the rope and use that to cross the cavern without walking across that suspicious floor. Robin had no real desire to discover what, precisely, was lurking beneath.

There was some silent discussion. Savra and Drev, in particular, were not thrilled by the idea of crawling along the rope, but no one was able to come up with a better idea—at least, not one they could easily communicate if they *did* have one—so they set to it. The hardest part was actually slipping into the cavern one at a time and climbing up the rope ladder to the ledge; Robin kept eyeing the holes in the floor as he did so.

He was the last one up, and he'd be the last one across. If he had to, he could grow wings and fly, after all. The only reason he wasn't doing so right now was because they had no idea what need there might be for magic before they made it safely out the other side. This was not a place where they could set up camp and try to meditate and restore one's energies.

Robin couldn't wait until he had an illusion that would let him fly more easily almost all of the time. Not long now. He knew just the spell, and it was Tier Three. He was getting so close.

Jhess crossed first, the rogue almost running across the rope, her balance was so precise. Drev followed much more slowly, hand over hand, inching himself along. Even then, he nearly slipped and fell, the give in the rope betraying the sureness of his grip.

Breath caught in Robin's throat. Would the mage fall, hitting the ground and altering whatever it was beneath them?

Drev wasn't a force initiate for nothing, however. Purple-white sparks flew, and Drev used minor telekinesis of some kind to steady himself. Robin let his breath out slowly. He did not need stress like that!

Vance was next, quick and sure, borrowing grace from some acrobat of legend or other. Robin could only shake his head at the man's efficiency. He was barely using a wisp of power, just enough to give him an edge. He needed to have more conversations about what techniques Vance used for efficiency.

Savra took Drev's approach, slow and careful. She, however, made it across without incident.

Then it was Robin's turn. Nerves had made his palms sweaty, and the silken fibers of the rope beneath his hands felt slippery. He moved along, using the same method as Savra and Drev, but moving more quickly. The beat of his heart drove him on, too nervous to go slowly. Let every second telescope into a potential whirlpool of mistakes?

No, thanks. Robin felt the need to move.

Then it happened. The rope slipped. Maybe it was the knot work; maybe it was bad luck or the negative effects of [Touch of Wild Magic], but whatever it was, the rope suddenly went slack beneath Robin, losing a degree of tension and dropping him precipitously toward the floor of the cavern ten or so feet below.

His hand slipped. He grabbed for the rope, but the silken fibers twisted out of his grasp. Robin's arm windmilled, a frantic attempt to stabilize himself and arrest his downward momentum.

Misfortune fouled his attempt, and Robin felt himself fall. Instinctively, he reached for his shapeshifting ability to turn himself into something with wings, but the fall was not that far. His mind was distracted, and he hit the ground with a *thud* before he could perform any changes.

The sound of scales over stone exploded as long, sinuous forms rose from each of the holes in the floor, a forest of writhing snakelike shapes. Some were barbed with crystal spines, some had three-clawed appendages like hands on the ends, and some blinked crystalline eyes around as they whipped back and forth, searching for their prey.

Robin froze as several eyes nearby locked on him.

Shit.

Chapter 11

Robin dropped the illusion of a cloud of shadows over himself; it was instinct at this point. Usually, it served him in good stead.

This time, however, he was not so lucky. While those tentacles ending in eyes flailed about a bit, looking for where he had gone, others seemed to have no trouble questing for him by feel. The way this thing had reacted to the rock, maybe it had some sort of ability to sense tremors or movement in the stone around it?

No way out of it; Robin was going to have to expend some magical energies. First, however, a distraction. Robin pulled several small rocks from his storage and threw them around the cavern. Where they hit, tentacles lashed out, confirming his suspicions that some kind of tremor sense was at play.

Not enough tentacles were distracted, though. Mostly only the ones that had gone for the rocks that had fallen within the perimeter of his shrouding illusion.

Still, Robin took advantage of it, shifting his body and making use of **[Assume Quality]** to get himself a set of wings, take the form of a winged elf.

He launched himself into the air, pulling the illusion up around him as he did so. Unfortunately, he was not really a master of flight, and there were tentacles writhing all through the space, grasping blindly for whatever they could get. Most of them were currently concentrated on searching the floor near where he had been and where he had cast his stones, but others were questing further, higher. Three had even found the rope strung across the cavern and were coiled around it. Robin could see it straining under their force. Any moment now, it was going to snap.

Missiles of force and several daggers flashed through the cavern; Drev and Jhess were attempting to provide covering fire so he could get away. A few tentacles were hit, including one eyestalk that got severed by a particularly sharp throw from Jhess, and the whole cavern went wild with their trashing. A keening that scraped at the edges of Robin's sanity wailed up from beneath the cavern's floor. Whatever was down there was *mad*.

Robin fired off a couple [Lesser Witch Bolt]s in opposite directions to keep the thing's attention from focusing on any one space. It didn't seem to be trying to feel out where Drev and Jhess were crouched with the rest of the party atop the ledge, but there was no guarantee it wouldn't.

He needed to find a way to fly to safety through the forest of waving tentacles, distract the fucking thing, and get out of the cavern with the rest of his party.

Robin's wings strained, gaining him a few more feet in height. There were no thermals to ride, and while he was lighter, he wasn't so accustomed to this form that he could fly with ease. Still, he was glad to be a bit above the roiling mass of tentacles questing along the floor. Most of its prey must simply walk past. That they'd made it this far without provoking the thing argued for that as well.

So. Step one. Rejoin his party on the ledge without getting caught and without drawing any attention to their location.

Step two. Figure out a way to clear the tentacles blocking the exit and make a speedy getaway.

Robin was under no illusions that they'd be able to easily slay whatever this was. The bulk of the thing was protected by the shield of rock that was the whole fucking floor, his [Bardic Lore] wasn't offering him any hints as to what it might be, and the party was low on massive firepower.

Some temporary magical items would be really handy right now. Scrolls, or wands stuffed full of [Lightning Bolt]s and [Fireball] spells. Or just an emergency [Teleport] or [Move Through Stone]. Short range would do it.

Ugh. No point worrying about what he didn't have. He needed to come up with a solution using what he *did* have. Starting with what he knew.

The thing used both sight and vibration. Both of those could be fooled, but the overlap was a bad pairing for a lot of his illusory tricks. The tentacles could be severed, and they didn't seem to have any kind of fast regeneration that he had seen. Also, based on the reaction to his earlier attacks, they didn't really like fire; not that many creatures did, mind you.

And another thing: while there were a lot of them, their range was limited. Most of the tentacles straining around the edges of the holes reached around ten feet into the air and no further. A few rose higher, but it was a minority. That meant the party could focus on clearing an area of tentacles and not have to worry about the whole cavern taking the opportunity to attack them as they did so.

One of the lashing tentacles waving near him brushed against his left wing and immediately constricted, tearing two feathers. Robin saw red stars. It was like having a lock of his hair ripped out by the roots, but somehow even spikier.

He forced himself to ignore the pain and clawed desperately for some more altitude, moving away from the tentacle as fast as he could, as now others were concentrating in the same area.

Robin managed to evade the grasping tentacles, but then one with an eye on the tip suddenly fired a beam of flaming red light and nearly singed off his right wing. He ducked into an instinctive spiral, dodging, but nearly slammed into a tentacle lined with nasty-looking barbs and weeping green fluid.

They needed to get out of here, now.

Robin fired off three more witch bolts before, with a grimace at the expenditure of energies, he conjured an **[Invisible Servant]** onto the ledge opposite where the rest of his party was standing, instructing it to throw any random pebbles it could find around the cavern, so long as they were away from where he was flying or where his party was hiding.

He sent a quick illusion to convey a message to Jhess. The rogue wouldn't like him breaking into her stores, but in light of how it might help them escape, well, maybe she'd make an exception.

He had to dodge a few more tentacles before he was able to send the rest of his plan to his party. Bruises and lacerations and even a few scorches from near misses with fire rays from the increasingly irate eyestalks were adding up, and his shoulders were beginning to scream. He needed to train his flying more. A lot more.

Eventually, however, at the cost of several more small wounds, he managed to arrange everything.

Robin was tiring fast, and he was very conscious of the fact that if it weren't for his shapeshifting and ability to use **[Visual Phantasm]** at will, he would long ago have fallen prey to the questing tentacles below.

Power. He needed more power. Always more. This was a dangerous world.

Wondrous, but dangerous.

Robin bent his attention to queuing up some distractions via [Lesser Phantasm]—he was ready to pump pure sonic hell through his illusions. When they went off, they would signal several things, provided his team had gotten all of the instructions and went along with them.

The first illusion began to wail, having run down the timer of silence that Robin had programmed into it. A horrendous screeching began, echoing from all corners of the cavern; Robin had spread the spells equidistant around the perimeter.

The tentacles went mad, lashing about, searching for the source of the noise.

Bolts of pure force and several daggers flashed out, drawing attention away from the exit while Vance, powered up and ready, leapt to the ground and began chopping through tentacles like a farmer sowing wheat. When a semicircular area had been sufficiently cleared, Drev dropped a few discs of force down, blocking much of the tentacles' reach as the nearby uncropped ones writhed madly, trying to stop the invaders causing so much pain and havoc.

Robin took the opportunity to fly up and over the writhing tentacles toward the exit, dropping down on the inside of Drev's barrier as the rest of his party slipped down from the ledge and sprinted for the exit.

It was not a noble end to a battle, nor was it a victory as such. Robin didn't much care, however, so long as they all made it out alive.

Sometimes, you didn't go for the kill. Sometimes, you went for the quick escape, if it meant you could live to see another day.

***

Robin moved slowly down the tunnel, wincing. After the confrontation in the cavern, crossing the rest of Silinir's territory had passed without event. He'd used [Healing Note] to take care of the worst of his wounds, but his left shoulder still stung, the feeling of those lost feathers itching in a way he'd never be able to scratch.

His eyes flicked over his character sheet, and he grimaced. He'd gained some experience from that conflict, but not as much as he'd hoped. It looked like even though he'd used some illusion spells, the fact that most of the plan had come down to brute force and simple distraction had somewhat limited his gains.

Sighing, he distributed the points, bumping his proficiencies as much as he could. If they managed to succeed in Nilsiir's quest, he had a feeling the resultant surge of experience would tip him right over into Tier Three, which, yeah, he would welcome, but he also wanted to make sure he wasn't letting too many of his skills fall behind. There were several numbers noticeably low that he should shore up.

So he did.

"This is it," Jhess called.

Robin looked up, converting his last spare experience points and dismissing the illusory interface before his eyes.

Jhess was pointing at a blank stretch of wall. Robin mentally checked the map Nilsiir had shown them and thought the rogue was probably correct. It was an otherwise unassuming stretch of passageway, about two-thirds of the way between one decorative sconce and the next.

"Now, we just need to find the way in. Find the trigger mechanism which opens the hidden door," the rogue said, carefully running her fingers along the stonework.

"Well, it's unlikely to be hidden by illusion," Robin noted, carefully examining the area. "In a city of illusionists, that would have too much risk of drawing attention. So there'll be a physical element to it, most likely. That would fit with Urkhan's mindset and that of his followers as well."

"I wish we had Ruprecht," Jhess complained. "He could just absorb the area and find the door for us that way."

It would be nice. And Ruprecht had certainly had a way with hidden passages! Weighting them in such a way that they worked like traps, and even large sections of stone could be moved with relatively little force . . .

Robin blinked. Force. Brute force. Could it really be that simple? But it would fit with what he knew of Urkhan and Melusk and Tarin-Tiran.

"Vance," he called. "Can you boost your strength as high as you can and then just start pressing—hard—against this wall to see if anything shifts? You'll need to be incredibly strong, stronger than any two or three of the brawnier peoples of Tarin-Tiran might be, I think."

"For a short period, I could probably manage it," Vance said. Power flared, and the librarian seemed denser.

And his hair was suddenly very long and very shiny.

Then he pressed against the wall. Once, twice, *there!*

On his third attempt, a section of the wall simply slid back. There should have been the scraping sound of stone on stone, but the soundlessness that cut off all noise around them spoke of a simple [Silence] enchantment of some kind.

Vance stepped back, revealing the entryway to a hidden room.

They'd found the first potential hiding spot!

Chapter 12

*T*he room Robin and the rest of his party found themselves in was small, but lushly appointed. It had been so tightly sealed that there wasn't even an appreciable amount of grime on things, just a small layer of very fine dust. Iron and gold were the most prominent metals, and red satins and velvets had been used liberally. There was a desk with an attached bookcase, a few small chests, some kind of sideboard or standing wardrobe, and a small but lush bed.

Jhess had claimed the chests, and Drev and Vance were carefully going over the place for hidden secrets. Savra was consulting her coin, and Robin?

Robin had called dibs on the desk, earning him glares from both the mage and the librarian. He'd ignored them. They could look at the books once they finished their scan, but he wanted first crack at the papers in the desk.

It wasn't locked, though it could have been. No wards apparently, either. Melusk seemed to have put a lot of stock in this place not being found. Justifiably, apparently, as it had remained untouched for centuries.

Ransacking the desk turned up several sheets of clean parchment, as well as quills and ink, sealing wax, and even a strange iron signet. Probably something to do with Melusk's dedication to Urkhan. After checking each one for hidden messages or other secrets, Robin dropped them into his storage.

Meanwhile, Jhess was swearing to herself. The chests, at least, appeared to be trapped. On the plus side, that argued for there being something worth guarding in them.

Robin refocused on the papers. There were a couple of scattered bills; scraps which Melusk might have kept for scratch-paper purposes or some other reason; letters, mostly inane braggadocio shouting at rivals—both political and romantic—but no secret missives to his cult of support or anything convenient like that.

One book sat on the desk, a thin ribbon marking a place halfway through. Robin opened it, and his eyes widened.

Melusk's journal! Now he was getting somewhere!

He looked up at the bookshelves he had only glanced at earlier. They were all journals! Melusk's secret thoughts, all laid out before them! Oh, this was good.

Robin quickly read the contents of the final page, Melusk's last thoughts before the fall of Tarin-Tiran.

It was not a pleasant experience. **[Tongue of the Fallen Tower]** translated it easily enough, but every word seemed to strike at his eyes as he read it, power and cruelty in every line of script. What language it was, he did not know, but from the feel of it, it had something to do with Urkhan. Maybe a secret temple tongue? As good as a secret code, for most purposes.

"Can you read this?"

Robin heard Drev asking Vance the question with half an ear, but he was so absorbed in reading the journal that he didn't do more than make an absent note of the fact.

"No," Vance replied. "Some kind of temple tongue? Our bard doesn't seem to have any issue with it, though."

Robin ignored them and focused on reading.

Melusk had been a piece of work and a piece of shit, but scanning quickly through the earlier journals, it seemed at the beginning he hadn't been any worse than your average aspiring politician. At some point, however, he'd been converted to the worship of Urkhan. An easy thing, considering his ambition and lust for power and control. Even his early journals whined constantly about the lack of respect shown to him and the chaotic nature of society in Tarin-Tiran.

"You could have just moved, asshole," Robin muttered.

It was rough going. He had the end and the beginning, but the middle was hard. There were too many journals to easily pinpoint events like when he had decided to take over the city, or how he'd first subverted Leivniz. It was taxing enough just trying to untangle his plan from the egotistical and ranting entries in the later journals.

Melusk needed an editor, badly.

But some things became clear. Terrifyingly so.

"I think I found what Gis and his dogs are looking for." Robin's voice was a thread poised to snap.

Motion in the room stilled as all eyes turned to him.

Robin turned, a grim look on his face, and held up the journal. On the open page was a detailed drawing of a crude and brutalist crown, surrounded by increasingly illegible notes. Its points were blocky, squared off things, and a large gem like a slitted, burning eye was inset front and center.

"What is that?" Jhess asked, her hand on the top of the chest she had just disarmed.

"The crown of Kharvec'Na, apparently," Robin answered. "It's an artifact of incredible, brutal power. Whosoever successfully dons it can issue irresistible commands, almost at will. Makes it really easy for wannabe tyrants to pull off successful coups."

"Melusk had it? Did he use it? We didn't see anything like that in any of the illusions." Vance frowned. "There has to be some catch that prevented him."

"A big one. The crown itself is sentient and, if these notes are correct, is incredibly strong-willed in its own right. One wrong move by the wearer, and suddenly, they're just a meat-puppet for the mind inside the crown." Robin sighed. "A former tyrant and High Priest of Urkhan, of course."

"So Melusk was too afraid to try his luck?" Drev asked. "Or didn't get the chance to for some reason?"

"He was certainly planning to try, but the journal doesn't say what, if anything, stopped him. He was afraid, though; I can tell that much." Robin flipped through a few more pages. "And he was convinced that there were secrets to the crown that he had not been told. Seems like the Church of Urkhan isn't the most trusting of environments. Imagine."

"If anyone, let alone a Disciple of Urkhan, gets their hands on that crown . . ." Savra's voice was ominous as it trailed off, painting a horrible picture in the minds of all assembled.

"Yeah. Being on the receiving end of Gis's little [Command]s and [Suggest]ions has been bad enough," Robin complained. "If he had this . . ." He shuddered theatrically.

"So we make sure he doesn't get it. We get there first and figure out how to destroy it," Drev said firmly.

"Won't be easy," Jhess spoke, "considering how hard it was to get to this place. And these traps are no joke. That crown is going to be better hidden and better defended."

"And divine artifacts—rather, artifacts of any kind are notoriously difficult to destroy," Savra added solemnly. "Many have only a single way in which they might be destroyed. Cast into a specific volcano or touched by the hand of a singular deity or immortal personage."

"I'll keep going through the journals," Robin said. "There might be more clues in here. Hopefully, the rest of you will find some more useful stuff."

"Let's see!" Jhess opened the chest in front of her, eyes gleaming. "Hello, my shiny friends!"

Shinies? Rerebos perked up and flitted across the room to peer over the rogue's shoulder.

Robin kept reading. A phrase kept coming up in relation to the crown: the primum command. Melusk was terribly concerned with phrasing it correctly. It sounded like there was only one command—perhaps the first one—which you could give to the spirit within that it was bound to obey. All other effects could only be accomplished through a battle of wills, and if the spirit managed to subvert an order enough, it could usurp the will of the wearer. Not what you'd want.

High priests and tyrants weren't necessarily known for being weak willed, either.

Melusk had line after line in various permutations trying to come up with a command that could encompass as many future commands as possible, with slight variations in wording between each of them.

I command you to issue all commands as I bid you, exactly as I word them, with the full strength of your power behind them.

It looked like part of Melusk's issue was that if the command was too general, there were ways around it, and if it was too specific, there tended to be all manner of loopholes. It was akin to trying to get a wish from a malevolent djinn. The crown appeared to have several powers, and they worked in different ways. It was difficult to boil everything down to a single command which would put the crown fully at the mercy of the bearer.

Ah! Some stories of past bearers of the artifact. Some had died because they had too carelessly issued commands to their followers, which the crown had reached out and enforced in unexpected ways. One king had ordered a rebellious food taster to make sure none of his food was ever poisoned. The crown had reached out, enforcing the command and further empowering the servant with a measure of magic. The servant, compelled by the crown, had then starved the king to death.

Hey, if you didn't eat anything, you could be sure nothing you ate was poisoned.

The crown could be resisted, as could most mind-influencing spells, but it was difficult. The will and the power in that thing were titanic, if Melusk's journals were to be believed. And nowhere in Melusk's journals or notes could Robin find any mention of how to destroy this thing. His [**Bardic Lore**] was equally unhelpful.

It was enough to make a guy want an iron will, or a ring of mind shielding.

Robin didn't have either of those, but he did have a free point he could spend on enhancing his mental resistance. Which stat was that again? He called up his character sheet.

Ah, yes. *Resilience*. It governed resistance to mind-influencing effects, how long his mental energy could last, and other similar things.

Robin considered what they had learned, and the path most likely in front of him. Then he grimaced. No point holding on to that extra point any longer. If he was going to need it for anything, it would be for this.

He put the point into *Resilience*. If his mind was going to ever need shielding, this was going to be one of those times.

"Come on," he said. "We've learned as much as we can here. Let's find that crown before that evil old fucker can."

Robin Parker

Heritage: Shadeling, Paragon
Profession: Bard
Tier: 2 (Effective Level: 9)
Experience: 50
Spell Points: 27
Bardsong: 9 uses

Properties

Free Ranks Available: 1

Physical
    -Strength: 11
    -Dexterity: 14
    -Fortitude: 11
Mental
    -Intelligence: 17
    -Cunning: 25
    -Resilience: 14

Social
- -Charisma: 15
- -Manipulation: 13
- -Poise: 16

Proficiencies

Free Ranks Available: 1

Physical (9/9)
- -Athletics: 7
- -Brawl: 7
- -Dodge: 11
- -Melee Combat: 6
- -Pilot: 5
- -Ranged Combat: 11
- -Sleight of Hand: 10
- -Stealth: 12
- -Survival: 8

Mental (9/9)
- -Arcane Lore: 10
- -Bureaucracy: 7
- -Concentration: 11
- -Crafting: 9
- -Healing: 8
- -Insight: 12
- -Learning: 9
- -Natural Wisdom: 6
- -Perception: 12

Social (9/9)
- -Animism: 6
- -Deception: 12
- -Empathy: 10
- -Expression: 11
- -Gossip: 9
- -Intimidation: 8
- -Persuasion: 10
- -Socialize: 9
- -Streetwise: 9

Peculiarities

Blessing of Rhyth
Tongue of the Fallen Tower
Mark of the Trickster
Chronicle of Infinite Visions
Mask of Myriad Faces
Initiate of the Craft
Illusion Focus
Metamagic Initiate
Improved Familiar Bond x2
Effortless Illusions
Metamagic Specialty: Duration

Perks

Wayfaring Stranger
Shard of the Shattered Manymind
Mark of Fairy's Favor
Touch of Wild Magic

Spells

Cantrips* (*no SP cost)
   -Lesser Phantasm*
   -Cutting Words*
   -Legerdemain*
   -Lesser Nightmare Curse*
   -Lesser Witch Bolt*
   -Minor Repair*
   -Lesser Charm*
Tier 1 (1SP each)
   -Visual Phantasm*
   -Healing Note
   -Whispers from Beyond
   -Minor Enchanted Slumber
   -Invisible Servant
   -Familiar Bond
   -Wizard's Armor
Tier 2 (3SP each)
   -Assume Quality (Special)
   -Lesser Mindreading

-Sorcerous Mark
-Phantasmal Mouth
-Lesser Figment

Bardsong

Command Attention
Song of Arcane Power

Chapter 13

$\mathcal{R}$obin began conjuring the illusory runes which would allow Nilsiir to manifest in this room and take it as his own while the rest of his party ransacked the place for anything of remote value. Robin himself would have loved to swipe the desk, but there wasn't enough room in his storage ring for it at the moment. Not that he really needed the leftovers of a follower of Urkhan.

Jhess had emptied the chests of their stored riches in coin. There were still several vials which seemed to have once contained potions and the like, but those had cracked or turned to stone or otherwise suffered some kind of ill effect, possibly from a wave of wild magic passing through the room at some point.

Robin frowned. He'd completed the runic array, but everything had remained the same.

"What's wrong?" Drev asked, noticing his expression.

"Do you see anything wrong with this?" Robin gestured to the illusion in front of him. "I can't see any errors, but nothing is happening."

Drev, Vance close behind him, stepped up to the illusion tracing its ways around and across the room, and went over the runes carefully.

"I don't see anything wrong," Drev said finally. "All of the runes look correct."

"Agreed. So maybe the runes aren't the problem," Vance added. Then he snapped his fingers. "Or *these* runes aren't the problem!"

"Of course!" Robin wanted to kick himself. "They aren't integrated into the network!"

"The what?" Vance glanced at him. "*Net-work?*" the librarian sounded the word out in English.

Robin's heart spiked against his ribcage, but he forced himself to casually repeat it in the common tongue of this land, "Net-work. Because it's like the runes are all connected like a net in order to do their work," he explained. "It's a phrase from my land."

"Ah, and the net has no draw line, so it simply floats about doing nothing!" Drev nodded. "It needs to be connected to the wider runic structure."

"Hopefully that's all it takes, yes." Robin made a show of looking around. "And there is none in here because Melusk wished to remain hidden. So where is the closest . . . probably one of the lights on the wall outside."

Robin muttered to himself as he paced back out the exit and squinted and worked at the wall until he uncovered the runic structure he was looking for. He was going to have to narrow the area to make it all fit. There was only so much space he could encompass within the illusion without hitting the limits to his conjuring. Still, it would be enough for Nilsiir to manifest.

Then it would be up to the illusory high priest to figure out how to expand their hold on the area.

The magic sparked at Robin's fingertips, and the illusion suddenly flared into reality, burning new runes across the stones in a lopsided circle—Robin couldn't quite reach the walls.

"Ah! Thank you." Nilsiir began to look around them. "So this is where the old bastard was holed up."

"One of several," Robin said, gesturing with one of Melusk's journals. "Though not the one where he was keeping his biggest weapon—"

"Or even any of his good magic items," Jhess complained.

"Well, that was rather cheap of him," Nilsiir quipped. "But I can't say it's out of character. I wouldn't be surprised if he had a tomb somewhere already fitted to receive his undying dominion before things went pear-shaped there at the end."

Please no. Robin did *not* need that kind of energy flying around in the universe when he still had to find this crown and destroy it before Gis could get his knobbly old fingers on it.

"Any idea which of the next two locations is likelier than the other?" Robin asked. "I don't think Gis and his people will be wasting any time in searching these places out; they'll already know where to look, while we're still somewhat guessing."

Nilsiir waved their hand, and the room around them changed. Well, first a series of runes arced up from the existing structure to subsume the nearby walls and *then* the illusory high priest twisted nearby reality to match their whims, transforming the former hideaway of Urkhan's lackey into a joyous monument to what appeared to be a series of racy pranks with Melusk as the (sometimes literal) butt of the joke.

Robin tore his eyes away from the shockingly detailed mural and looked at Nilsiir expectantly.

The high priest conjured a map, and their eyes went distant.

"There," they finally said, pointing to the further of the two options. "That is the likeliest place. Fiara agrees."

"I think so as well," Savra spoke quietly, staring with wide eyes at the coin in her hands.

"Why?" Jhess glanced over, a flicker of concern in her eyes. "What do you see?"

"There is woe in each direction, but a sliver of weal as well at the location High Priest Nilsiir points. But the woe I sense if we do not follow this suggestion . . ." Savra shuddered.

"Well, that pretty much seals it then, doesn't it?" Vance asked, looking around. "And it's not like there is much more we can accomplish here. Robin, do you have the map? The best route to take to get there?"

Robin studied the illusion Nilsiir had conjured.

"We can move fast by cutting through Silinir's territory again, or slightly more slowly while navigating around it," the bard said. "It's a risk either way, but I've got both routes memorized."

"Speed," Drev suggested reluctantly. "I think we need to take the risk, and it doesn't look like it's much of the dungeon's territory we'd need to cross."

"It's likely to be quite dangerous territory, though, this deep," Vance reminded him. "But I agree. Speed first."

"Wish us luck," Robin told Nilsiir. "Looks like we're taking the shortcut."

"Good luck! Now what are you waiting for?" Nilsiir looked at them. "Off you fuck!"

***

The party stood at a fork in the tunnels. To the left was the longer route, the safer route. To the right was the faster route through Silinir's territory. Even though they had all agreed to take that path, they still paused. This was the point of no return. After this, there would be no going back.

Robin caught Savra flipping her coin again. So even the seeress was having doubts? Interesting.

Well, you couldn't be fast if you were also dead, and the last time they'd cut through Silinir's territory, they'd faced a tentacled horror that none of them had been able to identify, and if they'd been slightly less paranoid and simply walked across the floor, it very well might have maimed or killed one or more of them.

This world really was like playing a game with a hostile dungeon master sometimes.

"We've already made our decision," Robin heard himself say.

"We have," Vance agreed.

"Nothing wrong with reevaluating in the face of new information, though," Drev added. "If we have any."

Savra shook her head.

"Jhess," the mage asked, "think we should do a quick scout ahead on each tunnel before we decide?"

"It's not a bad idea, if we think we can take the time." The rogue scratched her nose. "But I thought the whole point was that we didn't have the time. We're racing someone else for the prize here, aren't we?"

I smell something. Rerebos suddenly stirred on Robin's shoulder.

What is it? The bard tensed. *Which tunnel is it coming from?*

Stupid nose is much worse than tongue, the little dragon complained. *My own form is so superior to this stupid disguise!*

Hold that thought.

"Ree-Ree senses something," Robin whispered, motioning the party to modulate their volume. "He's not sure where it's coming from, but I don't think we're alone down here."

Jhess held up a hand, and the party stilled, silencing themselves. The rogue carefully lowered herself down to the tunnel floor and gently pressed her ear to the ground, first in the direction of Silinir's territory, then in the direction of the tunnel taking the long way around, and finally behind the party, back down the way they had already traveled.

Then she cocked her head, a quick and violent movement that nearly made Robin jump out of his skin.

She looked like a frelling possessed woman in a horror film!

"I think I hear something down the tunnel behind us." Jhess squinted back down the way they had already traveled.

The party stilled, all straining their senses to catch a whisper of what the rogue had heard. The chittering of crysrats? The scrape of hooves on stone? Or—

Voices!

Just a few soft syllables came wafting out of the velvety darkness to catch at the party's ears. Robin strained, but he couldn't make out what was being said. It was unfortunate, but the syllables alone told him more than he wanted to know. Because his trained bardic ear recognized both tone and timbre to several of those fragmentary words.

Robin knew that voice!

Gis!

Chapter 14

That's Gis and his party!

Robin conjured the words with **[Visual Phantasm]** as his mind immediately began to race. There was the opportunity for an ambush here, for some trickery. Every option that came to mind was a gamble, however.

The tunnel forked here. It would be easy to redirect Gis down one or the other pathways with a simple illusion, provided they were not moving carefully. But should they send Gis and company down the longer route and risk the shortcut, or take the safe path themselves and send Gis into Silinir's territory, hoping the priest would be destroyed or delayed by what might be found there?

Robin wished he knew what kind of map the priest was using. That would make the decision easier. But he didn't, and there was no time to dwell.

Retreat toward Silinir's territory. We need speed. I'll delay with illusion and catch up. Jhess, be careful while scouting!

The party nodded and slipped away as Robin whirled to carefully examine the floor, ceiling, and walls around this juncture so he could match them seamlessly with an illusion. Behind him, the sound of his friends faded into the darkness. Ahead of him, the sounds of Gis advancing slowly grew. Robin quickly stepped back into the tunnel on silent feet and conjured what he hoped would be a seamless illusion to block the way.

Thankfully, the air down here was still; no whisper of movement which might give things away. Robin moved to the tunnel's wall and pressed his back to it so he'd have partial cover from the approaching party and so he could see down the tunnel he hoped to effortlessly guide Gis down.

All too soon, someone broke his field of vision. Robin stiffened and clamped down on the urge to gasp in alarm. It was the last of the hobgoblin scouts, looking very much worse for wear. The brute paused and sniffed, but then shook his head and plodded dully on. He was clearly exhausted. Good for Robin! Exhausted people made mistakes.

Maybe a whisper of breath escaped his lips, or maybe Gis's status as disciple had enhanced his senses, but as the high priest passed the illusory wall behind which Robin hid, he paused, eyes narrowing.

"Sir?" one of the two brutes in armor asked. "Do you hear something?"

Robin froze, breath caught in the clutch of his lungs. He didn't move. He didn't dare so much as turn his head. His eyes were fixed fast to Gis's face.

Fortunately, the evil old man kept his eye patch in place, the snake that lived in his skull safely hidden away. Its heightened senses would not be brought into play. At least, they hadn't been yet. And there was no way Robin was going to simply stand here and wait for the worst to happen.

Time for a distraction.

Robin flexed his fingers silently through the motions of [**Lesser Phantasm**] and conjured the soft sound of a falling stone as far down the tunnel as he could.

Gis's head whipped around as the scout called out in response to the sound. The whole party went on high alert, but their attention was focused ahead, not to the sides, and they swiftly moved off down the tunnel.

Robin let out a long, slow breath, mentally renewing the illusion so it would last as long as possible after he left. Hopefully, Gis and company would be long gone by then and have no reason to backtrack.

He turned and made his way quickly after his friends, using his mental connection with Rerebos to guide him and assure himself that everything was fine with them so far. Now, they just needed to get through the shortcut intact and find the room and crown before Gis could catch up to them.

***

Robin panted. If he never saw another tentacle, it would be too soon! Thankfully, Jhess had spotted the formation in the cave floor, and this time they had taken extra care while traversing the ropes they'd strung across the cavern, making it through without incident.

There hadn't been any other major encounters in Silinir's territory. Robin wanted to call it good luck, but his recent experiences told him it was just the Scales of Fate balancing in advance of some seriously bad luck.

"It's got to be around here somewhere," Vance said, almost growling in frustration.

Robin had led them to the section of ruins marked by Nilsiir's map. These were in as good repair as the last section, and while that alone wasn't enough to raise suspicion, it did indicate they were in the right spot. There was no way Melusk's hiding place would have crumbled away.

"Try here." Jhess was squinting at a section of stone. "I'm not sure, but I think the color is slightly different."

Vance grunted and threw his enhanced strength against the wall once more. This time, it moved!

"Let me check for traps," Jhess said, ducking inside. "There weren't any last time, but better safe than sorry."

Robin almost bounced with nerves. They'd bought themselves some time, but Gis and his party could show up any minute now, and the last thing they wanted was to be caught in a dead end when that happened.

"Hu—" he began.

"Don't tell me to hurry up!" Jhess called over her shoulder. "Dead is slower, I promise."

So he waited with the rest of the party as Jhess did her thing. The rogue found a poison-needle trap and two trip wires attached to acid sprays, but nothing else. Drev confirmed there were no magical traps he could detect.

Inside Melusk's second hiding space was a small chamber almost identical to the last one. There was a desk and a small bookcase, several chests, a small bed, and little else. The main difference, however, was this room had paintings hung all across the walls. Not murals. Paintings.

"These have to be magic," Drev said. "They should have cracked and aged beyond all recognition by now, but they're as fresh as the day they were painted. Yet I cannot sense any magic in any of them."

"There are spells which conceal magic," Robin noted. "Maybe the frames are enchanted with those somehow? Both to preserve and hide the magic? No use creating a little hidey-hole like this if the magical signature gives it away."

"Look at this one," Jhess called softly. "The ego on this asshole."

Robin moved to look at the painting Jhess was pointing to. It was a portrait of Melusk; he recognized the man from the illusory scenes they had encountered earlier. He stood in a richly detailed hall—the architecture matched that of Tarin-Tiran, actually. He wore ermine and scarlet and there was a distinct crown upon his head. It was a brutalist, ugly thing, and it matched the description of the crown and the sketches Robin had found in the man's journals.

"Subtle he was not," Robin drawled. "Like so many of Urkhan's little pests."

"We could have company at any moment," Drev reminded them. "Let us see if we can find the crown and get out of here before that happens, shall we?"

"Indeed," Vance said. "Shall we turn our senses to seeing what magic might be present, yet hidden?"

"I'm going to check the chests," the rogue spoke. "He might have thought the place hidden enough not to need to hide the crown as well."

"I'll check behind the paintings for secret caches," Robin said. Too many stories from his old world where safes were concealed behind paintings.

"Now you're thinking like a proper rogue." Jhess smiled approvingly. "I'd not heard of that one, but good thought."

Robin began moving the paintings as the rest of his party began searching the room with means both magical and mundane. He found nothing but blank stone walls, Savra's divinations turned up nothing, and while Jhess had managed to disarm the traps on the chests, again all they found was bits of silver and gold, with the occasional jewel thrown in for variety.

There was no sign of the crown.

"I don't understand it. Something like that should be radiating a powerful magical signature," Drev said in frustration. "But I sense nothing of the kind. Maybe it's not here."

"Or maybe it's right in front of our noses," Robin replied. "Think about it. We know the paintings are magical, but they don't read as magic. Maybe the enchantment isn't there to hide how magical they are, but to hide the aura of the crown? Or both. But the point is, maybe it's—" Memories of moving paintings and stories of jumping into chalk murals and other works of art surfaced in his mind.

Robin reached out to gently probe the painting of Melusk with one finger. "Maybe it's somehow *in* the painting?"

The canvas was strangely cool beneath his touch, but nothing immediately happened.

"Melusk would certainly have access to the funds needed for such a thing," Vance noted thoughtfully.

"Too bad we can't trust Nilsiir enough to just summon them and have them do that reality-warping thing they do. That would probably make the crown pop right out." Jhess sighed.

"There's a reason Nilsiir didn't ask us to do that," Robin said. "We need to deal with the crown first. I'm willing to bet there's some danger to Nilsiir which the crown represents. Not that we're likely to ever know what it is. The secrets that priest keeps . . ." Robin shook his head.

"If it is in the painting, and that is a large if," Savra spoke, "how do we get it out?"

"Vance, check the desk for anything that looks like a command word; you read more quickly than I do. Let me know if you encounter any temple tongue." Robin kept staring at the painting.

"Most magical items do have an activation word or sigil of some kind," Drev agreed. "Perhaps there is a clue to it concealed in the frame?"

"What would happen if we just cut the crown bit free from the rest of the painting?" Jhess asked, dagger in hand. "Seems like that might work."

"It also might cause the dimensional space the crown is in to be lost on another plane, or the loosing of such energies might destroy us, possibly even suck us into whatever space the crown is held in."

"Evil magical crown lost in another world? Doesn't sound too bad to me." Jhess shrugged.

"Let's call that plan B," Robin said. "I'd rather not risk any of the other possibilities Drev mentioned if we can help it."

"Fine," Jhess replied. "I'll help Ree-Ree keep watch, then. Call me if you find something physical to disarm or unlock."

Robin and Drev nodded, most of their attention still on the painting, as Drev began cycling through common activation phrases for magical items, though it was clearly a long shot.

The painting was smooth and cool beneath Robin's fingers, but even when he carefully searched it with all of his senses, he found no hidden messages nor runes, no switch triggers or other clues. The bit of the painting which replicated the crown felt noticeably colder than any other part, so they had to be right that the crown was in there, but how to get it out?

A flare of alarm suddenly blasted across his mind. Rerebos had spotted something!

"Shit," Jhess cursed, ducking back into the room. "We've got company. Any luck with that crown?"

"Not yet," Drev answered.

"Then grab the painting and let's go! We can figure out how to get the ugly jewelry out of it later, when we're not about to have an angry disciple up our collective ass." Jhess was practically vibrating with nerves.

Robin grabbed the painting.

"It's stuck to the wall! It won't come off." The bard cursed.

"Leave it, then!"

"I'm not leaving it," Robin snapped back. "If Gis gets this, it's game over. He could use it to dominate the entire continent."

"Then we take our chances cutting the bitch out," the rogue said, advancing with her dagger.

"Whatever you do, do it fast," Vance urged. "I can hear them. They'll turn the corner any moment now and see the gap in the wall."

Robin's mind whirled. There had to be a trick to this! Something obvious he was missing!

But what?

Chapter 15

*T*he enemy was coming.

Robin's mind flew through potential options.

The enemy was coming.

Think! This was an artifact of Urkhan, hidden in a magical safe commissioned by a follower of—*of course!*

"Come!" Robin ordered, placing his finger on the painted image of the crown and focusing his will and magical energies on the act of *commanding* it to appear.

And it did.

The crown was heavy in his hands and burned with a cold and pitiless power. Robin could have sworn he saw the great eyelike jewel blink at him, but surely that was his imagination, right?

Right?

"Great!" Jhess exclaimed. "Now let's get out of—"

"Too late," Vance called, throwing his strength against the stone and shoving it back into place. "They're already here."

"But now we're trapped!" Jhess shouted.

"But they can't target us with their spells or ranged attacks," Drev said, immediately realizing why Vance had done what he had done.

"But we're *trapped!*" Jhess threw her arms up in the air. "How are we supposed to get out now?"

There was a great *thud*, and the section of the wall that was the secret door shuddered slightly. Vance braced himself against it, holding it in place.

"I think they noticed it closing," the librarian said drily. "Options?"

"Fight our way out. Find a secret door which has so far eluded us. Use magic to call Nilsiir and hope for the best. Or"—Drev glanced at the artifact in Robin's hands—"figure out how to use *that* against them."

"Jhess, can you reset any of the traps? Can we use those if we have to fight?" Robin asked, turning the crown around in his hand. "Drev, check the other paintings for anything that looks like a magical secret door or transportation spell. I think that's more likely to be Melusk's escape plan than another physical exit."

"Fine." Jhess's hands flew into action while Drev just nodded and turned his attention to the paintings. Savra flipped her coin, over and over, looking for ways out of this mess, and Vance kept his back to the door, holding the stone closed with all his might. Rerebos flitted around over their heads, radiating frustrated anger and a little bit of fear.

Robin thrust his mind into the well that was his **[Bardic Lore]**. There had to be something in there he could use now that he'd read through all of Melusk's theoretical attempts to make the crown bend to his will. What phrasing could he use to bring the crown to heel?

Because Gis and company were banging at the gate.

Literally.

He could hear the muffled cursing and scraping of stone on stone as they tried to force the door open, though they'd have to work harder if they wanted to overcome Vance's enhanced strength and the power of a strategically placed wedge of wood that he had broken off the chair and used as a makeshift doorstop.

"How are we coming on that alternate exit?" Vance yelled.

"Nothing so far!" Drev shouted back. "Savra?"

"I do not see any other way out of this room," the seeress replied. "We leave via that door alone. Or—or not at all."

Was that hesitation?

"Savra," Robin called. "What else do you see?"

The seeress glared at him.

"Nothing," she said defiantly.

"Savra! We need to know all the options here!"

There came the sound of stone grating on stone, and the wall began to crack as the passageway was slowly forced open from the outside.

"Tell him, Savra!" Vance shouted. "I'm not sure how much longer this will hold!"

"Fine!" the seeress snapped. "Our only ways out are through that door or via the crown! I can see no more than that! But the crown holds a way for us to leave this place. It comes at an incalculable cost, however. I have never seen such a sea of woe!"

Robin turned the artifact over in his hands. It was round, like a portal, and it held the key to their escape; that much was clear. If only Savra could divine the best phrase to use to command its power!

There were no clues he could see. No mystic runes in an ancient language he could conveniently read with [Tongue of the Fallen Tower], or any moving parts to manipulate and activate an effect without actually having to wear the thing.

No. If he was going to use the thing to get them out of this mess, to make sure that Gis didn't get his gnarled old hands on it, there was only really one option.

"Jhess," he spoke. "Be sure to stick a dagger in my heart if I go mad from the power or anything like that."

"What?" The rogue blinked at him, but before anyone else could respond, the bard acted.

Robin raised the crown and placed it defiantly upon his brow.

And it burned. Burned with a cold fire unlike anything he might have ever imagined. There was a sense of incredible age, of a cruel intelligence that watched the cycling stars pass as eon crumbled into eon and cared for nothing save that it endured, that it retained its power and might.

Time slowed around him, and the world slowly faded away from Robin's conscious mind. The field of stars burned in the darkness, one large red specimen beginning to pulse and grow, coming nearer and nearer until he could see it was the stellar twin of the gem inset in the crude crown he now wore upon his brow.

The presence within the crown beat down on him, wave after wave of crushing willpower seeking to drive him to his knees. The stars around him screamed in their spheres, a trilling, agonizing cacophony that grated on his soul like nails on a chalkboard. A crushing pressure wrung the breath from his lungs, and his head throbbed with cold fire in a slowly tightening vise. Every sense that could be assaulted was assaulted, and Robin knew he was trapped in a battle of wills unlike any he had heretofore experienced.

It was a no-holds-barred, take-no-prisoners assault on Robin's mind and senses. It beat at him from every direction, via every sense. A merciless, never-ending attack which drove him relentlessly back and back.

He wanted nothing more than to scream at the top of his mental lungs for it to STOP!

Somewhere in the midst of the cacophony, that thought prompted a single moment of clarity, undisturbed by the tempest all around. Of *course* the entity within the crown wanted him to order it to stop! That would use up Robin's first command! The only one the crown was a hundred percent bound to obey.

"That's not going to work," Robin forced himself to say calmly.

He had no idea if he was speaking aloud or only in the vaults of his mind, but his voice cut through the noise all around, so he suspected it was the latter.

The assault on his senses abruptly ceased. The malevolent will he had sensed withdrew and focused into a single point, the burning eye that had once been a star hanging before his eyes.

Robin could feel it weighing him, looking for weaknesses. Then came a sense of demand, mixed with query.

The crown wanted to know Robin's first command.

But Robin had no idea what that should be, yet. Had no idea how much time he had before he had to make a choice. He felt that time, here—within his mind or within the crown—moved more slowly than it did in the wider world around him, but it was not stilled.

Play for time. Find out more. Perhaps there were clues in here which could help him.

"It is customary when doing business that the negotiators meet face-to-face," Robin said, careful not to issue demands or speak anything which might be conceived of as a command. "Would you be willing to reveal yourself to me, that I might know who it is I am dealing with?"

The eye that burned before him blinked before it began to slowly whirl until it spun out into three identical eyes, the slits of each pupil pointing toward the space in the center of all of them. These eyes were set into a massive floating bulk of flesh which thinned out in nine separate places to coil into tentacles, each ending in their own bloodshot burning eye.

Three mouths, one between each of the central three eyes, split into wide and disturbingly angular smiles full of jagged teeth. A purple tongue slunk out of one to slide over the central eyes, cleaning them.

"Hello then, pretender. Face-to-face we meet, as you asked."

Robin's [Bardic Lore] screamed at him. This was entirely unexpected. He had thought he'd be facing a human priest of Urkhan, or a pious warlord or fallen paladin type. But no.

The tyrant inhabiting the crown, the guiding force behind its magic, and the mind that constantly strove to subjugate the will of anyone who wore the crown wasn't even human!

A tyrant of nine eyes and three!

Chapter 16

Robin stared at the aberrant monstrosity floating in front of him. Tyrants of nine eyes and three were creatures of monstrous appetites and monstrous wills, which some tales said came into being through sheer force of madness and personality. Other tales said they originated on other planes or other worlds, and merely used the force of their monstrous wills to travel between places, forcing themselves on a reality which suited their wishes when they could not find what they desired nearby.

This was the mind inside the crown; the mind which Robin must now contend with for mastery of the arcane forces within.

"Well, pretender?" the thing spoke. "You asked and have received. What would you have of me? You clearly know something of the power of the crown."

Those eyes. This had to be what the specimen on a dissection table felt. Or would feel, were they alive to sense the coming of the scalpel. Robin felt flayed and filleted and plumbed for his secrets.

"What is it you think I do not know, then, of the powers of the crown?" Robin asked, again careful not to phrase anything as a command.

Tyrants were often egotists, and egotists could sometimes be persuaded to brag. Maybe there would be a clue here—as long as he was careful. The legends of these tyrants of eyes had them in possession of a canny and cunning intelligence, in addition to great power and will.

"Clearly, you know that the commands you may issue to me are limited, or else you would not be so careful issuing your first one." The eyes tracked Robin's figure. "You are a bard, and you stink of illusions, so you must have some measure of cleverness, though likely not nearly as much as you fancy you have."

Ouch. So the tyrant was a bitch as well. Great.

"Do you truly think me so great a fool as to come here without some idea of what I might face? Do you have any idea how extensive the notes the last follower of Urkhan left were?"

If the bitch wanted to chat shit, it would find Robin was more than ready to throw down.

Had that been a flicker of unease? It was so hard to tell, looking at that alien visage. Not to mention the thing didn't even have a body to betray it. It was all mind and old magic and madness.

"You are none of Urkhan's, and I can taste the stink of that idiot Rhyth upon you, so yes, I do think you a great fool. You may command me once, but I suspect your will will hold out no more than that, can hold out no more than that, and were it not for—"The thing fell silent.

Not for what?

One command. One irresistible command. That was what Melusk had been trying to spin into a chain of irresistible commands, like someone try-ing to wish for more wishes when the genie was irrevocably evil and liked nothing better than to twist the intent behind every word.

"Quickly now," the thing taunted him. "You have only a little time."

Misty aurorae grew out of the hollows of space, the pockets of darkness, all around. Within each, Robin caught glimpses, scattered shards of what was occurring outside his body as he wrestled with the crown in the vaults of his mind.

Vance's face was frozen in a mask of panic as he was forced back, the stone door he was braced against finally giving way before the efforts of Gis's party. Time still flowed like honey, Robin could see and sense that, but even honey ran out of the jar eventually.

Jhess was trying to stab one of her daggers between the stone of the door and the stone of the floor to act as a metal doorstop. A cloud of purple-white sparks hung about Drev's person, his mouth open in a slow-motion chant of some kind. Defensive force, probably.

Savra was clearly deep in prayer, her hand on Robin's shoulder. Was she attempting to channel divine guidance his way? If so, he could use every scrap he could get!

He couldn't see Rerebos, but he could still feel their connection, muted and distant as it was. The little dragon was . . . alarmed? Excited?

There was definitely some greed there.

"Oh dear, it seems like your friends are very close to dying," the tyrant keened, speaking in an eerie three-part harmony with itself. "And I sense one of my brothers in Urkhan coming, a fellow disciple! He will wrest that crown from you if you do not issue a command quickly! And if you lose the crown, you will lose all. All will, all freedom, all of your *friends*."

The laugh that broke free from those triplicate lips twisted Robin's spine through non-Euclidean geometries and sent shock-wave shivers through his core.

Rhyth, but he hated this thing! Its very existence made his skin crawl, but more than that, it was twisted and knew just which buttons to push to make him squirm. He honestly didn't know what would be more satisfying: bending it to his will or destroying it utterly.

Destroying it would be safer. Making it bow before him would be more satisfying.

Or would it? Robin paused. He was wearing a magical artifact on his head, one inhabited by the spirit of an egotistical tyrant. Was that his desire for conquest, or did it come from the crown? How fast could this thing infect his thinking?

The saying was that power corrupted, but what power usually tended to do was simply make people more of what they already were. How that might square with constantly battling the dead spirit of a magical monstrosity stuck in a crown, however, was not something he'd had to philosophically contend with before.

The urge to dominate the tyrant receded before the force of Robin's thoughts, unable to contend with the personality that gave rise to them. Probably not his desire for conquest, then. This thing was fucking insidious!

Robin eyed the tyrant floating in front of him.

"All it takes to save them is one command, though, is that not correct?" Robin drew a slow, satisfied smile across his face, looking for a response from the many eyes of the thing before him. "Could not the right command bring anyone, even you, low? As long as it is the first one?"

Was that a twitch in one of the outer orbs? A quiver of fear in that tentacle?

The first command was irresistible. That was the key. Robin's mind began to gnaw at an idea, but he needed more time for it to coalesce.

"And how am I to even know if these visions that you show me are true? I've met Urkhan, and I have met his priests, and are they not as full of lies as they are of ambition? Does it not seem second nature to them?"

"Blasphemy!" the tyrant roared from all three of its mouths. "The mighty Urkhan has no need for lies! Main strength alone is the foundational stone of our faith, of our god's immutable power!"

"That's not the Urkhan I know, but hasn't it been a very long time since you last communed with him? How long have you been stuck down here, alone, with no one to wear you and no conduit to the outside realm? It's been thousands of years, has it not? What god or mortal might remain unchanged throughout so many centuries? Does not religion shift and change like the tides, albeit more slowly?" Robin couldn't resist needling the tyrant while playing for what little time he could.

In response, he got another blast of sense-shattering keening from the thing, and a wave of hateful pressure battered at his psyche. Robin took a deep breath and let it wash over him.

Let the tyrant rage. Let the stars around him burn with their dispassionate fire.

Robin was on the verge of a breakthrough.

One command. One single command which the crown—the spirit within the crown—had no choice but to carry out.

Artifacts have only a single way in which they might be destroyed . . . Savra's voice echoed out from the vault of his memory.

A single command that was irrefutable. A single way in which the crown might be destroyed. Robin turned the idea over in his mind, examining it for weaknesses.

He found a few. Of course he did. But . . .

The visions in the aurorae shuddered and changed, time speeding up like honey warming in the sun. The entrance to the room was open, and the light of spellfire flared in the darkness beyond. But were the visions truth or lie? The tyrant had seemed so offended at the thought of lies, and Robin hadn't detected any canny cunning in that reaction. Maybe he was nearly—

"Out of time, little bard," the tyrant of nine eyes and three gloated, echoing Robin's thoughts. "If you wish to command me, you have only moments left before the chance, like the crown, is snatched from you forever."

The thing wasn't wrong.

Fine. Time to roll the dice.

Robin straightened, casting defiance into the burning eyes before him.

"I've got your command right here," he said. "Heed me now and heed me well, for my first and final command to you is this: I command you to destroy yourself and this crown that is your vessel utterly, leaving no wisp of its power or your being behind."

Robin felt the crown at his brow suddenly blaze with a cold fire. He quickly reached up and plucked it from his head, holding it before him in that void full of stars where he floated in his own mind.

The aberrant and malevolent spirit frothed and raged before him, eyes bloodshot and pulsing with impotent fury. It could not resist that dreaded command, though it fought with everything it was. The blood-red cracks in its eyes spread to its very flesh, reaving it asunder and allowing waves of hateful red energies to flare free.

"Curse you!" it spat. "I, Zuarmaska, Disciple of the Mighty Urkhan, curse you, pretender! With my dying breath, I bind thee and mark thee! You shall regret this action, and you shall rue the day you set yourself against the God of Tyranny! I—You—"

It struggled to spew more vitriol, but the cracks in its being had spread too far. Small explosions rippled across its body, venting magic and life force into the starry void like bloody nebulae. The three central eyes were the last to go, glaring hatred at Robin to the very last.

And he felt the weight of the curse settle on him with a certainty which told him, as sure as morning would break tomorrow, that he would have a notification from his system about it once he was free of this place.

The crown that had been in his hands was so much floating silver stardust around him. He felt time rubber-band around him, yanking him out of this swiftly dissolving mental space as the last of the crown's magic dissipated.

Then he was back in his body, back in Melusk's hidden room, with spells and steel flying as Gis and his party forced their way inside. Some of the clarity of that other realm lingered, just long enough for him to note where everyone stood, himself in the center, surrounded by a small circle of rust-red dust.

The weight on his temples was no more.

The crown was gone! Destroyed utterly by the only power it would ever—could ever—bow down to: its own.

Chapter 17

*W*hat have you done?"

Robin looked up into the face of Gis, Disciple of Urkhan, towering in the entrance to the hidden room. Shock and outrage warred across the old man's cadaverous features, and hatred sparked in his eyes.

"Vanquished Zuarmaska, one of your fellow disciples, and destroyed an artifact of your usurping pig of a god. No big," Robin said. He and his friends were cornered. Might as well go big with pissing the enemy off.

Gis's eyes bulged, and the knight in front of him and slightly to the left bellowed in fury.

Robin's eyes flashed over his assembled opponents. Gis was the largest threat, of course, followed by the mage. The woman in robes didn't seem to have improved her mood any from the last time Robin had seen her. The hobgoblin scout was lurking in the hall, mostly out of the way but in a prime position to snipe with a few well-placed arrows or crossbow bolts.

They seemed to have lost one of the hulking brutes. The other, still with them, was closest to Robin's party. That was the one who had just bellowed in fury. His armor was battered and much the worse for wear, and Robin felt a quick flash of pleasure at the sight, knowing he and his friends had likely been the cause.

Thank you, Ruprecht!

Gis spat out an order, and the dark knight at the fore launched into action, his sword sweeping toward Vance and engaging the librarian in a brutal exchange of blows. Vance managed to hold his own, but not without taking a nasty blow to the arm, where blood began to seep through the paper armor which usually provided such incredible protection.

The mage fired off several missiles of magical force, but Drev's protective spells flared, entirely negating them. The mage growled in fury, and sooty red flames sprang to life in her hands.

Drev's force protections would have a harder time dealing with that.

Jhess flung daggers, forcing Gis to expend precious seconds uttering a warding spell to turn the mundane steel away from his flesh, while Savra shouted a [Healing Note], sealing the worst of Vance's wound before Robin had the chance to.

The bard flexed his will and called on [Visual Phantasm] to cloud the room in coiling smoke, moving it as best he could to provide cover for the party and hide them from the searching eyes and flaming spells of Gis and his minions. It was far from a perfect solution; the terrain was against them, and Vance was already engaged in combat. He and the dark knight were moving too quickly for Robin to effectively try and blind the enemy warrior.

"Clear!" Drev called.

Robin conjured an open space in the illusion, and a barrage of purple-white missiles scattered among the enemy. None did much damage, but all hit with at least some effect.

"I will rip your soul from your body and use it to light our campfire," the enemy mage screamed at Drev.

"It certainly sparks with more magical talent than yours does, you third-rate magician!" Drev snapped back.

Ha! Looked like he was rubbing off on his party members a bit.

Robin's mind raced. So far, they were holding their own, but the party was already taking damage. There was no other way out of this room, and Gis was clearly more powerful than Robin or any of his friends were. In an extended confrontation, they were in a very, very bad position.

Maybe he shouldn't have been so hasty in destroying that fucking crown.

Then it hit him. He and his party didn't *need* to fight Gis or face the priest and his party alone! They had allies nearby. All he needed to do was pull off a quick spell and hope Nilsiir was waiting impatiently for more territory to be added to their domain. If he was lucky, the high priest might even be able to call on Fiara as backup.

A vulpine smile stole across his lips. All he needed was a few moments to formulate the image in his mind, then he could will it into being with [Visual Phantasm], no magic words or gestures needed!

So long as he could connect his illusory runes to the wider network of magic that ran throughout the ruins of Tarin-Tiran. There were none inside Melusk's hiding place, after all.

Fortunately, Robin had taken care to mentally plot the location of the runic structures which powered the lights in the hallway. With the help of his various perks, he was able to visualize where he needed the illusion to appear to connect it to the wider runic network. Holding everything perfectly in mind was more difficult, but thankfully, he'd had a lot of practice recently. He knew exactly the runes to use and the positions to place them in. This room was nearly identical to the last one, and so the degree to which he had to alter his illusion to fit was also a nonissue.

"Honestly, Gis, you should have turned back the minute you saw me," Robin said, keeping the priest in place for the next crucial moment as he aligned everything perfectly in his mind. "Because unlike you, my friends like me. And here in Tarin-Tiran? I've got friends in high places."

Robin smiled and snapped his fingers dramatically, willing the structure he had visualized to manifest via [Visual Phantasm]. Runes flared to life as the magic connected, and suddenly, Nilsiir was standing in the room between the Disciple of Urkhan and Robin's party.

"Ah! Success! Congratu—"The illusion of Nilsiir paused, noticing Gis.

Silence fell, and Nilsiir's face took on a grave and terrible mien. The high priest's will flashed through the room, warping its reality to suit their will, and Robin and his friends suddenly found themselves behind protective bulwarks, angled arrow slits the only way to view what was happening in front of them.

"You." Nilsiir's voice was as smooth as a razor parting a carotid artery and as coldly furious as a nitrogen volcano. "You are trespassing on sacred grounds. You bring with you the presence of this city's most hated enemy. You dare to stand before me, now, after all the damage that parasite of a god you pray to has caused."

Nilsiir's form rippled and changed. Robin couldn't see it, but he could see the faces of Gis's compatriots, and he was suddenly quite glad he had no idea what form Nilsiir had assumed.

Fear was writ large across every face but Gis's, but even in the old man's face, fear warred with hatred and horror.

"Avert your eyes!" the priest of Urkhan shouted. "Do not meet the nightmare's gaze!"

The advice came too late for the mage in the group. She screamed and lashed out wildly, firing spell after spell at Nilsiir. They all flashed through them, doing nothing. Nilsiir, whatever appearance they had taken, was still only an illusion. Even after the woman had exhausted her store of magical energies, she continued to gesture and chant to no avail, her throat catching and blood running from her eyes until she collapsed onto the floor in a shuddering heap.

"Idiot!" Gis raged.

The priest of Urkhan snatched a scroll from the case at his belt and began chanting in a loud voice. The hair on the back of Robin's neck stood on end. Those syllables! They were dripping with power. That was a Tier Seven effect at least! Had to be.

The spellcasting rose to a crescendo, and Gis raised one arm dramatically, pointing a bony finger at the apparition that was Nilsiir.

But nothing happened.

The Disciple of Urkhan blinked and stared dumbly at the High Priest of Rhyth.

Nilsiir's voice answered, a deep and mocking tone in every syllable.

"If you're going to attempt that level of magical disruption, you really should be sure that your opponent doesn't have a spare [Counterspell] at hand to negate the effect. Especially if you need to rely on magical items to do so, when your opponent has the leashed energies of an entire city to draw upon!"

Nilsiir's laugh chilled Robin's blood, and he was an ally!

Gis swore and shouted a single word, an amulet at his neck flaring as he did so. The Disciple of Urkhan vanished along with the rest of his party, teleporting to safety. Well, most of his party. The downed mage remained, a cooling corpse on the floor, and Robin spotted the hobgoblin scout turn and flee down the tunnel.

But the threat was over. The crown had been destroyed, and Nilsiir had been granted not one but two sections of the city which had once been disconnected and isolated to increase their powers.

That was some serious quest progress right there, and the flood of notifications Robin sensed just outside his line of sight agreed. The most satisfying of them all, however, was the *ding* he felt in his bones.

Robin smiled as a sense of power flooded throughout his body. He'd breached the barrier between levels and ascended to Tier Three!

Time to make a few choices!

Chapter 18

$\mathcal{R}$obin sorted through his leveling options and notifications as the rest of his party looted the mage's corpse and bound their few wounds, and Nil-siir hummed to themself and redecorated the room, banishing the bulwarks they had conjured during the fighting.

Naturally, it was the curse that caught his eye first. The tyrant's words had indeed resulted in a perk. Though given how annoying it had the potential to be, *perk* didn't seem like precisely the right name for it at the moment.

Congratulations! (?) You have been awarded the perk [Enmity of Urkhan]!

You have destroyed a divine artifact of Urkhan and slain what remained of one of his disciples! For your efforts, you have been cursed by a tyrant of nine eyes and three!

Effect(s): *Those faithful to Urkhan will have an instinctual suspicion and dislike of you, making it more difficult to deceive them in relevant situations. However, individuals with an inherent enmity toward Urkhan or his faithful will be more inclined to like or trust you, so it's not all bad!*

Robin dismissed it and the other general notifications in favor of opening his character sheet and making some key selections there. His free property rank went into *Cunning*, as usual. And he had enough experience even after tiering up to rank his *Deception* up to the new maximum.

His peculiarity choice had been planned out in advance as well, so Robin went ahead and finalized that, taking **[Improved Metamagic Specialty: Duration]**. With that in play, he was well positioned to make the most of his limited (for now) store of magical energies.

The magic he was able to weave into his music, **[Bardsong]**, had more options available as well, and Robin quickly chose **[Suggest]** as his option there. Having been on the receiving end of the magical version, it was too tempting to pass up, and as a **[Bardsong]** effect, it was technically not a spell and therefore could bypass certain protections. It came with its own limitations in exchange, of course, but Robin could work with that.

He was just about to delve into spell selection when Nilsiir's voice rang out in his mind.

I sense you have ascended in the ranks of power. Congratulations! This calls for some rewards, in addition to what I owe you for completing these little tasks for me.

Images and words began to flash through Robin's mind, a compressed stream of information like a montage. Time went wild around him, and he flashed between living every moment of every lesson and feeling that time flew by like a coursing stream.

Congratulations! You have learned the spell [Lesser Figmentation]!

Congratulations! You have learned the spell [Refined Phantasm]!

Congratulations! Secret lore acquired! [Mercurial Illusions]

In addition, knowledge of all manner of other illusion spells and the benefits to each appeared in his mind, together with odd tricks and refinements he could master as he continued on his path to power. One of these he was already very well positioned to take advantage of, so he quickly opened his interface and selected **[Phantasmal Steed]** as his free spell for this level.

Robin felt he was finally getting somewhere. The new power felt comfortable, almost substantial. It was a far cry from the higher tier magics he'd been witness to, but it felt like he was finally past the introductory levels of power, that he was finally equipped to start really having some fun.

And what do you intend to do now? Nilsiir asked. *Will you explore the ruins of this city more, or will you embark upon a quest with a bit more . . . meaning?*

I think you know, Robin answered without speaking. *Or you wouldn't ask.*

It's best to ask, never assume.

Then I'll tell you now that I intend to make the restoration or rescue or rediscovery of Rhyth my quest, the bard said. *Too much has been lost with his absence, and I would see him returned.*

Ah. I am very glad to hear that. Very glad.

Robin suddenly looked over to the illusion of the High Priest of Rhyth. With all their power, it was easy to forget that they were irrevocably bound to Tarin-Tiran and the magics here in the city. That would certainly make questing to restore one's god a difficult proposition. Especially as it wasn't clear how much faith, if any, an illusion provided, versus one of the faithful.

Though considering Rhyth was a god of illusion . . . Robin gave a mental shrug. That was more advanced theological thought than he was prepared to engage in.

If you are undertaking this quest, you will need some protections.

Robin felt, rather than saw or heard, Nilsiir wrap a shrouding enchantment around him.

Thrice protected, thrice veiled. Keep three secrets in your heart, and the spell shall hold. Bury the most precious deep—the one which pertains to your plan to restore our Lord.

Of course Nilsiir would sense that! Though Robin himself had barely registered the idea, half formed as it was from recent events. Still, he did as he was bid and hid the secret deep within his heart, feeling the magic settle around it.

The other two secrets should be things you can afford to lose, if you must. Most will stop after unveiling your first secret, some few may persist to the second, but I know of none who ever delve deep enough to uncover the third, and not even the hand of a god may pierce the epic spell around you, so long as you do not stand directly before them and do not give them a reason to truly look.

I understand.

Urkhan took much; from this city, from Lord Rhyth. Nilsiir looked suddenly sad. *Restoring what was lost . . . well, you may find you need to wrest it from divine hands of steel. Still, there are many fragments of Rhyth's power yet scattered across the many lands that dance around the sun. It may be that you might gather enough to spark Rhyth's return without directly confronting Urkhan or the highest of his servants.*

I will find them. I will return Rhyth to us.

Robin felt a fierce determination well up within him. He had a purpose to bend his newfound power to! Not that gratification or wonder or fame were not enough, but this was different. Annealing.

Then my blessings go with thee, my son.

Nilsiir's tone was serious. Robin didn't like it. He didn't trust it. He felt certain that another shoe would drop soon, possibly making a squeaking noise as it did so.

Now gather up your share of the loot! If you don't hurry, your friends will leave you nothing! Quickly now! You have a victory to enjoy!

Robin didn't need to be told twice. He smiled at the high priest and dove into the postbattle glow. The mage had had a couple useful magical items, but they went to Drev and Vance. Robin got a share of silver and gold, however.

"Here," Nilsiir suddenly said, a small chest rising up from the floor. "The party would not be complete without your final member, now would it?"

The chest opened of its own volition, revealing Ruprecht's core.

I hear congratulations are in order! Though it's a pity about the artifact. Absorbing that would have—

"Given you fatal indigestion," Nilsiir interrupted. "You may not have eyes or a stomach, but that doesn't mean your senses can't still be bigger than your capacity!"

Robin laughed and went back to using **[Lesser Phantasm]** to flavor and spice the celebratory food and drink the party was partaking in.

It was a perfect evening. He had magic and a growing store of wealth. He had a purpose and the makings of a quest. He had friends and a new world to explore.

But all good things must come to an end, and Robin, drunk on success and wine, should have seen this coming. He should have known.

"Now," Nilsiir announced. "Everyone gather round and congratulate Robin! He has performed a great service for Tarin-Tiran and for his god, and it will be good for him to be surrounded by friends as he embarks upon the next adventure."

Laughing and drunk, the party did as the priest bid. A small part of Robin's mind began to scream a warning, but it was too late.

Never party with a trickster unless you are *sure* you are the cleverest one in the room.

A quest notification appeared before him, but Robin didn't have time to read through it before the illusory high priest spoke again.

"Farewell, Robin! Thus do I send you on your journey with what blessings and knowledge I can provide, even in this lessened form. Oh, and sorry about this, but we really can't have you knocking about the place. After destroying that crown like you did, all of Urkhan's might will be focused on finding you. Best I send you off someplace far away where it will take those idiots a nice long time to find you again. Ta-ta!"

Wait, what?

"Nilsiir! No, wait! Nilsiir!" Robin shouted but it was too late. The illusory high priest had raised their hands, and a wave of magic seized Robin bodily and cast him through the space between to lands unknown.

Robin had just enough time for one final thought before the world vanished around him.

Fuck me!

Here endeth the tale of *The Secrets of Tarin-Tiran*!

Robin Parker

Heritage: Shadeling, Paragon
Profession: Bard
Tier: 3 (Effective Level: 10)
Experience: 45
Spell Points: 36
Bardsong: 9 uses

Properties

Free Ranks Available: 1

Physical
  -Strength: 11
  -Dexterity: 14
  -Fortitude: 11
Mental
  -Intelligence: 17
  -Cunning: 26
  -Resilience: 15
Social
  -Charisma: 15
  -Manipulation: 13
  -Poise: 16

Proficiencies

Free Ranks Available: 1

Physical (9/9)
- Athletics: 9
- Brawl: 10
- Dodge: 11
- Melee Combat: 9
- Pilot: 8
- Ranged Combat: 11
- Sleight of Hand: 12
- Stealth: 12
- Survival: 11

Mental (9/9)
- Arcane Lore: 12
- Bureaucracy: 8
- Concentration: 12
- Crafting: 9
- Healing: 9
- Insight: 12
- Learning: 11
- Natural Wisdom: 8
- Perception: 12

Social (9/9)
- Animism: 8
- Deception: 13
- Empathy: 11
- Expression: 12
- Gossip: 11
- Intimidation: 10
- Persuasion: 11
- Socialize: 10
- Streetwise: 11

Peculiarities

Blessing of Rhyth
Tongue of the Fallen Tower
Mark of the Trickster
Chronicle of Infinite Visions

Mask of Myriad Faces
Initiate of the Craft
Illusion Focus
Metamagic Initiate
Improved Familiar Bond x2
Effortless Illusions
Metamagic Specialty: Duration
Improved Metamagic Specialty: Duration
Mercurial Illusions

Perks

Wayfaring Stranger
Shard of the Shattered Manymind
Mark of Fairy's Favor
Touch of Wild Magic
Enmity of Urkhan

Spells

Cantrips* (*no SP cost)
   -Lesser Phantasm*
   -Cutting Words*
   -Legerdemain*
   -Lesser Nightmare Curse*
   -Lesser Witch Bolt*
   -Minor Repair*
   -Lesser Charm*
Tier 1 (1SP each)
   -Visual Phantasm*
   -Healing Note
   -Whispers from Beyond
   -Minor Enchanted Slumber
   -Invisible Servant
   -Familiar Bond
   -Wizard's Armor
Tier 2 (3SP each)
   -Assume Quality (Special)
   -Lesser Mindreading
   -Sorcerous Mark
   -Phantasmal Mouth
   -Lesser Figment

Tier 3 (9SP each)
 -Refined Phantasm
 -Phantasmal Steed

Bardsong

Command Attention
Song of Arcane Power

Epilogue

Meanwhile, in a faraway land . . .

"Lord Redhand, General Alaria reports that the troops are in position. She requests your approval to proceed."

"She may have it," Lord Redhand said absently to the servant, most of his attention on the tactical map shimmering before his eyes. "Tell her to press hard on the left flank. It will not appear so, but they are weak there. A concentration of new recruits in veteran armor."

"Yes, my lord." The servant bowed and all but ran out of the room to relay the message.

Lord Redhand continued to study the map. The next battle would be decisive. If his forces succeeded here, then Vertei would be his, and the next step in his campaign could commence.

The warlord shook his head. The idiocy of the Vertein! They had the most defensible land on the entire continent, and they barely took advantage of it. A few strategically built forts to seal the passes, and they could be all but unassailable once magic was discounted. Food would be a problem, of course, considering how mountainous the region was, but still. They could be doing much more with very little. He would teach them that lesson then move to make Vertei the center of his growing domain.

His hand strayed to the pouch at his belt, crafted from an eerie gray reptilian hide, and his thoughts spiraled around the item concealed in an ornate box within.

The need to see it was growing too strong once more. The man who called himself Lord Redhand rose and moved around the perimeter of his tent, making sure everything was secure. Once he was satisfied, he stuck his head out of the entrance and issued orders to the guards outside to take up position around his pavilion so that no inch of it was unguarded, then told them he was not to be disturbed for any reason for the next hour.

It would take at least that long for Alaria to begin her assault. Nothing should go wrong in the meantime. Nothing that couldn't wait.

Once he was certain he would be alone and unobserved, Redhand carefully opened the pouch and withdrew the ornate box from within. It was slightly bigger than his hand, made of wood, and inset with an interlacing pattern of ivory, bone, and silver. The triune face of a beautiful and terrible goddess was worked into the center, playing-card style, and lacquered with black and gold.

Lady Fortune. Lady Chance. Good and evil. Weal and woe. And the razor line which balanced them all.

Redhand carefully set the box on a small camp table and seated himself next to it. The lid slid smoothly in its grooves as he removed it. Too smoothly. Inside the box was nestled a deck of worn yet still beautiful cards. The design on the backs was that of the goddesses on the box, although each time he opened it, the colors were different.

This time, the cards were a bright and starry blue mixed with highlights of black and gold.

Nothing he had read or experienced had given him any insight as to what the changing colors might mean. And he had looked. The damned deck had provided him with so much power and so much suffering that he couldn't help but seek out more of its secrets.

Not that many were forthcoming.

It was divine in origin, this artifact, and its powers were potent enough to tangle the threads of fate. There were minor cards and major cards, and at least three suits which he himself had personally seen, as well as at least one wild card.

The Fool.

Redhand shuddered at the memory of the card, the way its eyes had followed him from all angles, the mocking turn of its mouth. Maybe it would have looked on him with a kindlier visage if he hadn't—

He crushed the thought and took a deep breath, freezing over these weak musings, these pointless feelings. What mattered was power. What mattered was the balance of risk versus reward.

Of course, to know the risk he needed to know more of the deck and what it contained. He had a list of every card he had drawn so far, and his best accounting of what, precisely, the effects had been, but it was a frustratingly small sample, and the deck never seemed to get any smaller, no matter that the cards vanished from his hand shortly after drawing them.

Well, usually.

He hadn't counted the cards; he couldn't quite dare. It seemed far too close to drawing every single one of them, and there was no way that calculus ended well for him.

For anyone.

The deck seemed to whisper at him, calling him to draw a card, seize his fortune. His fingers hovered over the rectangle of pasteboard, almost—but not quite—touching it. Touching was something he'd forbidden himself from doing. Not until he knew more of his chances. It was too dangerous otherwise.

There was too much he'd already lost, in spite of all the power and wealth he'd gained from the deck.

Mentally, he recounted a litany of the cards he had drawn and the fair and foul fortune each had brought him. Twelve minor and three major arcana had he drawn from the deck. The minor effects were not so bad, enough that he'd be willing to risk it if those were all the deck contained.

But the major arcana? No. Those were terrifying specters of dire possibility which loomed over everything else. One of the few witness accounts he had found described a man drawing a card from the deck and being forced to confront Death itself.

The man had lost.

No. His odds were still too poor. Redhand drew back, closed the box, and sealed it within its pouch once more. The deck was more problem than opportunity, now.

Redhand needed to focus on more pressing matters.

He was going to take Vertei. He was going to occupy the castle at the heart of the domain. He was going to make the place the most defensible location on the continent.

And then he was going to bury the bastard deck deep in an impregnable vault until he could pry all its secrets loose and extract every last measure of power it had to offer.

About the Author

Tom O'Bedlam is the author of Trickster's Song. His writing is a madcap mixture of bad jokes, obscure references, and music of all kinds from pop to metal to traditional ballads, all tied up with a deep and abiding love of tabletop role-playing games. He should know better, but he doesn't. O'Bedlam lives in London, has more adventures than he should but less than he would like, and never turns down a pint of cider in a cozy pub. You can find him and more of his work on Patreon at www.patreon.com/tomobedlam.

DISCOVER
STORIES UNBOUND

PodiumAudio.com